MURDER
AT
SEDGWICK COURT

by Margaret Addison

A Rose Simpson Mystery

Rose Simpson Mysteries (in order)

Murder at Ashgrove House
Murder at Dareswick Hall
Murder at Sedgwick Court

Chapter One

'So here it is,' said Cedric, sixteenth Earl of Belvedere, waving a hand nonchalantly about him. Notwithstanding the apparent carelessness of his gesture, the young man's action managed to encompass everything in sight. 'This is Sedgwick Court, as far as the eye can see, don't you know? Ancestral home of the Sedgwicks and all that.'

There was a sharp intake of breath from his companion and then silence as she took in the view, somewhat overcome by the scale of it all. Of course, she had expected to be impressed. After all, Lavinia had raved about the house and had gone on and on about how immense it was. A great mid-eighteenth century, neo-Palladian mansion of a place that had been in her family for generations. And Rose was not disappointed by the reality. The house was all her erstwhile friend had claimed it to be and more, and had anyone asked, she would have readily admitted that it quite dwarfed both Ashgrove House and even Dareswick Hall. The building was indeed a colossal palace of a place with its smooth, plain alabaster-coloured exterior; its corner towers topped by pyramidal roofs; and its great Corinthian columns, which flanked the entrance porch, combining to give the overall impression that Sedgwick Court was a great temple from ancient Greece, risen from the ruins and transported to 1930s England.

Yes, the young earl's companion had expected to be impressed by the dwelling that was Sedgwick Court. What she had not expected, however, was the great expanse of the country estate itself, landscaped on an immense scale by a follower of the great Capability Brown. She marvelled at the park with its sunken ha-ha fences, confusing the eye by giving the impression that each piece of the parkland, no matter how differently managed or stocked, was as one for as far as the eye could see. She admired too the impression given of one single body of water which, Cedric had just explained to her, was in reality a number of expansive lakes cut into the ground at different levels. Close up they were seemingly unconnected, but from afar the impression given was of a river that ran right through the landscape.

'It's breathtaking,' Rose Simpson uttered at last.

These words of wonderment sounded sadly inadequate even to her own ears, but what else could one say when greeted by such a view? It was not just that the very sight was impressive, but also that she was actually here at all with Cedric. It was quite unbelievable given their reasonably short acquaintance, everything that had happened and their very different stations in life. She had thought that she would never set eyes on Sedgwick Court. She had believed that it was some utopia forbidden her. And yet there she was, a London shop girl, guest of the landed gentry.

'I'm awfully glad you like it, Rose,' Cedric said, sounding proud and embarrassed at the same time. 'Of course, you're not seeing it at its very best. I really ought to have waited until spring or summer to show it you. That's when Sedgwick looks its most glorious, with the sun reflecting on the water, the place all green and lush, and the flowers abundant and all that sort of thing. You wouldn't believe how many artists have approached us to paint the view. But I just couldn't wait for you to see the place. I think it the most wonderful place in all the world, don't you? Of course, I know I'm biased and all that, but it is rather delightful, don't you think? Even in winter when it looks a bit forlorn and brown, there's still something about it, don't you agree? I mean –'

'It's quite, quite lovely,' Rose said, clasping his hands in hers. It was all she could do not to spin him around and embrace him there and then. 'I can see why you love it so. There's something quite magical about it, as if it's not quite real. And I suppose it isn't really, is it?'

'No,' agreed Cedric. 'It's all been landscaped within a whisker of its life. And can you see that, on the top of the hill over there? You can just glimpse it between the trees if you look carefully.' Rose followed where he was pointing into the distance, his arm outstretched.

'I think I can see something,' she replied, screwing up her eyes in concentration as she studied the horizon. 'Why, it looks like a miniature castle, or at least a castle ruin,' she exclaimed in surprise.

'Yes,' agreed Cedric, 'but it isn't real. That's to say it isn't really a castle ruin or even the remains of one. It isn't the remnants of some Norman castle allowed to fall into disrepair or destroyed by a fire.'

'Isn't it?'

'No. It was just built to look exactly like that. A castle relic. It's nothing more than what is termed an eye-catcher. A folly if you will, that is specifically designed to draw one's eye into the wider landscape. It was built on a whim to satisfy some young countess at the time who thought it would be rather nice to catch a glimpse of a distant castle from the window of her boudoir. A lot of old rot, of course, and rather a waste of good stone as it has no purpose, but Lavinia and I found it rather a hoot to play in when we were children. You can just imagine it, can't you? Lavinia was the fair damsel in distress and I was the gallant knight come to rescue her from the clutches of some villainous baron, although I'm afraid that I always fell rather short.'

Rose laughed. She could picture the scene well. For she could imagine the young Lavinia dressed in all her finery trying to look gracious and demure while all the time fighting the desire to shout out orders and instructions to her younger brother. Try as he might, she thought it unlikely that Cedric would have lived up to her expectations of how a noble knight should behave when faced with danger and adversity.

'You might well laugh,' grinned Cedric. 'Lavinia was awfully bossy. Sometimes I wondered whether it wouldn't have been better if the roles had been reversed and I had been one of the princes in the tower and she had been the one come to rescue me from wicked old King Richard. But this place is simply littered with them. Eye-catchers and follies, I mean.'

'How marvellous.'

'There's one that looks all the world like a temple, and another one is a bridge which serves absolutely no purpose as it's over nothing at all. Not even a stream or a ditch. My father and his father before him let some of them fall into disrepair, but I'm determined to restore most of them to their former glory. They're wonderful places to have picnics and whatnot.'

Rose smiled. His enthusiasm was contagious and yet this mention of Lavinia had stirred up bitter-sweet emotions within her. She had once counted Cedric's sister, Lady Lavinia Sedgwick, as one of her closest friends. And it had been through Lavinia that she had first made the acquaintance of the Earl of Belvedere, or Viscount Sedgwick, as he had been then. Lavinia had taken up a bet with her brother that she could earn her own living for six months. She had decided to fulfil the bet by working in a dress shop and it was there that she and Rose had met and formed their friendship. Working side by side, they had buoyed each other on to cope with the mundane and tiring work, although Lavinia had been excused from dealing with the most difficult of the customers. The proprietor, Madame Renard, had not wished to lose the most attractive addition to her shop. Lavinia's presence had been good for business. Being attended to by a member of the British aristocracy had gone down well with the most snobbish and class conscious of her clientele. So, although Lavinia had been spared the most tedious aspects of the job, and had not been expected to sweep the floor or wrap up garments in brown paper in preparation for being sent to customers on approval, she had experienced some aspects of what the role of being a shop girl entailed, and she had found a friend in Rose.

Despite their very different positions in society, Rose had considered their friendship to be a strong one, albeit acknowledging at the same time that in all likelihood it would be temporary in duration. She had been fully prepared for the friendship to run its course and fizzle out once Lavinia had finished her time at the shop and returned to her privileged life. What Rose had been less prepared for was Lavinia's open disapproval and opposition to the obvious mutual attraction between Rose and Lavinia's brother. She had met him by chance at a weekend house-party hosted by Lavinia's aunt, to which Cedric had not been invited. The party had not been a success, culminating in death as it had done, and such an occurrence had done nothing to endear Rose to Lavinia, who believed that her friend had in some way been partly responsible for the tragic events that had unfolded. As a consequence, communication between the two had faltered and Lavinia had fled to the Continent, leaving her brother to pick up the pieces of their shattered lives and manage as best he could to deal with the aftermath.

'I think we should take a tour of all the follies this afternoon,' continued Cedric. 'Some of them really are rather impressive, even if one or two are in a dilapidated and dejected state. I know it's the middle of December and all, but it's dry and sunny. If you wrap up warm in all your furs and whatnot I daresay you won't feel the cold. Nothing better than a brisk walk on a day like this and ... oh, I say, I wonder what's up ...?'

Cedric broke off abruptly as his attention was drawn to the strange and unexpected spectacle of two of his upper servants hurrying, one could almost say running, towards him, while all the time trying rather unsuccessfully to maintain a dignified appearance. This was not helped by their attire of black trousers, waistcoats and tailcoats giving them the appearance of waddling penguins.

'What can Manning want, I wonder? And by Jove if that isn't old Torridge scuttling after him! I had no idea that the old chap still had it in him, not by the way he usually totters around. More than once I've thought of offering him a chair, and I would have done too if I didn't think he'd be offended.'

Rose looked on fascinated. Manning, the under-butler, appeared to have gathered pace even as they watched. Although, in another moment, catching sight of them studying him, he slowed to a more sedate step and Rose thought how he must wish that they were still studying the horizon so that he might break into a run unobserved by his master and his master's guest. Even though there was some distance still between them, Rose caught the flicker of a look of annoyance cross his face, quickly replaced by a dignified expression. She was reminded that, according to Cedric, the young man was still being trained up to replace Torridge in due course when the old man saw fit to be pensioned off to live out his days in a cottage on the estate. Apparently he was clinging to his occupation, reluctant to give into retirement and old age. Rose secretly thought that he did not want to leave his new master when he had so newly come into his title. No doubt the old man thought he had a responsibility to his old master to support his son the best he could.

Or perhaps secretly Torridge did not think that Manning was yet quite up to the job. She pitied the younger man having to endure the old butler looking over his shoulder, observing his every move as he tried to impart his years of wisdom on the art of being a butler in a great house such as Sedgwick Court. Notwithstanding Manning still being under a form of apprenticeship, the fact that Torridge was not far behind him, indeed was gaining pace and himself looked as if he wished to break out into a run, made Rose feel anxious. Something obviously was afoot as Cedric had speculated. Was something dreadfully wrong? Surely it must be. This feeling was reinforced as she caught the concerned look on Torridge's face. Something had happened.

Rose looked across at Cedric and saw that he too was as apprehensive as she was. His face looked clearly worried, his mouth set in a straight line and she saw that he clenched his fists as if preparing himself for the worst. She caught his eye and realised that the same thought had suddenly crossed both their minds, preposterous though it was. On the two previous occasions that they had been at house-parties together, murder had occurred. It was nonsensical to think it was a pattern, not when she thought how often they had met up in London since the unfortunate events that had occurred at Dareswick Hall. But even so she realised that in that moment they both feared the worst. Surely death had not come to Sedgwick Court. Oh, how very unfair if it had, considering everything that Cedric had been through …

'My lord,'

Manning's words recalled Rose to the present, banishing her daydreams. And, as the under-butler addressed his master, she was relieved to see that he was not trying to keep a stiff upper lip in the face of adversity. The news he had to impart was not catastrophic in nature after all. He was just excited and trying to keep his emotions in check as any good butler would. And, as if to dispel any lingering doubts about whether or not they were about to hear some appalling news, he blurted out: 'She's back, my lord, she's returned.'

Torridge, who had all the while been making his way laboriously towards them, had by this time caught up Manning and, after stopping for a moment to catch his breath, wheezing in rather an alarming fashion, all but pushed aside the younger man who retreated with a somewhat sheepish look.

'What Manning is trying to say, my lord,' said Torridge, addressing his master, and then breaking off for a moment to cast the unfortunate under-butler a look which would have turned milk sour, 'is that her ladyship has returned from her travels. Lady Lavinia has just arrived back home, my lord.'

'Lavinia's back!' Cedric put a hand to his chest and in that moment Rose realised how much he had missed his older sister, how much he had felt abandoned by her to deal with the aftermath of the Ashgrove tragedies. It was true that Lavinia had probably been most affected of anyone by what had transpired, but even so, how could she have just escaped to the Continent and left Cedric to cope with it alone? Even as she thought it, Rose knew that she was being unreasonable. Who could tell how she would have felt in similar circumstances?

Some five or six months had elapsed since Lavinia had up and fled, and Rose realised that she was feeling nervous at the prospect of renewing their acquaintance. She contemplated what had brought Lavinia back now. She wondered whether somehow unconsciously they had called her back, she and Cedric, whether by uttering her name at Sedgwick Court, her childhood home, and recalling memories of her they had summoned her home. Of course it was all nonsense, Rose knew that. It was perfectly understandable that Lavinia should think of family as Christmas fast approached, and on the heels of that to have a sudden longing to return home. She had been away long enough and the scandal and speculation surrounding the events that had occurred at Ashgrove had long since died down and been superseded by other matters, other gossip.

Such as what had occurred at Dareswick Hall, thought Rose gloomily. She wondered whether news of those murders had reached Lavinia's ears. Perhaps that was the reason for her coming back. Whatever the reason, she could not help feeling apprehensive about Lavinia's unexpected return, or rid herself of a ridiculous feeling of foreboding, as if their carefree weekend had disappeared with Lavinia's arrival. Of course, it was illogical, she told herself. However, Lavinia's presence was certain to change these few snatched days with Cedric at Sedgwick, not least because Lavinia was unlikely to be pleased by Rose's presence at her family home. If nothing else it was an indication that the fledgling romance that had begun between Cedric and Rose at Ashgrove had developed further in her absence. Oh well, thought Rose, she has only herself to blame for that.

'Lavinia!' Cedric's sudden exclamation recalled her from her musings and she looked up to see a figure in the distance making its way quickly towards them through the formal gardens and across the parkland. It was engulfed in a fine great wool coat edged in silver fox fur at cuffs and neck and complemented by a fur hat that hid the figure's face so completely that anyone at this distance, except for Cedric, would have been uncertain as to the figure's identity. For one second, although she knew that she was being unfair to Cedric, given the look of delight that had lit up his face, Rose prayed that it was not Lavinia, that the servants had been mistaken.

While she was thinking these uncharitable thoughts, Cedric had leapt forward as if to make his way towards the figure. Rose meanwhile remained where she was looking on, reluctant to intrude on the family reunion. But before she knew it, Lavinia was upon them, standing a few feet from her, embracing Cedric warmly, her shrill, infectious laughter carrying on the winter's air. Peeping under her fur hat was the same platinum dyed hair that Rose remembered so well. She was equally sure that under the great coat Lavinia would have the same willowy figure. Immediately Rose felt herself fade into the background, her own looks overshadowed by her erstwhile friend's.

As if suddenly aware of Rose's presence, Lavinia looked up and caught her eye. Rose took in her even, delicate, aristocratic beauty, so very different to her own plain looks. Lavinia had always had a tendency to look aloof. Now she looked something else too. Annoyed, Rose was sure of it, although the look of annoyance, if that was what it was, crossed her face only momentarily, hastily replaced by a look of superficial pleasure.

But Rose had not been fooled. Lavinia did not want her there. And something else, she was sure of it; her being there had upset Lavinia's plans.

Chapter Two

'Oh, Ceddie, I've missed you terribly,' exclaimed Lavinia, disentangling herself from her brother's embrace. 'I can't tell you how good it feels to be back here at Sedgwick, darling Sedgwick. I had a ball on the Continent, an absolute ball, but it's so good to be home, I can't tell you.'

'I say, Lavinia, you do look awfully well. But why ever didn't you write to say you'd be coming home, or send a telegram or something?' asked Cedric, holding her by the shoulders a little away from him so that he could take in her appearance. 'You could have telephoned.'

'Really, Ceddie, must you go on and on about it?' Lavinia laughed. 'If you must know, I only decided at the very last minute to come home. I had a sudden longing for Sedgwick and to see you too, of course. And then I thought what an awfully wonderful surprise it would be for you, me being home in time for Christmas.'

Lavinia looked up and feigned surprise as if she had only just become aware of Rose's existence. Rose meanwhile stood hovering awkwardly in the background.

'Why, Rose darling,' Lavinia said, 'I didn't see you there hiding in the shadows. This is a surprise,' she paused deliberately before adding: 'A wonderful one, of course.'

Cedric beamed, looked at Rose and grinned, his eyes shining. How easily he was taken in by his sister, Rose thought, and she felt a sudden stab of tenderness towards him. It wasn't that he was naïve or simply couldn't see Lavinia for what she was. Rose knew he just desperately wanted Lavinia to accept their relationship, which had developed in her prolonged absence.

'Hello Lavinia.' Rose said the words as warmly as she could muster, although her feeling of uneasiness had grown, spreading over her like a veil and making her feel a little sick.

'I must look a fright,' Lavinia was saying to Cedric. 'I've been travelling all day. I simply haven't stopped for a moment, I was far too anxious to see you and be back here. You know what I'm like once I've set my mind to something, impatient and all that. Why, I think Torridge was even shocked by my appearance when he first saw me, weren't you?' She flung a somewhat affectionate look at the head-butler, who was doing his best to protest while at the same time not wishing to appear to contradict his mistress. An impossible task by anyone's standards.

'Now, I really must wash and have a little lie down, or I'll be fit for absolutely nothing. You wouldn't believe how tiring travelling is, it absolutely drains one. Torridge, tell me, is my room ready for me, say it is?'

The butler nodded in a rather hesitant fashion, Rose thought. No doubt there had been a great deal of activity going on among the servants in the time between Lavinia's unexpected arrival and her journey towards them through the gardens and parkland. In her mind's eye, Rose saw the housekeeper and housemaids scurrying around busily in Lavinia's room like ants, polishing and dusting, putting out fresh linen, using an Electrolux suction cleaner on the carpet, sweeping the grate and laying the fire.

'Do come with me, Rose,' Lavinia said carelessly over her shoulder as if it were some throw away remark. Rose did her best to hide her surprise. 'It would be so nice to have a little chat after all this time,' Lavinia continued. 'And you can fill me in on all the gossip. You can tell me all about Madame Renard and her dreadful little dress shop.' She stopped and turned, addressing Rose sharply as if a sudden and far from pleasing thought had suddenly occurred to her. 'I take it you are still working in Madame Renard's shop?'

'Yes, I am,' said Rose casting a last look at Cedric before setting off in Lavinia's wake. She noticed that, while he was apparently grinning, there was a slight look of apprehension on his face which he was doing his best to conceal. Perhaps, Rose thought, he is as unsettled as I am by his sister's sudden reappearance.

Meanwhile Lavinia had set off back to the house at quite a pace and Rose had to hurry to catch her up. She noticed that Manning was undecided as to whether he should follow them or not, while old Torridge had remained behind with his master, no doubt to discuss the revised arrangements for dinner, which Lavinia's sudden arrival had brought about. It seemed to Rose that in those few minutes since Lavinia's appearance everything had changed, and probably not for the better. The crisp December air which a few moments ago had been bright and embracing, now felt chilly. It was as if the very weather was waiting for something to happen. Quite ridiculous of course, Rose admonished herself for letting her fancy run away with her. Lavinia had been nothing but charming towards her, even if she had clearly hoped that only Cedric would be there at Sedgwick to greet her on her return. But one thing was certain, Rose thought, no matter how one looked at it, it certainly wasn't going to be the quiet few days that she had envisaged.

'Miss Denning, I can't tell you how good it is to have you back,' said Mrs Broughton, the cook at Sedgwick Court, as the lady's maid bustled into the servants' hall.

'And good to be back it is too,' said Eliza Denning with feeling, sinking onto one of the chairs drawn up to the table. 'My throat's that parched for a good, proper, English cup of tea, I can tell you, Mrs Broughton. Mustn't complain as I know there's many a woman in my position who'd give their right arm to travel as I've done these past few months. But I tell you, Mrs Broughton, those foreigners don't know how to make a proper cup of tea, so they don't. It's either brewed so strong you'd swear it was treacle, or so milky you'd never think it had seen a tea leaf.'

'That doesn't surprise me, Miss Denning, so it doesn't. They prefer coffee on the Continent, so I've heard. Horrible, strong, bitter stuff too. Now, you just sit there and take the weight off your feet, and Dolly here will get you a nice cup of tea, won't you, girl? Why, I think I might join you.'

She glanced at the kitchen maid, who scuttled off to fulfil the task assigned to her. Presently two steaming cups of tea and their accompanying saucers were deposited in front of the two women, and Eliza took a grateful sip.

'Ah, that's better. Honestly, Mrs Broughton, I think half the time those foreigners don't even let the water boil, the number of lukewarm cups of tea I've drunk since I've been away.'

'Well, you're back home now,' said the cook comfortingly, taking a sip of her own tea, 'and that's all that matters. Things can return to normal, or as normal as they can be with a new master in place. You'll feel as if you've never been away, so you will.'

'But will they?' asked Eliza, removing her hat and depositing the hat pins on the table. 'Return to normal, that is? I'm not so sure about that. You've probably not heard from Mrs Farrier yet, but her ladyship's only gone and invited her new friends from the Continent to come and stay, hasn't she?'

'No!' The cook looked clearly alarmed. 'Why, Mrs Farrier's said nothing to me about it.'

'I expect she's only just been told about it herself. I did beg m'lady to write, but she'd have none of it. She wanted to surprise her brother, so she did. Although I'd say she's had something of a nasty surprise herself, what with Miss Simpson being here. I'm not one to gossip, as you know, but I rather think she was hoping that his lordship might set his cap at quite another young lady of her acquaintance.'

'Indeed?' said Mrs Broughton, leaning towards her conspiratorially. 'And who might she be, when she's at home, this young lady to whom you're referring?'

'Miss Emmeline Montacute, that's who, heiress to the Montacute fortune. You must have heard of her surely, or her father at least? He, no I tell a lie, his father I think it was, was the founder of those great Montacute department stores you hear so much about. Them that sell readymade clothing and household items and the like. Travelling on the Continent, she was, she and her companion, just like m'lady, and they got to talking. Quite taken with each other they were. Before long everything was "Miss Emmeline thinks this" and "Miss Emmeline thinks that" as if Lady Lavinia had known her for years. Still, I was pleased to see some colour come back into m'lady's cheeks.'

'Well, I never. And is she one of them, then, that's coming to stay here at Sedgwick? Mrs Farrier will be tearing her hair out getting the rooms ready.' The cook paused as her thoughts went to the housekeeper who'd already been into the servants' hall to grumble about Lavinia's unexpected arrival.

'She is indeed, Mrs Broughton. And happen we'll have one of those foreign counts staying under our roof as well! I tell you, it's going to be all go here, so it is!'

'Yes,' grumbled the cook rousing herself. 'And like as not I'll have to go about changing the menus. What suits a shop girl and the like, is hardly likely to meet with the approval of an heiress and a count, even if he's foreign, to say nothing of Lady Lavinia. Her ladyship likes her food all fine and dandy, so she does, not like his lordship.' She gave a heavy sigh. 'Well, I can't stay here gossiping, Miss Denning. Not when there's work to be done.' And she was gone to round up the scullery and kitchen maids, to inform them in no uncertain terms that they'd have to work their knuckles to the bone over the coming days, so they would. So they'd better start bucking their ideas up right now, or they'd have her to answer to.

As soon as they had made their way into the house, Lavinia tore off her hat and coat and handed them to one of the waiting footmen who was conveniently lingering in the hall. Before Rose had time to take a breath, her friend was already mounting the great oak staircase, seeming to take two stairs at a time, so that Rose was forced to hurry after her, scurrying behind her like a wayward shadow.

'Oh, I do hope that Eliza's seen fit to unpack my cases and put away my things,' Lavinia was saying. 'The girl was desperate to get to the servants' hall and catch up on all the gossip, and I daresay one can't blame her. Even so, it is rather trying when all one wants to do is have a lie down in one's own room among one's own things without being surrounded by cases and travelling paraphernalia. Why, if I have to see another trunk, I think I'll scream ...'

Her voice trailed off as, reaching her room, her fears proved unfounded. Her clothes had either been hung up in the wardrobe or taken to the laundry, and her various bottles, potions and other such toiletries were arranged neatly on her dressing table.

Lavinia gave a sigh of relief. Rose, for her part, marvelled at the speed by which the various servants must have worked to ensure that the room was tidy and welcoming. A fire had even been hastily laid and was burning gently in the grate so as to give the newly awakened room some warmth, without making it seem stiflingly hot or stuffy.

'I say, it is good to be home.' Lavinia surveyed her room with something akin to satisfaction before throwing herself onto the bed. 'One never quite realises how much one misses it until one returns after being away. Poor Eliza. The girl was so homesick. I think she was on the verge of upping and leaving me, and would have done too, if I'd stayed away for one more night. You should have seen her face when I said we were returning to Sedgwick. It was an absolute picture. It was all she could do not to hug me.' Lavinia looked around the room. 'Everything's just as I remember it, although smaller somehow. It seems an age since I was last here, what with working in that ghastly little dress shop in London, and then of course after everything that happened at Ashgrove ...' Lavinia's voice faltered and she idly caressed her bedspread with her hand as if it gave her comfort to do so, like some long forgotten toy suddenly unearthed. 'Such a very long time ago that I was last here, almost like another life.'

Her words hung in the air as both girls became lost in their own thoughts and memories. They remembered the events that had occurred at Ashgrove House, which had resulted In Lavinia's sudden flight to the Continent. Rose, who had remained standing in the doorway, hovered and fidgeted awkwardly with the corner of her handkerchief, her eyes averted from her friend. Meanwhile, Lavinia had moved to her dressing table, installed herself on the stool positioned in front of it, and was regarding her reflection critically in the fine oval mirrors.

The silence became unbearable like some tangible unwelcome presence. If no one spoke soon, Rose thought, she would surely scream or be forced to run from this claustrophobic room out into the comforting vastness of the parkland where she could gulp large mouthfuls of country air.

'Lavinia,' she said tentatively at last, 'I can't tell you how sorry I am about everything, I – '

'Don't!' Lavinia said abruptly, banging her hand down sharply onto the dressing table, threatening to shatter its surface, to say nothing of the glass above. In the mirror Rose could see her eyes blazing, brimming with emotion. 'Don't say anything. I don't want to talk about what happened at my aunt's house. I want to forget that anything ever did.' She turned in her seat and looked at her friend imploringly. 'Oh, I know one can't really, but one can try. And even if it's not possible to forget, it doesn't mean one has to go on and on about it over and over again until one gets

14

quite sick of it. I'm sure I'll go quite mad if I think any more about it. And it won't change anything if I do, will it? So what's the point? I am so very tired of wondering what might have been had things not happened in the way they did. And I daresay I blamed you and Ceddie at the time, although I realise now it wasn't really your fault, none of it. Now', she turned back to regard herself in the mirror, 'don't you dare get me started or I really won't be able to stop. It will be like releasing the flood gates and all that. Don't you see, Rose? I want to look forwards not backwards.' She dabbed at a stray tear.

'Lavinia – '

'I could sob for England, I can tell you; really I could. But what's the point? Besides,' Lavinia smiled suddenly as if she were trying to force herself to be bright, 'I already look a perfect fright after all this travelling. Even the servants think so. Travelling and crying and sleepless nights. The effects of which are really dreadfully awful for one's complexion.' She gave a little laugh and proceeded to powder her face. 'That's better, my nose doesn't look quite so shiny. I don't look as if I'm coming down with a cold or anything horrid like that. Now, you wouldn't be a dear, would you, and brush my hair for me? Eliza usually does it, but she's probably regaling the servants with exaggerated descriptions of our travels.'

So that was how Lavinia wished to play it, was it? Rose could hardly blame the girl and if she were truthful, it was a relief. She picked up the hairbrush and began addressing Lavinia's luxurious locks, marvelling as always at her beauty which always seemed exaggerated in comparison with the ordinariness of her own looks.

A comfortable silence followed, interrupted only by the sound of hair being brushed. Rose was pleased to have some occupation, even if she did feel a bit like a servant. And all the while Lavinia concentrated on repairing her face.

'I must say, I was rather surprised when Torridge informed me you were staying at Sedgwick,' Lavinia said, seemingly carelessly, but looking at Rose's reflection in the mirror out of the corner of her eye all the same. 'What with it being almost Christmas and all that. I'm surprised Madame Renard could spare you. It must be one of her busiest times of year.' The hand applying the powder suddenly stopped in mid-air as if a thought had just occurred to Lavinia. 'I say, Rose, you haven't been staying here with Ceddie by yourself, have you? There'll have been dreadful gossip in the village if you have.'

Rose wanted to laugh, inappropriate though it would have been under the current strained circumstances. It was, however, on the tip of her tongue to ask how she could possibly be considered to be alone here with Cedric when there must be upwards of a dozen servants residing within the house itself, to say nothing of the estate staff who tended to the grounds. Instead she said: 'No, of course not. Vera Brewster's here and so is Theo Harrison. They arrived a day or so before I did.'

'Vera Brewster!' Lavinia made a face in the mirror. 'How ghastly for you, you poor thing. You must have been bored stiff. Honestly, I don't think I've ever met a duller woman. Oh, I know,' she added quickly, seeing that Rose was about to protest. 'One would have to say she's awfully nice and pleasant and all that, but all the same dreadfully dull. You know, she's only a few years older than us, can't be more than twenty-eight or twenty-nine, but all she can think about is church bazaars and organising the rota for doing the flowers in the church, or overseeing a beetle drive to raise money for widows and orphans. Very worthy and all that, but I ask you, how very dreary. I suppose it's having a clergyman for a father and having to step up to the mark with her mother dying so young. Still, I'm sure that she'll make Theo a wonderful doctor's wife. They've been engaged for absolutely years, you know.'

'Well, I think she's rather nice,' said Rose, abandoning the hair brushing and sinking onto Lavinia's bed.

'Yes, well you would,' said Lavinia, not unkindly, as she played with a wayward curl, 'but then you do tend to see the best in everyone, Rose, even me. But you have to admit that Vera doesn't make much of an effort to be interesting, even in her appearance. I mean, she's probably got a good figure under all those unflattering clothes she insists on wearing, but one would never know it. Of course, there is nothing wrong with wearing tweed in the country, but why choose such nondescript shades of grey or brown? And if one must, at least make sure that the cloth isn't sagging and the hems aren't coming down. Really, she ought to make an effort. I know Theo's only a country doctor and all that, but he's frightfully ambitious and rather handsome in a country doctor sort of way, don't you

16

think? All the old biddies love him, can't get enough of his bedside manner. If Vera's not careful, one of them will leave him a fortune in her will and he'll up and open a practice in Harley Street and leave her behind.'

'Really, Lavinia, you do talk a lot of old rot,' retorted Rose, relieved that Lavinia seemed to be her old self again. 'I happen to think they're very fond of each other, and just because you're obsessed by clothes and your appearance doesn't mean every woman has to be.'

'Good old Rose,' said Lavinia smiling. 'Putting me in my place. I've missed you, you know, I really have. We had some fun times together in that dress shop, didn't we? I would never have been able to have stuck it out for as long as I did if you hadn't been there. Are those two awful girls still there? Now, what were their names ... let me think ... Oh yes, Sylvia and Mary, such horrid girls. Anyway, enough of reminiscing, I'm rather more interested in hearing about what you've been up to lately. I read about all that dreadful business at Dareswick Hall. It had me enthralled, of course, but the poor Athertons. I say, Rose, murder and death and all that do seem to follow you around, don't they?'

'Or Cedric,' put in Rose. 'He was there too, you know.'

'I do. You've been seeing rather a lot of my brother recently, haven't you?' Lavinia said suddenly, catching Rose off guard. 'Awfully good of you to be there for him when I wasn't, but really I'm back now.'

Rose felt herself blush, but Lavinia was still smiling sweetly, as she adjusted her hair.

'Do you wish me to leave, Lavinia?' Rose said somewhat coldly, feeling nevertheless obliged to offer to go given the circumstances, even though it was the last thing in the world she wanted to do. To leave Cedric now, when she had only just arrived at Sedgwick, it was almost more than she could bear ... She took a deep breath and tried to ensure that her voice remained steady. 'Really, I would understand it if you did, Lavinia. I can quite see how you might just want to have a quiet Christmas this year here with your brother.'

'And leave me with Vera and her beau?' Lavinia gave a look of disdain.

'I'm sure they'd leave too. They wouldn't think you rude if you were to ask them to. Why, I think Vera's likely to suggest it given everything.'

'Yes, I suppose she might. It would be just like her. She'd consider it the right thing to do and then no doubt complain about me to Theo all the way home. But no, I don't want any of you to go. Really, there's no need. I was dreading this first Christmas, you know, Cedric and me alone in this vast place, rattling around. So I did something about it. I've invited some friends I made on the Continent to come and stay. Actually they should all be arriving tomorrow.' Lavinia turned in her seat so she could face Rose. 'So you see, we'll be quite a house-party. It will be great fun, see if it isn't.' She smiled sweetly.

Somewhat apprehensively Rose returned her smile. While her heart leapt at the prospect of not having to leave Cedric, she could not rid herself of a somewhat irrational feeling that the next few days were likely to be anything but fun. She acknowledged also that the sense of foreboding that she had experienced earlier had returned, only now it was more intense.

Chapter Three

On leaving Lavinia to finish her ablutions, Rose came across Vera Brewster in the hall. She happened to look over the great oak banister and glimpse her from the staircase before she herself was observed by Vera. To her surprise the young woman was pacing the black and white tessellated floor below in a seemingly agitated manner, which immediately awakened Rose's curiosity. From what little she had seen of Vera, Rose had taken her to be a calm and collected sort of person. Her interest was further piqued as it became clear that Vera had been waiting for her. The woman's face adopted an eager but anxious expression as soon as she spotted Rose, and she stopped her pacing abruptly, as if she had been caught doing something of which she was ashamed.

'Oh, there you are, Rose,' the woman began, wringing her hands. 'Tell me. Is it true? Has Lavinia really returned?'

Rose nodded. The woman's manner was definitely restive and now that she was standing up close to her Rose thought her forehead looked moist and clammy. As if suddenly aware of her appearance, Vera put a handkerchief to her brow, but if anything it seemed to make matters worse. Yes, she was definitely on edge which seemed, from Rose's limited knowledge of her, out of character. Try as she might, she found it difficult not to think of Lavinia's less than flattering description of the girl, which was still ringing in her ears.

'Of course I always supposed she must one day, it's just that …'

'Yes?' Rose said encouragingly, intrigued by the woman's manner. Cedric had indicated that Vera Brewster was a longstanding friend of both himself and his sister. And yet Lavinia had spoken disparagingly of her and Vera in turn seemed on edge about Lavinia's return.

'It's just that I happened to pass the housekeeper just now,' Vera was saying. 'She was muttering angrily to herself under her breath. From what little I could make out it was something about more guests and heiresses at that. I just wondered what it all meant, that's all. Did Lavinia say anything to you about it?'

'No,' Rose said carefully, watching the woman's expression closely, 'not exactly. She did mention she'd invited some acquaintances to stay, some new friends she'd made on the Continent, but she didn't say who they were. I suppose one or two of them might be wealthy. After all, only the rich seem to be in a positon to travel for pleasure these days. But all she actually said was that it was going to be something of a house-party.'

'Oh, so I didn't mishear. I hoped I had.' Vera's voice had fallen to little more than a whisper and the colour had quite drained from her face.

To Rose's eye Vera looked distraught, as if her greatest fears had just been realised, which seemed ridiculous in the extreme. All her reactions appeared to Rose wholly disproportionate and she could not help feeling some resentment towards her. Sedgwick was Lavinia's home after all. Why shouldn't she invite guests to stay if she wished? Why should Vera be so crestfallen? To make matters worse, she could not help but notice that the hem of Vera's skirt was indeed coming down in one place, and the jumper she was wearing was both shapeless and a particularly unpleasing shade of brown. She fought the urge to try and persuade her to change her jumper for a fitted blouse, and to offer to mend her skirt before Lavinia caught sight of her.

'Oh, it's nothing, really it isn't.' Vera spoke hurriedly, as if she had become aware that Rose might think she was behaving rather oddly. 'It's just that I was so hoping that it would be a small house-party, well hardly a house-party at all given that it was just to be the four of us. I'm not very good at dealing with lots of people. I never know what to say. I'm always putting my foot in it or else I get nervous and say the most boring, inane things, one wouldn't believe.'

Rose nodded sympathetically although she was not convinced by Vera's explanation for her agitated manner. It seemed to her that a woman in Vera's position, heavily involved in arranging church events and good causes as she was, would be well versed in dealing with large gatherings to say nothing of handling the members of the nobility who were persuaded to open her father's church fetes and bazaars.

'Oh, I know I'm not explaining myself very well. And you probably think I am being very unreasonable. Why shouldn't Lavinia come home and bring any number of friends with her? It's just ...' Vera faltered and looked away into the distance apparently lost in her own thoughts.

Rose was just wondering whether Vera had forgotten she was there when the woman turned to her, her face now flushed.

'Tell me, Rose, have you ever been in love, really in love, I mean? So much so that you feel you would die if it wasn't returned?'

Rose, taken aback, was for a moment lost for words. Whatever she had expected Vera to say, it was not this. Perhaps it had been a rhetorical question, for Vera did not wait for an answer, did not seem to expect one even, but ploughed on.

'I was wondering whether you and Cedric felt that way about each other. Oh, I know it's none of my business, but it's always so hard to analyse other people's relationships, isn't it?'

'I suppose it is.'

'From a distance the people concerned might appear quite contented, but scratch the surface and one might find all sorts of things wrong. I'm so afraid that we might be like that, Theo and me, I mean. I know that if one were to scratch away at our surface, I'd be perfectly happy underneath, just as happy as I am above. But it's Theo I'm concerned about. I'm so desperately afraid that he might be unhappy with his lot. With his current life as much as with me. We're not enough for him you see, even if he's not aware of it yet.' Vera smiled sadly. 'It would be just like him not to know. He's so wrapped up in his work, you see, that he might not feel anything yet, not see the wood for the trees.'

Rose certainly did not see. What was more, she was startled that Vera should see fit to confide in her, a relative stranger. Should she apologise to Vera and say that she didn't quite understand what she was saying? But she would feel uncomfortable doing so, afraid that to be voicing such a sentiment would awaken Vera to the fact that she had made Rose privy to her most intimate thoughts. Sooner or later she felt sure Vera would come to her senses and bitterly regret confiding her inner most fears. But what to do now? Rose looked around the vast hall helplessly, seeking a chance of escape or a diversion of some sort. But the hall was strangely empty of everyone, even the servants, and her mind had gone unhelpfully blank of ideas.

'Don't you think I'm right?' continued Vera, apparently oblivious to Rose's discomfort. 'I suppose I'm rambling on a bit, but I thought it all made perfect sense, at least to me it does. But, no, I suppose for you it's different. And I don't suppose for a moment that it would matter so very much to Theo and me if it wasn't for *her*.'

'Whom?' Rose could not help herself from asking, despite her good intentions not to become involved in what appeared to her essentially a private matter.

'Why, the heiress, of course,' answered Vera, as if that explained everything.

'Oh, there you are, Cedric,' Rose said, coming across him at last in the formal gardens giving some instruction or other to the head-gardener. 'I wondered where you were.'

'Torridge wanted to talk to me about the arrangements for Lavinia's guests, you know, whether they were bringing their own maids and manservants and that sort of thing. Couldn't help him one jot, of course. Mrs Farrier really needs to talk to Lavinia about it, but my sister was far too busy talking to you. I say, how is she?''

'She seems quite well. Almost back to her old self, I'd say.'

'I'm awfully glad she's returned and all that,' said Cedric, 'but it's a pity she saw the need to bring a lot of friends with her. She's only just made their acquaintance, hasn't she? I hope they won't be too frightful.'

'I was one of her friends, in case you'd forgotten,' teased Rose. 'If she hadn't seen fit to bring me on a visit to your aunt's, we'd never have met.'

'True. And she's almost her old self, you say?'

'She appears to be on good form. Prepared to let bygones be bygones, I think, but she doesn't want to talk about what happened at Ashgrove. So I wouldn't mention it if I were you, not yet. I'm sure in time she'll want to talk to *you* about it all, but for the moment she'd rather not go over it. I don't believe she thinks it would do any good.'

'Righto. It's just good to have her back.'

'I also wouldn't mention what happened at Dareswick. She's read about it, of course. She seems to be under the impression that I attract murder wherever I go. '

'What absolute rot,' said Cedric, tucking her arm through his, as they set off idly back towards the house. 'She could just as easily say that about me. But I'm awfully glad to hear that she's all right. I was afraid that she might never come back, you know, make her home on the

Continent or in America. I was afraid that Sedgwick might hold too many sad memories for her.'

'I think it has something to do with the time of year,' Rose said, 'you know, with Christmas approaching. It made her think of family and so, of course, you.'

'Well, whatever Lavinia's reasons for coming back, I'm just jolly pleased she's here. And if she doesn't want to talk about what happened at Ashgrove, well, that's fine by me. Let's concentrate on the here and now, shall we? Did she happen to mention who her new friends were whom she'd invited to come and stay? Torridge mumbled something about her mentioning to him a foreign count of some sort.'

'Vera said that the housekeeper was grumbling about an heiress. I say, Cedric,' Rose stopped walking and clutched at his arm, 'Vera was behaving very oddly just now. She seemed jolly put out that Lavinia had returned and that she had invited some guests to stay.'

'Vera has always been rather jealous of Lavinia and very possessive of that doctor of hers. For all I know she might have good reason, but I don't know how Theo puts up with it sometimes. Usually she's fine but –'

'She kept going on about unrequited love and how she loves Theo more than he does her.'

'Did she? Oh dear, that must mean that she's ... I thought she'd stopped all that.'

'All what?' But before Cedric had a chance to answer, Lavinia was upon them, her hair expertly arranged, her face exquisitely powdered.

'Oh do come inside, you two. It's cold as anything out here. And I want you to see my new dress, Rose. It's from one of those famous houses in Paris. I forget which one, because I visited quite a few while I was there and bought ever so many gowns. I want you to see the one I'm going to wear to dinner tonight.'

'I'd like to see it,' said Rose.

'It was frightfully expensive,' continued Lavinia, 'but absolutely divine. Oh, don't look at me like that, Ceddie. You don't understand how important fine gowns are to a girl like me. You might like going around in faded tweeds or plus fours or whatnot, and I daresay it's very different for a man, but I'd simply die if I had to go around in the sort of get-up Vera wears. How she expects to keep a man like Theo interested in her, I can't imagine ...'

Too late Rose and Cedric became aware of Vera Brewster emerging from behind a rosebush a few feet from Lavinia. There must have been something in the expression on their faces, for it caused Lavinia to stop her incessant chattering mid-sentence. She looked behind her, turning around as she did so. At once she spotted Vera and moved a step or two backwards towards her brother as if seeking out his protection. There was a silence relieved only by the faint sound of digging, by one of the under-gardeners, in a far distant part of the gardens. The three stood there staring, wondering how much of Lavinia's speech Vera had actually heard. It was possible, Rose thought, that she might have caught none of it, or just the odd word, although the look of mortification on Vera's face indicated that if nothing else she had caught the general gist of what Lavinia had been saying.

But before Lavinia could even attempt an apology of sorts, Vera had turned on her heel and was half running, half stumbling, back to the house. There was nothing any one of them could do but look on in horrified silence at the retreating figure, with its shapeless jumper and sagging skirt, moving further and further away from them as if in flight.

Chapter Four

It seemed to Rose that the additional guests arrived in dribs and drabs. First to arrive had been the heiress, Emmeline Montacute, with her companion, Jemima Wentmore. The former had been exquisitely turned out: her clothes good, make-up skilfully applied and hair well-dressed, the overall effect being one of a young woman of beauty, although how much of this was due to the girl's own natural prettiness and how much to art and fine clothes was hard to tell. What could not be concealed however, was her enthusiasm. Her face beneath its carefully applied powder and rouge was animated, and excitement flowed from her, seeming to light up and warm the winter's day. And there was something delightfully infectious about her mood. Even Rose felt the apprehension she had initially felt at the prospect of the arrival of such illustrious guests begin to lessen and ebb away.

In comparison Jemima Wentmore appeared a much more insignificant character, a shadow even, the portrait of a woman sketched in grey. But this initial impression, Rose thought, was somewhat misleading. Jemima was prettier than on first glance she appeared to be. But, unlike Emmeline, she had not tried to accentuate her looks, rather the reverse was the case. Her clothes were well made but quite plain and a little drab, as if her intention had been to deliberately make herself look dull and less interesting than she might have looked had she been decked out in clothes that were of a brighter hue.

'Did you oversee the packing of my things, Jem?' asked Emmeline over her shoulder. Embedded as she was in ermine, she was in the process of allowing the footman to take her luxurious fur coat and hat.

'Yes, of course, Emmie, there's no need to worry,' Jemima answered, unbuttoning her own dull coat, innocent of any fur trimming. Standing behind Emmeline, she appeared immune to the infectious qualities of her friend's presence, if anything she looked rather exasperated.

Poor thing, thought Rose, I suppose it must be rather trying looking after an heiress. Less charitably Lavinia whispered to her a little while later: 'Detestable girl. It's a pity she has to be here to spoil things. And the situation's made all the worse in that one simply doesn't know what

Jemima's role is. I mean to say, is she some dependant of the Montacute household or Emmeline's paid companion? And of course I can't possibly ask Emmeline. But the way Jemima speaks to her; calling her "Emmie", if you please! But that does suggest that they are relatives of some kind, doesn't it? And Emmeline will insist on calling her "Jem", not "Jemima", which really is all rather confusing and over familiar, don't you think? I mean, what is one expected to do? Especially as Jemima will insist on fading into the background at any gathering and suffer being talked to as if she is a lady's maid.'

Rose refrained from comment. Later, as she became better acquainted with the heiress, what became apparent was that, while Emmeline might put upon Jemima, she considered her to be a confidante rather than just an upper servant.

'Oh well,' continued Lavinia, sighing prettily, 'I suppose there is nothing for it but that a place must be laid for Jemima at table for dinner and she be given one of the better guest rooms.' She smiled as a thought struck her. 'I say, Rose, it's jolly fortunate that the little bedroom next to Emmeline's grand one while rather small is elegantly furnished. Quite the thing.'

Rose had at first been somewhat surprised at the level of hostility Lavinia felt towards Jemima who, at worst as far as she could see, was insipid and a little boring. But after analysing Lavinia's dislike of the girl more thoroughly, she realised her friend was simply jealous of the girl's friendship with the heiress. It might be Lavinia that Emmeline was having fun with, laughing and giggling together at some trivial matter with Jemima in the background merely looking on, but it was her friend-cum-companion's advice and opinion that Emmeline sought, not Lavinia's.

Next to arrive had been Felix Thistlewaite, a pleasant-looking, freckled face young man with sandy coloured hair, which seemed to insist on standing up on end, making him look a little dishevelled. His valet or manservant, if indeed he had one, had obviously not made a good job of turning him out. But the overall effect made him look interesting and slightly eccentric rather than not groomed. Rose, looking at his clothes more closely, noticed that while his tweed jacket had been darned in one or two places and was a bit antiquated as to cut, it had once been very good. As the days went on and she saw more of his clothing, she noticed that they were all in a similar condition, and wondered if they had been borrowed or inherited from some relative. Certainly they did not fit him particularly well, for they had a tendency to be too big on the shoulder. But if the young man was embarrassed by his appearance, he did not show it.

'I say, Lavinia, it's quite a place you've got here. Have the others arrived yet?' Felix Thistlewaite cast his gaze around and Rose wondered if he was looking for one person in particular or whether he was referring to the Continent party as a whole. Certainly his glance appeared anxious, possibly nervous, which was at variance with his otherwise relaxed demeanour.

The final guest to arrive had been Count Fernand who had cut quite a figure, not least by his rather bizarre appearance. Lavinia, Cedric and Rose had all happened to be in the hall when he had arrived and so were present to see him enter dressed in full top hat and tails despite it being only mid-afternoon. That in itself was unusual but would not have caused any one of them to catch their breath. What had was that the man wore a waistcoat of scarlet crushed velvet and a full length black cape or cloak which almost touched the ground, and was lined with a vivid crimson silk.

On seeing that he had an audience of sorts, the count had unfastened his cloak himself and swirled it in the air much in the style of a matador trying to attract the attention of a bull. Instinctively, as one, they had all taken a step backwards, almost as if they had been afraid a bull would miraculously appear out of thin air, or perhaps more reasonably that they would be struck by the swishing cloak as it cut this way and that through the air under the control of the count's dextrous fingers. Notwithstanding this, Count Fernand made compelling viewing, and even Cedric and Rose who both considered the theatricals to be a little absurd, looked on intrigued and not a little bewitched by his performance.

It would all have been rather comical or ridiculous, Rose thought, had the count not been so very tall and handsome, and had not the rather strange attire suited him superbly. The man himself looked nothing less than exotic. Cedric was tall, but this man was taller still. His hair was so black that it had a blue sheen to it and his skin, slightly olive in hue, contrasted well with the whiteness of his shirt. There was a thumb length scar on his right cheek which gave his face a slightly roguish air, adding greatly to the sense of mystery and perhaps even a touch of danger, which seemed to exude from him. Certainly, Rose thought, as a figure of a man he could be nothing but admired. Even so, it became apparent that her view was not shared by all, for she was standing close enough to Cedric to hear him whisper a shocked and rather disgusted 'Good Lord!' under his breath. The spell was broken and she bit her lip to stop herself from giggling. She hoped desperately that the count had not overheard his host, although the man himself appeared to be currently engaged in profuse bowing to his hostess, finished by the brush of his lips on her hand, the result of which had Lavinia in raptures, giggling away very prettily.

Rose was curious to see how Count Fernand would be received by the rest of the party, both by those with whom he was already acquainted, and by those to whom he was a stranger. She trailed behind him as they entered the drawing room. Cedric, she saw, was very inclined to fall back and walk with her, but as host felt obliged to lead the way. The count at once made his way across the room to Vera and gave a spectacular bow before kissing her hand. Vera in turn gave a startled "Oh!" and withdrew her hand as if it had been stung by a wasp. Felix Thistlewaite, Rose noticed, was trying hard not to laugh. If the count was disappointed by Vera's reaction to his greeting, he did not show it but instead proceeded to bow to the rest of the party in his unique flamboyant way.

Theo Harrison, Vera's fiancé, merely raised his eyebrows and frowned slightly but otherwise looked unperturbed and, if anything, rather bored. Rose remembered Lavinia's description of him as being rather handsome in a country doctor sort of way. She was inclined to agree with her. Physically he was not as imposing as either Cedric or Count Fernand, being only of average height, but his features were even and regular, and the country air had given him a healthy glow. His well-cut tweed jacket and flannels fitted him well and suited both him and his surroundings admirably. He might not have the ostentatious dress of the count, or such an extravagant manner, but there was something quietly steady and authoritative about him all the same that demanded respect. Rose envisaged that his bedside manner was likely to be very good, firm but kind and perhaps more importantly reassuring. She imagined he was well-liked and respected by his patients in equal measure. It did not surprise her in the least therefore that Vera should hold him in such high esteem and love him in such a doting way.

Count Fernand had been exuberant in his greetings of everyone, but particularly the women. Rose herself had not been neglected for she had received her share of elaborate bows and had her hand kissed fervently. But she was aware also that the count's eyes seemed to comb the room as if he were looking for someone in particular who was not present. Felix had behaved in a similar manner when he had entered the drawing room a couple of hours before. The only members of the party missing were Emmeline and Jemima, who had withdrawn to their rooms shortly after their arrival on the pretext of having a rest and a wash after their journey. Now she reflected upon it, Rose remembered overhearing Felix asking Lavinia where they were, a little while before the count's arrival. She told herself that she should not read too much into this, this desire to see the heiress and her companion. It was after all to be expected and hardly very surprising if one thought about it, for of course they must all have become well-acquainted during their stay on the Continent.

Rose wondered afterwards, as she had wondered about Lavinia's sudden arrival, whether thinking of them, rather than just coincidence, had caused the two women to join them at the very moment that they did. It was just as Vera, having sat down in an armchair as far away from the count as possible, was idly turning the pages of some magazine and was therefore distracted. Theo on the other hand, having earlier become rather bored with the conversations and gone to the window to look out, had turned at the sound of the door opening and glanced back into the room.

Before they entered the room, the women's footsteps were heard in the hall, and at once both Count Fernand and Felix had looked up expectantly. Their air of anticipation seemed to have been picked up by the rest of the room as if it were contagious. For everyone else, with the exception of Vera, stopped what they were doing, not in a sudden, abrupt way, but more coming to a dwindling stop. People took a step or two away from each other, the better to turn around and study the door, and conversations that had begun faltered and faded in an awkward, embarrassed sort of way as if the speaker had suddenly became aware that his listeners had become less attentive or interested in what he had to say.

Their attention was being drawn instead to something more fascinating behind his shoulder.

So it was that when the door finally opened the two newcomers found that all eyes were turned on them as if it were supposed that they might create a more spectacular sight than even the count in all his finery. In addition to this, the room was in almost complete silence, save only for the noise of Vera flicking the pages of her magazine, apparently oblivious to everything and everyone else.

Emmeline entered the room first somewhat apprehensively, followed by Jemima in her wake, as if she were her bridesmaid carrying her train. Emmeline made a very pretty sight, if not quite so bizarre a one as the count. She wore an elaborately embroidered silk and velvet dress and appeared quite as beautiful as Lavinia, with dark chestnut locks compared with Lavinia's fair ones. Her eyes were shining and she was clearly delighted to see again the friends she had made on the Continent, and to make new acquaintances.

There was an openness about Emmeline's manner which was engaging. After an initial, awkward silence, she laughed her infectious little laugh and the tension and apprehension in the room was broken. The room was relieved. Conversations were resumed and the silence that had momentarily filled the room retreated to the edges. It was almost as if there had been no waiting, no nervous anticipation in the room. Almost, but not quite.

It was true that the count was now happily engaged in conversation with Emmeline and, after pausing for a moment, Felix likewise had made his way to Jemima and was talking to her earnestly, so that the majority of the party were taken up with talking or listening to one person or another. But Rose was still aware of a strong energy in the room, as sharp as anticipation and suppressed excitement. She looked around and her eyes alighted on Theo Harrison standing alone by the window, sufficiently removed from the others so as not to be obliged to enter into any of the various conversations. What arrested her attention was the frozen look upon his face. She noticed also that he was clutching the window frame as if for support. Rose followed his gaze to see what had affected him so deeply, to see what he found so very fascinating that he stood transfixed as if he no longer knew where he was and was oblivious to those around him. A quick look around the room reassured her that no one else had noticed that he was looking peculiar. And then she identified the one person whose presence he acknowledged, the one person who had arrested his attentions and caused him to stare dumbfounded. For his eyes were fixed on Emmeline Montacute, so intently that surely he saw no one else.

Rose studied Emmeline closely. On the surface she appeared to be giving her full attention to Count Fernand, listening with enthusiasm to whatever it was that he was telling her, smiling, laughing, and saying the odd word of encouragement in the appropriate place. But her eyes were not on the count, at least not exclusively so, for every now and then her gaze wandered, darting back and forth between Count Fernand and Theo Harrison. To Rose she seemed very aware of the doctor's presence. The expression on her face remained unchanged, but Rose noticed that her skin glowed a becoming shade and she imagined that the girl's heart was beating faster, as if her attention had been caught by something of far more importance than the general chatter in the room. It was as if a sudden connection had sprung up between the heiress and the doctor that had them both bewitched. Time might indeed have stood still for all the attention they gave it, and they might as well have been the only two people in the room for all the notice they took of the others.

They only have eyes for each other. As soon as Rose was struck by this thought she looked instinctively towards Vera to see if she had noticed anything untoward. But Vera was still engrossed in her magazine. She had been upset, Rose recollected, when first told of Emmeline's imminent arrival at Sedgwick, yet now here she sat calmly, turning the pages of her magazine as if she had not a care in the world. Rose gasped inwardly. Whatever Vera had been afraid of, she was sure that it had not been this. She stared at Vera, willing the woman to look up and yet at the same time praying that she did not. But Vera continued to read, her head bent over the page, blissfully unaware that her world was about to fall apart.

Chapter Five

'So you see,' Vera was saying, 'poor Theo just can't help himself, trying to ingratiate himself with someone like Emmeline Montacute.'

Vera gave a little laugh which even to Rose sounded false, as if she were trying to make light of something that was upsetting her a great deal. It was the day after the arrival of the party from the Continent and they were sitting in the drawing room having afternoon tea, their eyes drawn to the lively discussion going on between the doctor and the heiress.

Emmeline, who it must be said had a general tendency to giggle at any opportunity, was laughing happily at whatever Theo was telling her. Theo in turn appeared to be basking in her attentions, his face quite animated. Rose, although she had made a conscious effort to try not to, had been unable to tear herself away from watching the relationship developing between Theo and Emmeline. Both parties had been tentative at first, each almost going out of their way to avoid eye contact, but following dinner that first night, it appeared that they had both lost a little of their reserve and had seemed to gravitate towards each other in the drawing room over coffee almost unwittingly. They were like moths drawn to a light, as if an invisible thread were pulling them unwillingly together, or at the very least, something beyond their control.

'He thinks that he should like so very much to be a fashionable doctor, whereas I just know that he would simply hate it,' continued Vera, drawing her chair closer to Rose's so that they might not be overheard.

'Is that so?'

'He's much better suited to being a country doctor, you know, but he just can't see it. I daresay it would be very grand to have consulting rooms in Harley Street and name the aristocracy among one's patients, but really it isn't Theo. He would never be happy just scolding mothers and daughters who overdo it in the London season, or patting the hand of Lady So-and-So who fancies she has a temperature or is feeling unwell when there is absolutely nothing wrong with her at all. Theo is not the sort of doctor who would be content to prescribe some harmless tonic at some outrageous sum.' Vera paused to sigh and give a smug little smile. 'No, he wouldn't be satisfied at all. Because you see, medicine really is his thing. He wants to treat real illnesses that affect ordinary people.'

This was at such variance to what Vera had said to her two days before that Rose was quite at a loss as to how best to answer. She opened her mouth to speak and thought better of it. For, although it had occurred to her to point out that Vera was contradicting what she had said previously, she was reminded of the condition in which she had found Vera awaiting her in the hall that day. The woman had been clearly distressed and distracted and she did not wish to say anything that would induce a relapse. But this time Vera was wanting some encouragement before proceeding with her tale, and was looking at Rose expectantly for just such a response. Rose dragged her mind back from contemplating Vera's previous agitated state to the present conversation, which in all honesty she had only been listening to with half an ear.

'And a country practice offers that?' Rose said at last. 'Real illnesses?'

'Oh, yes indeed. You get all sorts of illness in a village such as Sedgwick, because you get people from all walks of life. And you don't know how good it makes Theo feel, to make a real difference. He was able to save Mr Collins's arm. It has healed quite nicely, with no more lasting damage to it than a ghastly scar, which is just as well as Collins has nine mouths to feed. He's a stone mason by way of trade and needs two arms to carry out that job.'

'Yes, I suppose he does. Tell me, Vera, have you always lived in Sedgwick?'

'Yes, and so has Theo, even if he has the air about him of someone who has grown up in town. But we've both lived here all our lives. Theo's father was the village doctor and his father before him. Daddy came to Sedgwick a year or two before I was born, and has been ministering to his flock here ever since.'

Further discussion on the subject was prevented by the arrival of Lavinia, who insisted that they should all go for a walk in the grounds while there was still some light. Rose in truth was relieved to have an excuse to escape Vera's company. It was not so much that she disliked the woman, more that she felt ill at ease in her presence. Was Vera really blind to the true nature of the relationship developing between Emmeline and Theo? She certainly acted as if she were, not seeing what was being played out blatantly before her very eyes and indeed, unfortunately, was becoming increasingly apparent to everyone else. Perhaps she was intentionally deluding herself, Rose thought, desperately clinging to the notion that Theo's only interest in Emmeline was that of a potential patient of standing who might be useful in furthering his career. Or was Vera well aware of what was going on, and had consciously chosen to ignore the situation and pretend to be ignorant?

They set forth as a group, Cedric in front pointing out the ha-has, the various lakes which appeared as one, and the follies dotted around the estate, much as he had done when he had shown them to Rose. She felt a sudden stab of regret that it was not just the two of them walking through the grounds, with perhaps Vera and Theo trailing slowly behind. To be alone here at Sedgwick with Cedric she realised suddenly was what she wanted more than anything in the world. She didn't want to share him with the others, to stand back while he played the jovial host. Why, oh why, had Lavinia seen the need to bring these friends back with her, to expect Cedric to fall in with her wishes and entertain them?

As if in answer to her question, she caught sight of the count walking at Lavinia's side, his dark head bowed towards her so that they could carry on some private conversation which had Lavinia in fits of giggles. If the light had been better, Rose had no doubt, she would have seen a rosy blush upon the girl's cheek. The count and Lavinia ... yes. Rose could see that the notion might hold some attraction to her friend. He was tall and dark and mysterious. Lavinia had hinted at wars in his homeland which had caused him to flee, and the noble cause for which he was fighting to restore order to his land. It all sounded very romantic. Just Lavinia's sort of thing, Rose thought not particularly kindly, as she was momentarily feeling some resentment towards Lavinia and her guests.

Vera was doggedly following Theo, who looked minded to put some distance between them and catch up with Cedric. Vera appeared to be talking to him quite seriously, with never a glance at the various things of interest being pointed out to them by Cedric. Rose supposed that she had seen these all many times before in the light and saw no need to give them a second glance in the dusk. But Theo, Rose could tell, was annoyed, as if he found her conversation irritating. Rose wondered idly whether she was giving forth on the virtues of being a country doctor. Whatever she was saying was not being received at all well, for the doctor stopped and turned suddenly and looked directly at Emmeline who was walking with Jemima. Rose fancied that he tried to catch the girl's eye, but she was unaware of this being herself engaged in deep conversation with Jemima, which necessitated them walking closely together, almost huddled. They appeared to be talking in whispers and Rose was surprised to find that their conversation did not appear to be littered with Emmeline's usual laughter. She wondered what they could be talking about so seriously. Meanwhile, she noticed that Vera was glaring at Theo, and looked undecided as to whether to give him a piece of her mind or pointedly forsake his side. Really, Rose was far from sure which one of the two she felt most sorry for.

'Well, Miss Simpson,' said Felix Thistlewaite suddenly, making her start, 'and how do you find Sedgwick Court? Quite a stately pile, don't you think? How the other half live and all that.'

There was something quite innocuous and endearing about his manner which resulted in Rose not taking offence at his words or assumed familiarity, for she did not think that his intention was to be rude. Rather he seemed only to want to speak the truth as he saw it, and there was something rather naïve about him that she found appealing. He seemed to her very young, although at five or six and twenty he was a few years her senior.

'I must apologise, Rose. May I call you Rose? You must think me very rude and impertinent to speak so of our host and hostess's hospitality. It's jolly decent of Lavinia to invite me here and on the basis of the merest of acquaintances too. If you had told me a few weeks ago that I would find myself the guest of an earl, why, I would never have believed you!'

Rose looked up into his freckled face and smiled. She had had little opportunity to have a proper conversation with Felix Thistlewaite up to now, but she found herself warming to him as she had not to the other guests.

'I'm jolly glad Lavinia invited me,' Felix was saying, 'and I'm awfully glad you and even Miss Brewster are here, although she does seem to be giving that doctor of hers a time of it, doesn't she? But what I mean is I was afraid that it was just going to be a lot of toffs and it's not at all. And Lord Belvedere seems a very decent sort of chap, although of course you don't need me to tell *you* that.'

Rose blushed. 'You met Lavinia on the Continent?' she said, partly to change the subject and also for something to say.

'Yes, I met them all in Florence and we visited all the galleries and gardens and palaces together. We made quite a party, I can tell you. I was there courtesy of my Great Aunt Maud, in case you think I am a gentleman of independent means. Unfortunately I'm not. I'm due to start as an articled clerk in some awful backstreet London office in a few weeks' time. This is my last opportunity to pretend that I am a young man of leisure.'

'I see,' said Rose smiling.

'My Great Aunt Maud is very much of the opinion that gentlemen, even those as poor as church mice like myself, should do the European grand tour. Unfortunately, if anything it has made me even more dissatisfied with my lot.' He paused a moment and looked over towards the huddled couple of Emmeline and Jemima, still engrossed in whispered conversation. 'I say, she is rather wonderful, isn't she?'

'Emmeline? Yes, I suppose she is.'

'No, not Emmeline. There is nothing very wonderful about *her*. She is exactly as one would imagine an heiress to be, awfully spoilt, you know, used to getting her own way and commanding everyone's undivided attention and all that. No, rather I was talking of Jemima. How that poor girl puts up with her, I can't imagine. She's treated more like a servant than a relative. And yet she is a distant relation of Emmeline's, you know, but as poor as anything. She fulfils the role of companion from what I can gather, and hates every minute of it I shouldn't wonder.'

'Yet the way that they call each other by their Christian names, surely that implies they are more friends than employer and employee, doesn't it?' said Rose. Indeed, the way the two girls were huddled so closely together suggested to her that they were exchanging confidences.

'That's just Emmeline's way,' Felix replied rather dismissively. 'It means nothing. She still treats Jemima like a lady's maid, expects her to do her hair and put out her clothes and all that. I've heard her speak to Jemima quite rudely and the poor girl takes it in her stride with never a bad word said. Why, if I had my way I'd take her away from it all, I can tell you.'

Rose looked up at him, somewhat taken aback by his frankness. Felix had the grace to blush.

'Sorry, I shouldn't have said that. Why, I haven't even told the girl herself how I feel about her. But I'm in no position to offer her marriage, at least not until I've done a few years of this articled clerk lark.' He groaned. 'I daresay she wouldn't have me. A girl like that could do a damned sight better than a fellow like me.'

Rose looked up and caught Jemima looking at Felix. There was something in her look which made Rose think that Felix's feelings for the girl might not be unrequited after all. At the same time Rose wondered what there was about her that made people feel that they could confide in her their innermost hopes and fears. First there had been Vera and her fear that mixing with grand society would increase Theo's desire to become a fashionable doctor. And now here was Felix, a man with whom she had hardly even passed the time of day, confessing his love for Jemima. He hadn't said it was a secret or that she should keep the knowledge to herself, but she assumed that he would not want it broadcast. She thought too that Emmeline was ignorant of Felix's feelings for her companion. Even if his feelings were reciprocated, she thought it unlikely that the reserved Jemima would confide in Emmeline on such a matter. No, Emmeline might confide trivial confidences to Jemima but, from what she had seen of Jemima, the girl kept herself to herself, remained on the edge looking on, an observer of the party rather than a participant. What a strange girl she is, thought Rose, I can hardly make her out. She watches us all so intently, listens to our conversations and yet does not offer up a view unless specifically asked for one.

It was only as they made their return journey to the house in the dark that another thought occurred to Rose. It hit her so forcibly, and so suddenly, that she actually stopped in her tracks causing Vera to walk into her and Felix to give her a concerned look and ask if anything was the matter. In truth she was not sure how to answer him. For only now had something struck her, something that seemed to make no sense at all given their respective stations in life. But, as she recalled those huddled figures, it was as if she were seeing them in a new, much clearer light. What was it that Emmeline was seeking so desperately from Jemima? Did she have a constant need for reassurance or was it a desire for something else? Was she not after all looking to Jemima for something more, approval even? And if she was, then surely that could only mean one thing. The heiress was afraid of her companion.

Chapter Six

Rose mulled over the curious relationship between Emmeline and Jemima while she was dressing for dinner that evening. As a consequence, without thinking, she dressed with the same haste that she employed when getting ready for a day in Madame Renard's dress shop when she had little, if any, time to spare. Still engrossed in her thoughts, she neglected to consult her wristwatch before descending the staircase and, much to her dismay, found that she was the first down. She admonished herself for having been so preoccupied with thinking about the heiress and her companion to the exclusion of all else, for she did not relish the prospect of having to wait for her fellow diners to join her in the drawing room for cocktails. There was Vera's magazine to read of course while she waited, but otherwise little to do but stand around rather self-consciously, and awkwardly, alone.

She had just made up her mind to return to her room when the door of the drawing room opened, thus preventing her escape. Before she could speculate as to the identity of the newcomer, Count Fernand walked into the room, dressed in his usual flamboyant finery, which did not look so very out of place in the evening. If he was disappointed to find that she was the only one down, rather than the much favoured Lavinia or Emmeline, he did not show it. Rose wondered, after a moment of awkwardness on both their parts, whether he wasn't after all a little pleased to have an opportunity to speak to her alone.

'Ah, Miss Simpson.' He came towards her and gave a low bow. 'We are the first down, are we not? What does this signify, do you think? Are the others a little slow or are you and I a little too eager to partake of our cocktails?' He gave her a disarming smile.

For the first time Rose saw his appeal. There was something so charming and affable about his manner that she found herself laughing with him. She had had few occasions to converse with him since his arrival, his attentions having usually been directed towards Lavinia and Emmeline. Receiving his undivided attention as she now was, and thus experiencing the full force of his personality, she began to understand why Lavinia had invited him to stay at Sedgwick. The man certainly had a knack of making himself agreeable. There was something appealing too about his quaint way of speaking, coupled with his voice with its foreign accent. The effect of which was to make his words sound more fascinating than perhaps they really were.

'This is a very beautiful estate that the young earl has, is it not? Lakes and parkland as far as the eye can see and all beautifully tended. England is certainly a green and pleasant land, is it not, for the likes of the Earl of Belvedere? And Lavinia is indeed fortunate to live here. To have a brother who is so attentive, she is most lucky, is she not?' He looked at her keenly and smiled, the whiteness of his teeth contrasting attractively with his suntanned skin. 'You are an old friend of Lavinia's and our Lord Cedric's. You know them well?' He learned forward unexpectedly and Rose instinctively took a step back. There was still the same charming smile upon his face, but something had changed. All at once he seemed to her a little less affable, more prying even. Perhaps he was aware of the direction of her thoughts, or conscious that at any moment they might be joined by the others, for his next words were said abruptly, with a degree of urgency about them.

'They are close are they not, Lavinia and her brother? They care about what each other thinks? They do not like to do anything of which the other might disapprove? Tell me, am I right?'

'Yes, indeed,' Rose said quickly. 'I think it unlikely that Lavinia would behave rashly, if that is what you are asking me. Certainly not in respect of anything that would change her situation irretrievably.'

His abruptness had demanded a candid answer, and so she had responded in such a fashion. Yet she was still quite unprepared for the look of fury that had appeared momentarily on the count's face before he had recovered his equanimity. Worse, she had actually believed for one second that he meant to strike her. For one ghastly moment the handsome face had become distorted and ugly. The transformation was fleeting, but the damage was done. For the awful image stayed with Rose long after, so that it still appeared clear in her mind's eye when she retired for bed that night and rose up before her as she tossed and turned in her bed clothes. The mask had slipped and she had caught a glimpse of the man beneath the gorgeous façade.

That Count Fernand was dangerous she now had little doubt. And he had manipulated her, deliberately lulled her into a false sense of security with his charming manner before putting his impertinent question to her.

Rose made her excuses and left the drawing room as quickly as she could. The thought of attempting to exchange polite conversation with the count while waiting on the others to arrive was now unbearable, given that she saw him in a different, more sinister, light. Undoubtedly he would think her rude rushing off, but better that than to stay and fear angering him further. The question now was where to go. The obvious course of action was to retreat to her room and wait until she was sure at least one or two of the others had gone down, before retracing her steps to the drawing room. But she was not in the mood for solitude. Besides, she felt the need to warn Lavinia about the count or, at the least, to ascertain how deep her feelings were for the man.

'Oh, it's you, Rose,' Lavinia said, catching sight of her out of the corner of her eye, while gazing as ever at her own reflection in her dressing table mirror. 'I didn't think it could be Eliza. No doubt she's still arranging Emmeline's hair. I do wish Emmie had brought her own lady's maid with her. Eliza's not going to have time to do *my* hair. Well, I suppose I'll manage. I don't suppose you could …?' She caught the look on Rose's face and thought better of it. 'No, don't worry. I'm sure I can manage …'

'Lavinia, how well do you know Count Fernand?'

'Well, hardly at all,' replied Lavinia, twisting a piece of her hair one way and then the other to see how it looked. 'Why do you ask? Don't you think him handsome? He is quite the most charming man I have ever met. His manners! He really is – '

'Are you very fond of him, Lavinia?' Rose interrupted, asking her question anxiously. She came into the room and hovered by the bed, clutching her hands.

'Well, of course not,' retorted Lavinia. 'But his company is delightful, and he's so attentive, just as if he finds everything I have to say of the utmost interest, fancy that! And he tells the most wonderful stories. That scar on his face, the one that makes him look so jolly good looking, why he told me all about how he came by it. It was just as one would imagine, a duel fought over a woman's honour.'

'Lavinia – '

'Oh, I don't believe a word of it, of course. He probably just slipped on some ice, or something frightfully boring like that. No, what I am trying to say is that his stories are awfully amusing. I could simply sit and listen to him for hours. I think it's that foreign accent, don't you? It makes everything he says sound so frightfully more interesting than it really is, don't you think?'

'Thank goodness,' Rose said, perching on the end of her friend's bed and visibly relaxing. 'I was afraid that you might think him a man to break one's heart over.'

'Not I,' replied Lavinia, cheerfully. 'As it happens, I wasn't quite sure which one of us he liked best. He seemed awfully keen on Emmeline when we were on the Continent. But why are you so interested in what I think of him?' She turned and looked at Rose suspiciously. 'You're not in love with him yourself, are you?'

Rose could not help but detect a hopeful note in her friend's voice.

'No, of course not. If you must know, I don't like him very much.'

'Oh, is that all.' Lavinia sounded bored and returned her attention to gazing at her reflection. 'Well, he's my guest, not yours, and I find him interesting which is all that matters. Now, if that's all – '

'I'm sorry,' Rose said hastily. 'I wanted to ask you something else. No, not about the count,' she added quickly, as Lavinia looked about to protest. 'It's about Emmeline and Jemima. It's the strangest thing, but I cannot get the impression out of my mind that Emmeline's a little scared of Jemima? I can't think why that should be, can you? I mean, Jemima's her companion.'

'Well of course Emmeline's afraid of Jemima,' Lavinia said dismissively. 'And with good cause I can tell you. She reports everything back to Emmeline's father. The poor girl told me that she can't sneeze without Mr Montacute being told about it. One can't really blame him, of course. He's just over protective of his daughter, has been ever since the kidnapping attempt.'

'Kidnapping attempt, what kidnapping attempt?'

'Oh, Rose, you must have heard about it. It was in all the newspapers at the time. They were full of nothing else, what with Emmeline being sole heir to the Montacute fortune, and only being a girl of fourteen or fifteen at the time. They were very lucky that the kidnap didn't succeed. You must remember all the rumour and gossip surrounding it. There were reports at the time that all sorts of prominent people had been involved in the plot; you know, bankers, policemen and politicians, although I don't think anything was ever proved.'

'Really?'

'Emmeline told me her father became quite ill with the worry of it all. He didn't know who he could trust. So he bought some stately mansion in the remote Highlands of Scotland and Emmeline has been living there with him like a recluse ever since. Well,' Lavinia admitted, 'not quite a recluse, because her father has held the most spectacular balls and parties for her there, but he is always very careful who he invites and the place is heavily fortified with an army of servants who man all the doors and windows and patrol the grounds. Emmeline says that it's quite like living in a palatial prison.'

'How awful. Tell me, how long has Jemima been companion to Emmeline?' Rose asked intrigued. 'Presumably she's living under the same conditions?'

'Only about a year or two, I think,' replied Lavinia. 'I think Mr Montacute was afraid his daughter would become bored with her own company when he had to leave Scotland from time to time on business. So he invited Jemima to come and stay and of course she's frightfully grateful to him. Her family are in rather a poor way.'

'And yet he … Mr Montacute that is, is quite happy for his daughter to go on the Continent and stay here at Sedgwick? I have to say, Lavinia,' said Rose, 'I've seen no sign of Mr Montacute's servants manning the doors and windows here or patrolling the grounds. I daresay they do it all very discreetly and with the minimum of fuss, but even so …'

'Ah, well, about that,' said Lavinia, going very pink and suddenly finding the pattern on the wallpaper surprisingly absorbing, so much so that she was not obliged to look her friend in the eye. 'As it happens Mr Montacute doesn't know she's here.'

Before Rose could respond in any way to this startling revelation, there was a tap on the door and Vera entered the room, looking somewhat surprised to find Rose already ensconced there.

'Lavinia … Oh, I say, I hope I'm not intruding? I just wondered if I could borrow – '

'A dress?' enquired Lavinia rather unkindly. 'Surely Vera you're not going to wear that old black frock again? Haven't you rather done it to death already?'

'Lavinia!' exclaimed Rose, shocked.

'Oh, don't worry, Rose' said Vera, carelessly. 'You don't need to protest on my account. I'm quite used to Lavinia's ways. She doesn't mean anything by it.'

'Actually, this time I do. Wouldn't you rather like to borrow one of my dresses, Vera? Eliza could do something with your hair and I could make you up. Oh, do say yes, it would be such great fun, wouldn't it? Rose?'

Rose nodded, not knowing quite what to say or what she thought of the proposal. It seemed to her that it would take more than a well-groomed Vera to tear Theo's eyes away from Emmeline. Perhaps though it was worth a try.

As it happened, Vera was having none of it.

'I'm not some mannequin or doll for you to dress up, thank you very much,' Vera said rather crossly. 'Clothes and make up really are not my thing at all, as you well know, Lavinia. Besides, Theo likes me just the way I am.'

'Are you sure about that?' Lavinia said rather coldly.

'What exactly do you mean by that?' cried Vera defensively, a wild gleam appearing in her eye.

'Only that Theo seems to be enjoying the company of Emmeline Montacute rather too much for my liking …'

Lavinia let the sentence drift off into silence, which for a few moments no one in the room seemed inclined to break. Rose looked desperately first at Lavinia and then at Vera, wondering what to do for the best. Privately she thought Lavinia had gone too far. Vera's face had become quite ashen and she was clenching and unclenching her hands in an agitated manner. Finally, when the silence became almost too much to bear, Vera sank herself onto the bed beside Rose and said resignedly:

'He's hoping that she'll help further his career, that's all. I won't say I like it. I want us to stay here in Sedgwick, but you know what Theo's like. He has ideas of becoming a fashionable doctor. But he wouldn't like it, not really, I know he wouldn't.'

Vera's voice to Rose's ears sounded strained, as if the woman were trying to convince herself of the truthfulness of her words. Rose felt desperately sorry for her and rather angry towards Lavinia for upsetting her so. Yes, she admitted rather grudgingly to herself, Lavinia was just saying what everyone else secretly thought, but really, there were ways to go about it and this was not one of them.

'Come on, we'd better go down,' Rose said, to put an end to the conversation. 'They'll probably all be waiting on us, wondering where we are. I'm sure that we'll be dreadfully late.'

Lavinia was through the door even before Vera had risen to her feet. Rose stayed back and took Vera's hand in hers, squeezing it for a moment.

'It'll be all right, see if it isn't. You mustn't take any notice of Lavinia, I know I don't.'

Vera nodded and gave a feeble smile that did not reach her eyes. Somewhat miserably she followed Rose downstairs. But, even as Rose made her way down the grand oak staircase to the black and white tiled hall below, she knew with almost certainty that everything would not be all right, for she felt it in the air.

Chapter Seven

'We'll be late. Do hurry. Everyone will be waiting for us, or should I say *you*,' Jemima said, staring at Emmeline's reflection in the dressing table mirror.

Emmeline did not turn around, but instead studied herself critically in the mirror.

'I'm certain they won't mind waiting a moment or two for us. There's something missing, don't you think? I need some sort of necklace or trinket to set off this frock. Lavinia always seems to be absolutely draped in diamonds.' She opened her jewel box and toyed with the jewellery inside, letting the necklaces and bracelets fall through her fingers, pausing every now and then to hold up one or two of the most eye-catching pieces so that they caught the light.

'Lavinia wears far too much jewellery,' Jemima said. 'It's as if she were going to a ball. I daresay she's trying to impress you,' she paused, 'or Count Fernand.'

'You're no doubt right. But I am rather tired of wearing this string of pearls. Of course,' Emmeline added hurriedly, 'they're very fine and understated and all that. I daresay they show breeding, but ... well, they're something a maiden aunt might wear. I'd like to wear something different tonight, something that will make even Lavinia gasp.'

She shut the jewel box and waited for Jemima to respond. There was an awkward pause, and she thought for an awful moment that Jemima wouldn't say anything, wouldn't make it easy for her, and that she would be forced to ask outright.

'You mean ...' Jemima said at last, and then stopped.

'Yes, oh, yes!' Emmeline said excitedly, swinging around on the stool. 'Couldn't I, just this evening? Just this once? Surely it isn't too much to ask?'

'They're too precious, too valuable. We should have asked Cedric to lock them in his safe.'

'We can do that tomorrow. I'll wear them tonight, and then you can do with them as you will tomorrow.'

'I still – '

'Oh, please don't let us argue about it,' implored Emmeline. 'Surely it's not too much to ask, is it? Why, I'll only be wearing them for a few hours at most, and then I'll hand them over to you to look after and lock away in Cedric's safe as you see fit. And I promise I won't make a fuss about wearing the pearls after that.'

'Oh … very well,' said Jemima, resigned but still full of misgivings, 'wear the diamonds tonight if you must.'

Vera, Rose noticed, watched Theo and Emmeline closely over dinner. For once, however, they appeared to have little to say to each other, so that Emmeline's usual giggling chatter was directed to those around the table as a whole, rather than to the doctor exclusively. Rose silently breathed a sigh of relief. If Vera's suspicions had been aroused by Lavinia's words, then there was nothing in Theo and Emmeline's behaviour to prove them founded. She wondered idly whether the two had had some form of a disagreement, or perhaps conversely they had decided only to be more discreet in their conduct.

Whatever the position, the dinner passed pleasantly enough and, when the gentlemen joined the ladies later in the drawing room after their cigars and port, agreeable conversation flowed. Any lingering tension in the atmosphere thawed. A fire crackled and burned brightly in the grate, and the various jewels worn by Lavinia and Emmeline sparkled every now and then in the light from the chandeliers.

And yet there was still something about Emmeline Montacute that seemed to mesmerise them all. Even those outside her immediate circle of Theo, Lavinia and Count Fernand, felt drawn to watching her. The onlookers, feeling excluded and yet equally intrigued, were silent for a time, busying themselves with sipping their drinks or lighting, and puffing at, cigarettes to give themselves something to do before they turned their gaze from her and entered into their own conversations.

Rose had just come to the conclusion that the evening was going to pass off without incident, when Vera, who had been particularly quiet all evening, opened her mouth and spoke in an unnecessarily high voice, the effect of which was to cut, like a knife, through the various conversations going on in the room.

'It must have been awful for you, being kidnapped, I mean.' Vera's words were directed towards Emmeline who immediately paled. She attempted to stutter a reply and then gave Jemima a look of such distress that Rose feared she might be going to faint. Theo, obviously of the same opinion, leapt to her side, clutched her hand and put an arm around her to support her and thus prevent her from falling.

'Vera! Really how could you?'

Theo almost spat out the words over his shoulder and that, together with the accompanying look of fury on his face, saw his fiancée visibly retreat to the corner of the room, reeling from the hatred and emotion expressed in those few words. Jemima meanwhile was grim faced and was clutching at the back of the armchair she happened to be standing behind. She had remained where she was during the outburst, and only now did she venture forward to go and stand before Vera, her eyes blazing with barely concealed emotion.

'How dare you! How could you be so unkind as to mention that? What sort of a person are you?'

Jemima's eyes had a wild look about them and she seemed close to tears. Felix went over to her quickly and showed her to a chair on which she sank down heavily, sobbing quietly into her handkerchief. Felix knelt down before her, whispering words of comfort, before bestowing a look on Vera which equalled Theo's in its ferocity.

Vera retreated further to the edges of the room and looked as if she wished to disappear into the shadows. The others meanwhile had been standing around in amazement, not quite believing that they were witnessing such a spectacle in the drawing room of Sedgwick Court. To make matters worse, out of the corner of her eye, Rose saw one of the footman endeavouring to keep his face expressionless. She had little doubt that news of the incident would soon be spreading around the servants' hall like wild fire. Inwardly she cursed Vera for behaving so rashly and Lavinia for her meddling, which she felt had made the situation worse, and which she was far from certain had been well meant.

The outburst had created an uncomfortable atmosphere among the party which threatened to spoil the rest of the evening. Certainly everyone appeared at a loss as to what to say or do to restore the agreeable ambience that had previously prevailed. Cedric looked particularly ill at ease. No doubt, Rose thought, because he felt as host it was his responsibility to repair matters. She caught his eye and saw the look of desperation on his face.

'Lavinia,' Rose said quickly, 'do you remember those silly games that we used to play in the dress shop when Madame Renard's back was turned and we had a particularly difficult customer to deal with?'

'Y-yes,' said Lavinia, 'although I'm not sure that I can remember …'

'Oh, they were very silly games,' Rose said, lightly. 'But it made me think about parlour games. Don't you think it would be awfully fun to play some now?'

'Oh, rather,' Cedric said quickly.

'You mean charades or pass the slipper?' Lavinia said with distaste and frowned. 'I've always been absolutely hopeless at charades and, really, I've never quite seen the point of pass the slipper.'

'Parlour games are for children, I think, are they not?' said Count Fernand, joining in the conversation. 'But I agree with Miss Simpson that games can be fun. You ladies, you like fine gowns and fine jewels, do you not?'

'Of course,' agreed Lavinia. 'A woman can never have enough diamonds. I never tire of looking at my diamonds and seeing how they catch the light. I do think diamonds look beautiful in candlelight, don't you?'

'I do. You say you like to look at your diamonds, and yet I think you have never looked at them, not properly.'

'I can't think what you mean by that,' said Lavinia, 'I look at mine all the time, don't you, Emmeline? Well I would, only Cedric insists that I keep them locked up in the safe when I'm not wearing them.'

'Oh, yes,' agreed Emmeline, rallying, 'all the time, don't I Jemima?'

All eyes turned to the heiress's companion, but Jemima said nothing, as if she were still lost in her own little world of despair.

'I'm always opening my jewel box just to look at them,' Emmeline continued. 'And diamonds are my absolute favourites.' She turned to look at Jemima, who still appeared absorbed in her own thoughts. There was a moment's hesitation before she went on excitedly, but nevertheless almost whispering: 'Especially the Montacute Diamonds.'

'The Montacute Diamonds?' exclaimed Lavinia, with equal excitement. 'Do they really exist?'

'I think I've read about them somewhere,' said Felix, showing some interest in the conversation for the first time. 'They're supposed to be worth a king's ransom, aren't they?'

'Yes, oh, yes!' exclaimed Emmeline, detaching herself from Theo and going over to the count. The colour had returned to her face and it appeared that she at least had been quick to regain her composure. She threw a glance at Jemima who had stopped crying and was now sitting quietly, although she still looked pale and agitated. 'They are magnificent, aren't they, Jem?'

Jemima nodded, but again said nothing. Undeterred, Emmeline went on, obviously determined to veer the conversation away from talk of the attempted kidnapping.

'There's a necklace, a tiara, two broaches, a ring, some pendant earrings. I've probably missed out one or two other things, but one gets the gist. A complete suite of jewels, Max. The centrepieces in both the tiara and necklace are frightfully beautiful. Large, yellow and internally flawless diamonds mounted in platinum and rose gold and surrounded by ever so many white diamonds.'

'They sound magnificent,' exclaimed Lavinia.

'They're awfully pretty,' agreed Emmeline, 'really they are. Of course they're so frightfully valuable they're kept at the bank and only brought out and worn on very special occasions.'

'How did your father come by them?' enquired Cedric.

To Rose, he sounded a little bored of the conversation, but determined to play his part.

'M-my father didn't,' Emmeline hesitated slightly for a moment. 'My grandfather acquired them from an Indian prince, I think, and gave them as a present to my grandmother. I don't believe the prince really wanted to sell them. The story goes that he went hunting big game with my grandfather and that they entered into a wager over who could shoot the most tigers. The prince was very confident that he would win because he spent nearly all his time shooting big game. He wagered the diamonds. But Grandfather was a very good shot, even if he was more used to shooting rabbits and pheasants than he was tigers. He won the wager much to the consternation of the prince, and brought the diamonds back home to England with him.'

'The poor prince,' said Lavinia. 'He can't have been very popular with his subjects ... is that what you call them in India? Or is it just in England, and then only when one is referring to a king or queen? No, don't tell me. I say, though, I wonder if they are cursed, the diamonds I mean? Perhaps they were cursed on leaving the shores of India.'

'Oh don't say that,' Emmeline said, shivering slightly.

'What nonsense, Lavinia,' said Cedric. 'You do talk absolute rot sometimes.'

'But it is such a pity to have to keep such beautiful jewels locked away,' murmured the count.

'Yes, isn't it,' agreed Emmeline with feeling, 'frightfully dull and all that.'

A few moments of silence returned to the room and the uneasy atmosphere that had lifted temporarily threatened to return. For it seemed that no one else could think of anything to say, as if their thoughts were with the unfortunate prince who had behaved so rashly. And for some unaccountable reason, conversations that had begun before Vera's outburst could not be continued or sustained, and no one could think of any new subject to discuss.

'Whatever did you mean just now, Max, when you said that you thought I'd never properly looked at my diamonds?' Lavinia persisted, addressing Count Fernand.

'What I meant,' explained the count, 'is that you girls do not look at them closely. 'No, no, no.' He held up his hand as Lavinia was about to protest. 'You look to see how the diamond looks on your finger, how well the necklace sits on the nape of your neck and makes your skin glow. You do all this, yes, but you never really look into the diamond. To do that, you need to use one of these.' He produced something from the breast pocket of his dinner jacket that looked like a miniature magnifying glass.

'Whatever is that?' asked Lavinia, intrigued.

'It is a jeweller's loupe,' replied the count. 'Fine jewellery is a great fascination of mine, and diamonds in particular. I regard myself as something of an expert.' He smiled and held out the lens to Lavinia. 'With this little lens, you can see how fine your diamonds really are. You can see if there are any cracks or chips around the edges and you can see the diamonds' many facets. Why, you can even see if any of them have large inclusions or blemishes. Perhaps you want to examine the little claw settings. Are they secure and holding your diamonds fast? Or are they loose? Are you about to lose your beautiful diamonds like this?' He snapped his fingers loudly for dramatic effect and Lavinia squealed excitedly.

'I say,' whispered Cedric to Rose. 'He's a bit much, isn't he?' Why does the chap insist on being so theatrical? I mean to say, his clothes are bad enough, but this?'

'But he is rather good at it, isn't he,' Rose replied, 'putting on a show, I mean? And it has made everyone forget about Vera's spiteful remark about kidnapping. I really can't imagine why she said what she did. I suppose she was deliberately trying to be hurtful.'

While they had been talking, Lavinia had insisted that she have a go at looking at her diamond earring through the jeweller's loupe. The count, eager to oblige, stood just behind her and showed her how to hold the loupe between her index finger and thumb and to place it half an inch or so from her eye.

'You keep the loupe steady by resting it against your cheek … yes … just like that. Now, hold your diamond just a little above your line of vision, so that you can look into it … Yes, hold it here.' He took her hand gently, 'Just a little distance from the loupe … exactly so, yes. Now, tell me, is it in focus?'

There proceeded a number of excited exclamations from Lavinia as she regarded the diamonds in her earring.

'Oh, I can't see any blemishes, can you? They look absolutely wonderful, don't they? Do take a look, Max.'

'Remarkable,' agreed the count, courteously.

'Oh, but what about Emmeline's necklace?' asked Lavinia, admiring it rather grudgingly from where she was standing. 'I say, it does look rather grand.'

'Oh, yes, do let me have a go,' answered Emmeline with enthusiasm. 'Of course it's not a patch on the Montacute diamond necklace, is it, Jemima?'

Her companion nodded, but said nothing. To Rose Jemima suddenly appeared rather anxious, having emerged from her contemplations.

'Now, you must show me how to do it, Max,' Emmeline said. 'Just as you showed Lavinia.'

'Emmeline ...'

'Yes? What is it, Jemima?' The heiress looked annoyed as if she thought Jemima was determined to spoil her fun.

'Well, I don't know whether it's wise to – '

'Oh, no harm is going to come to it,' snapped Emmeline. 'I do wish you wouldn't fuss so. Now, Max, what do I do?'

'I should like to see your necklace very much,' said Count Fernand, 'but if you think ...' His sentence trailed off.

It was obvious to everyone present that the count felt rather uncomfortable at being instrumental in the disagreement between the two girls. Rose wondered whether he regretted bringing out his loupe.

'Well, I wouldn't mind having a look too,' said Felix rallying. 'I've always wanted to look at diamonds as a jeweller would. You'll need to tell me what to look for though. No need to worry, Jemima,' he looked at her tenderly. 'We'll be careful with the necklace, I promise.'

'Yes, rather,' agreed Cedric, moving forward and there were similar murmurings uttered by the rest of the party, who followed his lead, with the exception of Vera, who remained silent and abashed in the corner, and Jemima who still looked anxious despite the various words of reassurance.

The others gathered around Count Fernand and waited impatiently for Emmeline to undo her necklace, which did indeed consist of a very splendid array of diamonds, which glittered invitingly in the chandelier light. It was not lost on them that Jemima made no move to help her with the task.

At last the necklace was unfastened and Emmeline was positioned with the loupe so that she could examine the diamonds. The others then took it in turns to have a look at the necklace, which was passed from one to another. They were not, as Emmeline said, the Montacute Diamonds, but they generated as much interest among the party as if they had been. Jemima alone watched the proceedings like a hawk.

The necklace had come full circle and now it was the turn of the count to examine them. Slowly, the loupe to his eye, he passed the jewels between his fingers, his dark head bent over them as he turned them this way and that to catch the light. After a few moments of deliberation he returned them to the heiress.

'Well?' demanded Emmeline. 'How do you find them?'

There was a slight pause before the count replied: 'They are exquisite, truly exquisite.'

'There's been ever such a to-do in the drawing room,' Charlie, the footman, said to Eliza in the servants' hall as he passed her on her way to help Lavinia undress.

'Well, I can't say I'm surprised,' replied Eliza, 'not with Miss Montacute carrying on the way she is with Dr Harrison. Who'd have believed it? Poor Miss Brewster. Anyone can see she's that upset by it all. Disgraceful I call it. But look here, Charlie Barker, you watch your tongue. Don't you go around gossiping or you'll have Mr Torridge to answer to, so you will.'

It was only later when Eliza sat with Mrs Farrier in the housekeeper's little sitting room, indulging in a last cup of tea before retiring to bed, that she confessed: 'I'm that worried, Mrs Farrier. Something's brewing, so it is. It can't go on like this. Something's going to have to give. And what that'll be I'm sure I don't know. Who'd have thought Dr Harrison would've behaved like a love sick young puppy at his age, and with Miss Brewster here too. I feel for that young woman, really I do. She's taking it awful hard, even if she's pretending she's not.'

'Ay,' said Mrs Farrier. 'It can only lead to trouble one way or t'other.'

The two women sipped their tea in companionable silence and gave a collective sigh. But as each sat there contemplating the worst, it never occurred to either one of them just how awful the worst might be.

At the same time that the housekeeper and the lady's maid were having their discussion in Mrs Farrier's sitting room, a similar conversation was being held upstairs behind closed doors in one of the guest bedrooms.

'I wish that dreadful woman had never mentioned kidnapping,' Emmeline half mumbled, taking her necklace off and placing it carefully in her jewel box.

'Yes. It's made me realise how very foolish we've been. Oh, we shouldn't have come here, really we shouldn't. Whatever were we thinking?' Jemima stood by the door, wringing her hands. 'I'm frightened, oh, I tell you I'm frightened. We should never have done it!'

'I'm sure nothing's going to happen,' said Emmeline. Despite her reassuring words, she sounded anxious. 'We've just allowed ourselves to be frightened by that awful woman. All the same, *he'll* be returning from abroad any day now. He mustn't find out what we've done. There'll be all hell to pay if he does.'

'You're right. He mustn't find us here. Listen,' Jemima grabbed Emmeline's hands and forced the girl to sit down beside her on the bed. 'I know what we'll do. We'll tell Lavinia some tale about being called away on some family business or remembering another engagement, or some such thing, and we'll go back home.'

'But I must speak to Theo first, before we do anything. I suppose you won't want me to tell him the truth? Oh, I wish you'd let me, I do really. There's a possibility he'll still love me when he knows the truth, don't you think so?'

'I can't answer that, but you can't tell him the truth, not while we're still here. Promise me you won't. Promise.' Jemima held Emmeline's hands so tightly that the girl winced, but Jemima did not let go until Emmeline had nodded.

'It's not safe,' continued Jemima, speaking with a degree of urgency. 'I'm not saying you can't ever tell him the truth, of course I'm not. You'll just have to wait, that's all. There's nothing to stop you writing to him when we're away. He does seem very taken with you. But you must be careful. Really, must you make it so very obvious to everyone how in love you are? Vera Brewster strikes me as an unstable sort of a woman. A dangerous woman to cross, I'd have said.'

Emmeline looked so crestfallen, that Jemima sighed and patted the girl's hand.

'Have it your own way,' Jemima said. 'I suppose there's no harm in waiting a day or two before we leave, but no longer mind you. I can't get the feeling out of my head that it's dangerous for us to be here at Sedgwick. I thought we'd be safe here, but I think I was wrong.'

Chapter Eight

The following morning, when Rose came down to breakfast, she was surprised to be greeted by a scene of sorts, this time between Lavinia and Jemima, who appeared to be engaged in some form of a dispute in the hall. Both women were glaring at each other and Lavinia's voice was quite shrill with indignation. Jemima was regarding her with obvious irritation.

'I've told you already, Jemima,' Lavinia was saying in an annoyed tone of voice, 'Emmeline's gone out riding with Cedric. Really, I don't know why you have to go on about it so. Why shouldn't she go out riding without you? Must you follow her around everywhere like a shadow?'

'How could you be so irresponsible? She's no good on a horse at all. She'll hurt herself, she's bound to fall off!'

'Nonsense! She'll be perfectly safe with Cedric. He'll have put her on one of our steady horses, I expect. Merrylegs or Moonstone. And anyway, why should you worry? I was only reading in some newspaper or other how well Emmeline rode to hounds. If she can manage riding miles at a time and jumping dozens of stiles and fences, then I'm sure she'll manage quite well riding one of our hacks around the estate. And besides,' Lavinia stood up tall and glared at Jemima, 'I won't be spoken to like that, not in my own house and certainly not by the likes of you.'

What would have happened next was anyone's guess, but fortunately Rose was relieved of the necessity to intervene by the arrival of Manning who, even to her untrained eye, looked somewhat flustered. As was usual, Torridge tottered in his wake looking suitably composed.

'What is it, Manning? What is it now?' snapped Lavinia, still in an ill humour.

'It's Miss Montacute, m'lady. It appears she's taken something of a tumble from her horse. Miss Denning's had a look at her and says as she thinks it's no more than a few cuts and bruises, but the young lady is quite shaken up, she's …'

He faltered to a stop as Jemima hurried out of the hall to see to her mistress.

Before Lavinia herself had an opportunity to say anything, Cedric, in full riding dress, came striding into the hall.

'A word if you please, Lavinia, in the library,' her brother said coldly, at the same time glaring at his sister, so that it was more a command than a request.

Rose had never known the earl look or sound so angry. With a twinge of regret she noticed that he hardly acknowledged her presence, so intent was he on his purpose. Lavinia meanwhile looked about to open her mouth and protest. On reflection she obviously thought better of it, for she followed Cedric reluctantly into the library, where the door was shut firmly behind her. Rose was left standing in the great black and white tiled hall, with only the dull and austere portraits of the Sedgwicks' ancestors for company.

'Whatever were you thinking, Lavinia, asking me to take Emmeline out riding?' demanded Cedric, as soon as the door was closed behind them. 'You told me she loved riding. I'd be surprised if she's ever ridden more than a few times in her life.'

'Nonsense!' protested Lavinia. 'I read something in an article about her riding to hounds and keeping up with the pack. One can hardly do that if one can't ride, can one? Although I daresay some of the details may have been embellished by the newspaper reporter.'

'I'd say they were! Greatly exaggerated more like. Thankfully Cryer had the good sense to saddle up Moonstone and not Captain. Really, Lavinia, I doubt if Emmeline had ever done much more than trot. You should have seen the look on her face when I suggested that we go for a bit of a gallop. Thankfully we hadn't quite got into a canter before she fell off.'

'Well, no real harm's been done then, has it? A few cuts and bruises, that's all, isn't it?'

'Lavinia –', Cedric began, before his sister interrupted him.

'You needn't go on and on about it, or look at me like that, Ceddie. I'm sure I've learnt my lesson and all that. I just thought it would be a frightfully good thing if I could tear Emmeline away from Theo for a little while, that's all. How was I to know that the silly girl would fall off?'

'You may be able to persuade others that your intentions were honourable, but it doesn't wash with me, Lavinia. I know you too well. No, I think your plan had more to do with keeping Rose and me apart than Theo and Emmeline.'

The conversation between the siblings had been so short that Rose was still in the hall when Lavinia came out of the library.

'Really, Rose, people will make such a fuss about things, won't they? First Jemima, and then Cedric. Why, I've lost count of the number of times I've fallen off a horse. You just get straight back on and don't make a song and dance about it.'

With that, Lavinia hurried off into the breakfast room. Rose held back from following her and decided instead to go into the library where she found Cedric poring over an old atlas.

'Sorry about all that,' Cedric said looking up and smiling. 'I suppose no real harm's been done, no thanks to Lavinia. But I shudder to think what could have happened if Emmeline had been riding Captain instead of Moonstone. I do wish Lavinia hadn't invited those people here.'

'So do I.'

'Of course, it's her home as much as it is mine, but it makes everything so dashed awkward. If only Harrison wouldn't make it so damned obvious how infatuated he is with Emmeline. One can hardly blame Vera for making ructions. It's jolly rotten for her. I've a good mind to have a word with him.'

It was on the tip of Rose's tongue to say that matters had only been made worse by Lavinia's antics of the evening before, but she thought better of it. Instead she asked Cedric what he was doing with the atlas, which was spread out before him on a carved oak, octagonal library table.

'Trying to find the country where our Count Fernand hails from,' he said, studying a page. 'I say, Rose, did you happen to catch the name of the place? I'm dashed if I can remember what he said, although that's not surprising since the man was mumbling at the time. I wonder if it was deliberate. But one doesn't want to admit to one's guests that one wasn't listening.'

'No, I'm afraid I can't recall. I'm not even sure that he told me ... Cedric, I don't like him very much, do you?'

'Not a jot. There's something damn odd about him.' Cedric shrugged and closed the book with a bang. 'It wouldn't surprise me if he'd bought his title from some god forsaken country or wasn't a count at all. I mean, all that swishing of his cloak and scarlet waistcoat business. It's a bit much, isn't it? I don't mind telling you that I've been awfully anxious about him ever since he began paying his attentions to Lavinia. At first I thought it was Emmeline he had his eye on, but of course that was before Harrison threw his hat into the ring.'

He linked Rose's arm through his and they made their way out of the library.

'I don't think he is who he pretends to be, either,' said Rose.

'No,' agreed Cedric. 'I don't trust the fellow at all. I don't trust him one little bit.'

The words were no sooner out of Cedric's mouth when, strolling into the hall, they walked straight into the count himself, who appeared to be loitering there with no apparent intent. Cedric immediately went a bright shade of red, but if Count Fernand had overheard their conversation he gave no sign of it and smiled at them affably.

Rose looked at the count anew, contemplating Cedric's suspicions. It was only then that the rather bizarre notion occurred to her that Count Fernand might not be the only impostor at Sedgwick Court.

After breakfast, Cedric advised Rose that he had a meeting arranged with his estate manager, who was such a capable and competent sort of fellow that it shouldn't take long at all. After that he would be all hers and would join her for a stroll in the grounds as there were still one or two items of interest that he had to show her, and no doubt would have done already, had they not been disturbed by the unexpected arrival of Lavinia and her guests.

The morning promised to be a fine one for a walk, providing one was wrapped up well before venturing out. The lure of the gardens and park seemed to Rose too tempting to wait for Cedric. Besides, she had a sudden desire to leave the guests and their various associated complexities and complications behind. Exploring the grounds alone and taking in the beauty that was Sedgwick Court seemed a suitable means of whiling away the time before Cedric joined her.

Rose had just decided on this course of action when she was joined in the hall by Vera who, on discovering Rose's intentions, asked if she might accompany her on her walk. At a loss as to how she might politely refuse, Rose reluctantly acquiesced, while severely admonishing herself for having remained in the hall dithering. The truth was she did not relish Vera's company. She thought the woman was either likely to be quiet, nervy and on edge, or else give full vent to her feelings towards Lavinia's guests. Neither scenario was particularly appealing.

The door of the breakfast room opened again and this time Theo Harrison came out looking none too pleased, in Rose's opinion, to find Vera standing there. If Vera was aware of his displeasure, she did not show it. '

'Theo, won't you join us?' cried Vera. 'Rose and I are going for a walk in the gardens. It's such a delightfully crisp morning, don't you think so? Such a shame to waste it by being inside.'

'Not now, Vera,' replied Theo, in a tone that was hardly friendly. Indeed he barely looked at her.

To Rose it was obvious that the doctor had not forgiven his fiancée for her behaviour of the night before. Vera, however, appeared oblivious to this, for she kept pressing for him to join them.

'For goodness sake, Vera. I have some medical matters to attend to, some writing up of notes and so forth. I have not got time for this.'

With that he was gone, mounting the stairs two at a time, leaving Vera to look after him somewhat dejectedly.

'He works too hard,' she said to Rose, 'but he won't be told.'

They made their way to the formal gardens, which looked rather bleak in winter, there being a dearth of flowers in bloom to brighten the landscape. Only the marigolds seemed to be thriving, shining bright orangey-yellow in the thin winter sunshine. How wonderful it would be to see the gardens in the spring and summer, Rose thought, when they would be at their best. She wondered whether she would be invited, if Lavinia had her way.

To Rose's relief, Vera appeared on good form, chattering happily about Theo's work in the village and her own charitable work.

At length, Vera declared: 'I daresay I took what Lavinia said last night too much to heart. She does love to shock and say things are black when they are quite obviously white. I can't think where she got that ridiculous idea that Theo was in love with Emmeline, or she with him come to that.'

Rose decided to say nothing. If Vera had resolved to bury her head in the sand, then who was she to make a fuss? Far better that than Vera try and put the cat among the pigeons as she had done the previous evening. While a part of her thought that the adoption of such an approach should at least make for an agreeable and peaceful evening, another part of her wished that Vera would confront Theo in private to determine his feelings for Emmeline, and to persuade him to rein in his caddish behaviour.

Poor Vera, Rose thought, as they wandered rather aimlessly around the gardens. They happened to be talking about the latest church bazaar that Vera had become involved with and the poor quality of the clothes donated, when they rather unexpectedly came across Jemima and Felix sitting on a stone bench overlooking the rose garden. Due to the positioning of the bench and the fact that the two were seated facing away from them, the two women were placed in the rather uncomfortable position of being able to observe Felix and Jemima while themselves being unobserved.

If they were tempted to make their presence known, then the intimate manner in which Felix and Jemima were sitting together, hands clasped tightly and talking earnestly and quietly to one another, rather deterred them from doing so. The most discreet and appropriate course of action seemed to be to change course, and this is what the two women did, but not before they had caught a few words of Felix and Jemima's conversation.

'I'll be absolutely miserable in London without you, Jem. If only I didn't have to make my own way in life. I daresay I can make a reasonable living in the legal profession if I put my mind to it, but it will be a few years before I can support a wife. Will you wait for me, do you suppose? Is it too much for me to ask of you? Tell me it isn't?'

'I'll wait, Felix, although Scotland is so very far from London. We'll write of course, but we'll hardly see one another.'

'Oh, I don't think I can bear it,' groaned Felix, putting his head in his hands. 'I say,' he looked up suddenly, 'couldn't you get a positon in London? It would be too horrid and beastly for words if I never saw you.

I'm afraid that it might take me years and years to make a go of it in the law. Of course, I'll try, really I will – '

'What if, 'Jemima interrupted, speaking slowly, 'we didn't have to wait? What if I could get my hands on some money now, what then?'

Vera and Rose did not hear any more of their conversation, or indeed how Felix had answered Jemima's question. The scene they had just witnessed made Rose think of Cedric and the many intimate words that they had exchanged. How she wished that he was walking beside her now and that they could escape to some secluded part of the grounds to exchange confidences.

'Poor things. They seem very much in love, don't they?' Vera said, obviously moved by their plight.

Rose wondered whether it made her think of her dwindling relationship with Theo. She could not imagine that he had ever spoken to Vera so tenderly, particularly given the way he had snubbed her company this morning. Perhaps Vera was thinking the same thoughts, certainly she appeared on the verge of tears.

'Let's walk on to the lake,' suggested Rose hurriedly.

She thought it unlikely that they would encounter anyone there other than the odd gardener or estate servant. In this however, she was to be sadly mistaken.

As soon as she heard the first sounds of laughter, Rose knew they should turn back. Vera, however, thought otherwise and quickened her stride.

'Vera, no ...' But Rose's words trailed off into silence.

The effect of her words seemed only to encourage Vera onward. For there was now a grim, determined look on the woman's face that indicated she would not be swayed. Indeed, if anything, she increased her pace so that Rose was now running to keep up with her. For a moment Rose wondered whether to shout out some form of a warning, to give the others sufficient time to disappear, or at the very least, stand apart. But she had hesitated for too long and now it was too late. For Vera had turned the corner so that the hedge that had obscured her vison was now behind her and the inevitable scene, the one that she had both most feared and obdurately refused to believe was possible, was now playing out before her eyes.

Rose turned the corner and saw the scene as if through Vera's eyes. The man was Theo Harrison, but not the staid country doctor that she knew. He might resemble him physically but there the similarity ended. This man seemed relaxed and younger, and was playfully chasing Emmeline Montacute beside the lake, he laughing, she giggling and shrieking hysterically, as if it were all the most marvellous game. And for them it was, because even as the two women looked on, Emmeline stopped running and turned and Theo catching up with her, pulled her towards him until they collapsed into each other's arms.

Rose tore her eyes away from Theo and Emmeline and looked at Vera, who was trembling and staring in disbelief. For a moment, Rose did not know whether Vera was going to faint or march over and confront her fiancé. But in the end she did neither. For the doctor and the heiress, with eyes only for each other, and thus totally oblivious to the presence of the interlopers, had walked on. Vera, after staring at their retreating backs a moment, clenched her hands and, ignoring Rose completely, turned on her heel and ran back to the house, every now and then stumbling blindly, but nevertheless persistently carrying on.

Chapter Nine

'Careful, Vera, you'll break that glass if you're not careful,' Lavinia said, 'they are rather precious, you know. They've been in the family for generations, haven't they, Ceddie? By the way, is your headache better, Vera? You must be awfully hungry missing luncheon. I did ask cook to send up a tray, but when it came back, she said it had been barely touched.'

'I'm afraid I wasn't very hungry. I feel better now, though,' answered Vera, staring forlornly at a bit of the carpet. They were standing in the drawing room having cocktails before dinner. It was the first time that she had come down from her room since the incident at the lake and, although Rose was relieved to see her, Vera had barely spoken a word, and seemed unnaturally calm given the circumstances. Lavinia, having done her hostess duties as she perceived them, seemed unconcerned and taking Rose by the elbow steered her to another part of the room out of earshot.

'Really, Rose, Vera is being very silly. If Theo were my fiancé, I wouldn't put up with such behaviour.'

Rose blushed and was glad that, with the exception of Cedric, she had told no one about the scene at the lake.

'He's making a fool of her,' Lavinia carried on. 'If I were Vera I wouldn't stand for it. I'd take him aside and tell him what's what. But knowing Vera she won't do that. She'll just look at him with those sad, doleful eyes and be a martyr, or else things will get too much for her and she'll cause a scene which will be very embarrassing for all of us. And Theo won't think any the better of her for it. She'll drive him away.'

Unlike Lavinia, Rose felt more sympathetic towards Vera and her plight. As she stood regarding her she was aware of a tangible tension in the room, which seemed to emanate from the woman like a perfume. Vera had moved and was now standing at the very edge of the room, on the periphery between the drawing room and the hall as if she were in two minds whether to come back in or turn around and walk back to her room or out of the house. She was staring fixedly at Emmeline and clutching at the top of an occasional table positioned just inside the door, having abandoned the wine glass which stood discarded on the table. Her hands were clenched, Rose noticed, and her knuckles had gone quite white.

How highly strung she is, Rose thought. It won't take much to send her over the edge. She's like a spring that is waiting to unravel, and instinctively she moved towards her and took Vera's hand before she could do damage to the table top with her fingernails.

For a moment, Vera just stared at her, a blank expression on her face as if she did not know where she was, or what she was doing. Perhaps she saw in Rose a kindred spirit, or a compassionate one at least, for the next moment she was venting the emotions and feelings that she had been keeping bottled up inside her all day.

'Look at her! You have to applaud her, don't you? The way she manages to keep them all enthralled. Why, they're hanging on her every word. Even that strange fish, Felix, is rather taken with her I fancy. And look how much she is enjoying all the attention. I think that's the worst of it, don't you? You'd think she'd be used to it by now, wouldn't you? Instead she behaves like a child let loose in a sweetshop. Men must flock to her wherever she goes. Beauty and wealth, what a very winning combination. Do you ever feel how unfair it all is for women like us, Rose? How can we possibly compete with the likes of Emmeline Montacute?'

'Vera ...'

'And she has Theo quite bewitched. Just look at the way he is looking at her. Oh, it's enough to make one sick, it really is. Before she arrived, Theo and I were quite content you know, in a quiet, unassuming sort of a way. She doesn't care that he and I are engaged to be married and have been for simply ages. She doesn't care that he's mine. That doesn't bother her at all. Perhaps it amuses her, to take a man away from another woman. And it is not as if she will want anything to come of it. She won't want to marry a country doctor, or even a fashionable doctor, come to that. Oh, if only Theo were not so very weak. I-I don't think I can bear much more of this.' Vera snatched her hand away from Rose's and stifled a sob by putting her handkerchief to her mouth.

Rose looked around quickly. All the while Vera had been talking, her voice had been rising and becoming shriller. However, standing apart from the others as they were, no one else appeared to have noticed. Or at least if they had, they were pretending not to have done. How wretched Vera looked. Her unhappiness was making her ill. It can't go on like this, Rose thought, Vera becoming more miserable by the hour. She felt annoyed with Theo Harrison for putting his fiancée in this position. How could he behave so inconsiderately? Could the doctor really be so mesmerised by Emmeline Montacute that he was oblivious to the distress he was causing to the woman to whom he was engaged? The sooner Cedric spoke to Theo the better, and Rose made a mental note to remind him after dinner.

'Theo is behaving very badly,' she said aloud to Vera. 'He must realise how unhappy he is making you. But if you are so very miserable, must you bear it? Why don't you think up some excuse and leave? If you hate it all so very much, why stay?'

'Must he? I don't know. I don't believe he realises and even if he did, I don't think he cares. And we don't discuss such things, he and I. It's all rather awkward, you see, and then again I can't seem to get a moment alone with him. *She's* always there. It's as if he's forgotten I am here, as if I've faded into the background and he can't see me. Perhaps I have become invisible to him. Do you think so? I couldn't bear it if I had. Oh, I know that the sensible thing would be to leave, but I just can't do it, I tell you, I can't. And while I'm still here, there's a possibility that he'll come to his senses, isn't there?'

Vera turned away to stare at Theo and Emmeline. Her timing was unfortunate in that she caught them at that moment being particularly flirtatious towards each other. Emmeline had her hand on Theo's arm as if she were trying to draw him towards her, and she must have spoken to him very quietly for he bent his head towards her as if trying to catch her words. She giggled suddenly and Theo grinned. Vera flinched as if she had been struck. She spat out her next words through clenched teeth, saying them with such hatred and fury, that they sent a shiver down Rose's spine.

'How can they? I hate them, I tell you I hate them! I wish they were dead!'

Looking around desperately, Rose noticed that Lavinia too was bristling around the edges, for the count also appeared a little taken by Emmeline. Unlike Vera, Lavinia was not content to remain on the edges, but instead did her best to infiltrate the little group of Emmeline, Theo, the count and Felix, and to some success. The count immediately switched his attention to include her and soon her laughter filled the air to rival Emmeline's. And all the while Vera looked on and sought refuge in her glass rather than following Lavinia's example and joining in.

Once dinner was over, Lavinia had given the signal for the ladies to depart the dining room and leave the men to their port and cigars before they joined the women in the drawing room for coffee. Cedric had always enjoyed this time after dinner. It was an opportunity for the men to relax and talk more easily and freely among themselves, and on subjects of little interest to the women. This weekend, however, was different and he sighed, for he had found that the present company of men, consisting only of the three of them as it did, was not inclined to linger in the dining room.

For one thing the count seemed disinterested in male company and conversation, and Harrison too, who had in the past enjoyed this tradition of male camaraderie, appeared eager now to re-join the ladies as soon as was politely possible. As a consequence, the business of cigars and port was unusually rushed and, after a short while, the port was carried into the drawing room.

Tonight, though, Cedric was keen to prolong the ritual in so far as the doctor was concerned. Breaking with tradition he suggested to Count Fernand, who looked distinctly bored at the prospect of staying behind, that he re-join the ladies. It was Cedric's intention that he and the doctor would follow shortly. As Theo Harrison looked at him quizzically, Cedric played over in his mind what he wanted to say and the approach to take. It seemed to him that he was obliged to adopt the role of the older man, even though in reality Theo was probably some eight or ten years his senior. He sighed. The whole business was going to be damned embarrassing and awkward for both of them, but he supposed he was resigned to that.

Cedric rose from his seat and began pacing the room so that he would not be obliged to look the other man in the eye. He also felt that by standing while the other man was seated gave him the upper hand.

'Look here, Harrison,' Cedric began, without preamble, as soon as they were alone. 'I daresay you'll think it none of my business and all that, and I feel dashed embarrassed raising it, but anyone can see you're infatuated with Emmeline Montacute, and that it's making Vera damned miserable.'

'Now, look – ', began Theo angrily, going a deep shade of crimson.

'I appreciate that under normal circumstances it would be none of my business what you get up to,' Cedric interrupted hurriedly, having anticipated that the doctor would make attempts to protest. 'But while you're staying in my house I'll ask that you refrain from making Vera upset. I will not have my guests made miserable.' He glanced at the ceiling a moment, before carrying on quickly in case he lost his nerve. 'And besides, Vera is an old friend,' he paused, 'as of course are you.' He sighed. 'Dash it all, can't you see how it's putting everyone on edge? For goodness sake, Harrison, think what you're doing. Is Emmeline Montacute really worth losing your head over?'

'I suppose you think I should concede defeat now and throw in the towel,' Harrison answered, bitterly. 'I would have thought you of all people, in love with a shop girl as you are, might appreciate how it is to love outside your station.'

'I do,' replied Cedric coldly, resenting the way in which the doctor had referred to Rose. 'But I'm not engaged to marry someone else. I'm not saying that nothing can come of it, of course I'm not, but what I am saying is that you must consider Vera in all this. If you feel so strongly about Emmeline then you owe it to Vera to tell her and break off your engagement.'

Theo glared at the table, and clutched the bottle of port with one hand, his face white with barely concealed fury.

'Are you aware that Vera saw the two of you down by the lake this morning?' continued Cedric more gently. 'How do you think that made her feel? Why do you think she's kept herself shut up in her room all day?'

'She s-saw us? Oh, my God!'

It was as if the doctor had received a sharp slap across the face. For his expression immediately changed, and now a look of anguish crossed his features. Almost trembling, he buried his head in his hands.

'I thought she was going for a walk in the gardens, not by the lake.' Theo groaned and then raised his head. 'Oh, you're right, of course you're right. I've behaved like a cad, I know. I didn't mean to hurt Vera, but I couldn't help myself. I can't explain what I feel for Emmeline. I don't even understand it. All I know is that I have never felt this way about a woman before, and I doubt that I ever will again.'

Cedric felt a touch of compassion. 'You need to resolve the situation one way or the other, old chap,' he said more kindly than he'd spoken before, coming over and laying his hand briefly on the other man's shoulder. 'Otherwise I'm afraid I'll have to ask you to leave.'

Having anticipated that Theo would be annoyed with him after his interference in what was after all essentially a private matter, and fearing that Vera might be tempted to make a scene, Cedric had entered the drawing room with a topic of conversation in mind that was likely to engage his audience without leading to ructions.

'I say, Lavinia, why don't we take everyone to see the maze tomorrow.'

'The maze? Oh, Ceddie, that's a wonderful idea,' squealed his sister, clapping her hands in delight. 'Oh, Emmie, you'll simply love it,' she said, turning to the heiress. 'And it's just as good to do in the winter as in the summer, because the maze is made of privet or yew, or something like that, isn't it, Ceddie?'

'Box,' said her brother. 'It's a hedge planted maze and the hedge is box. We're jolly lucky that it wasn't destroyed when the natural landscaping and sweeping views were introduced at Sedgwick in the eighteenth century. But Lavinia's right, it's just as dense in winter as it is in spring or summer. It was based on the maze at Hampton Court Palace, you know, although not as big, of course. Even so, the hedges are still about six and a half feet tall and two or three feet wide.'

'My goodness!' exclaimed the count. 'And how much area does it cover, this maze of yours?'

'About a third of an acre all told. Takes about a quarter of an hour or so to reach the centre, providing one doesn't take a wrong turn of course.'

'Oh, Cedric, there's that frightful story about the housemaid, isn't there?' exclaimed Lavinia. 'Didn't she arrange to meet her young man at the centre of the maze one evening but he was called away on some job or other? And she couldn't find her way back out in the dark and got terribly lost in the maze and no one knew where she was.'

'Something like that,' agreed Cedric. 'It happened a long time ago, some thirty or forty years ago, I think. The story goes it was two days before she was discovered half mad and dying of thirst.'

'Yes, and ever since then a copy of the plan of the maze has always been kept in the butler's pantry,' said Lavinia, 'because few of the servants knew how to find their way through the maze and so it took simply ages to find her and get her out.'

'I'd like to see this maze,' said Felix. 'Can't say I know what the one at Hampton Court looks like.'

'It's trapezoidal in shape, as is ours,' said Cedric. 'If you wait here, I'll go and get a copy of the plan from the library. There's a sketch in one of the old books about the house.'

Within minutes, the young earl had returned with a large book bound in calf leather. Everyone with the exception of Lavinia, Vera and Theo, gathered around Cedric with varying degrees of enthusiasm so that they might look over his shoulder.

'Of course, you've both done the maze before, haven't you?' said Lavinia.

Her question was directed to the engaged couple, who were standing as far away from each other as possible. Although Vera, Rose noticed, was trying desperately to catch her fiancé's eye. But Theo was resolutely looking the other way, when not looking down at his hands or staring at the floor. Rose assumed he was thinking over what Cedric had said and considering what course of action to take.

The others stared at the plan, which was done in watercolours and ink. To Rose, the maze looked like an inverted triangle with the tip cut away.

'You see,' said Cedric, pointing down at the page, 'one enters the maze here at the bottom in the middle. Then follow the path round to the left, go all the way up to the top, come back down again, almost as if you were retracing your steps, along to the right, back up to the top, across to the right, down a bit and then bear to the right, up again, go to the left, back around to the right and then all the way down, and follow the hedge around until you go up through the middle and reach the centre.'

'Golly, it sounds awfully complicated,' said Emmeline, 'I'm sure I'd get frightfully lost like that poor maid.'

'Not if you had a copy of this plan with you,' pointed out Felix. 'If you take the right path, you only go through a bit of the maze.'

'Yes,' said Cedric, 'but one needs to hold one's nerve. The temptation is to veer off onto one of the other paths and get frightfully lost.'

'Of course Cedric and I know the maze like the back of our hand,' Lavinia said with some pride. 'Don't you remember, Ceddie, how as children we used to go and hide in the middle when Mother wanted us to do something we didn't want to?'

'Yes, and we used to take picnics there. One of the gardeners set up a small wrought iron table and two chairs in the centre for us to use. They're still there as far as I know.'

Afterwards, Rose wondered what would have happened if they hadn't discussed the maze that last evening. If talk had moved to other subjects, would the tragic events that were to happen next day still have occurred? It was true that she had felt the tension in the room, even if it was not as tangible as it had been the night before. But when she finally went up to bed that night Rose had no sense of foreboding. The last thing on her mind was death.

Chapter Ten

The girl who called herself Emmeline Montacute woke up with a start. Although it was still pitch black, for one awful moment she was afraid that she had overslept despite using the old schoolgirl's trick of putting a hairbrush under her pillow to ensure that she did not sleep soundly. But that was the trouble with December, it was so very dark. The majority of the day was dark, or half-light at best. Full daylight brightness was scarce, existing for only a few precious hours of the day. And half past five in the morning was not one of those hours.

She switched on her bedside light and looked at her wristwatch to check the time. Good. She had overslept by only ten insignificant minutes or so. No harm done. She threw off her bedclothes, climbed out of bed and went to the window, where she lifted the curtain and peeked outside. Even had it not been so dark and so far away, she wouldn't have seen what she was looking for. Because she realised only now that her room was facing the wrong way. She shuddered, not only with the cold, because really these grand old places were always so draughty, but also because outside was as pitch black as she had been afraid it would be. Really, the prospect of venturing out in the dark was most unappealing. She thought back to the day before, and the end of the evening in particular, and wondered how she had managed to convince herself to keep this secret assignation. She assumed that the consumption of fine wines with dinner and the warmth of the fires that had blazed in the fireplaces of the house, including in her own room, had lulled her into a false sense of comfort, so that she had forgotten that in the hours before daylight the house would be cold and dark, and outside even more so.

But there was nothing she could do about it now. Although of course really there was. She had not after all given her word that she would be there, for she had been given no opportunity to do so. The temptation to creep back into bed, pull the bedclothes up to her neck and go back to sleep was very enticing. But she thought back to those too brief moments during the previous day, when they had whispered and giggled together, always careful lest they be seen or overheard. It had all been exciting, a bit of an adventure even, and goodness knows she had had little of that, cloistered as she had been in her overprotected existence. She took a deep breath. It would be fun. And it wasn't as if she would have to clamber around in complete darkness. She had had the foresight to procure an electric torch, and although she was not wholly confident that the beam would be anything but feeble, it was surely better than having no light at all.

Before she could think better of it she threw on a thick tweed skirt and an angora jumper. It was not the most becoming of outfits of course, but at least she should be warm. Besides it would be well hidden beneath her blue serge coat with its grey fox fur collar, which she thought became her rather well, even, or perhaps especially, in the half darkness.

She looked at her wristwatch again and then adjusted the collar of her coat. She must be quick. In houses such as these the servants rose early, she knew, and she had still to make her way downstairs without making a sound and to draw back the bolts of the door that had been selected, being one of the few ones in the house that did not also need to be unlocked with a key. But if she didn't look sharp she would find herself colliding with some poor scullery maid, who no doubt would scream the place down and give their game away.

Quietly, she opened her bedroom door and stood a moment listening before venturing out. Then she flew down the stairs like a shadow, her hand all the while on the bannister lest she fall or slip in the darkness. She felt most vulnerable crossing the vast black and white tiled hall. How she longed to switch on a light or turn on her electric torch, but it would be far too much of a risk. She consoled herself with knowing that once outside it wouldn't matter. Meanwhile she stole through the house like some errant ghost. The door was located and she was relieved to find that the bolts slid back with almost no sound. She stepped out into the early morning, the cold air hitting her face and making her hesitate for a moment, wondering whether to go on. Had she realised at the time that her life lay in the balance, she would have stopped and thought more deeply before venturing out. Instead she admonished herself for her cowardice and went to meet her fate.

'Mrs Farrier, Mrs Farrier!' cried Dolly, running into the servants' hall and catching herself on the edge of the table in her hurry. Despite being excited, she kept her voice down, for the news she had to impart was of a sensitive nature.

'What's the matter, girl,' demanded the housekeeper, her head already busy with the preparations for the day ahead, so that she did not give the maid her full attention.

'Miss Montacute, Mrs Farrier. She's not in her room. I knocked on her door as usual and there being no answer, which didn't surprise me as she tends to sleep heavy, I went in. But when I'd opened the curtains, after putting her cup of tea down on the bedside table, I saw how her bed was empty. It had been slept in, mind, because the sheets and blankets they were all twisted and ruffled just like she'd been tossing and turning in bed. But there were no sign of her.'

'No need to make such a carry on, Dolly,' said Mrs Farrier briskly. 'Like as not she was in the lavatory, or perhaps she's gone to have a chat with that friend of hers, Miss Wentmore. Don't you go making mischief where there's none, my girl.'

'I checked the lavatory and the bathrooms and I went into Miss Wentmore's room next, to take in her tea, and she wasn't there neither,' protested Dolly. 'There's no sight nor sound of Miss Montacute, really there isn't, Mrs Farrier, and I looked everywhere, so I did.'

'Well, perhaps you didn't look properly, or perhaps she's gone out for a bit of a walk.'

The housekeeper tried to keep the worry out of her voice. There was likely as not a perfectly innocent explanation for the girl's absence. She was not one to jump to conclusions and fear the worst.

The main thing was to give no hint to Dolly that she feared anything was amiss. Goodness knew there was little enough between Dolly's ears at the best of times but, while she might lack sense, she wasn't above gossiping with the kitchen and scullery maids and other housemaids. And the housekeeper knew well from bitter experience that once a rumour started, it had a life of its own.

'That'll do, Dolly. Get on with your work now. And if I hear any gossiping on the matter I'll know where it started and you'll feel the back of my hand, so help me, if you don't.'

Dolly fled, quite frightened into silence, leaving Mrs Farrier to ponder over what was to be done. Given the time of year and the darkness of the hour, it was highly unlikely that Miss Montacute had gone for a walk in the grounds. It was just possible however that she was in the room of one of the other young ladies having a chat. Anything was preferable to the alternative, and she was relieved to catch no hastily whispered words passing between the manservants concerning the discovery of a woman in any of the gentlemen's rooms when they were taken in their morning cups of tea. Presumably the girl had had enough sense about her to hide herself under the bedcovers or else lock herself into a convenient dressing room or wardrobe before her presence was discovered and her character ruined.

The housekeeper tut-tutted to herself. She could have told anyone who cared to ask her that there was going to be trouble. She had been forewarned. She knew it as soon as her ladyship had informed her that guests had been invited to arrive on the morrow. And not just any guests neither. An heiress and some sort of foreign count, whatever that was, although from what country he originated no one seemed to know or have heard of. Mrs Farrier didn't hold with foreigners. Give her a good Englishman any day.

In her long career, Mrs Farrier had unfortunately inevitably had experience of the destruction of young ladies' reputations. But she had no wish for Sedgwick Court to be tarred with those kind of goings on, thank you very much. And it wasn't just the interests of the family she was considering. That sort of thing brought shame on the whole house; the servants would suffer and all. No, the matter had to be contained.

The housekeeper decided to confide in Mr Manning, the under-butler. It would do no good to have a word with Mr Torridge; the shock might do for him. When she did speak to the butler, it was a relief to receive reassurance from him that no reports had reached his ears that any of the gentlemen's rooms were inhabited by anyone other than their expected occupants. Notwithstanding this, she felt compelled to put the case before her mistress.

'Good heavens, Mrs Farrier, whatever are you doing here?' Lavinia, propped up in bed as she was against her many pillows, sipping her tea, was most taken aback and somewhat perturbed by her housekeeper's unexpected appearance in her room at such an hour. 'I was expecting Denning, not you. Is anything the matter?'

Lavinia, when told of her guest's disappearance, did not appear unduly shocked. In truth, she was far more interested in speculating as to the identity of the gentleman who might be harbouring the wayward girl. Although she did not altogether trust him, she hoped that it did not prove to be the count. The devil inside her took a malicious delight in supposing that it might be Dr Harrison. That would certainly give Vera something real to moan about and tear her hair out over. Still, she had a duty to protect Emmeline's character, or at least thought she did, given that Emmeline was her guest. But lurking at the back of her mind was also the worry that the girl had disappeared or got into difficulties. What should one do for the best? She had half a mind to summon Jemima and put the matter to her. But what if Emmeline should turn up in a few moments. She would hardly welcome her companion's interference, and Jemima was just the sort of girl to consider it her duty to inform Mr Montacute of his daughter's nocturnal activities. There was only one thing to do, she decided, and she did it. She summoned Rose to her presence.

'Disappeared!' Rose took the matter far more seriously than her hostess. Even Lavinia noticed that Rose's face had lost some of its colour. 'Lavinia, we must organise a search party immediately. She may be hurt or in some sort of danger.'

'Pah!' Lavinia made a face, although Rose's reaction to the news had alarmed her. 'We'll do nothing of the sort. You've seen the way that she's been behaving. It's far more likely that she's in one of the men's rooms. She's probably hiding in Theo's wardrobe as we speak! No, the important thing is to try and protect the silly girl's reputation, although she really doesn't deserve it. I can't tell you how much I regret inviting her to stay.'

Mrs Farrier was hastily summoned and it was agreed between them that nothing would be done, and no mention would be made of the girl's disappearance, until after breakfast. While everyone was at breakfast, the bedrooms would be hurriedly searched by some of the most trusted servants, as would the other rooms in the house such as the drawing room and the library lest the girl had curled up in a chair there and fallen asleep over a book or magazine.

All the men, Rose noticed, came down to breakfast. Theo was the last to come down and none of them, she thought, looked as if they were trying to conceal a guilty secret. Although Theo very obviously was doing his best to avoid catching Vera's eye. She in turn picked at her toast and ate nothing, making no attempt to help herself to any of the bacon or sausages under the silver salvers. Vera was clearly still miserable. Whatever one said about Vera being rather pathetic in the way she clung to Theo like a limpet, hardly letting him come up for air, one couldn't help feeling sorry for her. Theo Harrison, Rose thought, had behaved abominably.

Emmeline did not appear at breakfast, although both Rose and Lavinia kept looking expectantly at the door praying that she would. Rose found herself on tenterhooks. Try as she might, she could not share Lavinia's optimistic view that the girl was engaged only in some sort of indiscretion. Increasingly she felt that something was very wrong. The feeling bubbled up inside her and she longed to tell Cedric who, oblivious to there being anything wrong, was happily tucking into a plate of eggs and kidneys. Only Jemima made any reference to Emmeline's absence from the breakfast table, to which Lavinia answered hurriedly that she believed she had a headache and was breakfasting in her room. A general muttering of commiseration and the wish that she would feel better soon went around the table. Other than that, no one appeared particularly perturbed or concerned. Indeed, Rose thought she had even detected the faint shadow of a smile appear on Vera's face, which had been hastily suppressed.

It was not until after breakfast, when Lavinia and Rose sought out Mrs Farrier, that it became apparent that any hopes either might have had that the girl's disappearance would resolve itself without their interference were dashed. All the rooms had been thoroughly searched by the servants and no sign of Emmeline had been found. And she had not taken the opportunity to crawl out from some wardrobe and return to her room while the others were breakfasting. Her room remained empty and abandoned, her bed unmade.

The housekeeper had asked Eliza Denning, who was acting as lady's maid to Emmeline for the duration of her stay, to look through the girl's wardrobe and ascertain if any items of clothing were missing. As far as Eliza could tell, not being overly familiar with the girl's clothing, her blue serge coat with its silver fox fur collar and matching hat were missing but nothing else, except perhaps a tweed skirt and angora jumper, although she could not be quite certain about these items. But it did indicate, if nothing else, that Emmeline was not in the house and had ventured out. This theory was further substantiated by Manning advising that one of the French windows had been discovered unbolted, when he himself was sure that he had bolted it last night.

Rose noticed that for the first time Lavinia looked worried; she herself was seriously concerned. Emmeline had been missing for at least three hours and probably a lot longer. Where had the girl gone and what had happened to her? She was suddenly aware that Lavinia had clutched her hand as if instinctively, unconscious of what she was doing.

If Lavinia had said to Jemima that they had indeed found Emmeline Montacute in a compromising position in one of the gentlemen's bedrooms, the effect could not have been more devastating. For Rose thought for all the world that Jemima Wentmore was about to become hysterical.

'Why didn't you tell me as soon as you were aware that she was missing?' Jemima had demanded furiously. Her face, Rose noticed, was quite ashen, as if she herself had experienced a sleepless night.

'Pah! And have you run off to her father as soon as you were back home to tell him what his daughter had been up to?' retorted Lavinia, equally angrily.

'But isn't it obvious that she's been kidnapped?' Jemima sobbed.

The tears that had been all the while threatening to fall did so freely now, unchecked. Rose was pleased that they had had the foresight to take Jemima aside to tell her the news away from the others. The three of them were, in point of fact, in Lavinia's exquisitely, and expensively, furnished boudoir.

'Nonsense! You know as well as I do that it's far more likely that she went off to keep some sort of romantic assignation,' Lavinia retorted. 'And now that all the men have been accounted for, unless of course she's formed an attachment to one of our footmen and is stuck in one of those stark little bedrooms in the servants' quarters, we must suppose that she arranged to meet the man in question somewhere in the grounds. And for some reason, which I have to admit escapes me at present, she has been detained. No doubt she's in one of the follies,' Lavinia paused a moment and then added gleefully: 'I understand our housemaids use them often as convenient places to meet their sweethearts.'

There was a certain gleam in Lavinia's eye which made Rose wonder whether Lavinia herself might not have done something similar in the past.

'She must have fallen asleep, I suppose,' continued Lavinia. 'Although how she came to, I can't possibly imagine. I mean to say, most of those follies are jolly draughty places even in summer let alone winter. But, more likely as not, as soon as we mention to the others that she is missing and propose a search of the grounds, the man in question will hasten to where she is and bring her to us with some implausible story that we shall all pretend to swallow. Either that or he will suggest a likely location where she might be found.'

'Yes, I suppose that's possible,' said Jemima, sounding less than convinced.

Although some colour had returned to Jemima's cheeks, her hands continued to play with the fabric of her skirt, as if she must pull and clutch at the material to stop herself from wringing her hands and tearing out her hair.

She thinks we are clutching at straws, Rose thought, as do I. We're all clinging to the notion that everything will be all right, even though in our hearts we know it won't be.

Chapter Eleven

The atmosphere of anxiety was further heightened once the men had been informed that Emmeline was missing. Rose was to remember the expression on Cedric's face long afterwards, a mixture of anger at not having been told earlier, and concern at what they might find. He had drawn Rose aside so that he could speak to her for a moment without being overheard by the others.

'I'm worried, darling. It was particularly cold last night. Do you think Emmeline went out in the night or sometime early this morning? If it was last night, I'm jolly afraid she may have died of hypothermia or exposure by now.'

'Ssh!' said Rose, quickly, because she had just noticed that Jemima was standing not so very far from them and that she was looking at them intently, as if she had heard Cedric's whispered words. Certainly she looked close to tears. Rose took Cedric's arm and led him further away.

'Apparently her bed had been slept in, so the maid thinks. Hopefully that means she went out this morning rather than last night. She was also wearing a hat and coat, so perhaps she hasn't got so very cold. Poor Jemima's convinced that she's been kidnapped, but Lavinia and I think it's far more likely that she arranged some clandestine assignation. Although why she hasn't returned by now I can't imagine, particularly as all the men are present. But that was why we didn't say anything earlier. We were worried about the damage it might do to her reputation.'

'If that's the case then hopefully Harrison or that count fellow will come forward and suggest where she might be found.' Cedric only looked slightly more relieved. 'Why did the fellow leave her to return alone, that's what I can't understand?'

'Well they are sure to have taken particular care that they were not spotted returning to the house together, just in case someone happened to be up and about or looking out of their window. Tell me, if you were to arrange to meet someone secretly as Sedgwick, where would you choose to meet?'

'You've said that the servants have searched all the rooms, including even the lumber rooms and attics, while we were all at breakfast? Well then, if not in the house itself, I imagine one or other of the follies that are dotted around the estate. And of course there is always the boatshed down by the lake.' Cedric gripped her arm suddenly, so hard that she was obliged to stifle a cry. 'Oh my god, Rose, you don't think that she went out on the lake do you? You don't think we are going to find her drowned?'

'No, I don't,' said Rose quickly, although a vision of Emmeline in a white gown drifting like the drowned Ophelia, her dark hair spread out and tangled, interwoven with river weeds and bedecked with flowers, came unbidden before her eyes.

A search party was hastily established, made up of Cedric, his sister, their guests and servants. Rose overheard Vera making her excuses to Lavinia for not being one of the party, claiming a headache and the beginning of a cold. Rose saw her try to make eye contact with Theo before she departed to her room. But the man gave her no second glance, his mind apparently fully preoccupied with recovering the missing girl. His face was an unbecoming shade of grey, and there was almost a wild look to his eyes. It was all Cedric could do to stop the doctor from running off to try and find Emmeline by himself. But the Sedgwick estate was large, and Cedric sensibly argued that members of the search party be given specific areas to explore to ensure that as much ground be covered as quickly as possible.

In the back of all their minds was the possibility that the girl might be found in a compromising situation. With this in mind, it was decided that Cedric and his guests should be given the task of searching the nearest follies and the boatshed. The servants were despatched to search the lake, the woods, and the follies located furthest from the house. Rose and Lavinia were assigned the formal gardens to search, and a time agreed when they should all meet. Each group of searchers was given a hunting horn to blow to let the others know if they discovered Emmeline. Although no one alluded to it, Rose thought that it was probably a relief to them all to have a medical man among them.

Armed with blankets and flasks of coffee and brandy, the search party set off. Just as they were leaving, Rose happened to look up and caught a glimpse of Vera looking out at them from one of the windows. On realising that she had been spotted, she had quickly stepped back out of sight, but not before Rose had seen a look of apprehension on her face.

The search party was in a focused mood, with words exchanged regarding the firming up of plans in respect of the various search areas. Cedric, as the young earl and host, was very much in command of the expedition while, every now and then, being obliged to digress from his plans to rein in Theo who, pulling at the bit, was desperate to set off as soon as possible. This would of course have been permitted if there had been any indication that he had any idea where the girl might be found. It soon became clear, however, that he was as much in the dark as the others. The fact that none of the men seemed to have any idea, or even offer any suggestions, where Emmeline might be found weighed heavily on Rose. If they really did not know then the possibility of a clandestine assignation faded and the possibility of a kidnapping became more credible.

Rose looked over at Jemima. It was clear that the same thought had crossed her mind. She seemed to be all but shaking and had given up any attempt not to cry. Felix, obviously concerned, was fussing over her, whispering positive words of encouragement, while at the same time trying to persuade her to return to the house, which she resolutely refused to do.

The party made a sombre procession across the estate, every now and then losing a couple or so of its members to search a particular area. When they had first started off there had been some chatter, but this had soon died down and all but fizzled out as the members of the party faced the reality of the situation. While a feeble sunlight fought its way through, it was a bitterly cold day, and few thought it likely that anyone could have survived long outside without warm clothes. Rose had caught snatches of the servants' conversation before it too had faded. She heard them saying that the temperatures at night had been freezing and that a heavy frost had covered the estate at dawn.

It was a relief to Rose that she and Lavinia were among the first to break off from the main party to search the formal gardens. It was good to have something to do, even if the task seemed fruitless, for Rose thought it highly unlikely that Emmeline would have come to harm so near to the house, unless she had stumbled and hit her head and lay unconscious on one of the paths. This did not appear to be the case. The gardens were quite deserted and when Rose looked up to scour the horizon to try and judge the progress of the others, the trees looked sadly naked and forlorn, stripped as they were of their autumn leaves.

After an hour or so, Rose and Lavinia gave up searching and went to wait for the others, straining their ears to hear the welcome sound of someone blowing a hunting horn. But no such sound was forthcoming. Lavinia kicked at the gravel path and looked close to tears. Not only was Emmeline her friend, but as hostess she had an additional responsibility for her, particularly as she was aware that the girl had defied her father and left the safety of her Highland home. Awful as it was, it seemed that the most likely explanation for Emmeline's disappearance was that, as Jemima had dreaded, she had indeed been kidnapped.

'Rose, Rose!'

Rose was awakened abruptly from her musings by the sound of Lavinia's excited voice.

Gone was Lavinia's listless manner of a few moments ago. Instead she was pulling at the sleeve of her friend's coat for all she was worth.

'The maze! No one's looking in the maze! Don't you remember Ceddie going on and on about it last night? We were going to make a game of it today, don't you remember, see which one of you could get to the middle first?'

'I do,' said Rose, 'but surely you're not suggesting that Emmeline might be there? Whatever would have made her go there in the dark?'

But even as she said the words, the memory came back to her of Cedric telling them the story of the maid who had arranged to meet her lover in the maze. They had all crowded around him to look at the plan and he had explained how the maze should be navigated. It was just possible, she supposed, that Emmeline had arranged to meet Theo there. But why hadn't she returned? After all, Theo obviously had, for he had come down for breakfast, and was now engaged in the search for the missing heiress. If he knew where she was, why had he not suggested that they explore the maze? Perhaps he had not wanted to let on that they had met there, but there were ways around that, surely? Far better that Emmeline's reputation be ruined, than that she died of hypothermia.

Not one to be discouraged from doing anything once her mind had been made up, Lavinia rushed off to the maze leaving Rose to stand around aimlessly, waiting for the others to arrive. This they did in dribs and drabs, and in answer to questioning looks, each shook their heads. They had seen no sign of Emmeline. The news that Lavinia had gone to search the maze, was greeted with an eager hopefulness and they proceeded to make their way there, following in Lavinia's hasty footsteps.

'How long has my sister been gone, Rose?' enquired Cedric, leading the way.

'Oh, about three quarters of an hour or so,' replied Rose, consulting her wristwatch.

'That's strange. It only takes about a quarter of an hour to get to the centre of the maze, and I daresay only ten or twelve minutes if one were to run. She should have been back by now.'

'Perhaps she decided to explore the other parts of the maze,' suggested Felix. 'If Emmeline has got lost in it, she more than likely took a wrong turning and has veered off from the main path.'

'You may be right,' agreed Cedric.

But Lavinia's prolonged absence had given an urgency to their steps, so that they were almost running by the time they came across the maze. Rose realised that she had already passed it several times during the course of her various walks in the grounds but that she had mistaken it for a hedge enclosing pasture.

Cedric took them to the entrance and they peered in. Even in the daylight the maze looked formidable. For it was impossible to look over the hedges that enclosed the paths because of their height, or through them due to the density of the box, and so the effect was one of being confined. The party huddled together behind Cedric who took the lead and alone looked undaunted.

'We'll make our way to the centre of the maze first,' Cedric said, 'and then if we don't come across them we'll spread out and take the other paths. If we have to do the latter, one or two of you might well become lost, but there's no need to worry. Lavinia or I will be able to find you and lead you out.'

'I suppose there's no use in us calling out?' asked Felix.

'No, the hedge is too dense, it muffles out sound. If we call out to Lavinia, she won't hear us.'

The search party followed Cedric, veering off to the right here, going back to the bottom there, ignoring paths which they felt certain were the ones that should be taken, but deferring each time to Cedric's judgement. Rose tried to visualise the plan of the maze that they had studied the night before, but, for the life of her, she had no idea where they were or whether they had taken the right path or not. If Emmeline had indeed undertaken this journey in the dark, then she might well still be wandering around now in the light.

When she studied the plan of the maze afterwards, Rose realised that they had not been so very far from reaching the centre when they came across Lavinia and Emmeline. They had been making their way back down so that, as the crow flew, they were near the start of the maze, although the entrance was obscured from them by a vast expanse of hedge. They had just turned the corner. If they had proceeded down the path that stretched out before them, and then turned right at the end as they had intended, they would very soon have come to the centre of the maze. But the scene that greeted them as they rounded the corner had the effect of stopping them in their tracks. Indeed, the leaders halted so abruptly that those behind Cedric and Felix, who had not had an opportunity to fully take in the scene, stumbled into them, and there ensued a few moments of confusion.

Lavinia, oblivious to their presence, with all colour drained from her face so that she resembled more a ghost than a living being, was standing over what at first sight looked to be a bundle of clothes strewn out in a heap on the ground. As they edged nearer, the newcomers saw that the bundle took on a form that eventually revealed itself to be that of a body. And, as they came closer still, they recognised it as Emmeline, still and lifeless on the ground, the side of her head disfigured by a gaping wound, the blood from which was glistening in the weak sunlight. But more shocking still was the realisation of what Lavinia, standing there motionless as if in a trance, was holding clenched so tightly in her hands. A silver candlestick covered with blood.

Chapter Twelve

Cedric was the first to regain his senses insomuch as he ran forward a stride or two before stopping and calling out his sister's name.

'Lavinia!' There was an urgency in his voice that was not lost on anyone present. 'Put down that candlestick and come here.'

All the time Cedric was speaking, he was walking very slowly towards his sister, his arm outstretched, as if he feared that any sudden movement would scare her or make her panic-stricken. There were those present who assumed she must be of unsound mind. They held their breath, not certain what she would do, being cornered as she was.

Lavinia gave no indication that she had heard her brother, and remained transfixed by the grim scene before her, swaying slightly. As soon as Cedric was standing beside her, he snatched the candlestick from her and flung it away from them as if it were diseased. Lavinia did not resist.

'Rose, take my sister back to the house and get her washed and cleaned up, please.'

He spoke abruptly, not even bothering to turn his head to look at her. But Rose heard the emotion in his voice that he was trying so hard to contain. They watched with fascination as he produced a handkerchief from his breast pocket and walked over to the discarded ornament. Bending down to kneel beside the candlestick, Cedric then gingerly proceeded to wipe it.

'Lord Belvedere, I must protest,' exclaimed Felix, running forward. 'The police won't want us to touch anything. They will expect everything to be left just as it is.' He turned to address Theo. 'That is right, isn't it, Harrison? You're a medical man, aren't you, you must have come across a suspicious death before?'

'Rose, come here quickly,' said Cedric. He spoke as if he had not heard Felix and was issuing a command; indeed, he was almost shouting. 'Take my sister away from here. Have her change her clothes and get one of the servants to burn what she's wearing.'

As if by common accord the others, who all the time had been moving forward, turned and studied Lavinia's clothes. From where they stood, the clothes did not look particularly blood spattered, although there were some light smears of blood on them.

'But my lord – '

'Shut up, Thistlewaite,' Cedric shouted, 'this doesn't concern you. Rose, please do as I say.'

'Cedric, no, whatever are you thinking of?' Rose said, appalled.

Rose had never seen Cedric like this. She had never heard him sound so insistent or determined, and although she did not want to oppose him if she could possibly avoid doing so, she could not bring herself to do as he asked.

As if aware of her hesitation, Cedric turned and gave Rose a look of such desperation that she felt his pain as if it were her own. He was beyond reason, she knew. Later he would bitterly regret what he had done, but now he was resolute. She could argue with him, but it would do no good. She hesitated for a moment longer. She reasoned that whatever fingerprints there might have been on the candlestick were not there now. The harm had already been done. Cedric had tampered with the evidence and the police were certain to make no end of a fuss about it all, and rightly so in her opinion. Cedric would have to deal with them later and explain his actions the best he could.

What decided Rose in the end was her own eagerness to remove Lavinia from the scene. The girl looked quite ill with the shock of it all. There was no knowing how long she had stood there, poised over the corpse. Rose shuddered at the thought. She consoled herself that, although the damage had been done with regard to the candlestick, there was nothing to stop her from disobeying Cedric's final request. She could keep the soiled clothes intact.

Rose hurried over to Lavinia and put her arm around her shoulders. The girl was visibly shaking now and offered no resistance at being guided out of the maze. Rose only hoped that she would be able to retrace her steps without getting lost. Rose threw one final glance over her shoulder before she left. Theo Harrison had now collected himself sufficiently to examine the body and feel for a pulse. Felix Thistlewaite meanwhile was continuing to protest at the destruction of evidence, and Cedric was telling him to go to the devil. Jemima and Count Fernand were standing a little removed from the others, the former clearly in shock and the count doing his best to comfort her. It was a pitiful scene and she was glad to leave it behind.

It seemed a long way back to the house. Lavinia walked so slowly, and had to be constantly encouraged to keep going. Left to her own devices, Rose thought the girl would simply have stopped and slumped to the ground. She was concerned that Lavinia had not uttered a word since they had discovered her standing over Emmeline's body. On reflection though, she thought that perhaps it was just as well, for she had no wish to hear her confess to the crime. As they stumbled along, Rose half dragging Lavinia, Rose did not allow herself to think of the murdered body in the maze, or that the man she loved had so easily and willingly taken the law into his own hands. There would be time enough for that later. She would not let herself dwell on that now. Rose permitted herself only to feel relief that she had been given something constructive to do, something that would use all her energies and concentration.

She realised later that Lavinia's lady's maid must have been watching from the window, because Eliza came hurrying out long before they reached the house. She took Lavinia from Rose and, without asking what had occurred, ushered her mistress inside, leaving Rose to trail behind.

'What has happened? Is Emmeline all right?'

Unseen by Rose, Vera too had come out of the house and was tugging at the sleeve of her coat, a wild look in her eyes. Something distracted her for she let go of Rose's sleeve and stared across the gardens. Turning around Rose saw what had caught the woman's attention. For in the distance she saw the remnants of the search party returning home. Although the party was still quite far away, it was obvious even to the most casual observer that they were walking in a sombre fashion, and that Emmeline was not among them.

'There's been an accident, Vera. Emmeline's dead.'

Rose realised as soon as she had uttered the words that she had spoken too bluntly. She should have softened it somehow, but she was too exhausted from the shock of it all, and having to physically support Lavinia half way to the house, to think properly.

'Dead!' All colour drained from Vera's face and she clenched her hands. 'No, she can't be. She can't be dead. Ah my God, what have I done? I never meant to – '

But Vera never finished her sentence for, as Rose turned to stare at her, trying to take in what she was saying, the woman slumped to the ground. Vera had evidently fainted.

'Leave me alone, Eliza,' Lavinia said wearily, her voice barely above a whisper.

Her lady's maid, regarding her with concern, hesitated a moment before carrying out her instructions. In her opinion, her mistress was in no fit state to be left alone.

'It's all right, Eliza', Lavinia said sighing. 'I want to see Miss Simpson. Get her for me now, will you?'

Rose was waiting on the landing not far from Lavinia's door. As she passed Eliza she noticed that the lady's maid was carrying the clothes Lavinia had been wearing.

'Miss Denning, let me have those please.' Rose made to take them from her but Eliza snatched them back.

'No, miss. They're going for the wash at once, so they are,' answered Eliza. Her manner was hard and unyielding, verging on impertinence. 'Otherwise there'll be no getting out the stains. This fabric here marks something rotten.'

'No, you can't …'

Rose's sentence faltered as Eliza hurried away from her, and out through the green baize door leading to the backstairs. She would have followed her into the servants' territory and wrestled the clothes from her had Lavinia not chosen that very moment to become distressed, calling out as if she feared to be alone. The matter having been decided for her, Rose reluctantly went instead into Lavinia's bedroom, closing the door firmly behind her.

'Is she really dead, Emmeline, I mean?' asked Lavinia.

There were tears in Lavinia's eyes as she clutched at her gold chintz bedspread, and to Rose she sounded exhausted.

'Yes, at least I think so.' Rose sat down on the bed beside Lavinia and held her hand. 'Theo was checking for a pulse when we left, to make absolutely certain.'

Almost to herself Lavinia said: 'Poor Theo, it must be awful for him. I didn't consider him at all.' She turned to Rose and spoke slowly, almost

90

reluctantly, as if she feared the answer to her question. 'Do they all think I did it? Do they think I-I killed Emmeline?'

'I don't think anyone knows quite what to think,' Rose replied truthfully. She might have reassured Lavinia that everyone considered her innocent but, had she done so, she knew she would have been lying.

'Cedric thinks I did it, doesn't he?' Lavinia said, bursting into tears and mopping at her eyes with the back of her hand. 'That's why he asked you to take me away, isn't it? Oh, how could he think it of me, how could he?'

'He was just concerned about you, as we all are,' said Rose, choosing her words carefully, and passing Lavinia a handkerchief.

Rose was pleased that the girl was at last showing signs of emotion, and made no move to comfort her. She felt certain Lavinia would feel better after a good cry. Perhaps they all would.

'You've had a great shock. It must have been awful for you.'

'It was. I can't tell you how awful it was, Rose. I just couldn't believe what I was seeing. I couldn't believe it was Emmeline. She was so bright and always laughing, and so full of life. And th-that thing on the ground, it was so d-dead and not like a real person at all. It certainly wasn't like Emmeline. I couldn't believe it was her at first, I couldn't. I just went on staring and staring at it, and then I saw the blood and …'

To Rose's relief Lavinia faltered in the middle of her sentence, her voice having risen hysterically during her account, which had alarmed Rose considerably. She moved now and put her arm around the trembling girl.

'Ssh, it's all right. Try not to think about it anymore. Try and put the image out of your mind.'

Of course, Rose thought, it was easier said than done, having herself had recent experience of being alone with a murdered corpse.

'Y-you don't think I killed her, do you, Rose?' Lavinia asked, urgently. There was a desperate look in her eyes, and she clutched at Rose's hand so tightly that the girl winced.

'No, I don't. Of course I don't,' Rose said quickly, trying to sound more confident than she felt.

'She's dead,' said Theo, crouched over Emmeline's body, and telling them what they already knew all too well. 'Oh my God, how could anyone ...'

The doctor broke down, covering his face with his hands. Cedric and Felix stopped their arguing and both looked uncomfortable. It was not often, if ever, that either of them had witnessed a man cry, and certainly not under such tragic circumstances.

'There, there, old chap', said Cedric, awkwardly. 'This is dashed distressing for you. Let's get you back to the house, there's nothing more you can do here. The poor girl's beyond all help now.'

He bent down and, taking Theo by the elbow, began to steer him out of the maze, all the time thinking how inadequate his words of condolence sounded even to his own ears.

'We can't just leave her here,' protested Theo, struggling to free himself from the surprisingly firm grip Cedric had on his arm.

'No, we can't,' agreed Jemima, rushing forward. 'I'm going to stay with her.' Her eyes were red-rimmed from crying, and her skin blotchy, but other than that she appeared remarkably composed.

'You'll do no such thing,' said Cedric firmly, and addressing Count Fernand none too politely he added: 'Take Miss Wentmore and Dr Harrison out of the maze and wait for us at the entrance will you?'

'I'll do that,' offered Felix, keen to be by Jemima's side.

'No, the count can. I want you to stay here with me. We need to check the rest of the maze. For all we know the murderer may still be here lurking behind one of the hedges.'

With that, Cedric proceeded to explain to Felix the various paths that made up the maze so that they could decide between them who should search which areas.

'I say,' said Felix, as soon as the others had turned the corner and were out of earshot. 'Why wouldn't you let me escort Jemima out of the maze? A fat lot of good our count will be. And Harrison is not much better, poor devil; he's quite done in by it all.'

'I don't trust that fellow,' answered Cedric frankly, 'the count, I mean, not Harrison. And besides, he'd no doubt get himself lost in the maze.'

'Who's to say I won't?' retorted Felix, amicably, although he appeared satisfied with Cedric's explanation. 'But I say, old chap, I know it's frightfully rotten for you and all that, but I mean to say, isn't this searching business an awful waste of time?' He averted his gaze so that he was looking up at the sky rather than at Cedric. 'What I am trying to say is, we already know who the murderer is, don't we?'

As Felix had predicted, the search of the rest of the maze proved fruitless. There was no one crouching behind the hedge on any of the more obscure paths. The two men made their way back to the entrance to the maze where they met up with the others. Felix at once went over to Jemima but she withdrew from him. It was clear to all from both her manner and posture that she wished to be alone.

Cedric, leaving one of the estate servants to stand guard at the entrance to the maze with strict instructions not to admit anyone, headed the party back to the house. It was a mournful procession that returned. Barely a word was spoken between them as each was lost in their own thoughts, trying to come to terms with what had happened as best they could. Notwithstanding their sorrowful state, they walked at a fair pace as if to put as much distance as possible between themselves and the scene of violent death.

It was not long before the remnants of the search party made out the two young women in the distance making their own slow progress to the house. They were there to witness both Rose discharging Lavinia to Eliza's care, and Vera's sudden appearance. And although they could not hear what she was saying, they saw clearly that the woman was in an agitated state as she tore desperately at Rose's sleeve. The look of horror on her face was not lost on them, the way her mouth fell open and she slowly released Rose's arm. As they looked on she balanced precariously on the edge of consciousness, before tottering and falling in a crumpled heap at Rose's feet.

Chapter Thirteen

'How is she?' Cedric demanded, as soon as Rose joined the others in the drawing room. More quietly he said: 'Did she say anything?'

'Your sister's still in shock, as you'd expect,' Rose answered wearily, sitting down on one of the Queen Anne chairs, and suddenly feeling very tired. 'Her lady's maid is with her now. But I think she will be all right.'

'But did she say why she did it?' Felix asked, interrupting their conversation.

The intrusion was unwelcome. Cedric glared at Felix and Rose averted her gaze to stare at the carpet miserably.

'I mean to say, it's awful and all that to ask,' persisted Felix, apparently undeterred by his reception, 'but the police will want to know. Personally I always thought that Lavinia and Emmeline got on like a house on fire. It just goes to show how wrong one can be.'

'Thistlewaite!'

Cedric leapt towards the man and Rose thought there was a real possibility that he was going to strike him. The count was obviously of the same opinion and moved surprisingly quickly to intervene. His dark, physical presence between them was effective in holding the two men apart. And although Cedric continued to glower fiercely at Felix, he made no move to push Count Fernand aside. Even so, Felix backed away a step or two, obviously frightened by the reaction his words had caused.

'Everyone is very upset, I think,' said Count Fernand soothingly, in his heavily accented English. 'What has happened is most tragic. We say things without thinking, just as they come into our heads. We need to think a little bit before we speak, I think, do we not?'

Rose did not know what to think. Part of her admired Felix for being so resolutely determined to find out what had happened however unpleasant the truth might prove to be. But another part of her felt only that he was goading Cedric, even if it were unintentional, and she wished he would leave well alone. There would be time enough later for accusations and incriminations when the police arrived. Most of all she wanted time alone to consider what Cedric, normally so upright and law-abiding, had done, and the part she herself had played. She thought of

Lavinia's blood-smeared coat, which now no doubt was freshly washed and drying in front of the fire in the servants' hall. She stifled a sob in her throat. What had they done?

'Lavinia didn't do it, or at least she says she didn't,' Rose said at last.

But even as she spoke it suddenly occurred to her that Lavinia had said no such thing. Admittedly Lavinia had been very worried that everyone would think she had killed Emmeline, but she had not actually denied doing the deed. Rose went over their conversation quickly in her head. Lavinia had been afraid that Rose thought her guilty and wanted her reassurance that she believed her innocent. If she really had something to hide, would she have been so persistent? And more importantly, thought Rose, warming to the idea, would Lavinia really have waited for them to find her standing over Emmeline and holding in her hand what they all believed to be the murder weapon? How easy it would have been for her to have fled the maze instead or, if there had not been sufficient time to do so, to hide in another part away from the main path until the coast was clear.

'Well, of course she didn't do it,' Cedric said with conviction. 'That goes without saying.'

Even so, the young earl looked relieved by Rose's words. She studied his face closely and fancied she saw signs of something else, or perhaps it was just that she wanted so much to see another emotion etched on his face for all to see. She wanted him to feel a sense of guilt for what he had done, tampering with the evidence. Now that Lavinia was not standing before him, a bloodied candlestick in her hand, did he bitterly regret the rashness of his actions in his futile attempt to protect her?

'If you were so very sure of your sister's innocence,' said Felix quietly, from the relative safety of the other side of the room, 'why did you wipe off any fingerprints that there might have been on that candlestick, and insist that Lavinia leave the scene and be cleaned up? It seems to me that you thought she was guilty like the rest of us. Only, unlike us, you decided to do something about it. I think you'll find that the police will take a pretty dim view of your actions, messing about with the evidence and all that.' A sudden thought struck him. 'I say, I take it you have telephoned the police, or at the very least instructed your butler to do so?'

What might have resulted in an uncomfortable silence with Cedric finally being obliged to admit that the police had yet to be summoned, was prevented by Theo entering into the proceedings. Up to then, the doctor had been sitting so quietly in the corner, his head buried in his arms and uttering not a word to anyone, that his presence in the room had been all but forgotten.

'Be quiet you two, damn it,' Theo snapped.

The doctor had not spoken loudly, but there had been sufficient anger in his voice to reduce the two young men to silence. He began to pace the room, and every now and then he passed a hand through his hair in an agitated manner. His face looked haggard and he had an unhealthy grey hue to his skin. To Rose, he seemed to have aged ten years since breakfast.

'Lavinia hadn't just killed Emmeline if that's what you're getting at, Thistlewaite,' Theo said quietly, but in a doctor's authoritative voice. 'Sh-she'd been dead a few hours from the look of h-her corpse …'

Theo gulped and they all wondered whether he would go on or break down and weep again. Somehow though he managed to regain his equanimity, the physician in him triumphing over the distraught lover.

'She'd been dead a few hours I'd say when we came across her. Of course we'll know more after the post-mortem.'

He turned to look with some contempt at Cedric. 'For God's sake man, telephone for the police. You should have done it ages ago, as soon as we discovered the body.'

'Yes, yes, of course old chap. It was very remiss of me,' said Cedric, getting to his feet. 'I'll telephone the chief constable, name of Whitmore, right away. I'll ask him to bring in Scotland Yard. Any luck and we might get the chaps who investigated the incidents at Dareswick and Ashgrove.'

The four of them were left in the drawing room, standing around awkwardly, not knowing what to do until the police arrived. In the end, Theo decided to retreat back into his own thoughts and chose a high-backed armchair at the other end of the room, which he pointedly turned towards the fire so that his back was to them. The count, who looked the most composed of all of them, walked over to the windows and looked out at the fine gardens that stretched out before him, before turning around and aimlessly picking up a newspaper which he then proceeded to read.

Felix appeared more inclined to talk, although he still looked a little sheepish from his dressing down by the doctor.

'I suppose you think that I spoke rather out of turn to Lord Belvedere, accusing his sister and all that?' Felix said, walking over to Rose and, although clearly addressing her, avoiding looking her in the eye.

'Well you certainly didn't beat about the bush, did you?' retorted Rose, not feeling altogether kindly towards him, even if she knew it was because she herself felt guilty. 'You're jolly lucky Cedric didn't punch you. I can't say I would have blamed him if he had done.'

'I only said what everyone else was thinking, but was too polite to say,' argued Felix, rather feebly. 'I probably wouldn't have said anything at all if the fellow hadn't gone about trying to destroy the evidence.'

'Cedric just wasn't thinking,' replied Rose defensively.

But Felix was right, of course he was right. And the police would see it that way too. Why, Rose saw it that way, and if Cedric was even half the man she took him to be, he would too. Why had he been so foolish and done what he had? She had no doubt that he had had the very best of intentions. He had been trying to protect his sister, but his actions had only made matters worse. Still, however badly she felt, however much she despaired over Cedric's behaviour, she was not about to say as much to Felix Thistlewaite. She did not wish to talk any more about it to anyone until she had had a chance to speak to Cedric alone. With considerable effort, because she did not feel so inclined, she made attempts to put an end to Felix's reproaches and her own guilt by trying to lighten the mood.

'I say, though, you'll have to curb your tendency to speak bluntly if you go into the legal profession, otherwise you'll frighten away all your clients.'

'You're right, of course.' Felix grinned and had the grace to blush. 'And it isn't very becoming is it, to admonish one's host?'

'I say, where is Jemima?' asked Rose suddenly, looking around the room.

It was only now that she noticed the girl's absence. Jemima had such a tendency to watch from the shadows of a room, seeming to perch precariously on the threshold between guest and servant, that her presence was never obvious or overstated at the best of times.

'Jemima walked back with you all, didn't she, I was sure I saw her?'

'Yes,' said Felix, 'but she insisted on going straight to her room. She wanted to be alone.' For the first time Felix looked worried. 'She's taken it all very badly, as you can imagine. Yes, indeed, she feels pretty shaken up about it all as one would expect. I don't mind telling you that I'm awfully worried about her. She's hardly said a word. She was trembling like a leaf when we were walking back, and her face was as white as d … well, yes, I might as well say it … death. I did try and insist that she stay here with us all in the drawing room, where it's warm and she'd have company, but she would have none of it. I hate to think of her sitting in her room alone. She refused even to have one of the maids sit with her.'

'Well, I can understand why she would want to be alone. It must have been a frightful shock for her. She and Emmeline were awfully close, weren't they?' said Rose.

'Yes, they were. Although I could never quite understand it, myself. Emmeline put upon Jemima something rotten, you know.'

Felix cast a look around the room before continuing in a slightly quieter voice than before. To Rose this seemed an unnecessary precaution for she felt it unlikely that Theo, with his back to them staring at the fire and the count, engrossed in his newspaper, had heard a word of their conversation up to now. Even so, she bent her head towards Felix in a conspiratorial way.

'In the first place it'll be frightfully rotten for her having to explain to old Montacute why they went against his wishes and left the mansion in the Highlands unaccompanied.' Felix sighed and raked his hair with his fingers, a gesture which Rose thought made him look very young. 'You see, the old man's always had a bit of a bee in his bonnet about his daughter being kidnapped after that first attempt. As a consequence, he's always insisted that either he or an army of servants should accompany the girls whenever they left the grounds. Well, one can imagine how tiresome that was for them. It isn't really any wonder that they decided to venture out alone when the opportunity arose, is it?'

'No, I suppose not.'

'As soon as he'd set off on his travels to goodness know where,' continued Felix, 'they upped and left. Of course it was Emmeline's decision to do so, not Jemima's, but I doubt Montacute will see it like that. Jemima really didn't have any choice in the matter. Once Emmeline had made up her mind, there was nothing that Jemima could do to change it, and she was obliged to follow her. She's been ever so worried that something might happen. But of course she thought it would be on the Continent, not here. They thought they'd be safe here at Sedgwick.'

If Felix intended to say more, he did not get the opportunity to do so. For just at that moment the door opened and Cedric reappeared, his face clearly showing signs of strain. Nevertheless his voice when he spoke sounded steady and firm.

'I've spoken to the chief constable and he's agreed to call in Scotland Yard. I hardly had to persuade the fellow. He doesn't think the chaps here are up to investigating a murder, certainly not the murder of an heiress at the home of the local aristocracy. Petty theft and poaching are more what they're used to. But he'll send over a constable for form's sake to stay here until the men from the Yard arrive.'

Felix went over to the French windows and looked out. Theo still stared into the fire and the count, after looking up briefly when Cedric came in, returned to perusing his newspaper. Rose went immediately to Cedric who, having delivered the information about the police, looked suddenly done in. She took his hand and led him to one of the settees placed at some distance from the others so that they could converse without being overheard, even by the belligerent Felix.

'I suppose,' began Cedric, 'you must think me awfully stupid, that business about Lavinia, I mean? All the time I was on the telephone to the chief constable, I kept wishing I had left things well alone.'

'Well,' Rose began and hesitated a moment before continuing because she felt so angry with him. 'I realise you were only trying to protect your sister, but whatever were you thinking, Cedric? What made you do such a thing? You could be arrested and, don't you see, you've only made matters worse for her.'

'I know, I know. It was a moment of madness, I promise you. Sitting here now in this drawing room, it's almost as if someone else had done it, not me. Say you forgive me, Rose.'

Cedric put his head in his hands, and Rose regarded him with a mixture of anger and compassion. She did not know what to say, and so said nothing. If truth be told, she was desperately afraid that he might not be the man she thought him to be.

'I'll have to try and brazen it out with the police,' Cedric said, and gave her a feeble smile. Rose squeezed his hand.

'We should have stopped you,' she said finally, and sighed. 'It was just such a shock seeing Emmeline's body lying there with her head all disfigured and Lavinia standing over her like that. I think we were all rather slow to take it all in. You'd taken the candlestick from her and wiped it before we could think to stop you.'

'It was a very stupid thing to do, I see that now,' admitted Cedric. 'And wrong, of course. To say nothing of foolish. For one thing, it's made it look as if I thought Lavinia had killed Emmeline, which of course couldn't be further from my mind.'

'It is now. But it wasn't then. When we first came upon the scene, a part of all of us jumped to the obvious conclusion that Lavinia had killed Emmeline. It was only to be expected given the circumstances.'

'Yes ... I suppose you're right.'

'We should have realised that there must have been an innocent explanation for why Lavinia was standing over the body as she was. I mean, for the life of me I can't imagine what motive Lavinia could have had for wishing Emmeline dead, can you?'

'Haven't an inkling. If only she hadn't picked up that damned candlestick. Did she tell you why she did?'

Cedric however did not remain silent long enough to allow her to answer. For this Rose was relieved, for it occurred to her that Lavinia had said very little. Of course, she had been in shock, probably still was, but even so ...

'I don't know what I'd do if you weren't here, Rose,' Cedric was saying. 'I'm not so very worried about the police. I can give them some cock and bull story about not thinking things through and being concerned that Lavinia be taken indoors into the warm ... which of course I was. To tell you the truth, I'm finding it hard to feel anything at the moment ... but I know that I will soon.'

'I know, darling. It's the shock of it all.' Rose said, holding his hand. 'It's too awful to think about.'

'It's not just the frightful way in which that poor girl died and the tragic waste of the life of someone who was ... well ... full of life. She was a sweet natured little thing, wasn't she, always so bright and laughing

'… But it's no good dwelling on all that now. It won't do any good, it won't bring her back.'

'No, it won't.'

'But what I can hardly bring myself to think about, darling, is that it happened here at Sedgwick.' He clung to Rose's hands. 'My ancestral home. The place where I spent my childhood. The place that I love most in all the world.'

'Yes, I know.'

'It seems terrible to think it when that poor girl's life has been so cruelly cut short, but what I am so afraid of Rose is that I will never feel the same way about Sedgwick again. And that it should have happened in the maze, the very place where Lavinia and I played for hours and hours as children and had so much fun. I wanted my children to play there, to have the same wonderful experiences I did, to – '

'It will be all right,' Rose said quickly. 'It isn't all spoilt, I promise it isn't. The police will find out who is responsible for poor Emmeline's death, and they will be punished. It'll take a little time, but you will love Sedgwick again, and life will get back to how it was. This house and grounds have a long history. Who knows what violent acts have occurred here in the past that have now been forgotten?'

Rose smiled at Cedric encouragingly. He wasn't being callous or thinking only of himself, she knew. It wasn't that he didn't care about Emmeline, for she could tell by the look in his eyes and the slight tremor in his voice when he spoke, that he cared a great deal. He did not view her death only as an inconvenience to be overcome or to be borne with dignity. He felt that he had let her down. He felt that he had let Sedgwick down and his ancestors that had gone before him. He viewed himself, she knew from their numerous conversations, as the current custodian of all that was Sedgwick Court and believed it was his role to protect and nurture the stately pile for future generations of Sedgwicks.

'Rose, will you find out who killed Emmeline? Say that you will, darling? I daresay Scotland Yard is very capable and all that, that they'd get there in the end. It's just that I have so much more faith in you. Look how you solved everything singlehandedly at Ashgrove and Dareswick.'

'I did have some help from the police,' Rose replied modestly. 'But I promise you I'll do my best. I know how important it is to you. Of course, if the police will let me that is,' she added as an afterthought.

Rose blushed suddenly for she could not forget how she had not been completely open with the police during the last incident that she had investigated. She had even gone so far as to suggest a possible alibi to someone she was trying to protect. Such actions had not endeared her to the police force or to a certain Inspector Deacon in particular. And now she had only made matters worse. What would the inspector think of her when he discovered that she had helped Cedric tamper with the evidence to protect Lavinia? Would he ever trust her again, or would he always view her with suspicion? How unbearable it was that Cedric had placed her in this dilemma. How she wished she had thrown herself against the green baize door and refused to let Eliza leave until she had given up the clothes.

She would have to try and make amends by telling Inspector Deacon everything she discovered as soon as it became apparent to her. It never occurred to her for one moment that she would not have the opportunity to do so.

Chapter Fourteen

The door to the drawing room opened and, with the exception of Theo, who was still sitting resolutely turned towards the fire lost in his own sad thoughts, everyone turned to ascertain the identity of the newcomer. A mixture of expressions appeared on the faces of those present, predominantly being ones of disappointment. Cedric had clearly hoped it would be Lavinia, while Felix was eager to discover how Jemima was bearing up. Only the count looked indifferent on finding that it was Vera who entered the room.

It was not lost on Rose that Vera came in tentatively, as if she were unsure of her welcome. She first looked anxiously at Rose and then scoured the room for Theo, who she did not see at first, seated as he was with his back to her. On locating him, she made to go towards him but Rose, who had anticipated such an eventuality, sprang forward and caught her by the arm before she had moved more than a couple of steps.

'Vera, I wouldn't,' Rose said gently, 'really I wouldn't. I daresay it hurts damnably my saying so, but Theo is pretty shaken up by Emmeline's death. I know it's jolly rotten for you, but I think you need to leave him alone for a while.'

Vera looked about to protest, but Rose had no intention of loosening her grip on her arm.

'Only for a little while, Vera. Surely you can allow him that? If you go to him now, you both may say something that you'll later regret.'

'But I love him,' said Vera so sadly that Rose felt a lump form in her throat.

How awful unrequited love must be, Rose thought, particularly in Vera's case where presumably Theo had once loved her enough to get engaged. She tried to put herself in Vera's shoes and imagine how she would feel if Cedric were to fall in love with someone else.

'I'm sorry, Vera, I really am,' Rose almost whispered.

'Is it true what the servants are saying?' Vera asked, brushing a tear or two hastily from her eye. 'Did Emmeline really die from having her head bashed in?'

Rose could not stop herself from looking appalled at Vera's bluntness.

'What I mean,' added Vera quickly, 'is did someone … kill her? She didn't, for instance, die from … the … cold?'

'No,' said Rose, somewhat frostily, 'she was murdered if that's what you're asking me.'

Was it her imagination or did Vera look relieved? Yet how could Emmeline being brutally murdered be considered favourable to her dying from natural causes? An unpleasant thought suddenly occurred to Rose and she held Vera's arm more tightly so that the woman winced.

'Just before you fainted, what did you mean when you said: "what have I done? I never meant to …"'? What did you mean by that, Vera?'

'N-nothing,' stuttered Vera, trying to pull away from Rose's grip. 'I meant nothing by it. I was just upset, that's all … It was an awful shock.'

'You didn't accompany us on the search. Why not? Did you know what we'd find?'

'Of course not,' protested Vera, although she looked frightened. 'I wasn't feeling very well, you know I wasn't. I said so at the time.'

'You may not want to tell me the truth,' said Rose, slowly, 'but it would be in your interests to tell the police. It'll only make matters worse for you if you don't. Vera, listen to me.'

Rose tried to get the woman to look at her, but Vera insisted on averting her gaze as if she would rather look anywhere but at Rose's face.

'Have it your own way then,' Rose said. She was too tired to argue with her. 'But the police are certain to find out the truth one way or the other.'

Silently cursing Vera under her breath for her being so obstinate and refusing to see reason, Rose had left the others in the drawing room to ascertain how Lavinia was faring once the first throes of shock had diminished. While she was eager to advise her friend that the others no longer considered her guilty of Emmeline's murder, she was honest enough to admit to herself that being left alone in the drawing room with only Vera, Theo and Count Fernand for company was too dismal an experience to contemplate. For Cedric had seen fit to leave shortly after Vera's arrival to consult with the servant guarding the maze. No doubt, she thought, he felt the need to make amends for his previous ill-advised behaviour in trying to protect Lavinia.

Mindful of her promise to Cedric that she would try to solve Emmeline's murder if it were within her power to do so, Rose was keen to ascertain from Lavinia if she had seen anything when she had first come across Emmeline's body in the maze. Although she acknowledged that if Theo was correct about the time of death, and Emmeline had been dead some hours rather than the few minutes that they had originally supposed, it was unlikely that Lavinia had seen anything at all. Nevertheless it was the excuse she needed to leave the room and the others behind.

At the top of the staircase on the landing, Rose was just about to make her way to Lavinia's room when it occurred to her that Jemima was still alone in her room, no doubt miserable and upset. She had been left alone too long, Rose thought. She might not want to join them in the drawing room, but it would be for the best.

'Jemima, it's me … Rose.'

There was no answer to either her gentle tapping on the door or to her calling out, and when Rose tried the door it held fast.

'Jemima, please open the door. I don't think it right for you to be alone. You mustn't shut yourself away at a time like this. Do come down. Felix is very worried about you as are we all, and the police will be here soon. They'll want to speak to you.'

Rose heard both the turn of a key in the lock and a bolt being slid back before the door opened. It occurred to her then that the girl was frightened as well as upset. She wished again that Emmeline's companion had not been left alone.

'Is *sh-she* down there with you all?'

The words, when they were uttered through trembling lips, were almost spat out with an air of disgust. Even in the dim light Jemima looked ill. She had half opened the door but still stood resolutely in her room, peering out. It was obvious to even the most casual of observers that she had no intention of opening the door any further or of inviting Rose to enter inside. There were dark circles beneath her eyes which in turn were red-rimmed and bloodshot. When she spoke, her voice was accompanied by sniffing and her handkerchief, which she held rolled up into a little ball in her hand, was completely wet. Her plain clothes did nothing to alleviate the general picture of misery and despair.

Rose could barely restrain herself from stretching out a hand to the girl. She knew, however, that if she did so such a gesture of compassion and kindness would be rejected. For Jemima appeared to her to be a solitary figure. Rose thought that even if it were Felix standing before Jemima now, the intrusion by him into her grief would not be welcomed.

'She?' It suddenly dawned on Rose to whom the woman was referring. 'Oh, you mean Lavinia? Jemima, listen to me. Lavinia didn't kill Emmeline, if that's what you're thinking.'

'We all saw her standing over Emmeline's body with that dreadful candlestick in her hand. It was smeared with blood. There was blood on her hands and her coat, there was – '

'Yes, yes,' interrupted Rose quickly, for the girl was on the verge of becoming hysterical. Jemima's voice had risen and become quite shrill and she was afraid of it carrying to Lavinia, only a few doors down in her own room.

'Lavinia didn't kill Emmeline.' Rose said the words slowly and deliberately, hoping that they would sink in. 'She just came across her body in the maze as we did. Theo said Emmeline had been dead for hours when we found her. Do you understand what I'm saying? Lavinia didn't do it?'

'Then why was she holding the candlestick?' asked Jemima doggedly, looking far from convinced.

'I don't know,' replied Rose truthfully. 'For some reason she decided to pick it up. Perhaps she did it instinctively finding it there on the ground. Whatever reason made her pick it up, she didn't do it Jemima. She didn't kill Emmeline.'

'Cedric thought she'd done it,' Jemima continued stubbornly. 'Otherwise why would he have done what he did? All that destroying – '

'He didn't think it through. He jumped to the obvious conclusion, as did we all,' said Rose hurriedly, 'But he was wrong. We all were. Think about it, Jemima. Why would Lavinia wish Emmeline dead? They were friends after all. It was Lavinia who invited her to stay here at Sedgwick. What possible motive could she have had for killing her guest?'

'But if what you say is true – ', began Jemima slowly.

'It means that someone else killed Emmeline … yes, of course it does,' said Rose quickly, pleased that Jemima was beginning to take in her words.

But if she had thought that Jemima would be relieved to discover that her hostess was not the murderer, she was mistaken. If it was possible, even more colour had drained from Jemima's face and her bottom lip had started to quiver. Jemima clung to the doorframe, as if for support, as realisation dawned on her.

'Someone else killed Emmeline,' she half whispered, 'Oh my God, no!'

'So they know I didn't do it?' said Lavinia, sitting up.

She had been reclining on her bed, bedclothes pulled tight up to her neck. She had been so still that Rose had at first thought she was asleep. But when she looked closely, she found that Lavinia had instead been staring into nothingness, her eyes wide open. And when Rose had spoken, Lavinia had roused herself quickly enough as if leaving behind some troublesome dream.

'Well, I suppose I should feel relieved, shouldn't I? That no one thinks I'm a murderess anymore, I mean? But the truth is that I don't feel anything at all … I still feel numb … I still can't quite believe what's happened, even though I saw her body with my own eyes and picked up that awful candlestick –'

'Why did you do that? Why did you pick up the candlestick, Lavinia? Why didn't you leave it where it was?' asked Rose curiously.

'I don't know … Why did I do it?'

Lavinia sounded vague. The look on her face showed clearly that she was trying to cast her mind back. She clung at her bedspread as the awful image sprung up before her, and she passed her tongue over her lips, as if she suddenly found them dry.

'Here, have some water,' said Rose, passing her the glass of water beside her bed. 'I wonder if it wouldn't be better for you to have some brandy.'

'I'll be all right in a minute or two,' said her friend, taking a few sips. 'It's just so frightful. But I want to remember why I did it, picked up the candlestick, I mean. It does seem such a strange sort of thing to have done, doesn't it? The police are sure to ask me, aren't they, and I haven't the faintest idea how to reply.'

'Did you see the candlestick before you discovered Emmeline's body?'

'Yes … now I come to think of it … I am sure I did. Yes … that was it.' Lavinia closed her eyes to enable her to think better. 'I came across the candlestick first. It made me stop, because I wondered what it was doing there. It seemed so out of place. It was gleaming in the sun and I thought how bright it looked, only it seemed to be smeared with something, and I wondered what it was. So I picked it up to have a look. I didn't know what it was, only that it was red. I didn't realise it was b-blood. All the time I was thinking: why would someone throw away a perfectly good candlestick in the maze? And then I thought that I recognised it, that I had seen it somewhere before.'

'Where had you seen it before, Lavinia? Here at Sedgwick?' asked Rose eagerly. 'Please try and think. It could be very important.'

'It seemed familiar, so I suppose I must have seen it at Sedgwick, mustn't I? But I'm not sure where. I wonder if I passed it every day without noticing it, as if it had become part of the wallpaper. Do you think that very likely, Rose?'

'Yes I do. We'll have to check with the servants to see if any of the candlesticks are missing.'

'Won't the police be doing that? Can't we leave it to them?'

'Yes, of course, it's just that – '

'It's just that Cedric has asked you to investigate,' said Lavinia, giving her an ambiguous stare.

'Yes, do you mind awfully?'

'That you intend to take it upon yourself to find the murderer, or that you're still in love with my brother and he with you?' Lavinia was looking at her closely, and Rose felt herself blush.

'Both I suppose,' she stuttered.

'Well, I would like you to investigate this murder,' said Lavinia. 'You seem to have quite a knack for it. Murder does seem to be rather attracted to you. I daresay that the police will get there eventually, but it may be rather good to have you there sleuthing away to keep them on their toes. I say, do you think it will be the same inspector fellow that investigated at Ashgrove? He investigated the murders at Dareswick too, didn't he? I thought he was rather handsome, didn't you? Not that I think he liked me very much. That sergeant of his certainly didn't.'

'Scotland Yard is being brought in to investigate Emmeline's death, and Cedric did ask the chief constable if it might be Inspector Deacon and Sergeant Lane.'

'Well, there you go,' said Lavinia. 'It'll be them.'

But as it happened, she was only partly right.

Neither woman was inclined to hurry downstairs to join the others in the drawing room. Rose found it pleasant in Lavinia's room, and the old feeling of camaraderie that they had shared in the dress shop seemed to have returned for some time at least. She assumed that Cedric was still out by the maze awaiting the arrival of the police. She very much feared that Vera had been unable to keep herself from going over to speak to Theo. The result of which was likely to have been ructions or, at the very least, a chilly reception. How she pitied the count, stuck as he was in the room between the two.

When Lavinia and Rose did at last begin to make their way downstairs, they stopped at Jemima's door on the way. Rose had previously arranged for Jemima to come down with them, as neither Jemima nor Lavinia had indicated that they wished to enter the drawing room alone. Both women anticipated being met with inquisitive stares.

Jemima still looked pale, but to Rose's relief she appeared more composed than before, holding herself upright with her head thrown back as if prepared to meet the onslaught of compassionate looks and stares that would greet her when she encountered the others. It would certainly be an ordeal, Rose thought, to someone who kept herself so much to herself. She noticed that Lavinia and Jemima both looked at each other warily. Rose wondered if Lavinia had overheard her conversation with Jemima, in particular the girl's assertion that Lavinia had killed Emmeline.

Despite her posture, Jemima still appeared hesitant at leaving the safety of her room. She closed the door behind her gingerly and held back from the other two, walking in their wake as she had always done with Emmeline. This suited Lavinia well enough but Rose hung back slightly, not wishing the girl to walk alone. In such a fashion they made their way along the corridor and across the landing to the top of the grand staircase leading down to the hall below.

All at once, Jemima seemed to come alive and dashed to a window, in the process almost upsetting a houseplant that was perched rather precariously in front of it on top of an Edwardian, mahogany plant stand.

'Whatever are you doing, Jemima?' asked Lavinia haughtily, her voice rather cold.

'I'm sorry,' Jemima said apologetically, making sure that the plant pot was securely positioned on its base. 'I was just wondering whether one could see the maze from here. It's silly I know, because even if one can, it'll only be the outside hedges, not the inside. But I can't bear to think of poor Emmie's body lying there all alone in the cold. I didn't even go over to see her, to say goodbye. I suppose it was the shock. I was afraid to go too close … afraid of what I might see. But I should have made myself, shouldn't I? I should have gone to her, I should – '

'Well, I should consider yourself lucky, if I were you,' interrupted Lavinia, both sounding and looking far from compassionate. '*I* saw Emmeline's body and it was frightfully awful, I can tell you. I saw all the blood and where – '

'We'd better go down,' Rose said quickly, noticing that Jemima had gone an unhealthy shade of greenish-white. 'The others will be wondering where we are.' She glared at Lavinia, who merely raised her eyebrows, made a face, and did not look the least bit repentant.

Silently they made their way downstairs, this time Rose bringing up the rear. She would have followed the two other women into the drawing room had her attention not been caught by the opening of the study door and hearing Cedric's voice from within. Her instinct was to go to him, but it was obvious that he had company and was in the middle of a conversation, odd words of which she could just make out. She looked at her wristwatch and was surprised by how long she had spent talking to Lavinia in her room. Unless she was mistaken, the men from Scotland Yard had arrived.

Rose decided to make her excuses and loiter in the hall. She realised then how very much she wanted the men to be Inspector Deacon and Sergeant Lane. If it were them, then everything would be all right. She had every faith in the inspector's police methods and skill at arriving at the truth. And he had considered her an ally rather than a hindrance, keen to obtain her views. Rose blushed, even though there was no one there to see her. The thoughts that she had had before came flooding back. There had been some unpleasantness when Inspector Deacon had realised that she had withheld some information from him and suggested an alibi to a suspect. Of course, she knew she had done it all with the best of intentions. But she could see how he might have been annoyed at the time. And now he would think she had done it again. Worse than that, he would think badly of Cedric. They would both go down in his estimations.

The door of the study opened further and a man came out.

'Sergeant Lane,' Rose said with relief, stepping forward. 'Oh I am so glad it's you and Inspector Deacon that they've sent. It would be too awful if it was anybody else.'

'Miss Simpson.' Sergeant Lane looked equally pleased to see her. 'I wondered whether you'd be here as soon as I heard that the murder had occurred in the grounds of his lordship's estate. I said to myself, so I did, I wonder if Miss Simpson will be there to give us a hand.'

'Well, I'd be very pleased to. Where is Inspector Deacon? Is he in there?' She indicated the study with a wave of her hand. 'With Lord Belvedere?'

'No, miss.' Sergeant Lane looked distinctly uncomfortable.

'What's the matter?' cried Rose, becoming worried. 'Where is Inspector Deacon? Why isn't he here with you? Who's in the study with Cedric?'

'That would be Inspector Bramwell, miss. It's him that's been sent down with me.'

'Not Inspector Deacon?' Rose felt fear rising inside her.

She knew instinctively something was wrong. A part of her did not want to know why Inspector Deacon was absent. But another part of her wanted to know very much. Even before she asked her question, she dreaded the answer.

'Where is Inspector Deacon, Sergeant? Why isn't he here with you?'

'I'm afraid he was shot, miss.'

Sergeant Lane's words hung in the air, and it was a moment or two before Rose could comprehend what he was saying. And if it hadn't been for the sergeant's quick thinking in grabbing a chair and placing her very gently in it, then she thought later that she would surely have slumped to the ground as Vera had fallen, on being told of Emmeline's death.

Chapter Fifteen

'Miss Simpson, Miss Simpson, are you all right?'

Out of the corner of her eye Rose could see Sergeant Lane's face peering over her full of concern. His voice sounded anxious. She thought she should say something to allay his fears, but she could not think of what to say; words seemed inadequate.

'I'm awfully sorry, miss, I daresay I should have softened it a bit. It'll be the shock, miss, on top of the murder that happened here. I wasn't thinking straight. Of course you'd be upset, knowing him as you did – '

'Was he hurt?' Rose said at last. 'When he was shot, was he hurt?'

She saw the pain and confusion on the sergeant's face. How ridiculous her question sounded even to her own ears. Of course he was hurt; he was worse than that. He was dead, lying on some slab in a mortuary somewhere, or perhaps he was already buried in the ground, the funeral long over and done with and all the time she had never known.

'Yes, miss, he was hurt bad,' said the sergeant. 'He was shot twice. We were investigating a burglary and … well, I won't go into all the details. But he was lucky too. One of the bullets went awfully near one of the main arteries so the doctor said. If it had gone any nearer that would have been it for him. The second bullet – '

'What … What are you saying?' cried Rose as the significance of his words finally sank in. 'Are you saying he's alive? He's not dead? Is that what you are saying?'

'You thought … Oh, miss, I've made a right mess of this, haven't I just?' exclaimed Sergeant Lane, chuckling in spite of everything. 'Lord, miss, no. Inspector Deacon's not dead. Like I said, he was badly hurt but he's recuperating and should be as good as new, except for his leg, that is. It's likely that he'll walk with a bit of a limp and he might need a stick, but there's plenty of poor blighters you see worse off than him.'

As if as one, their minds drifted off to the casualties of the Great War, of which Rose's father had been one. The men who had returned with troubled minds or with missing limbs, who were still common enough sights to remind those who had survived of the great sacrifices made by a generation of men.

'You're right, Sergeant,' Rose said quickly, getting up from her chair. 'I didn't quite understand what you were saying, and on top of the murder, well … I'm afraid I found it just too much. But I am quite all right now. And I'm jolly glad Inspector Deacon will be all right.'

It occurred to Rose that she had made rather a spectacle of herself. She was grateful that the sergeant had been the only person there to witness it. Thankfully none of the footmen were present so it would not form a part of servant gossip, and Cedric and Inspector Bramwell were still in the study in discussion.

'Do you see anything of Inspector Deacon while he's recuperating?' Rose asked. 'If you do, I'd be grateful if you would pass on my best wishes. And Lord Belvedere's as well, of course. Cedric will be as upset as I am to hear about him being wounded.'

'Yes, miss, I see a bit of him. He likes to keep his hand in, so to speak, you know, hear all about the cases that we're investigating. My guess is that he gets a bit bored like, stuck there all alone in his lodgings with just his landlady for company. But hopefully it won't be too long before he's back at the Yard. The place is not the same without him there, so it isn't.'

'We, that is, Cedric and I, were rather hoping you'd both be investigating this murder. What is Inspector Bramwell like? Is he any good?'

'He's got a fearsome reputation at the Yard, miss,' replied Sergeant Lane. 'You don't get to where he is without being good at your job. But he's a lot different from Inspector Deacon in his manner and how he tackles an investigation so I've heard, although I've not had the pleasure of working with him before. He'll not take any nonsense and, between you and me, he can be somewhat abrupt, but he gets the job done.'

'Goodness,' said Rose, 'he sounds rather frightening. But I'm awfully glad you're here.'

'Oh, he's that, miss,' agreed the sergeant, a twinkle in his eye. 'I think I'd better warn you that he's none too fond of amateur sleuths, so if you have a mind to investigate this murder yourself you'd do best not to say so to him.'

'Well, my lord, this is a rum go and no mistake,' said Inspector Bramwell, sitting himself down heavily in the seat offered him.

He was quite a bulk of a man and it occurred to Cedric that it might have been wise to have offered him a sturdier chair in which to take the weight off his feet. The young earl was doing his best not to show the disappointment he felt on finding that Inspector Deacon would not be investigating Emmeline's death. Unfortunately he had taken an instant and probably wholly unreasonable dislike to the fellow sitting in front of him.

'I feel pretty shaken up about it, I don't mind telling you,' Cedric concurred. 'No doubt Sergeant Lane has already told you that Miss Simpson and I have had some experience of this sort of thing. But it's somewhat different when it occurs in one's own home. I still can't quite believe it's happened, and the maze of all places, I – '

'Now then, my lord, I'm sure it's awful for you and all, but there's no use crying over spilt milk or pretending like it's not happened, because it has.'

'Oh,' said Cedric, somewhat taken about by the man's rudeness. 'I was just saying that – '

'I'm sure you were. But we've got a murder to investigate and there's no time to waste. We need to get down to business, so to speak.'

The inspector paused to give Cedric a particularly penetrating stare. It gave Cedric the opportunity to look at the man more closely. As he described him to Rose later, Inspector Bramwell was of middle age and of heavy build, and had small, watery grey eyes and a double chin. His suit and shirt, although both of reasonable quality, looked a couple of sizes too small for him so that the buttons on his shirt threatened to come undone, and his stomach bulged over the waistband of his trousers in a way that was not at all becoming. To make matters worse, he persisted in continually mopping his brow with his handkerchief during their conversation, although the study was far from warm, the fire having not long been lit. The variance in manner and appearance between Inspector Bramwell and Inspector Deacon could not be greater and Cedric found it disquieting. He felt his heart sinking.

'I understand there was some delay in notifying us of the death,' the inspector said at last, 'but we'll come to that later.'

Cedric felt himself go red and turned his attention to studying an invisible fleck of material that he had just noticed on his trouser leg. He spent a moment or two engaged in flicking it away, wondering how the inspector would take the news that in addition to his tardiness in notifying the police of the murder, some of the evidence had also been tampered with, and he again was the culprit. It was a moment or two before he looked up and met the inspector's gaze.

'I daresay I'll go about this investigation slightly differently to what you've been used to. Inspector Deacon and I do things differently, I'd imagine. No doubt he was mindful that the murders he was investigating were at the homes of the gentry and so liked to tread careful like, so as not to ruffle any feathers.' The inspector snorted and leaned forward in his chair. 'I work differently, my lord. I have no qualms about ruffling feathers. In fact, I rather enjoy it. And it makes no difference to me whether a murder's occurred in a slum or an ancestral home, or whether the victim is a lady of the streets or a member of the British aristocracy. Me, I treat them just the same. That's not to say that I don't care, because I do. They all matter to me and I'll do all that I can to see that those responsible are brought to justice.' He sat back heavily in his chair. 'I do hope I have made myself clear, my lord?'

'Perfectly, Inspector,' replied Cedric, quite at a loss as to what to make of the man.

'Right, now that we have got that out of the way, I'll ask you about who's staying here at Sedgwick. Friends and family, I gather, a proper little country house-party, am I right, eh?'

Cedric noticed that the inspector had an irritating habit of jabbing the air with his finger when putting a question. He decided there and then that he disliked the man very much.

'The people staying at Sedgwick this weekend, Inspector, are myself and my sister, Lady Lavinia Sedgwick. Miss Simpson, who is a friend of us both is here too, as are Dr Harrison and his fiancée, Miss Brewster, who are guests, and finally a number of acquaintances of my sister. Friends made during her recent travels on the Continent. I'm afraid I know very little about them, except that the woman who was murdered was Emmeline Montacute, of whom you probably know more about than I do myself.'

'Is that so?' said Inspector Bramwell. 'Well, suppose you tell me what you do know about your sister's new friends. Let's start with their names.'

'Very well,' said Cedric rather coldly.

He considered that it was a significant disadvantage for a man in the inspector's position to have such an unfortunate manner about him. His inclination was to be as unhelpful as possible, but instead he took a deep breath and decided to address himself to a space just above the inspector's shoulder so that he was not obliged to look the man in the eye.

'Well, first I suppose there is Miss Jemima Wentmore. She was a sort of friend-cum-companion to Miss Montacute, I think; her exact position was never made very clear. Then there is Felix Thistlewaite. I'm afraid that I don't know much about him except that he has a rich old aunt who was paying for him to go on a sort of European tour before he settled down to work as an articled clerk at some London legal establishment. Poor devil, his last few days of living the life of a man of leisure have been completely ruined for him.'

'Well, I'd say he was jolly fortunate to have gone on his European tour. Not all of us have a rich old aunt to treat us,' said the inspector. He looked at a place a little distance behind Cedric. 'Are you getting all this down, Lane?'

Cedric assumed that the sergeant must have nodded, for he did not hear him reply. He had forgotten that Sergeant Lane was there and imagined that was the inspector's intention. Suspects and witnesses were far more willing to speak freely if they were not constantly reminded that every word they uttered was being written down. He wished he could catch Sergeant Lane's eye for he considered Inspector Bramwell was unlikely to be the sergeant's cup of tea.

'Anyone else?' enquired the inspector, turning back to scrutinise Cedric, 'or is that the lot?'

'There's just Count Fernand,' began Cedric.

'Count Fernand?' said the Inspector snorting. 'Isn't he a character out of Dumas's *The Count of Montecristo*?'

'Very likely, Inspector,' agreed Cedric. 'Fernand Mondego, if I am not mistaken, was Count de Morcerf.'

'Well, and who's this fellow of yours, my lord, when he's at home?'

'I wish I knew. He's a count from a far off land, that's all I know about him. He's a dashed evasive fellow when it comes to providing details about himself. Damned if I know which country he hails from. When I enquired, when we were first introduced, why, blow me if the chap didn't mumble. I didn't feel I could ask him again. Awfully bad form you know, Inspector, to show one's not been listening to one's guest, what. But he gets on well with the ladies.'

Cedric noticed that the inspector was studying him closely. He wondered whether he had overdone things a bit and blushed. It occurred to him that the inspector might not be so much of a fool as he first appeared.

'So if I understand you rightly, my lord, you have certain reservations about Count Fernand?' Inspector Bramwell did not wait for Cedric to answer but turned instead to address the sergeant. 'Take a note of that if you will, Lane. Our Count Fernand requires some further scrutiny.'

There were a few moments of silence as the Earl of Belvedere and the inspector from Scotland Yard regarded each other. Cedric braced himself to face the verbal onslaught which was surely inevitable. Inspector Bramwell would require him to explain why he had deliberately meddled with the evidence and delayed telephoning for the police. And how he would answer, he was not quite sure. He had a story to hand that he had gone over and over in his mind but, now that he had come face to face with the inspector, he felt it wouldn't do. Inspector Bramwell was unlikely to swallow it. More than that, he realised, while Inspector Deacon would have been annoyed, he would have let it go with a reprimand. Inspector Bramwell was a completely different kettle of fish. He doubted very much whether he would be so obliging.

'Thank you, my lord. That will be all for the present time.' The inspector seemed to stifle a yawn. 'You may go back to the drawing room and join the others. We shall of course want to speak to you later. There'll be one or two questions that we shall want to put to you.' He turned his head to look at the policeman. 'Sergeant, I'd like you to talk to the servants now, hear what they've got to say for themselves.'

Sergeant Lane got up from his chair and taking his notebook and pencil with him made to leave the room. Having got to the door he half opened it, but lingered a moment or two as if reluctant to go.

'What?' Cedric looked at the inspector in amazement. 'I mean to say, don't you want to ask me some more questions? You haven't asked me anything yet about Emmeline; where I was when she was killed, who I think might have wanted to hurt her, that sort of thing.'

'All in good time, Lord Belvedere. By your own account you hardly knew Emmeline Montacute.' Inspector Bramwell looked up at the door, as if suddenly aware that Sergeant Lane had not left. 'Still here, Sergeant? Ah, is that footsteps I hear in the hall? Possibly the ladies have come down now?'

'Odious man, the inspector' said Cedric to Rose, when he caught up with her later in the drawing room. 'He's a damned rude sort of chap. Goes out of his way to be so, as far as I could tell. Can't make him out at all. He didn't ask me any questions about the murder, just said that he would speak to me later, and he's sent poor old Sergeant Lane off to interview the servants. Bring back Inspector Deacon, I say.'

He turned and for the first time registered the presence of the other women in the room.

'I say, I'm pleased you managed to persuade Lavinia and Jemima to leave their rooms. I got the distinct impression that the inspector was none too pleased that we hadn't all kept together in one room. Heaven knows what he thought either of them were going to do.' He studied them closely 'My sister at least looks to be bearing up quite well after the shock. That's to say she looks an awful lot better than she did in the maze. I'll just go and have a word with her. Do you think that I should offer my condolences to Jemima, or would that be bad form?'

'That would be kind. Tell me, is Inspector Bramwell really so awful, Cedric?' Rose asked, worried. 'Sergeant Lane said he was good at his job.'

'Oh, I'm not saying he's not sharp,' reassured Cedric, 'because I think he is. It's just that he seems to go out of his way to put people's backs up. And he has an odd way of doing things, although I suppose there must be some method in his madness.'

Chapter Sixteen

Having interviewed the servants, Sergeant Lane returned to the study. Although some considerable time had elapsed he was not unduly surprised to find the inspector in exactly the same position as when he had left him, namely settled comfortably in Cedric's buttoned-velvet captain's chair, and seated behind his large, walnut, estate desk. Due to his build, the sergeant had considered Inspector Bramwell to be more of a man for quiet contemplation than physical activity. He cast an anxious eye at the chair wondering how the spindles were bearing up under the strain of Inspector Bramwell's not insignificant weight.

'Ah, Sergeant, back are you? No doubt with some tales to tell. And I've not been idle, if that's what you're thinking. I've been finding out all there is to know about the unfortunate Miss Emmeline Montacute.'

Inspector Bramwell leaned back in his chair making it creak and Sergeant Lane wince. The inspector gave his subordinate a smug smile.

'Have you, sir?'

'I have. I hope it'll throw some light on the circumstances leading up to her untimely death. I find it helps to have a picture in my mind of the murder victim. As Lord Belvedere says, it seems she was an heiress. You've no doubt been in some of them Montacute department stores, Sergeant.'

'One or two, sir.'

'All over the place they are, least in all the big cities. Owned by her father, they are. She stood to inherit the entire Montacute fortune on his death, so she'd have come in for a pretty penny. Of course, we'll have to find out what happens to the money now she's dead. Who'll inherit the fortune, that's what we've got to find out.'

'It should be easy enough, shouldn't it, sir, to find out who'll inherit her father's fortune? All we need to do is have a word with the man himself. Speaking of whom, have you been able to notify him about his daughter's death?' The sergeant sighed. 'I think I'm right in thinking she was his only child. The poor fellow will be grief stricken.'

'Yes, she was an only child, and no I haven't been able to get hold of Montacute,' replied the inspector. 'I managed to get hold of Montacute's secretary though, a chap named Stapleton, who informed me the gentleman's off on his travels acquiring new merchandise to sell in his department stores. Went to New York, so Stapleton says, and been gone some two months all told. I thought we'd have to cable him but, as fortune has it, he's due to dock in Liverpool in a day or two. The secretary's making his way down there now so as to be there to break the news to him as soon as he disembarks. He's awful keen to make sure Montacute hears the news about the daughter from him, poor fellow, and not from the newspapers. Of course, we'll make sure one of the local constables accompanies him.'

'Well, I daresay that'll make our job easier,' muttered Sergeant Lane. 'I wouldn't have recognised the poor girl as being Miss Montacute. I can't say I've ever seen a photograph of the young lady in the society pages, which seems strange given her position.'

'That's because the old man has kept her cloistered away in the Scottish Highlands. There'd been a kidnap attempt made on Miss Montacute some years back, which you may remember. It was foiled just in time, but I understand it was a very close thing. It put the wind up Montacute something dreadful, so I'm told. He was driven half mad with the worry of it all, quite convinced another attempt would be made to snatch his daughter unless he took steps to ensure her safety. Not content with residing in as remote a place as possible, he also took measures to ensure that no photographs of his daughter ever appeared in the newspapers.'

'Yet, despite all that,' Sergeant Lane said reflectively, 'someone did manage to get to Miss Montacute.'

'They did indeed, and kidnap, or should I say a failed kidnap attempt, must be one of the motives that we shall have to consider. It would appear that the girl was rather reckless about her own safety when given the opportunity. She waited for old Papa to go off on one of his travels, which I am given to understand happened infrequently, and then did a moonlight flit, so to speak, with that companion friend of hers, Miss Wentmore. It was quite a shock for poor old Stapleton, who'd been charged with the daughter's safety in his employer's absence. Most indignant about it he was too. Said there was no reason for them to leave the way they did.'

'Oh?'

'Mr Montacute's only stipulation was that a number of servants should accompany them for their own safety. The secretary's been beside himself with worry. The girls had left no indication of where they'd gone or when they'd be back. He and the servants had been praying that they'd be returned and safely ensconced in the Highlands before Montacute arrived back from America.'

'Poor fellow, I don't envy his task,' said Sergeant Lane, producing his notebook and jotting down a few notes. 'I take it Montacute is likely to hold him partially responsible for his daughter's death?'

'The man thinks he's likely to lose his job over it,' confirmed the inspector. 'Damned unfair, of course, because girls are dashed independent these days. Stapleton tells me he holds Miss Wentmore responsible. He's of the opinion that it was all her idea. Says Miss Montacute would never have considered doing anything so foolhardy left to her own devices; says what happened is solely due to Miss Wentmore and the influence she had over the girl.'

'In which case I wouldn't like to be in her shoes when Montacute catches up with her,' Sergeant Lane said. 'I assume you'll want to interview her first. If Miss Montacute had any enemies or had received any threats to her safety then Miss Wentmore should know about them, shouldn't she?'

'All in good time, Sergeant,' Inspector Bramwell said, putting down the papers that he had been perusing during their conversation. 'I daresay Miss Wentmore will have information useful to our inquiry. But as I said to you before, I do things a bit differently to your Inspector Deacon. Me, I like to interview what I call the 'little people' first, what others might call the bit players. I daresay policemen like your Inspector Deacon would consider them insignificant and leave them till last to be interviewed. But as I say, I like to interview them first.'

'Why's that, sir?' enquired the sergeant, looking distinctly puzzled.

He was already at a loss as to why his superior had chosen not to question Cedric about the murder when they had had the opportunity. It had been painfully obvious, even to the most casual observer that the Earl of Belvedere had been rather put out at being dismissed in such a cavalier fashion.

'Because they have a tendency not to watch their words,' answered the inspector. 'They see all the goings on, so to speak, but are not so much a part of it. They are not hampered by the various loyalties that the main players wrestle with in trying to decide whether or not to impart information. No, it doesn't take much for our bit players to spill the beans, more often than not it just takes a bit of encouragement on our part. And of course the bit players have another considerable advantage over our main players.'

'And what's that, sir?'

'They see things more objectively.'

'I take it, sir, that you see Lord Belvedere as having a main role?'

Inspector Bramwell nodded.

'Well then, sir,' continued Sergeant Lane, 'I think you may have got it wrong in his case if you don't mind my saying so. He's an upright young man from what I know of him. I think you'd have found him forthcoming. It appeared to me, sir, that he was keen to tell you what he knew.'

'That's as maybe,' said Inspector Bramwell, rather dismissively. 'But his account will be somewhat tainted. I've seen it before with the likes of him. They believe they have a responsibility to their guests. Why, in one particular case I was investigating, blow me if the damned duke didn't do everything in his power to prevent me even questioning his friends.'

'Lord Belvedere's not like that, sir,' Sergeant Lane said.

'Is that so, Sergeant?' Inspector Bramwell looked at him rather sceptically. 'And yet we have it on the good authority of the local constable that it's more than likely that our earl tampered with the evidence before he called us in.'

Sergeant Lane said nothing and looked a little sheepish. To cover his embarrassment he turned the pages of his notebook. 'Do you want to hear what I found out from the servants, sir?'

'I do indeed, Sergeant. Treated right, they're even more forthcoming than the bit players. Now, what have they to tell us, I wonder.'

'Well, it seems, sir, that the deceased and the doctor had taken rather a fancy to one another,' began Sergeant Lane, keen to redeem himself in the eyes of his inspector. 'Quite taken with each other, they were. As soon as they laid eyes on each other if the footman's to be believed.'

'But wasn't Harrison staying here with his fiancée? Now ... what's her name ...?' The inspector glanced at his notes.

'Yes, sir, Miss Brewster. And as you'd imagine, she didn't take it at all well by all accounts. Proper upset, she was. Pretended not to notice what was going on, but she was that miserable all the time that all the servants were certain that it was going to come to a head, and it did.'

'Oh?'

The inspector had discarded his papers and looked up, waiting for the sergeant to continue.

'According to our gossip of a footman,' continued Sergeant Lane, 'Miss Brewster made some blasé remark about the failed kidnap attempt. Miss Montacute burst into floods of tears and Dr Harrison and Miss Wentmore had a right go at Miss Brewster, asked her how she could be so unkind. Our footman enjoyed it no end, said he hadn't seen as much fur fly not since Lady Lavinia announced her intention to work in a dress shop where, as it happens, she met Miss Simpson.'

'When did this outburst occur?'

'The night before last. After dinner in the drawing room it was, and in front of all the family and guests. The footman said everyone was standing there, staring in disbelief, wondering how it was all going to end. It was the count who came to the rescue and changed the direction of things by talking about jewels. Miss Montacute cheered up no end and told them all about the Montacute Diamonds, and she and Lady Lavinia took it in turns to look at their precious stones using the count's jeweller's lens.'

'Did they indeed? Well, well, well. I'd like to know how this count fellow fits into everything. The young earl didn't have a good word to say about him, made him sound like some character out of a storybook.'

'Do you think there's more to the count than meets the eye? I mean to say, how many gentlemen just happen to have a jeweller's loupe on them? It seems a funny sort of thing to carry in the pocket of your dinner jacket, doesn't it, sir?'

'It does,' agreed the inspector.

'And another thing, sir. The servants said he was a favourite among the ladies ... well, at least with Lady Lavinia and Miss Montacute. Could be quite charming, he could, had a tendency to amuse and flatter them.

The general feeling in the servants' hall was that he was trying to ingratiate himself with these two ladies in particular.'

'Was he, indeed? Did he have a particular favourite between the two?'

'Now, there's a thing, sir. The footman thought he had a slight preference for Miss Montacute, but subsequently turned his attentions towards Lady Lavinia.'

'I'll wager he didn't want to compete with the doctor fellow for Miss Montacute's affections. He sounds a fickle sort of a fellow to me.' Inspector Bramwell got up from his chair and began to pace the room. 'Interesting that, Sergeant.'

'Oh?'

'Is it just coincidence that he had a jeweller's loupe about his person and these two women have a pile of jewels between them? I doubt the other women would have been able to scrape together any jewels of much worth. We'll need to look at this fellow pretty closely, Lane.'

'Yes, sir. Apparently he wasn't the only one to have a bit of an eye for the ladies. Thistlewaite is sweet on Miss Wentmore and according to this footman, although the young lady in question has a tendency to keep herself to herself, it is generally believed among the servants that she feels something for the fellow.'

'Any more affairs of the heart that I should be informed about, Lane?'

'Lord Belvedere and Miss Simpson, sir.'

'An earl and a shop girl, whatever next!' The inspector chuckled. 'I'll wager the servants have a view on that. Still, there's many a member of the aristocracy who's married an actress or chorus girl in the past so I'm led to believe.'

'And Miss Simpson is not just any woman, sir,' Sergeant Lane said quickly. 'She's been very useful in solving some murders in the past. I happen to know Inspector Deacon holds her in high esteem. Miss – '

'An amateur detective,' groaned the inspector, 'that's all we need.' He held up his hand as Sergeant Lane showed signs that he was about to protest. 'And I don't care how highly thought of by your Inspector Deacon Miss Simpson is, she has no part to play in this investigation other than as a witness and possible suspect, same as everyone else in this house. Do I make myself clear, Sergeant?'

'Yes, sir, but – '

'No buts, please, Sergeant. I've had my fill of amateur detectives. They always think that they're so much cleverer than us policemen, always sticking their noses in where they're not wanted, and more often than not having to be rescued by the very people they ridicule as being incompetent.'

'Miss Simpson's not like that, sir,' began Sergeant Lane.

'Hmm, isn't she, Sergeant? But I'll hazard a guess that she's not above withholding information or protecting a suspect that she's taken a shine to, eh?'

There was an awkward silence.

'That's the trouble with people who fancy themselves to be amateur detectives,' said the inspector more kindly. 'They can't look at things objectively, not like we can. They should keep their noses out and leave us to get on with our jobs.'

'But, sir – '

'I think I've made myself clear, Sergeant.' The inspector's voice had now taken on an icy tone. 'I'll have no more said on the matter, do you hear?'

'Yes, sir. Oh, there's one other thing, sir, I almost forgot. After dinner last night they talked about the maze. Lord Belvedere showed them all a plan of it and explained in detail the route through. Apparently they were intending to make a bit of a game of it today, seeing how long it took for each of the guests to get to the centre of the maze. There was to be a prize for the winner, so I've heard.'

'Now that is interesting, Sergeant. When we saw the body in situ, I couldn't help but think how damned complicated that maze would be to navigate if one didn't have a map.'

The two policemen were disturbed from their deliberations by a discreet knock on the study door.

'Ah, good, hopefully we're about to get some coffee,' said Inspector Bramwell. 'Perhaps even a slice or two of cake if you managed to make a favourable impression on the cook while you were down in the servants' hall, eh Lane?'

The sergeant thought he detected a twinkle in the inspector's eye, and he blushed.

The inspector was however to be disappointed. For although a servant did indeed enter the room, he came empty handed.

'Oh, and what can we do for you, my man? What are you? Footman? Butler?'

'I'm under-butler, sir. Manning.' Every now and then the man glanced nervously at the door, as if he were expecting them to be joined any minute by someone else.

'What's the matter, man? Are you waiting on somebody, one of the maids or footmen perhaps? My sergeant here and I are rather parched. We could do with a pot of coffee and a slice or two of cake. Should we ring the bell or is that something you can arrange?'

'Refreshments are on their way, sir. But if I may have a word with you first?'

'If you must, so long as you do not dither about it. We are in the middle of a murder investigation, if you hadn't heard.' The inspector sighed and looked down at his papers.

'I am aware of that, sir, which is why I thought it my duty to come and see you.'

'Oh?'

Inspector Bramwell looked up from the desk, and for the first time regarded the servant with something close to interest. The man in front of him was approaching middle age and was dressed in the usual butler's attire of black waistcoat and tailcoat. There was a nervousness about his manner that the policeman found both disquieting and surprising, given the man's position as one of the chief servants of the household.

'Yes, sir. Although I am not sure that Mr Torridge will approve of my coming to see you.'

'And who's this Mr Torridge, when he's at home?'

'He's head-butler, sir. I'm not sure that he'd think it proper.' Manning bent forward slightly and said in a low voice: 'They don't hold with having policemen in the house, Mr Torridge and Mrs Farrier, she's the housekeeper, sir.'

'That's as maybe. But they can expect nothing else with a murder in the grounds. And you can tell them from me that we'll be here for as long as it takes to apprehend the murderer.' The inspector glared at the under-butler, his face even more florid than usual. 'Now, out with it man, why are you here?'

'I overheard talk between a couple of the guests, sir, regarding the murder weapon. Is it true that it was a silver candlestick?'

'And what if it were? What's it to you?'

'Do you know where it comes from?' interjected Sergeant Lane, before the unfortunate butler was obliged to answer the inspector's question. 'Does it come from this house?'

'Yes, sir, I think it does.' Manning, spurred on by the interest shown by the sergeant, turned his attention from the inspector to his subordinate. 'That's to say, a silver candlestick appears to be missing from the dining room.'

'What? I thought you fellows kept the silverware and crystal and suchlike locked up in your butler's pantry,' said the inspector, taking exception to being ignored.

'We do indeed, sir, the expensive silverware and crystal, that is. But not the ordinary, everyday silver; there's just too much of it. The candlestick in question, sir, was a very run of the mill affair and as such was not locked away but left out on the sideboard.'

'So it's missing, eh? What does it look like, this candlestick?'

'I can show you, sir. It's one of a pair. If you care to come with me into the dining room, I can show you the other one. It's still there.'

'Well, what are we waiting for?'

Sergeant Lane had never seen the inspector move so quickly. For such a heavy man, he was extremely agile.

They crossed the hall and followed the butler into the dining room. As they passed the drawing room, Sergeant Lane glanced at the closed door, imagining the Sedgwick family and their guests seated anxiously within, or else fretfully pacing the floor.

The dining room was a grand affair with its high, strapwork ceiling, wood-panelled walls and lavish furnishings, and the policemen paused a moment to take in the full splendour of the room. The butler meanwhile went straight to a large, bow-fronted Georgian sideboard, placed against the far wall. He turned to face the policemen, and indicated a tapered column, silver candlestick.

'That looks like the candlestick we found in the maze, don't you think, Sergeant?' said the inspector. 'An exact copy I reckon. Can't be absolutely certain without the other one in front of us to compare it with, of course. But I'd say that object could certainly do some damage.' He lifted up the candlestick to feel its weight. 'See how sturdy the base is, Sergeant? And you say, Manning, that this is one of a pair and the other is missing?'

'Yes, sir. It's usually just here, sir,' he indicated a spot on the sideboard.

'When did you last see it there?'

'Last night, sir. It was there when dinner was served and also when we cleared away. I know that because I remember checking to see that all the candles had been snuffed out and Jack, that's the second footman, sir, he'd forgotten to put out the candles on the sideboard. He'd done the ones on the table all right. Really, he's the most forgetful lad, whether we'll be able – '

'Right, so it was here last night after dinner. What about when you made your rounds before going to bed? Was it still there then?'

'I couldn't swear that it was,' Manning said hesitantly. 'You must understand, sir, that my attention is focused on checking that all the doors are locked and that the house is secure against intruders and fire and the like. I'd only have noticed the candlestick if the candle in it was still burning, which obviously it wasn't because as I've explained already I'd snuffed out the candles on the sideboard myself after the dinner things were cleared away. But,' he added hastily, as he saw the look of annoyance on the inspector's face, 'I like to think that if it had been missing, I'd have noticed it, unconsciously like. I like to suppose that I'd have gone over to the sideboard to see why things didn't look quite right. And then I'd have seen it was missing, sir.'

'Hmm. Well, suppose you're right, that means that the candlestick was taken either last thing at night after the house was all locked up and everybody gone to bed, or else in the early hours of this morning.'

'May I, sir?'

Sergeant Lane held out his hand to take the candlestick from the inspector, who was still clutching it in his plump hands.

'It's a nice piece, sir; solid but not too heavy.'

'We're not here to admire the silverware, Sergeant.'

'No, sir, what I meant was that it would not have been difficult to carry this candlestick out to the maze. It isn't cumbersome, and you wouldn't have to be particularly strong. Don't you see what I'm getting at, sir? A woman could have carried and wielded this candlestick just as easily as any man.'

Chapter Seventeen

It seemed to Rose that they had been left by themselves a very long time in the drawing room. With the exception of Cedric's all too brief first interview with the inspector, not one of them had been summoned for an interview to provide an alibi for the time of Emmeline's death. As a consequence, the mood in the drawing room became restive, and Rose wondered rather cynically whether that had been Inspector Bramwell's intention. Perhaps he thought everyone would be more forthcoming, having first been cooped up together almost beyond endurance. Certainly not knowing what was happening or where the police were with their investigation was unsettling.

What little conversation there was became desultory, for no one was minded to open up in the presence of murder. Most had retreated into their own solitary inner worlds, doing the best they could to cushion themselves from thinking too deeply about what had occurred. Nevertheless, the prevalent atmosphere in the room was one of incredulity. Close on its heels was fear, which seemed to cover the very surfaces of the furniture, ebbing out into the shadows like a fog.

Glancing around the room, Rose noticed that the most frightened of them all appeared to be Jemima. Fear exuded from her like an odour and, unless Rose was mistaken, the girl was even now trembling, the effect of which was to make anyone standing close to her feel instinctively nervous and on edge. Vera in particular gave Jemima one quick, frightened little glance before moving to the other side of the room. Felix, Rose noticed, had at first been inclined to go over to Jemima and offer his support, but he had been discouraged by the girl's resolute refusal to acknowledge his presence; if anything she physically drew back from him. She was only in the drawing room now because she had been obliged to join them, but her general demeanour was that of one who wished to be alone.

'What's keeping them from interviewing us, do you think?' Felix whispered to Rose. 'I'd have thought they'd want to get as much information from us as quickly as possible.'

'They're probably still examining the maze. Dusting for fingerprints and that sort of thing.'

But Rose felt the same uneasiness. It's just the waiting, she thought, it's not having anything to do but think. Cedric's summing up of Inspector Bramwell was still ringing in her ears, and she could not help a feeling of foreboding prejudicing her view of a man she was yet to meet. She stared at the door, willing it to open. Surely Sergeant Lane had spoken with the servants by now?

'Not that they'll find many fingerprints with his lordship having so considerately wiped them away,' Felix was saying. 'No,' he raised a hand as Rose made to protest, 'don't worry, I don't mean to start all that again. But you're familiar with this sort of thing, aren't you, murder investigations, I mean?'

Rose was about to admit, rather reluctantly, that she did indeed have some experience in this area when, looking up, she caught Jemima's eye. They had both been speaking quietly, huddled together a little way from the others, but even so she wondered whether Jemima had managed to catch a few words of their conversation. The girl was watching them closely now, she noticed, her eyes still red and swollen. After a brief moment's hesitation, as if she were deciding quite what to do, weighing up the various alternatives in her mind, Jemima came over to them. She was still trembling slightly, and Rose saw that Felix was looking at her anxiously.

'Do you know the policemen from Scotland Yard? Have you had dealings with them before?'

Jemima's voice was rather breathless. She put out a hand and clung to Rose's arm. It reminded Rose of Vera grabbing at her sleeve a few hours previously, and instinctively she stood back a step or two, but Jemima did not let go.

'You spoke to the policeman in the hall earlier as if you knew him. Are they any good these Scotland Yard men do you know? Will they find poor E-emmie's murderer?'

Rose noticed that Jemima stumbled over saying Emmeline's name, as if it were all still too raw, too much for her to take in.

'I can't believe it. I still can't believe she's dead.' The girl spoke the words quietly, barely above a whisper so that both Rose and Felix had to bend forward to catch her words. 'I keep thinking that she's going to walk into the room any minute and say that it was all a silly game.'

Jemima began to sob quietly. Felix helped her into a nearby chair and handed her a handkerchief, all the while looking on rather helplessly. It was plain to anyone who cared to observe that he did not know quite what else to do. Rose wondered why he did not take Jemima's hand, and pondered whether her being there made him feel awkward or shy. She would have walked discreetly away, only she was conscious that she had not yet answered the question that had drawn Jemima to seek them out.

'I know Sergeant Lane,' replied Rose finally, choosing her words carefully, 'and I hold him in the highest esteem. But I have never met Inspector Bramwell before, although I understand from Sergeant Lane that he has a very good reputation for getting results. Inspector Deacon investigated the two previous murder cases that Cedric and I were involved with, and he was very good. I expect Inspector Bramwell is of a similar calibre.'

'Oh?' Jemima stopped weeping and looked up. 'Why isn't your Inspector Deacon investigating this murder if you and Cedric think so highly of him? Can't Lord Belvedere insist that he does? I assume the aristocracy can do that, can't they? I would have thought they could.' She sounded indignant as if it were all Cedric's fault that Inspector Deacon was not there.

'It isn't up to Cedric, I'm afraid,' said Rose, trying not to become riled by Jemima's insinuation that Cedric was somehow to blame. 'It's the decision of the chief constable as to whether Scotland Yard is brought into an investigation or not and, as it happens, Inspector Deacon is not in a position to investigate Emmeline's death.'

'Oh? Why not?'

'Because he is indisposed. He was shot in the course of carrying out his duties,' Rose said bluntly.

On receiving this news, Jemima's eyes became wide with horror and Rose, feeling guilty, hurried on.

'It's not as bad as it sounds. He wasn't killed, but he was badly wounded, although he's expected to make an almost full recovery. But it does mean that he won't be able to investigate this murder.'

'That's a pity,' said Felix, appearing keen to take part in the conversation. 'Still, if you know the sergeant, and this Inspector Bramwell has a reputation for being one of the best in his field, I daresay we have nothing to worry about. I say, Jemima, are you all right?'

Jemima did indeed look pale and, if possible, she looked even more distressed than before, despite Rose's various assurances concerning Inspector Deacon's fate and Inspector Bramwell's competency to lead a police investigation.

'Yes, I'm all right,' Jemima said slowly, regaining her composure, but she walked away from them as if she no longer wished for their company.

'Jemima really needn't worry,' said Rose to Felix. The young man was looking forlornly at Jemima's retreating figure. 'As I said, Sergeant Lane's assured me that Inspector Bramwell is very good.'

'Perhaps,' said Felix almost whispering more to himself than to her so that Rose was forced to bend her head towards him to catch his words, 'that's the issue.'

Before Rose had an opportunity to ask Felix what he meant, the door opened and Sergeant Lane appeared. All eyes were immediately turned to stare at him, and the few conversations that had been in progress faltered. There was a general air of nervousness and trepidation in the room, now that the endless waiting was over, as everyone feared what was to follow. Cedric, who all the time that Rose had been talking to Felix and Jemima had been in whispered discussion with Lavinia, immediately came forward.

'I say, Sergeant, not before time. We're all feeling a bit like caged bears in here. I'm not meaning to criticise your police investigation or anything like that, and I'm not trying to teach grandmother to suck eggs, but I'm rather surprised that we haven't been interviewed before now. It can't help but make one wonder what you've been doing.'

'I'm sorry, my lord,' Sergeant Lane said looking, Rose thought, rather embarrassed. 'I can assure you we've been very busy. We haven't let the grass grow under our feet. As I told Miss Simpson, Inspector Bramwell likes to do things a bit differently from what you're used to.'

'Well, you're here now, and that's all that matters. Now, which one of us does your Inspector Bramwell wish to interview first? He said he'd be speaking to me again, but I expect he would like to interview Miss

Wentmore first, wouldn't he, being as she knew Miss Montacute better than all of us?'

Jemima, Rose noticed, looked particularly anxious at this suggestion. She appeared to have drifted towards Felix and was now holding his hand tightly, as if to give herself strength. Felix was regarding her with even more concern than before.

'I don't think Miss Wentmore is up to being interviewed yet,' Felix said quickly. 'Miss Montacute's death has been the most awful shock to her, as I am sure you can appreciate. Perhaps you might interview someone else first to allow her a little more time to compose herself and come to terms with what's happened.' He gave the sergeant an engaging smile.

'Not to fear, Mr Thistlewaite, is it? The inspector doesn't want to interview Miss Wentmore first. No, he has someone else in mind completely.'

'Good,' said Felix. He turned his attention to Jemima, who was looking relieved at the temporary reprieve.

'No, sir, as I say the inspector has someone else in mind,' said Sergeant Lane. 'The fact of the matter is, sir, that he'd like to interview you first.'

'Me?' Felix could not have sounded more surprised. He made no attempt to leave Jemima's side. 'There must be some mistake, Sergeant. I cannot imagine why the inspector would want to interview me first.'

'Even so,' replied the sergeant, firmly, 'he does. This way if you please, sir. We don't want to keep the inspector waiting, do we?'

For one moment Rose thought Felix was going to refuse to go. But if that had been his initial inclination, he obviously thought better of it. He turned to give Jemima one last look. For the first time she looked up and appeared to give him her full attention. It seemed to Rose that something silent and intense passed between them in that look, something that only they themselves could decipher; a secret look that meant nothing to anyone else.

Sergeant Lane coughed and the spell was broken. Felix made for the door to follow the policeman out. But Jemima, apparently on impulse, intervened. She sprang forward and then stopped a few steps away from him. Felix hesitated in the doorway as if unsure what to do. Rose could not make out the expression on his face, for he appeared to be experiencing a variety of emotions in those few moments. The whole room had become quiet, seemingly waiting to hear what Jemima had to say. But in the end she uttered only one word.

'Felix – '

'It's all right,' Felix Thistlewaite said quickly, 'everything's going to be all right, Jemima.'

As soon as Felix Thistlewaite entered the study, Inspector Bramwell thought that the young man looked ill at ease. There was something about his freckled face and unruly hair that suggested that he usually had a nonchalant approach to life which, when coupled with the beginning of laughter lines, indicated that he was generally of a cheery disposition. But that could not be said of him today. He had an anxious look about him, which was accentuated by his fiddling with one of the buttons on his jacket. The young man was definitely wary. Although whether there was more to his present demeanour than not surprisingly being a little overwhelmed by the situation in which he unexpectedly found himself was difficult to determine. Certainly his attitude was not uncommon.

In Inspector Bramwell's considerable experience no one, from whatever walk of life they might come, knew quite how to behave when faced with violent death. The subject of murder was not covered in any book on social etiquette. Murder, the inspector thought, had a tendency to bring out the best in people and also the very worst; the same, he thought, could be said of war, and involuntarily he shuddered. The Great War to end all wars did not seem so very long ago.

'Look here, Inspector,' said Felix, as soon as he walked into the room, obviously deciding to come straight to the point. 'I can't for the life of me think why you have decided to interview me first. I hardly knew Miss Montacute, and doubt very much if I can throw any light on her death. And I'm certain that I'm not in receipt of any information that would be important to your investigation. I'm not meaning to tell you how to do your job, but don't you think you'd do better starting with someone else?'

'All in good time, Mr Thistlewaite. Although I would be interested in knowing who you suggest I interview first.'

'Well, Lady Lavinia, of course.'

'Not Miss Wentmore? You surprise me, Mr Thistlewaite.'

The inspector spoke slowly, and left the words hanging in the air. There was an uncomfortable silence which neither man seemed inclined to break. Inspector Bramwell did not let his gaze falter. Felix meanwhile blushed and was looking everywhere but at the inspector's face.

'I take it from that, Inspector, that you are aware that I have formed an attachment to Miss Wentmore,' Felix said at last. 'But my reasons for suggesting that you interview Lady Lavinia first have nothing to do with that. She was the first person to come upon the body, hadn't you heard?'

'Indeed I had, thank you, Mr Thistlewaite. The local constable who was first at the scene was most diligent and informed me of that fact. No, I was rather surprised that you didn't mention Miss Wentmore seeing that she was Miss Montacute's friend-cum-companion.'

'She had nothing to do with Emmeline's death,' Felix said quickly.

'I'm not suggesting that she did, Mr Thistlewaite. I merely thought that you would quite understandably assume that as Miss Wentmore knew Miss Montacute rather better than anyone else here, well, she might be able to throw some light on why anyone would wish to kill the young lady.'

'I think I see what you're saying, Inspector,' Felix said, passing a hand through his hair. 'Although I am still a little confused. You still haven't explained why you have decided to interview me first.'

'There's no need to fret, Mr Thistlewaite. As to why I have decided to see you before any of the others, well, that's easy to explain.' The inspector paused to steeple his fingers, and looked at them briefly as if the questions he wished to ask were written on them. 'It's exactly because you are on the periphery of this inquiry that I've decided to interview you first. You are a member of this house-party but not at its core, so you have been present to witness everything but unlikely to have had a major role. I'll wager therefore that you're likely to be more objective than the rest. Now, sit down if you will, Mr Thistlewaite, and paint the scene for me. I'd like to know what it was like here at Sedgwick Court leading up to the tragedy.'

'Oh, if that's the case, then of course I understand perfectly.' Felix visibly relaxed and took the proffered seat, opposite the inspector, sinking back into its deep velvet upholstery. 'But I'm not sure I can be of much help. It seemed a pretty ordinary house-party to me, not that I've been to that many. Of course these surroundings are particularly fine, but the guests alas are quite ordinary, myself included.'

'You surprise me.' The inspector looked at him quizzically, and Felix at once appeared flustered again. 'I wouldn't have thought there was much that was ordinary about an heiress and a foreign count, to say nothing about the British aristocracy. But then again, I can't say I have frequented many house-parties myself. Have you, Sergeant?'

'What I meant,' replied Felix, clearly ruffled, 'is that putting aside rank and position in society and such like, it was just an ordinary house-party.'

'An ordinary house-party where one of the guests was murdered. Hmm … Suppose you tell us where you were this morning between about four o'clock and say seven o'clock?'

'I say, is that when Emmeline was murdered? I know it might sound rather strange, but it makes me feel better knowing that she hadn't lain out there all night. Frightful too, of course, to think that we were all fast asleep when the deed was done, blissfully unaware that anything was wrong.' Felix paused a moment before going on. 'So there you have it, Inspector, that's my alibi, not a very good one at that. I was in bed at the time, as I am sure everyone else was except perhaps one or two of the servants. I daresay the scullery maid rises early to light the stove, doesn't she? Unfortunately no one can corroborate my alibi.'

'Now, Mr Thistlewaite, you say it was an ordinary house-party. In my experience there's no such thing. When you gather a group of people together, particularly people from different walks of life, so to speak, and confine them in a place where they have only each other for company, even in a place as grand and beautiful as this one, then there are sure to be some petty squabbles and disagreements. Am I right?'

'I'm afraid there were a few,' admitted Felix.

'Perhaps you would be so good as to elaborate, sir?'

'Must I? It does seem rather a rotten thing to do.'

'May I remind you that this is a murder investigation, sir?'

'Very well. But if you are looking for a motive as to why anyone would want to murder Emmeline, I don't think I can provide you with one.' Felix sat up in his chair. 'Now, let me think. I suppose one had better start with the count. An odd sort of chap, but popular with the ladies, or should I say some of them. I think both Lady Lavinia and Miss Montacute were rather taken with him. When we were on the Continent, I had the impression that he was a little more keen on Emmeline than Lavinia, although he always made a point of being overly charming to both women.'

'And this led to a squabble between the two women here at Sedgwick?' The inspector sounded confused.

'Not really, no. But it might have put Lady Lavinia's nose out of joint a bit. One should probably not speak ill of one's hostess, not when one is enjoying her hospitality, but she always strikes me as a woman who is used to being the centre of attention. Hardly a motive for murder though, Inspector.'

'I agree,' said Inspector Bramwell gravely, 'particularly when Miss Montacute had shown a preference for Dr Harrison.'

'Ah, so you know all about that too, do you?' Felix sounded relieved. 'How well informed you are, Inspector. I suppose even in the best of houses servants still gossip. Or perhaps Lord Belvedere told you?'

He waited a moment or two before going on, but Inspector Bramwell was not forthcoming about from whom he had obtained his information.

'If you must know, it was dashed awkward for the rest of us,' said Felix. 'I mean to say, the fellow's fiancée was here, still is, of course. Awfully embarrassing and upsetting for Miss Brewster. She tried not to let it get to her. She tried to put a brave face on it. I daresay she thought it was an infatuation that would fizzle out. Still, jolly humiliating for her.'

'I see. Do you think Miss Brewster might have wished to do Miss Montacute harm?'

'What? No, of course not!' Felix jumped up from his seat. 'What a monstrous suggestion. You're putting words into my mouth, Inspector.'

'Sit down please, Mr Thistlewaite. We need to investigate all possible motives before we can eliminate them.'

'Which is why I didn't want to say anything, Inspector. This was what I was afraid of, that you'd twist my words,' Felix said, somewhat reluctantly sitting down again. 'My opinion, for what it's worth, is that if

Vera had decided to kill anyone it would have been that cad of a fiancé of hers, Harrison, not poor Emmeline.'

'Quite so. Now, let's move on to when Miss Montacute's body was discovered. I understand that Lady Sedgwick had gone on ahead to look in the maze for her friend. According to the constable's notes, the rest of the party, of which you were one, followed some three quarters of an hour later and found Lady Lavinia standing over the body with a candlestick in her hand. Is that right?'

'Yes, quite correct.'

'And everyone, quite understandably, assumed that Lady Lavinia had done the deed?'

'Yes. Of course, thinking about it now, it's quite ridiculous to think that Lavinia could have done anything of the kind.'

'But understandable given that you didn't know then that Miss Montacute had been dead some hours,' Inspector Bramwell said, briskly. 'Did Lord Belvedere tamper with the evidence at the scene?'

'Inspector!' The abruptness of the question had caught Felix unawares. He opened his mouth and then shut it again, reminding the inspector of a fish.

'It's a simple enough question, Mr Thistlewaite. Please answer me yes or no. Did Lord Belvedere meddle with the evidence?'

'Why don't you ask him?'

'Because I'm asking you. Did he, or did he not, tamper with the evidence?'

'Well,' Felix sank back into his chair, 'if you must know, he took the candlestick from his sister and wiped it. Then he instructed Rose to take Lavinia into the house to be cleaned up and have her clothes washed.'

'Did he indeed?' The inspector looked at him with interest. 'I take it no one took it upon themselves to try and stop him?'

'I jolly well did, Inspector,' said Felix indignantly, 'but the earl wouldn't listen to me, told me to go to the devil, would you believe? There was nothing I could do. Miss Simpson tried to reason with him too, but he was having none of it.'

'Didn't anyone else try to stop him?'

'No. I think everyone else was in shock, or just didn't think. We were all pretty shaken up, I don't mind telling you, seeing Emmeline's dead body like that and Lavinia standing over her with that damned candlestick in her hand.'

'Were you all there to see that?'

'Yes, everyone … oh … wait a minute. I remember now … Vera, Miss Brewster, wasn't there. She said she was feeling unwell, so she didn't join us in the search. I say, it's rather funny when one comes to think of it.'

'Oh, what is?' The inspector looked at Felix with renewed interest, and even Sergeant Lane looked up from his notebook, his pencil hovering above the page like a wasp.

'Well, Vera of course was not too fond of Miss Montacute and she didn't see her body, not like the rest of us. She didn't have to contend with trying to forget that awful image of Emmeline lying there – '

'Yes, what of it?'

'Well, Inspector, when we were making our way back to the house, we saw Miss Simpson in the distance with Lady Lavinia. She had just discharged her to the care of her lady's maid when Vera came running out of the house all hell-for-leather. Of course we couldn't hear what she said to Miss Simpson, or Rose to her come to that, but they must have been talking about the murder, mustn't they?'

'One would think so, yes.'

'Well, one moment Vera was tugging at Rose's sleeve, more than likely trying to find out what had happened, and the next moment she had slumped to the ground in a dead faint. Odd that, isn't it?'

Chapter Eighteen

'I don't see it as being very odd, sir,' said Sergeant Lane as soon as Felix Thistlewaite had left the room. 'It seems to me quite natural if Miss Brewster were of a delicate disposition. And even if she wasn't, mayn't she have fainted with relief thinking she'd get the doctor's affections back on the death of Miss Montacute?'

'Possibly,' said Inspector Bramwell, sounding far from convinced, 'although fainting with relief does sound rather fanciful and far-fetched to me. I'm not sure I've known any woman do that. You do realise though, don't you, that that second point of yours gives Miss Brewster a damn good motive for this murder?'

'I do. Other than that, Mr Thistlewaite wasn't very forthcoming, was he, sir? I mean to say, we already had our suspicions that Lord Belvedere had tampered with the evidence. If you ask me, sir, the earl would've admitted as much if we'd put the question to him.'

'I dare say he would, particularly now he knows Miss Montacute was killed a few hours before they discovered Lady Lavinia standing over her body. But it doesn't alter the fact, Lane, that his lordship did a criminal act in doing what he did. Now,' the inspector leaned back in his chair and, as always, the sergeant could not help wincing at the sound of the springs straining under the policeman's weight, 'to your other point. I happen to think Felix Thistlewaite was very forthcoming, although of course his intention was to be anything but.'

'I'm not sure that I follow you, sir.'

'He deliberately threw suspicion on Lady Lavinia who, I think we'll find, had little motive for wishing the deceased dead. And then Miss Brewster as soon as we told him we knew about the attachment that had formed between Dr Harrison and Miss Montacute.'

'I still don't think I follow you, sir,' said Sergeant Lane looking distinctly puzzled.

'Don't you, Sergeant?' Inspector Bramwell frowned at his subordinate, who averted his gaze and took a sudden interest in the cover of his notebook. 'Well, Lane, it's my view that he implicated Lady Lavinia because he knew we would not be able to form a case against her, and told us what he did about Miss Brewster because he was well aware that if he didn't someone else would. They all saw it after all, didn't they, Miss Brewster fainting in rather a spectacular fashion in front of the house? It was only a question of time before someone mentioned it.'

'I wonder whether she said anything before she fainted,' said Sergeant Lane, looking up from his notebook.

'Your Miss Simpson should be able to tell us that, unless of course,' the inspector paused to frown again at the sergeant, who sank back into his chair, 'she decides to keep the information to herself. But what interested me, Sergeant, was that young Mr Thistlewaite seemed to me to be deliberately going out of his way to divert suspicion away from someone else.'

Manning had entered the drawing room to supervise the serving of tea and coffee by the footmen. The man was standing rather awkwardly by the door, in two minds, Rose thought, as to whether to remain or depart. Rather tentatively he made as if to go over to Lavinia, as mistress of the house, but she was busy at that moment having a rather intense conversation with Vera, no doubt telling her in not too kindly tones to leave Theo to himself. Cedric, Rose noticed, was standing equally at a loss beside the doctor, supposedly with the intention of trying to comfort the man, who still looked distraught by what had happened.

She wondered if Cedric rather regretted having spoken to Theo the previous night about his conduct. She could not forget that it had been partly at her instigation that he had done so. The rather unpleasant thought crossed her mind that it might have played a contributory factor in Emmeline's death. She stared at Theo and tried to dismiss the notion from her mind, but it lingered stubbornly at the fringes of her consciousness. It's being cooped up in here, she thought, it's making me think all sorts of strange, irrational things. More to stop herself from thinking such thoughts rather than for something else to do, Rose made her way over to the butler, who looked relieved to see her.

'Is anything wrong, Manning?'

'I don't know that it is, miss. Not wrong as such. It's just that the kitchen were wondering what to do about luncheon, although it's rather late for it, I know. Only it didn't seem quite right to do anything about it before. His lordship didn't think anyone would be hungry, but it's quite a time that's elapsed since breakfast, so it is. Mrs Farrier, she's the housekeeper, miss, said fine dining wasn't the thing at all at a time like this as it could be seen as rather heartless and how it's also likely that no one will have much of an appetite.

'I think Mrs Farrier is quite right.'

'But it's put Mrs Broughton's nose out of joint, I can tell you, as she and the kitchen maid were working at the dishes all morning not knowing anything was wrong because we tried to keep things quiet like. Of course, I'd ask Mr Torridge what he thought we should do, as of course he'd know, but he's having a bit of a nap and I don't like to wake him given his age and all. All this has hit him very bad, miss. A murder in the grounds.'

'I'm sure it has, as it has us all,' said Rose soothingly. 'I think a little light soup would be best, perhaps a chicken broth, or suchlike?'

Privately she thought Manning very talkative for a butler. She doubted very much whether the revered Torridge would appreciate his deputy advising a guest of all the various goings on and musings in the servants' hall. But it also occurred to her that the butler might prove useful in furthering her investigations into Emmeline's death.

'Manning, I'm sure you've heard already that a candlestick was found in the maze. Lady Lavinia thought she recognised it. I wondered whether one was missing from the house. '

'Indeed, miss, as I already told the policemen. It's one of the candlestick's from the sideboard. It was there last night when dinner was cleared and like as not when I did my rounds, but not this morning, least I don't think it was. It was one of a pair and the policemen have taken the other one away to compare it with the one found, I suppose.'

'I see. Thank you, Manning.'

Rose was vaguely aware that where the butler had been standing was now a space, and that the man himself had left the room as noiselessly as he had entered it. She wondered if he had realised the significance of his words.

'I say, are you all right?' Cedric was beside her, his face full of concern. 'You look as if you've just seen a ghost.'

Rose put out a hand to him to steady herself. There was something very comforting about his presence. If only he would not leave her side and they could stroll in the grounds of Sedgwick arm in arm as they had done before the arrival of Lavinia and her guests.

'Cedric, it was one of us that murdered Emmeline.'

'Are you sure?' Don't you think it's just as likely to have been a failed kidnap attempt?' Cedric passed his hand through his hair. His face had gone white. 'I've been rather hoping that all this might not have had anything to do with Sedgwick, apart from Emmeline's body being found in the maze, that is ...'

'No, I'm afraid the weapon was taken from this house. Lavinia thought she recognised it and Manning's just confirmed that it was one of the candlesticks from the sideboard. I remember it now, what it looked like, I mean.'

'And you think that proves that whoever murdered Emmeline was someone in this house?'

'Of course it does. It can't mean anything else, Cedric, no matter how much we might wish it otherwise.'

'I suppose no one would think to break into the house and then go to the maze.' Cedric sighed. 'Even if they had, Manning would have told me about it if the servants had seen any signs of a forced entry.'

'And don't you see, Cedric? Every one of us would have seen the candlestick at each meal and known where to get it when looking for a weapon.'

'You're quite right of course, I didn't think of that.'

'There's more, I'm afraid. According to Manning the candlestick was still on the sideboard when the house was locked up for the night. No one from outside could have taken it unless they had broken into the house, and we have already established that did not happen. Besides, the maze is nowhere near the house. They would have had no reason to come here, unless...'

'Yes?' Cedric looked at her hopefully, grasping at anything that might suggest that the murder had been done by someone outside the house.

'I was going to say unless the murderer had arranged with Emmeline to come to the house and escort her to the maze,' said Rose. 'But it doesn't seem very likely, does it?'

'No.' Cedric shrugged his shoulders and looked despondent.

'And another thing. I don't think even Lavinia's guests knew the maze was here until you mentioned it last night. It's unlikely anyone else would have known of its existence unless they'd been here before.' She looked at him rather reprovingly. 'Even I didn't know about it.'

'Didn't you? Hadn't I mentioned it to you before? Of course I was going to show it to you.' Cedric suddenly paled. 'I say, what you said just now. You mean if I hadn't spoken – '

'No,' said Rose quickly, 'I think the murder would have happened anyway, only perhaps not in the maze. I say, I wonder what did make Emmeline decide to go there when it was still pitch black outside. That's what we've got to find out, Cedric.'

'Count Fernand, is it?'

Inspector Bramwell eyed the newcomer with obvious suspicion. The count had seen fit not to wear his scarlet waistcoat or full length black cape for the interview, but there was still an air of flamboyance to both his dress and manner that the inspector found irritating. What was more, he'd swear the man dyed his hair.

'Now how should I address you, sir? Your Illustrious Highness perhaps, or my lord or – '

'Sir, will be perfectly satisfactory, Inspector. In this country I do not consider myself a princely count. To everyone in this country I am nothing, no more important than the man who sweeps the street, but in my own country – '

'Which is?' the inspector interrupted sharply.

'I beg your pardon, Inspector?'

Was it the policeman's imagination, or did he see a flicker of fear cross the man's face?

'If you don't mind my saying, sir, everyone seems to be a little unclear as to which country you actually come from.'

'The country that I come from, Inspector,' said Count Fernand, having regained his composure, 'it is little and insignificant. You Englishmen, you will not have heard of it. If I tell you its name, it will mean nothing to you, nothing, absolutely nothing.'

The count's voice had risen all the while he had been speaking. The ensuing silence appeared harsh, broken only by the word "nothing" which seemed to echo around the room.

'Oh, I don't know about that, sir. I was particularly good at geography at school, so I was. One of my best subjects. Even now, I think I can tell you all the capital cities of – '

'I assure you, Inspector,' the count said, eyeing the policeman coldly, 'you will not have heard of my country.'

'That might well be, sir, but I'd still like to hear where you hail from.'

The inspector was greeted by another silence that threatened to become uncomfortable. He looked across the table at the handsome features of his companion and noticed that his forehead was furrowed and that he appeared to be finding a spot on the study carpet particularly fascinating.

'I tell you what, sir, suppose we help you out if we can, shall we?' said Inspector Bramwell, adopting a hearty tone and sitting back in his chair. 'My sergeant here will go into the library and see if he can find an atlas. I'm sure they'll have a fine one in a grand house like this one, where they must read plenty of books or at least have them on display. And then you can point it out to us on a map, your country I mean. You won't even have to say the name out loud, if you don't want to. It's just so my sergeant has something to write down in his notebook. What say you, shall we do that, sir?'

There was another awkward silence. The inspector was looking at the count so intensely that the young man appeared to physically recoil, shrinking back into his chair. Sergeant Lane had looked up from his notebook, and was watching the proceedings with interest. Count Fernand had entered the room with something of a princely swagger aimed at achieving maximum effect. Now he seemed to wish to disappear into the very chair in which he was sitting.

'No,' said the count, finally. He had uttered the one word scarcely above a whisper so that the sergeant, who was sitting a little distance from him, had to lean forward to catch what he said.

'I thought as much.' Any pretence at civility had disappeared from Inspector Bramwell's manner, to be replaced instead by something akin to contempt. 'Now listen to me, count. I will still call you count although I doubt that you have any more right to use that title than my sergeant here does. I see through you and so, as it happens, does Lord Belvedere. You are an impostor, sir; that is clear. I'll wager too that you are an Englishman. As to what your game is, I can't say that personally I'm very interested unless it has a bearing on this murder.' He sighed. 'Although unfortunately, tedious though it is, I feel duty bound to investigate your purpose for being here masquerading as someone you are clearly not.'

'It doesn't have any bearing on Miss Montacute's death,' the count replied sullenly, all traces of an accent having left his lips.

'Glad to hear it, although I will be the judge of that.' Inspector Bramwell got up from his chair and began to pace the room. 'This game of yours, adopting the disguise of some illustrious personage, what is your aim, young man?' He looked at the count, who purposely averted his gaze. 'Well, then, we'll just have to think the worst, won't we, Lane? Your intention, I imagine' said the inspector, turning back to address Count Fernand, 'is to ingratiate yourself with ladies of fortune. Whether you do this to travel the world at their expense or to receive gifts that will support you in your lavish way of life, who can tell? Perhaps you are even seeking an advantageous marriage?'

The inspector paused for a moment before going on. Count Fernand again refused to catch his eye or say anything.

'Very well. If that's the way you wish to play it, so be it. My only interest in you, as I have already said, is to establish whether or not you were involved in the murder of Miss Montacute.'

'I've already said I wasn't,' the count said, sulkily.

'Forgive me if I find it hard to accept your word.'

'Are you going to tell Lord Belvedere about my not being a count?'

'As I said before, he already has his suspicions. If you're worried that you will be required to vacate Sedgwick, you needn't be. No one is leaving this house until I say so. But,' the inspector fixed the man with a hard stare and said quietly, 'I wouldn't go proposing marriage to Lady Lavinia, if I were you, otherwise I might well feel obliged to advise the earl of the sort of brother-in-law he'd be gaining.'

The count stared at the carpet miserably, and said nothing. The inspector thought how ordinary he appeared without his foreign accent and his charm.

The policeman was interrupted from asking further questions by a rapid knocking at the door, followed immediately afterwards by the entrance of a young constable, clearly out of breath. Before the inspector could admonish him for entering before waiting for an answer, or indeed ask him what he wanted, the constable had bounded over to him and was whispering rapidly in his ear.

Both Sergeant Lane and the man who called himself Count Fernand looked on with interest. To the frustration of both men, neither could hear what was being said. Whatever it was, the inspector was giving the constable his full attention, and every now and then he uttered the odd exclamation, nodding his head as he did so.

The constable departed, closing the door carefully behind him and the inspector's attention reverted to Count Fernand.

'Now that we have got all that cleared up, let's get down to business and proceed with this murder investigation, shall we? I think we've wasted quite enough time on your dubious activities, young man. Right, without further ado, let me ask you where you were between four o'clock and seven o'clock this morning. And you'd do well to answer me truthfully, young man.'

'In bed, Inspector, but unfortunately no one can vouch for me,' the count replied, rather wearily. 'Is that when she was killed, Emmeline, I mean?'

'We think it was, yes. What can you tell me about her?'

'She was quite a sweet little thing. Awfully pretty. Tended to be happy and excited, although who wouldn't be in her position? Money no object and a doting father. How lucky some people are.'

'I gather that when you were all together in Florence you had a preference for Miss Montacute over Lady Lavinia, is that right?'

'Miss Montacute. Lady Lavinia. Both women lovely in their own way.' The count gave the policeman a feeble smile. 'But yes, my preference, as you put it, was for Miss Montacute.'

'Easier to ingratiate yourself with Miss Montacute than Lady Lavinia, I would imagine.' The inspector returned to his chair and sat down. 'Yet you made a sufficiently favourable impression on Lady Lavinia for her to invite you to stay here at Sedgwick.'

'Charm and flattery, Inspector. You should try it.' Count Fernand laughed.

'Perhaps I will. Now, what can you tell me about Miss Montacute and Dr Harrison?'

'I am sure that you have already heard all about it, Inspector. You don't need me to tell you.' The young man sighed and leaned back in his chair. 'I don't pretend to be any more observant than the next fellow, but suffice to say that I turned my attentions to Lady Lavinia. I am not one to indulge in unnecessary competition unless I have to. Having said that, what Emmeline saw in the fellow I can't imagine. A pretty boring, ordinary sort of chap, if you ask me.'

'I understand it created rather an unpleasant atmosphere, what with Miss Brewster being here too?'

'You can say that again, Inspector. The night before last Vera created a bit of a scene, alluded to the failed kidnap attempt concerning Emmeline. It happened some years back, you may remember it?'

'I do.'

'Poor Emmeline was pretty shaken up by it, I can tell you, and so was Jemima for that matter. She had a proper set to with Vera. At one point I thought she might strike her. Of course, Harrison had been sailing damned close to the wind. Miss Brewster may be rather dull, but she's not stupid.'

'I understand you took matters into your own hands, sir?'

'Did I?' For a moment Count Fernand looked confused, and then he laughed. 'Ah, you're referring to the diamonds aren't you?'

'I am.'

'A bit of a parlour game to entertain the ladies, Inspector. Wealthy young women always like to show off their diamonds and have others admire them. I knew Lavinia and Emmeline would want to see each other's gems so that they might compare them. Emmeline cheered up no end, I can tell you, particularly when she was given the opportunity to talk about the Montacute Diamonds.'

'So looking at the diamonds was just a sort of game, was it, sir?'

'It was, Inspector. The aim was to lighten the atmosphere and cheer everyone up.' The count began to look a little wary. 'Everything was a little fraught. I was only trying to help.'

'Do you always carry a jeweller's loupe on you?'

'I do, Inspector, but you needn't read anything into it.'

'Needn't I?

'No.' Count Fernand sighed. 'If you must know, I do it to impress the ladies. They respect a man who they think is knowledgeable about diamonds.'

'I don't doubt it,' agreed the inspector, before adding sharply, 'and are you knowledgeable about diamonds?'

'I like to think so.'

'What did you think of Miss Montacute's diamonds?'

There was a distinct pause before the count answered. He swallowed hard and took a deep breath.

'They were fabulous, Inspector, quite fabulous.'

'Righto, I think that's all for the time being, count,' Inspector Bramwell said.

'What?'

Count Fernand was clearly taken by surprise at being dismissed so abruptly. For a moment he remained seated, as if he thought he had misheard the inspector. He gave a quick glance at Inspector Bramwell, and seeing that the policeman appeared engrossed in his papers, made swiftly for the door.

'Ah, just a moment before you leave, sir.'

'Yes, what is it?' Count Fernand swung round, his hand still clasping the door handle.

'Yes, sir, just one more thing, or should I say two?'

'Yes?' the count snapped.

'You have admitted that you are not a foreign count.' Inspector Bramwell smiled at him warmly. 'I am rather interested to know who you really are. What's your real name, young man?'

'You said you had two things to ask me.'

'Did I? Oh, yes, so I did.' The inspector sat up in his chair and looked at the count with interest. 'Now what was it? Ah, yes. Are you by any chance a jewel thief?'

Chapter Nineteen

'It really is too bad,' said Lavinia scowling, the effect of which was to make her quite beautiful face plain and ugly. 'Expecting us to wait like this. I mean to say, why should they want to interview Max before me? I found Emmeline's body after all. They should want to speak to me first. And this is my house … well mine and Ceddie's. Did you see how they spoke to my brother first, Rose? I suppose it's because he's a man. I'm of no importance because I'm a woman.'

'I don't think they asked Cedric very many questions,' said Rose. 'They want to interview him again later.'

'Well, I'm tired of waiting. I don't know who that inspector thinks he is.'

'The man heading the investigation into Emmeline's murder.'

'Well, I've got far better things to do than stand around waiting for the inspector to condescend to summon me for interview. I'm not going to just stay here, especially with the likes of Vera and Jemima, who really are so dull and boring at the best of times, I – '

'Ssh, they'll hear you.' Rose looked around quickly at the other two women who, to her relief, appeared not to have heard Lavinia's rant. 'Do be quiet, Lavinia, and do be reasonable. This is a murder investigation, not a dull tea party.'

'Well, I'm bored and I still see it as quite an affront that the inspector decided to interview Felix and Max before me.' She grabbed at Rose's arm as an idea crossed her mind. 'I say, Rose. What about if I were to say to the constable over there that I had suddenly remembered seeing something when I came across Emmeline's body. The inspector would want to interview me then, wouldn't he? He wouldn't be able to get rid of Max quick enough.'

'I think that would be a very bad idea,' said Rose, holding on to Lavinia's sleeve as if afraid that her friend might really be about to carry out her threat.

'Well, I'm not staying here.' Lavinia threw off Rose's arm and walked straight over to the constable. 'I'm feeling rather unwell, Constable. You see, I can't get the image of poor Emmeline's body out of my mind. If I don't go and have a lie down, why, I think I might faint. You wouldn't want that now, would you?'

'Err, no, miss.' The young constable looked rather pale and fiddled with a button on his tunic.

'Lady Lavinia, actually,' Lavinia said, sweetly. 'My friend here, Miss Simpson, is just going to see me up the stairs. That's all right, isn't it? She'll be down again as soon as she's got me settled.' She turned her head slightly, so that she could talk over her shoulder. 'Come along, Rose. I'm jolly afraid I'm about to faint. Yes, I really think I am. I'm feeling rather lightheaded. Oh, thank you, Constable.' Lavinia smiled sweetly again at the policeman, who had offered her his arm to steady her.

Rose hesitated, in two minds whether or not to play along. From what she'd heard of Inspector Bramwell, she thought it highly unlikely that he would be taken in so easily by Lavinia's rather melodramatic performance. She also imagined that he would be far from impressed at discovering them absent from the drawing room. But, like Lavinia, Rose was finding being in one room with the others dull and oppressive. The chance to escape the confines of the drawing room if only for a few minutes was too tempting. Besides which, it would give her the opportunity she sought to put some more questions to Lavinia without being overheard.

'I thought you weren't going to play ball,' complained Lavinia, as they dashed up the stairs. 'I think we'll go to my boudoir, don't you?'

'You really are incorrigible, Lavinia,' Rose said, trying to keep up with her agile hostess. 'There'll be all hell to pay when the inspector finds out what we've done. He wanted us to keep together until we'd given our statements. And they won't know to look in your boudoir for us.'

'It will jolly well serve him right for keeping us waiting,' retorted Lavinia. 'He let Felix go to his room.'

'That's because he'd given his statement,' said Rose, following Lavinia into her boudoir. 'I expect he'll let the count too, when he comes out.' She hovered by the door. If she were to sit down, she felt that she might well be inclined not to leave. 'Are you feeling better now?'

'Better? Oh, yes, it was just the shock of finding her body like that.' Lavinia sank down thankfully on to a richly upholstered settee and curled her legs up under her. 'Ah, that's better. I say, I feel jolly hungry. I didn't eat much at breakfast because I was worried about Emmeline, although I was thinking more of her reputation at the time rather than anything more sinister having occurred to her. I never thought for a moment that she might be dead, and murdered at that. I was jolly hungry at luncheon, particularly as it was so late and only soup, but no one else seemed very interested in food. I thought people might consider it as being in rather bad taste if I was the only one to eat, my being the hostess and all that.'

'I really don't think you're half as heartless as you like to make out,' Rose said, deciding, despite her reservations, to sit down for a moment or two. 'Tell me, didn't you like Emmeline at all? I thought she was your friend. Aren't you even a little bit sorry that she's dead?'

'Well, of course I am.' Lavinia sighed and picked up a magazine, the pages of which she flicked through aimlessly. 'You know what I'm like, Rose. I just don't want to think about it. It's too awful. And it won't bring her back, will it?'

There were a few moments of silence as neither woman spoke, each lost in their own thoughts. Rose watched Lavinia flick through the pages of the magazine, hardly giving each page a proper glance. She found herself watching the pages being turned until Lavinia flung the magazine down on the table with a resounding thud.

'It's rather awful to say it, and I'd only say this to you, Rose … but I was becoming rather tired of Emmeline. I was even beginning to wish that I hadn't invited her to stay.'

'I thought you found her amusing.'

'Oh, I did on the Continent. We had the most absolute fun in Florence, even with Jemima watching over our shoulders like some mother hen. I thought we'd have just as much fun here at Sedgwick.'

'And you didn't?'

'Well, of course not, because Emmeline went all silly over Theo, didn't she? She didn't seem to be interested in anything else.'

Rose nodded, which Lavinia seemed to find sufficient encouragement to go on.

'Who'd have thought Emmeline would have lost her head over a man like Theo? Of course, one can see what he saw in her. I suppose for Emmeline it was just some little dalliance to pass the time of day.'

'Do you really think so?' Rose said. 'It didn't seem to me like that at all. It appeared to me she was genuinely fond of him. I'm certain Theo Harrison didn't view it that way, as just a dalliance, I mean.'

'I'm sure he didn't. Theo has always thought rather a lot of himself. But really! I mean to say, he can hardly have expected it to come to anything, can he? Emmeline's father would have seen to that. I can hardly imagine that he would be delighted at the prospect of his daughter marrying a country doctor, can you?'

'No ... I suppose not.' Rose pondered a moment or two. 'Which makes it all the more strange, don't you think? Jemima's behaviour in all this, I mean.'

'Now you come to mention it,' said Lavinia, 'I suppose it does seem odd.'

'If Jemima did report everything Emmeline did back to Mr Montacute,' continued Rose, 'I'd have thought she'd have felt obliged to do whatever she could to discourage an attachment from forming between Emmeline and Theo.'

'One would have thought so, yes. She gave poor Emmeline a hard time about everything else, so why not that? It would have been just the sort of spiteful thing she'd have done. Do you know, she never wanted to come to Sedgwick in the first place? Emmeline had to do lots and lots of persuading.'

'There's something else that's been worrying me.'

'Oh?'

'How did you first come to make Emmeline's acquaintance?'

'I've already told you,' sighed Lavinia. 'She was staying in the same hotel as me in Florence. She arranged for us to be introduced when we were both taking afternoon tea there one day. I remember thinking how very shy and timid she was.' Lavinia laughed. 'Jemima was absolutely furious about it. I suppose she wanted to keep Emmeline to herself.'

'I see. Was it an expensive hotel?' enquired Rose.

'What a very strange question to ask,' Lavinia said, looking at her friend closely. 'I assume there's something more behind your question besides just idle curiosity? But yes, I suppose it was quite expensive. I wouldn't have been staying there otherwise.'

'I'll ask you another question which you might find strange. Whose idea was it that Emmeline should go horse riding with Cedric yesterday?'

Lavinia blushed visibly and paused before answering.

'It was mine, as I'm sure you know full well already. I daresay you're just trying to make me feel bad about it, which is jolly beastly of you. I wasn't being very fair on you, I admit. But I shan't apologise, if that's what you're wanting me to do.'

'You were hoping that Emmeline might turn her attentions towards Cedric?'

'Yes. Oh, don't look at me like that, Rose,' Lavinia sat up on her sofa and looked earnestly at her friend. 'You know how much I like you. But really, Emmeline would have made my brother a very suitable wife. Surely you must see that, don't you? Hello … who's this?'

Lavinia's last remark was occasioned by the sound of feet coming up the stairs at a considerable pace, and making quite a noise.

'I'd better go,' Rose said, jumping up from her chair and making for the door. 'I've stayed here talking to you far longer than I intended. The constable will be wondering where I am. You stay here and rest if you like. I'll tell the policemen where you are.'

Rose had anticipated that it would be one of the constables or Sergeant Lane coming up the stairs to find her. It was however Count Fernand, who barely cast her a glance as he passed her on the landing and made for his room. She heard him slam the door behind him as she descended the stairs. Sergeant Lane was in the hall below and looked up at her entrance.

'Miss Simpson. I was wondering where you were. I couldn't see you in the drawing room when I looked in just now.'

'I was helping Lavinia upstairs. I'm afraid it's all been a bit too much for her. She's feeling unwell.'

Rose looked down at the black and white floor tiles, and had the grace to blush.

'I see. Well, perhaps you could go back into the drawing room now, if you will. I appreciate that you've been holed up in there for some time. If you want some air, the inspector has no objection to you all strolling about outside the window for a bit. But don't go far.'

'Doesn't the inspector want to interview me now?'

'Not just at this very moment, no. But it shouldn't be too long before he does.'

'If you don't mind my saying so, Sergeant, he does seem to be interviewing us in rather a strange order.'

'I'm afraid I couldn't comment on that, miss,' said Sergeant Lane, with a small grin. He looked around a moment to ensure that no one was about. He then proceeded to lean forward and speak more quietly so as not to be overheard. 'I'll say this though, miss. Inspector Deacon would have gone about things differently, so he would.'

I'm sure you're right, Sergeant.'

'And another thing, miss, although by rights I shouldn't be telling you this,' said Sergeant Lane speaking in a voice which was hardly above a whisper. 'I'd stay away from that count fellow. Lady Lavinia would do well to do likewise. And you might want to tell his lordship to lock up all his jewels while that young man is here.'

'Did you see that he went straight upstairs, Sergeant?' asked Inspector Bramwell when the policeman returned to the study.

'I did, sir,' replied Sergeant Lane. 'Our count fellow didn't speak to anyone. He passed Miss Simpson on the landing, but ignored her rather pointedly. My guess would be, sir, that he'll lie low in his room, so he will. Now that he knows that we're on to him. If you don't mind my asking, sir, how did you find out about him?'

'I had my suspicions as soon as Lord Belvedere expressed his reservations about the man and described his theatrical appearance. So I made some enquiries when you were down with the servants.'

'Oh?'

'It seems there are various young men of attractive appearance, like our count, staying in expensive hotels on the Continent, and trying to pass themselves off as someone they're not. More often than not they pander to the vanity of rich, middle-aged women with more money than sense. Our Count Fernand must have thought his luck was in when he met our Lady Lavinia and Miss Montacute.'

'I suppose the usual etiquette and niceties regarding social introductions go by the wayside when you're holidaying abroad, don't you think, sir?' The sergeant noted the puzzled frown on his superior's face and hastened to explain. 'What I mean to say, sir, is that I can't imagine that it is a regular occurrence Lady Lavinia inviting people to stay at Sedgwick whom she knows so little about. Why, they're almost strangers, aren't they?'

'Who knows what the aristocracy get up to,' grunted the inspector. 'And as to what people get up to on holiday abroad, I wouldn't know. Mrs Bramwell and I, we always take our holidays in Eastbourne. A lovely little seaside town that, if you don't know it, Sergeant.'

'I can't say I do, sir, although I've heard it has quite an impressive pier. But what about the diamonds, sir? Is that what the constable came in to tell you about?'

'It was, Sergeant. The men made a search of the rooms when we first gathered everyone into the drawing room, and they couldn't find Miss Montacute's diamonds, that we'd heard so much about. Despite being local fellows, they had enough gumption about them to check with Lord Belvedere that the diamonds had not been placed in his personal safe for safekeeping like.'

'And they hadn't? So that's when you wondered whether Count Fernand had stolen them, given the interest he'd shown in the diamonds?'

'Yes. It was something of a wild shot, of course, to ask him outright like that.'

'Well, I think it certainly hit home, sir. Did you see the look on his face when you asked if he was a jewel thief? He looked as if he'd seen a ghost.'

'Yes, but there's more to it than that, Sergeant. I already knew about the missing jewels. What the constable came hurrying in to tell me was that they'd found a jewel box hidden away on the landing.'

'Was it Miss Montacute's? Were the diamonds still inside it, sir?' Sergeant Lane held his breath.

'Yes, they were. That surprised you, didn't it, Sergeant?' said the inspector chuckling. 'You thought I was going to say they were missing.'

'Well, yes I did, sir.'

'The lock had been forced, though.'

'Oh, had it? And yet the diamonds were still there? That's a bit of a rum do, isn't it, sir? But perhaps the count panicked. He could have been afraid that we'd discover what he was up to. Decided to hide the diamonds at the first opportunity. Or at least remove them from his person or out of his room. Though the landing doesn't seem much of a hiding place to me. He'd have done better to bury them in the grounds somewhere.' The sergeant tapped the side of his head with his pencil. 'I say, sir, I take it no fingerprints were found on the box? No, what am I thinking? Of course there wouldn't have been. The count would never have been as stupid as all that.'

'Now, that's where you're wrong,' said the inspector with the air of a man who had left the best bit of his story to last. 'As it happens we did find fingerprints on the box ... but they weren't the count's.'

'Weren't they? Then who's were they, sir?'

In reply the inspector did not say a name out loud but wrote it instead on a piece of paper and passed it to the policeman. He awaited with interest his subordinate's reaction to the identity of the thief. He wasn't disappointed and chuckled to himself.

'Well, I never!' exclaimed Sergeant Lane. 'I say, sir, now that's a surprise, isn't it? Shall I go and ask the constable to get – '

'All in good time, Sergeant. There's no rush. The thief doesn't know that we're on to them. And I'd like to establish first, if I can, whether the theft of the jewels has anything to do with the murder of Miss Montacute. That's our primary concern, Sergeant. The issue of theft is secondary.'

'But it must be connected, mustn't it, sir? It's too much of a coincidence for it not to be. What are the odds of both a murder and a theft having occurred here within a few hours of each other? And the jewels belonged to the victim, didn't they? We oughtn't to forget that.'

'Even so, Sergeant,' Inspector Bramwell said firmly. 'I'd like our thief to be left wondering for a little while longer as to whether or not we've found the diamonds.'

'Who would you like to interview next, sir?' enquired the sergeant, trying to hide his disappointment.

'I think it's high time we interviewed your Miss Simpson, don't you? Let's see what she has to say for herself. And by the way, Sergeant ... you never did tell me what she was doing upstairs. I thought I'd left instructions that no one was to leave the drawing room until they'd been interviewed.'

'It appears, sir, Lady Lavinia had a bit of a turn. I suppose it all caught up with her, finding the body and all. She went up to her room for a lie down and Miss Simpson went with her to see she didn't come to any harm on her way up the stairs.' The sergeant saw that the inspector was regarding him cynically. 'The constable assured me Miss Simpson came straight down again.'

'Did he indeed? I very much doubt that she did.' The inspector gave a snort. 'That's the trouble with these amateur sleuth types. Always trying to find ways to poke their noses in and interview people behind our backs. Well, let's have her in, Sergeant.'

Chapter Twenty

'Rose. Oh, there you are, darling. It's seems simply ages since I last spoke to you. Are you all right? Where's Lavinia?'

Cedric was by her side as soon as she entered the drawing room, closing out the world behind her. He grabbed her hand and pulled her towards him, and together they walked hand in hand over to the far end of the room.

'Cedric. Oh thank goodness you're here. I was afraid that it was just going to be the others. I've hardly seen anything of you all day. And when I have, you've been with Theo.'

'I know. I'm worried about him, Rose. He's hardly said a word since all this happened. I jolly well wish the inspector would hurry up and interview him. Although I have to say I'm rather afraid what Theo might say. Hello ... they've opened the windows. Let's go outside, shall we?'

As soon as they stepped outside the cold hit them. It did not occur to either of them to go back for a hat and coat. Instead Rose snuggled up closely to Cedric, and he put an arm around her, drawing her to him protectively. She breathed in the fresh winter air. The murder seemed very far away as they stood in the feeble sunlight with eyes only for each other.

'That's better,' said Cedric. 'I suppose it wouldn't do if I were to kiss you, would it? Not the thing at all at a time like this. But I do want to so badly, Rose.' He sighed. 'If only this damned murder business was all over and done with. It could be just you and me here and to hell with the rest of the world.'

'Oh, Cedric ...'

Rose leaned back against him and felt his arm supporting her reassuringly. I don't want this to end, she thought. I certainly don't want to go back into that room. I want to stay in the gardens and forget about the murder and the fearful Inspector Bramwell. Aloud she said: 'They'll find us here, won't they? When they want to come out and interview us, they'll find us?'

'Yes, they're certain to. I expect they're spying on us now from the windows.' He paused. 'Oh, dash it all, the others are coming out. Can't they leave us alone for one minute?'

'It's only Jemima,' said Rose, turning to see who had followed them out. 'And she's walking in the other direction. I think she wants to be alone as much as we do. Oh … that's good, Theo and Vera appear to be staying inside.'

'I'm not sure that it's a good idea leaving them alone together,' sighed Cedric. 'But I'm tired of playing nanny, and they'll have to work things out themselves one way or the other. Hello … what's he doing out here?'

Cedric's last remark was occasioned by the figure of Felix coming out of the French windows of the library and striding purposefully over towards Jemima.

'Jemima, I must talk with you.'

The girl had turned with alarm at the sound of the approaching footsteps on the gravel.

'You shouldn't be here, Felix. The police haven't interviewed me yet, and they are certain to see you from the window.'

'Damn the police!' said Felix, with feeling. 'I had to speak to you.'

'I wish you'd go away.'

She turned away from him, and he thought how very dejected she looked.

'I wish everyone would go away and leave me alone.'

'Even me?'

Felix held his breath, waiting for her answer.

Jemima heard the urgency and hurt in his voice.

'I'm sorry,' she said, more gently. 'I just want to be by myself. I need to think. I need to think about what to do.'

'That's why I had to see you.'

He gently held the girl by her shoulders and turned her to face him. Jemima did not resist, although her natural inclination was to turn away.

'I wanted to tell you it's all right. Everything's all right.'

'What on earth do you mean by that?' demanded Jemima. 'How can everything possibly be all right? She's dead. My friend is dead!'

Her voice had risen hysterically. Jemima looked across at the others, and caught Rose's eye. The girl was looking at her quizzically, although Jemima felt certain that her words would not have carried given the distance between them. Even so she must try and compose herself and speak more quietly, she must …

'Shh!' Felix too was looking around anxiously. 'Listen to me, Jemima. It's awful, I know. A frightful tragedy and all that, but you have to be strong. What I meant before, when I said everything was all right, is that the police don't suspect you. They don't think you killed her.'

'Think I killed her?' Jemima's eyes had gone very wide. 'What do you mean? Why ever should they think that I killed Emmeline?'

'Because you had a motive. But I didn't tell them about it, Jemima, I promise I didn't.'

'What motive, Felix? What possible motive could I have had for wishing Emmeline dead?'

'Shh! I said keep your voice down. Do you want everyone to hear? As to motive, well, money of course, my dear. You said so yourself when we were in the garden yesterday. Don't you remember? It seems so long ago after everything that's happened, but we were saying how awful it was going to be for us having to be apart until I made enough money to keep us.' He held her by the shoulders. 'Don't you remember? You asked me what if you were able to get hold of some money.'

'I don't understand what you're saying, Felix. Are you saying I killed Emmeline for her money?' Jemima looked horrified.

'How else would you get hold of any money, Jemima? We both know you're as poor as a church mouse. I didn't understand what you meant at the time, but I do now. Jemima will have left a will, won't she? I'm sure she's left you something in it, hasn't she?'

'Yes, as it happens, Felix, she's left me a great deal of money.' Her voice sounded devoid of all emotion.

'There you are. I don't say I blame you. Emmeline treated you awfully.'

'Did she? I can't say that I noticed. She was my best friend.' Her voice fell to little more than a whisper. 'My only friend.'

She had withdrawn from him now, determined to put some distance between them.

'Nonsense. What am I to you, then?' retorted Felix, pulling her to him. 'I love you Jemima, you know I do. I would have waited for you,

you know I would have done. But what's happened has happened. It's no use crying over spilt milk.'

'How can you be so heartless?' cried Jemima, fighting back her tears. 'Losing Emmeline is bad enough, but to have you talking as if it doesn't matter, as if we will profit by her death, it's too frightful. I can't bear it, I tell you. I can't bear it.'

'Shh! Do you want everyone to hear? What is wrong with you, Jemima? I mind terribly that Emmeline's dead, of course I do. But there is nothing we can do about it now. I wanted to see you to say that I will stand by you. I won't say anything to the police, I promise I won't. But you've got to pull yourself together.'

'I don't understand. If you love me half as much as you say you do, how can you be so willing to believe I killed Emmeline?' Jemima said, trying very hard not to cry.

'Because it's the only thing that makes any sense. I don't want to believe it of you. It goes without saying I don't want to.'

There was a pause as Felix passed a hand through his hair looking miserable and confused.

'I say, Jemima,' he said suddenly, holding her away from him and searching her face for some sign or other. 'Are you really telling me that you didn't do it? Please tell me the truth, not just what you think I want to hear.'

'Of course I didn't do it.' Jemima had all but pushed him away from her. A moment later she was clutching at his arm so hard that her nails dug into his flesh and he almost winced with the pain.

'It's funny isn't it? You see, Felix, all this time I've been wondering whether you did it. I've been wondering whether it wasn't you who killed Emmeline.'

'Theo. Theo. Didn't you hear me?'

As soon as Jemima had left the drawing room on the heels of Cedric and Rose, Vera had run over to Theo, a look of consternation on her plain face. It was her first opportunity to be alone with him since the search party had returned with its woeful tidings. Up to now the others had thwarted any attempt made by her to speak to him. Although she acknowledged that their efforts had been well-meaning, done with the best

165

of intentions, it was a relief to know that she could now accomplish what she had been longing to do all day. She could approach the doctor and talk to him without fear of being intercepted or disturbed.

But now that she found herself standing right in front of the man she might as well have been invisible for all the notice that he gave her. He was staring beyond her into the fire, the light from the flames flickering on his face so that his features alternated from being spectacularly lit up to being half hidden and obscured by shadow. The effect was rather grotesque when coupled with the first signs of dusk, which was fast approaching, and which accentuated in stark contrast the artificial brightness of the room.

Involuntarily Vera shuddered and turned to look out of the window. Her eye was drawn to the other couples, particularly to Cedric and Rose, and she wished that they were Theo and herself, strolling as they often had through the grounds of Sedgwick Court in a companionable silence. Although, in their case, she noticed that Cedric and Rose appeared to be talking nineteen to the dozen, stopping every now and then to touch or discreetly embrace. It occurred to her that she and Theo had never behaved like that, even in the early days of their courtship. And then all at once, unbidden, she saw again the image that had so haunted her during the night. Theo and Emmeline laughing and embracing in the gardens. What had hurt her most, she realised now, was that she had never seen Theo look so happy or appear so young.

Vera bit her lip and stifled a sob. She mustn't let herself dwell on that awful image or what awful act it had compelled her to do. It didn't do any good to look back on the past and consider how one might have behaved differently. One could not undo what had been done. But it was easier said than accomplished. Now though, she must look to the future and try her utmost to restore things to the way they had been before Emmeline had come in their midst and caused such destruction. She must be strong for both of them, Theo and herself. But it was almost too much to bear, to stand in front of the man she loved so desperately, while all the time having him ignore her. Even worse than that, she thought he was not even conscious of her presence.

The next time his features were lit up by the flames she scrutinised his face closely, and noticed lines around his eyes that had not been there before. His skin, despite the yellow glow cast by the fire, looked grey and taut. She felt his deep unhappiness as if it were her own. Indeed it mirrored the misery she felt at the collapse and ruin of their relationship. Despite their shared feelings of desolation, she was aware of the gulf between them and wondered whether it could ever be bridged.

'Theo. Please.' This time she raised her voice slightly and accompanied her words by pulling at his elbow, an impatient, desperate gesture to make him aware of her. 'Let's go outside. Let's join the others. You've being sitting here staring at the fire far too long. It won't do you any good, you know, brooding like this.'

'Leave me alone, Vera.'

Theo's voice sounded weary and as if it came from a long way away. The doctor passed a hand over his eyes. She could not decide whether he did so because he did not wish to look at her or because he was tired.

'Theo – '

'For goodness sake leave me alone, Vera.'

He pushed her hand away with such force that she almost lost her balance. She wondered what he would have done if she had toppled backwards into the fire.

'Go away! How many times do I have to tell you? I've never hit a woman before, but heaven help me, Vera, I'll strike you if you don't leave me alone.'

For a moment she was so taken aback that she felt unable to move or do anything but gape, her mouth open, her eyes wide. Theo had never spoken to her like that before. On no occasion had she heard such venom in his voice. Indeed she had not known that he was capable of such anger. She could not have been more shocked if he had carried out his threat and struck her. If it were possible, she felt more wretched than before. Even so, a part of her longed to stand her ground and cling on to him. The others had been right to be concerned, to stop her from undertaking her self-destructive path. But she didn't want to let go. She was not prepared to lose after all that she had done. She desperately wanted to continue her attempts, no matter how futile, to reclaim him to her and banish all contemplation of Emmeline from his mind. But, even as these thoughts passed through her mind, she discovered that he had frightened her so badly that her instinct for self-preservation had already resulted in her recoiling from him, edging away towards the French windows where she stumbled into Jemima, returning from her walk.

'Well,' said Cedric, from his position seated beside Rose on a small wooden bench, her arm tucked comfortably through his. 'That didn't seem to go very well, did it?'

He was referring to the encounter between Jemima and Felix, which they had witnessed from a distance.

'No, I thought they seemed very wary of each other, didn't you? They weren't at all like that the other day.'

'I say, do you think they suspect each other of murdering Emmeline?'

'I don't know. Jemima certainly looked a little afraid of Felix, don't you think?'

'I do,' said Cedric. 'I can't quite make Jemima out, can you? She seems to keep everything bottled up inside herself while keeping us at bay. I wanted to commiserate with her on Emmeline's death, but she gave me such a reproachful look that I didn't dare go near her.'

'I think she's frightened, but what of, I couldn't say,' said Rose.

She looked back across the lawns at the grand Georgian mansion that had been the Sedgwicks' ancestral home since she did not quite know when, and then out across the parkland to the very edges of the estate. Her gaze took in the sunken ha-ha fences, the lakes and the eye-catchers, all of which Cedric had shown to her so proudly when she had first arrived at Sedgwick, blissfully unaware of what lay ahead. She remembered that she had caught her breath at the scale of it all, the sprawling estate that had been Cedric's childhood home.

She thought of the small terraced house that she shared with her mother, and which they found so difficult to maintain without the assistance of paying guests. Her eyes misted with unshed tears and blinking them away she allowed her gaze to stray reluctantly in the direction of the maze. Was it her imagination, or did the hedges appear darker and more dense? It was as if the maze had become some forbidden corner, closed off from the rest of the estate.

'It's no good, you know, Cedric,' Rose said, leaning her head against his shoulder. 'This talk of running away won't do. We can't pretend that things will resolve themselves, no matter how much we may want it.'

'I know. I was only saying out loud what I wished could happen.'
Cedric got slowly to his feet and pulled Rose up with him into a long
embrace. 'Of course you're right, my darling. I suppose I had better step
back into the role of the Earl of Belvedere, adopt my official façade and
go back inside now and face the inspector. I'll sit there meekly and have
my knuckles rapped, and be told that I am a disgrace to my country and
my class.'

'Does he know that you tampered with the evidence?'

'Yes, Felix was good enough to give me the nod about it before he
was frogmarched upstairs. He managed to give the constable the slip for a
few moments and dashed into the drawing room to tell me.'

'That was good of him.'

'Yes, wasn't it? Jolly decent of him. He said that the inspector
already seemed to know all about it, and put it to him more as a given fact
than as a question. He said it threw him completely off his stride, and that
before he knew what he was doing he was telling the inspector all about
it.'

'Poor Felix.'

'I say, I've just remembered something. I meant to tell you earlier but
didn't get the opportunity to do so. I was feeling rather guilty asking you
to investigate Emmeline's murder. I thought I ought to play my part and
undertake a little investigating of my own.'

'Oh?'

'Yes. I was thinking about when Emmeline and I went horse riding
yesterday. The girl was absolutely petrified and yet Lavinia claimed she
was an accomplished horsewoman. The two things didn't seem to tally.
When I took Lavinia to task about it later, she swore blind that she had
read in some rag or other about how well Emmeline rode to hounds.'

'It was Lavinia's idea that Emmeline should go out riding with you,
not Emmeline's. Although I suppose that doesn't really prove anything,
does it?'

'Ah, but that's not all. I told you that I did a bit of sleuthing of my
own.' Cedric gave a schoolboy grin. It lit up his face and made him look
very young. 'Inspector Bramwell had me going backwards and forwards
between the maze and the house a few times today answering questions
and pointing things out to the policemen. He was adamant that I should do

it and not a servant. Perhaps he regarded it as my penance for meddling with the evidence.'

'So what did you do?' asked Rose intrigued.

'I took the opportunity to go across to the stables and have a word with Cryer. He's our head groom. There's very little that Cryer doesn't know about horses and riders, and what there is, isn't worth knowing. The man absolutely devours every edition of *Horse & Hound* that I pass on to him.'

'So did you ask him if he had read anything about Emmeline riding to hounds?'

'I did. And do you know what he said?'

'No, but I'm certain you're going to tell me.'

'He said that he'd read somewhere that she was awfully good at keeping up with the pack and thought nothing of jumping hedges that others went miles out of their way to avoid.'

'Why, that doesn't make any sense,' cried Rose. 'If Emmeline was so at home riding to hounds, why should she be daunted at going out on a hack with you?'

'I can't begin to imagine,' said Cedric. 'I say, I hope she hadn't suddenly taken against me.'

'I'm sure she hadn't. Now … given what we now know of her exploits on horseback, there was no earthly reason for her being afraid of going for a ride around the estate. Unless of course she had a nasty fall that had suddenly put her off riding for life. But … no, that won't do. Cryer would have read about it. Unless ... and it really seems the only explanation … oh, but it seems too fanciful.'

'Unless what?' prompted Cedric.

'Unless Emmeline Montacute wasn't Emmeline Montacute at all.'

Chapter Twenty-one

'And you think that, why, Miss Simpson?'

Inspector Bramwell was looking at her as if she had gone quite mad. Even Sergeant Lane was looking a little embarrassed on her behalf as if she had said something rather ridiculous. On reflection perhaps she had. Rose sighed. She was beginning to wish that she had kept quiet about her suspicions, certainly until she had got the measure of the man sitting before her, his eyebrows raised and with an expression of incredulity on his face. Even Cedric, who had absolute faith in her detective abilities and had provided her with the evidence to support her suspicions, had thought her theory that the woman purporting to be Emmeline Montacute had been an impostor rather far-fetched. With a sinking feeling in her stomach, she realised she was beginning to have second thoughts herself.

'I've already told you, Inspector. The woman who was murdered had very little experience of riding a horse. Emmeline Montacute was an accomplished rider.'

'According to some article in a magazine? Well, where is this article, Miss Simpson? And even if it does exist, what does it prove?' Inspector Bramwell tapped the desk with his fingers as if the answer would be found there. 'I'll tell you what it proves. That the writer confused one rich young woman with another. It happens all the time I should imagine. No, Miss Simpson. You'll have to do much better than that to convince me that the murdered woman was not Emmeline Montacute.'

Rose opened her mouth to speak, but thought better of it. If nothing else, she was at a loss as to what to say. To make matters worse, she was conscious of the inspector looking at her through watery eyes which looked surprisingly alert. She blushed and to her annoyance saw a look of satisfaction appear on the inspector's face. He almost chuckled and proceeded to regard her with a paternal smile. He leaned back into his chair and she heard the springs strain under his weight. Her mind conjured up the not too unpleasing image of him falling through the seat of the chair on to the floor.

'Now then,' began Inspector Bramwell, his voice softening.

Rose immediately felt guilty for her uncharitable thoughts, and tried not to think of the sagging chair.

'This just goes to show you, Miss Simpson, why it's always best to leave things to the police to investigate. It's our job after all. It's what we're paid to do, and trained for.'

'But – '

I'm not saying you didn't mean well, miss, but it really won't do. We can't have members of the public putting their noses into things that don't concern them and muddying the waters with absurd suppositions. For one thing, it's not safe. There is a murderer among you, Miss Simpson, who I doubt very much will take too kindly to you stirring things up by asking awkward questions. You need to leave that for us to do.'

'Will you at least find out whether Emmeline Montacute is at her home in the Highlands?'

'We've already done that, miss,' Sergeant Lane said. 'Miss Montacute and Miss Wentmore aren't there. By all accounts they just upped and left without a word. The servants were most put out.'

'Thank you, Sergeant,' said Inspector Bramwell, giving his subordinate a reproving stare. 'Now, Miss Simpson. You mustn't take it into your head that we don't investigate matters thoroughly, because we do. And as to your concerns regarding whether Miss Montacute was Miss Montacute … well, you can put them to rest. Mr Montacute is returning from his travels and should be with us in a day or two. He'll officially identify the body, of course, and I think you'll agree that he'll know as well as anyone whether the body's that of his daughter or not.'

'Yes. Of course you are right. But perhaps you could arrange for him to see Miss Wentmore first,' suggested Rose. 'You see, if the body's not that of Miss Montacute, it stands to reason that the woman calling herself Jemima Wentmore is not Jemima Wentmore. You do see that, don't you, Inspector?'

'I do. We will of course be doing just that, Miss Simpson. Mr Montacute will want to have a few quiet words with his daughter's companion, I have no doubt, and we'll ensure that he does. So you see, everything's in hand. You needn't worry. We'll know the lay of the land as soon as Mr Montacute lays eyes on Miss Wentmore so to speak.'

'So you do think I could be right?'

'I'm not saying that, Miss Simpson. I'm not saying that at all.' The inspector frowned and looked at his notes. 'Well now, I think we've wasted enough time on this, don't you? May I remind you, Miss Simpson, that it is for us to put questions to you and not the other way around?'

'Yes, of course, Inspector. There are just one or two other things that make me think that the deceased is not –'

'Miss Simpson!'

'I'm sorry, Inspector. I won't say anything more about it,' Rose said hurriedly. 'Please do go on with your questions. What would you like to ask me?'

'Thank you. Did Lord Belvedere interfere with the evidence?'

'Oh!' Rose was taken aback by the abruptness of the question. 'Well … yes … I suppose he did. But I know for an absolute fact that he means to tell you all about it himself. He's very ashamed about it. He knows that what he did was very wrong. He would have told you about it himself already if you'd only given him an opportunity to do so.'

'Is that so? Well, perhaps while you're here, you'll tell me about it, Miss Simpson.'

'Of course. Now, let me see … yes, Lord Belvedere took the candlestick from Lavinia, wiped it and then asked me to see to his sister and take her up to the house.'

'And you didn't think to protest?'

'Of course I did, Inspector. I tried to, and so did Felix Thistlewaite. But it was no good. Lord Belvedere was not in a mood to be reasoned with.'

'Why was that?'

'I imagine it was because he was under the impression that his sister had just murdered Miss Montacute.'

'And is that what you all thought?'

'Yes, I suppose we did all think that at the time. Lavinia was standing over Emmeline's body holding a candlestick smeared with blood. It was difficult to think anything else.'

'I see.'

'But of course we know now that didn't happen. Emmeline was killed much earlier and really Lavinia had no reason to wish her dead. And … well … the candlestick, Inspector. I know it was very wrong of Lord

Belvedere to tamper with the candlestick and he feels absolutely awful about it now. But, really I don't think much real harm has been done, do you?'

'What makes you say that, Miss Simpson?'

'Well, it would have been awfully cold when Emmeline was killed. It was still jolly chilly when we set out to search for her. We were all wrapped up in coats and scarves. Don't you think, Inspector, it is far more likely than not that the murderer was wearing gloves when they struck Miss Montacute with the candlestick? And if that was so, they wouldn't have left any fingerprints, even if Lord Belvedere hadn't wiped them off.'

'Possibly,' conceded the inspector. 'Tell me, was Lady Lavinia wearing gloves when you found her clutching the candlestick?'

'Well … no, of course not, otherwise Lord Belvedere wouldn't have gone to the bother of wiping the candlestick, would he?'

'Ah! Then perhaps your theory is not quite as robust as you seem to think it, Miss Simpson. The murderer may well have been wearing gloves as you suppose. But I think it very likely they would have taken them off before they swung the candlestick in order to give them a better grip on the instrument. Just as Lady Lavinia removed her gloves to pick up the candlestick.'

'Oh.'

Rose wished she had kept quiet. For it occurred to her that by saying what she had done, she had only made matters worse.

'I understand the lady's maid came out of the house to see to her mistress?'

'Yes … I suppose I ought to tell you that she ran a bath for Lavinia, and … took the clothes she was wearing to be washed.'

'And you didn't think to stop her?'

'Yes … no, I ... Lavinia was in quite a state, as you can imagine. I thought a hot bath was just what she required. I was worried about her, Inspector. If you had seen her, you would have been too.' Rose put a hand to her forehead. 'I did try and stop the clothes being washed, of course I did, but everything happened so quickly, and then it was all too late and … I know I should not have let them out of my sight. But it was not as if they were covered in blood, far from it. There were only a few traces of blood on Lady Lavinia's coat from what I could see, smears from her hands or the candlestick, I imagine ...'

Rose faltered, discouraged from continuing by the look on the inspector's face.

There then followed an awkward silence. Rose glanced at the inspector and saw that he was regarding her closely. After a few moments he cleared his throat and Rose, taking a deep breath, readied herself to be severely admonished for her various shortcomings.

'Do you recognise these diamonds, Miss Simpson?' The inspector produced a diamond necklace from his pocket.

'Oh! Do I recognise ...? Let me see.'

Rose bent forward eagerly in her seat and took the necklace from him, holding it up so that she could study it closely. 'Why ... yes, I think it's Emmeline's necklace, the one she was wearing the night before last.'

'Are you sure about that, Miss Simpson?'

'No ... I've just said I'm not ... but, yes ... I think it is her necklace. You see, we all took it in turns to look at it through Count Fernand's jeweller's lens. I don't know much about diamonds, I'm afraid, but it looks to me to be the same necklace that Emmeline was wearing.'

'Thank you.' The inspector took the jewellery from her and stowed it back into his pocket. 'Now, Miss Simpson. I'd like you to cast your mind back, if you will, to the two days leading up to the murder. Just so you know, we're aware of Dr Harrison and Miss Montacute being rather fond of each other and Miss Brewster being made miserable by it.'

'Are you? I'm glad ... at least I think I am. It doesn't feel so much like speaking out of turn if you already know all about it. Vera was rather beastly to Emmeline the night before last because of it. She referred to her kidnapping and how it must have frightened her terribly. Both Emmeline and Jemima were awfully upset by it. That's why the count suggested that we look at the diamonds through his loupe. I think he thought it would take everyone's mind off what had happened.'

'And did it?'

'Oh, yes. Emmeline cheered up no end.'

'What about Miss Wentmore?'

'Jemima? No … now you come to mention it, Inspector, Miss Wentmore remained subdued. She kept herself apart from everyone. To tell the truth, I don't think she thought much of the count's game.'

'What surprises me most in all this, Miss Simpson, is that Miss Brewster did not try to put a stop to the relationship developing between her fiancé and Miss Montacute. Mr Thistlewaite informed us that he believed that Miss Brewster thought it was a mere flirtation or infatuation that would just blow over in time. Tell me, were you of that opinion also?'

'No. At first I don't think Miss Brewster saw it as any more than Dr Harrison trying to curry favour with someone who might be in a positon to further his career. Vera told me she thought he worked too hard. He had aspirations of becoming a fashionable doctor rather than a country one. She was concerned that when they were married he would want a London practice. She herself wanted to stay in the village of Sedgwick.'

'And later?'

'I think she realised that Emmeline and Theo were attracted to each other but tried to ignore it. But it made her miserable. It was only when …'

'Yes, Miss Simpson. Go on. What were you going to say?'

'I am certain that it had nothing to do with Miss Montacute's death.'

'I'll be the judge of that. Go on.'

'Well, on the morning before Emmeline's death, I decided to go for a walk in the gardens. Miss Brewster asked if she might accompany me. She then asked Dr Harrison if he would care to join us, and he declined saying he had too much work to do. He wasn't very polite about it, I'm afraid. I remember feeling rather sorry for Vera at the time.'

'I take it there's more to come?'

'Oh, yes, I'm just giving you the background, Inspector. We decided to walk on down to the lake. And that's when we came upon them, Dr Harrison and Miss Montacute. They were laughing and giggling and chasing one another. They were so obviously in love. I felt so sorry for Vera. Even now I can see her face, her look of disbelief. She was trembling, I remember that. It was quite awful.'

'What happened next, Miss Simpson?'

'She ran back to the house and kept to her room until it was time for dinner.'

'Brooding, no doubt.'

'She said she wasn't feeling well.'

'I daresay she would say that. But the fact remains, Miss Simpson, that less than a day later Miss Montacute was murdered.'

Rose felt a little sick. What if it transpired that Vera had killed Emmeline? How would she feel knowing that she had provided the police with some of the supporting evidence they required to send poor, wronged Vera to the gallows? She bit her lip and did her best to swallow the lump that was forming in her throat. For she had remembered Vera's mood the previous night. How the woman had watched while the man she loved had laughed and flirted with another woman, oblivious of her presence and seemingly uncaring of the pain he was causing her. Rose recollected also the very words Vera had uttered, spat through clenched teeth: "I hate them, I tell you I hate them! I wish they were dead!"

If she were now to reveal to Inspector Bramwell the words spoken by Vera while she was at her lowest ebb, what then? Would he keep an open mind and look for other suspects? Or would he decide that Vera was the murderer and not look elsewhere?

She looked up and noticed that the inspector was looking at her curiously. She wondered if her face revealed her various emotions.

'Are you all right, miss? You're looking a bit peaky if you don't mind my saying.'

Rose looked confused. She had not seen the inspector's lips move. And then she realised that the words had been spoken by Sergeant Lane and not his superior. She had half forgotten that the sergeant was there, scribbling down her every word. She slowly nodded although in truth she did not know how she felt.

'Now, perhaps you'll tell me about last night,' continued the inspector. 'I understand his lordship turned the conversation after dinner to the maze. Showed you a plan of it and described the path to take to get to the middle.'

'Yes, he did. It was going to be a sort of game today. To see who could make their way there first without the plan. You will have seen for yourself that it is quite a large maze, Inspector. Lavinia told us a story about a young maid going there once to meet her young man and getting terribly lost.' Rose sighed. 'It doesn't seem fair that Emmeline was killed there. She was so eager to see the maze.'

For a few moments no one spoke. In her mind's eye Rose saw again Emmeline, young and lovely as she had been; laughing and smiling as had been her way. Until now she had thought only of those affected by Emmeline's death and the unpleasantness of it having occurred at Sedgwick. Only now did she allow herself to feel the full horror of what had happened. How very awful it was that Emmeline, so full of life, had been done to death. What a waste of a young life.

'It's all right, miss. I only have one more question to ask you,' the inspector said rather gruffly. 'But it's an important one at that. I've been told Miss Brewster said something to you before she fainted. As I understand it she didn't join you in the search for Miss Montacute?'

'No. She wasn't feeling very well.'

'Dear me, not unwell again? Poor Miss Brewster. She does appear to suffer from bad health.' The inspector got up from his chair and started to pace the floor. 'Well, Miss Simpson? Did Miss Brewster say anything before she fainted?'

'Yes ... yes, she did.'

Rose heard again Vera's voice: "Dead! No, she can't be. She can't be dead. Oh my God, what have I done? I never meant to ..." She remembered she had asked Vera later what she had meant by it, and that the woman had been evasive. More than that, Vera had pretended that her words had meant nothing, and yet, of course, they must have meant something, otherwise why say them? Vera had been frightened, Rose remembered now. And she herself had been annoyed with her, certain in her belief that the woman was lying or hiding something.

She sat there for a moment in a quandary as to what to do. If she told the inspector what Vera had said, it might be the final nail in the coffin as far as confirming their suspicions of the woman. But what else could she do? And what if Vera was guilty? Wouldn't she want to see her brought to justice?

'Well, Miss Simpson? What did Miss Brewster say?'

Inspector Bramwell was watching her closely with those small, watery eyes of his which were surprisingly observant. Rose thought she heard a note of impatience in his voice. He knew full well that she was prevaricating.

'She said – '

At the very moment she was about to tell them about Vera's desperate confession, uttered in a moment of weakness before the woman slumped to the ground, the sound of running feet on the black and white tiles in the hall beyond diverted their attention. It was proceeded at once by the study door being flung open, the constable obviously having decided that the information he had in his possession was far too important to require him to stop and knock before entering.

'Constable! I am in the middle of an interview, I – '

Inspector Bramwell had jumped up from his seat at the interruption. Pinkish spots had appeared on the loose flesh of his cheeks like badly applied rouge, and his eyes appeared darker and less watery.

'Sir ... Sorry, sir.' The man put a hand to his chest while he caught his breath. 'It's just that we've received a telephone call from the mortuary, sir. They found something, the doctors did. On the deceased's body, sir. They found something that tells us who the murderer is ... well as good as. It's as good as a confession, sir, so it is. It's – '

'Hold your tongue, man!' The inspector swung around to face Rose. 'That will be all for now, thank you, Miss Simpson. I may wish to speak with you further. If I do, I'll send for you. But you may go now. Sergeant, see Miss Simpson out, will you?'

Chapter Twenty-two

'Well, darling, what did you think of Inspector Bramwell?' asked Cedric, as soon as Rose had re-entered the drawing room.' Was he as beastly to you as he was to me?'

'I'm not sure what to make of him,' Rose said, linking her arm in his as they made their way to the far end of the room. They chose a richly upholstered settee and sank down on to it, their hands still entwined and their heads bent closely towards each other.

'Cedric, I'm awfully afraid that I've made an absolute fool of myself over that business about Emmeline and Jemima not being Emmeline and Jemima, if you know what I mean? You should have seen the inspector's face when I suggested it to him. He didn't believe it for one moment, even when I explained my reasoning.'

'Well, more fool him, that's all I can say.'

'You are a darling, Cedric. But I know full well that you're not entirely convinced either, are you? The more I think of it, the more I believe I may have it all wrong, anyway. The real Emmeline Montacute and Jemima Wentmore aren't at home. The police have already checked. It's just as Lavinia told me. They left without telling anyone of their intentions.' She sighed. 'Anyway, I don't think it matters too much now. Emmeline's father arrives back from his travels in a day or so and is coming down to Sedgwick to formally identify his daughter's body, so we'll know one way or the other by then.'

'Is he indeed? Did you find out anything else from the inspector?'

'No, not really. He plays his cards close to his chest. Oh, wait a minute, there was something.'

'Yes?'

'He showed me Emmeline's diamond necklace and asked me if I recognised it.'

'Did he? I wonder why he did that.'

'Come to think of it, he asked me quite a few questions about the diamonds. He was particularly interested in the count's parlour game. The one involving the jeweller's loupe. I suppose it's because he suspects him of being a jewel thief. I explained how it had come about, the game, I mean.'

'Because of what Vera said? It was awfully cruel of her to bring up the subject of the kidnapping,' said Cedric. 'I say, Rose. You don't think Emmeline's death could have anything to do with a kidnap attempt, do you?'

'I don't see why not. I was just wondering that myself as it happens. It seems just as likely as diamonds or Theo's relationship with Emmeline and Vera's jealousy. Inspector Bramwell knew all about that too, Theo and Emmeline, I mean.'

'Do you feel any closer to knowing who did it?'

'I'm sorry, darling, I don't ... Oh, Cedric!'

'What, darling? Is something wrong?'

'I can't keep it to myself any more. I'm being awfully mean to you. Keeping the best bit of news to last.'

'Oh, and what's that?'

'They've discovered something. The police, I mean. Or should I say the pathologist? While I was being interviewed, a constable rushed in and said that they'd found something at the mortuary. It was on Emmeline's body. He said it as good as proved who her murderer was.'

'Did he indeed? I wonder what they've found.'

'Before we do anything else, we'd better find out what that fool of a constable was talking about,' grumbled Inspector Bramwell. 'Better not get your hopes up, Lane. Likely as not the fellow's got hold of the wrong end of the stick. It may be very little at all. The man has no sense. To come barging into the room like that and saying what he did in front of Miss Simpson of all people. I suppose it'll be the gossip of the drawing room by now.'

'Miss Simpson's not like that, sir,' Sergeant Lane said. 'She'll keep news of it to herself.'

'Pah! She'll tell Lord Belvedere at least, you know she will as well as I do.'

'I've arranged for the call to be put through here, sir.' Sergeant Lane said, keen to change the subject. 'It's a pity Jackson didn't ask for details before hanging up, although perhaps they wouldn't have given them to him. They'd have wanted to speak to you first, sir.'

'Well, at least the man had the sense to ask them to ring back before he hung up. I'd telephone the mortuary myself but they'd probably put me through to a different fellow than the one who rang up, who'd know nothing about this business. No … all in good time. I'll wait for them to telephone. Besides, I want to go over one or two things in my mind first.' He turned to look at the sergeant. 'Are you feeling hungry, Lane? I am. Isn't it time for tea? Go to the kitchen and ask them to bring in a tea tray, will you? Better still, pull that bell rope over there.'

'It's all right, sir, I'll have a word with one of the footmen. I think there's one in the hall. I hope you don't think it a liberty, sir, but, when I was seeing Miss Simpson out just now, I suggested to one of the servants that tea be laid in the library for the family and their guests. They were getting a bit restive seeing as they had been confined to the drawing room all day.'

The inspector snorted. 'Very considerate of you, Lane, I'm sure. Although they took their lunch in the dining room, didn't they? And we've allowed them a stroll in the gardens. That's not confining them to the drawing room in my book. Count Fernand and Mr Thistlewaite will be down for their tea too, no doubt. Have one of the constables keep an eye on them. I don't want them talking with those among the party we haven't had the opportunity to interview yet. Although happen the count will keep himself to himself.'

'Yes. I'm certain he'll want to keep his head down.'

Sergeant Lane left and returned a few minutes later having accomplished his mission on both fronts. As he had anticipated, a footman had been easily found. Much to his satisfaction also, he had seen the count safely ensconced in a corner of the library with an expression on his face, and an air about him that deterred any of the others from going over and speaking to him. Felix Thistlewaite too appeared unusually quiet and wrapped up in his own thoughts. With his back to the room, he had looked out of the window on to the grounds beyond, although he could see almost nothing given how dark it was now. He had given up even the pretence of this pursuit once the curtains had been drawn and the world outside shut out. Then the young man had stood rather awkwardly, clutching a plate in his hand but hardly eating a morsel. Every now and then, the policeman had noticed, he had stolen a glance at Jemima Wentmore, but she either did not notice he was trying to catch her eye, or else was purposefully ignoring him.

'What did you make of Miss Simpson's theory that Miss Montacute might not have been Miss Montacute at all, sir?' the sergeant asked as soon as he had closed the study door. 'It sounded a bit far-fetched to me, although, for what it's worth, there's usually something in what Miss Simpson has to say.'

'It that so, Lane?' Inspector Bramwell glared at his sergeant. 'Well you've heard my views on amateur sleuths, Sergeant. Their activities are not to be encouraged. Having said that, we'll have to look into it, more's the pity. There may be something in it and there may not.' He began to pace the room. 'We can't have Montacute being told that his daughter's been murdered only to find that she's alive and well in London. No. That wouldn't do at all.' He stopped his pacing and turned and glanced at the sergeant. 'We need to find out the truth before Montacute's ship comes in to dock.'

'Couldn't we just get the secretary chap down here? Stapleton. He'd be able to tell us if Miss Wentmore is who she claims to be, and if she isn't we could then have him look at the corpse.'

'We could. But I'll wager that we can find out easily enough by ourselves. While we're waiting for tea to arrive, go and have another look at their bedrooms, Miss Wentmore's and Miss Montacute's. Happen as not you'll find something in one of them that'll tell us one way or the other.'

'As you wish, sir,' said Sergeant Lane, somewhat reluctantly. He would have preferred instead to wait for the telephone call and find out if what had been discovered at the mortuary was really as important as the constable believed it to be.

'If they're not who they claimed to be,' said the sergeant, hovering by the door, 'they'd have to have some connections with the Montacute family, don't you think, sir? They'd have to know that the real Miss Montacute and Miss Wentmore were abroad at the time, else they'd be taking an awful risk. They might have got away with it on the Continent but they'd be taking a bit of a gamble here at Sedgwick if the ladies were back at home in the Highlands.'

'I'm not sure I follow all that, Lane. But we have it on good authority that Miss Montacute and Miss Wentmore are not at home. Although you might have a point there, Sergeant, about them having some connections with the Montacute family. But, from what we know of the real Miss Montacute, she lived the life almost of a recluse. There wouldn't be much mention of her made in the newspapers, if any. The impostors, if that is what they are, needn't have been afraid Lord Belvedere would open his copy of *The Times* over breakfast one morning only to find that Miss Montacute was reported as having gone to some society do or the other the night before.'

'What would be their game, I wonder, sir? Do you think it would be the same as the count's malarkey? They had a very valuable diamond necklace in their possession, we mustn't forget that, sir. That's of some interest, don't you think? Hello, there's the telephone.'

The inspector pounced on the instrument much as a cat would a mouse and held the receiver up to his ear. The sergeant meanwhile lingered by the door, reluctant to leave. He listened with interest to Inspector Bramwell's half of the conversation, which was disappointingly lacking in providing any clarity as to what had been discovered, consisting as it did of little more than grunts and one word answers.

'What!' The inspector had almost dropped the receiver in his excitement. 'Read it to me again, slowly this time mind … hmm … Are you sure it says that? It couldn't be some other initials? No? … Are you quite sure? … Very good … And where did you say you found it? … Have a man drive down with it to me at once, will you? … Of course I need it today! No it can't wait until tomorrow. I want to have it in my hand when I interview … Now listen to me, my man … What? … Yes, that'll do nicely. I'll expect it within the hour.'

The inspector hung up the telephone receiver and gave the sergeant a look of triumph.

'Well, sir? Was that young constable right after all? What have they found? Does it prove who the murderer is?'

'So many questions, Sergeant. But as regards the most important one … you could say that, Lane,' the inspector replied, grinning. 'As good as, anyway. Well, well, well. What a turn up for the books.'

'As good as proved the murderer? I'm not sure I follow you, sir.'

'Then I'll tell you, Sergeant. We now know why Miss Montacute went to the maze when she did. And what is more, we know the identity of the person she went to meet.'

'Do I take it then, sir, you won't be wanting to interview Miss Wentmore now after all?' enquired Sergeant Lane. 'Even if I do find something in her room or Miss Montacute's which would substantiate Miss Simpson's theory concerning those two ladies?'

'No, Sergeant. We'll speak to her later. I think our investigations are pointing us in another way, don't you?' He sat down heavily in his chair. 'You carry on with your searching of the ladies' rooms and then we'll have our tea. By that time the others should have finished theirs and that package will have arrived from the mortuary. I don't want to interview the doctor until I have it in my hands and can show him. Have a word with the servants and tell them they're to bring the parcel to me as soon as it arrives.'

'Here's the package you were asking for, Charlie,' said one of the hall boys passing over an envelope to the footman. 'You should have seen the motor the man was driving who brought it! He said he'd driven like the wind on account of the inspector requiring it immediate like. Said it was a valuable piece of evidence and that I weren't to lose it.'

'Did he, indeed? Sounds to me he said rather too much,' the footman said laughing. 'Don't let Mr Manning catch you passing on gossip.'

'Mr Manning's all right. It's Mr Torridge I'm scared of. Not that he'd be able to catch me these days, what with him being so doddery.'

'You cheeky young scallywag! I've a good mind to box your ears for you, myself.'

The boy laughed and ran off just as the under-butler appeared.

'What have you got there, Charlie? Is that the package the inspector's been expecting?'

'Yes, Mr Manning. It doesn't seem much, does it? Just an envelope. By the feel of it, I'd hardly have thought there was a letter inside.'

'Well, you'd best take it into the inspector, Charlie. It's not up to the likes of us to decide what's important and what's not in a murder investigation.'

Chapter Twenty-three

Both policemen eyed the doctor with considerable interest as he was shown into the study. They saw a man in his late twenties or early thirties, clean shaven except for a neat moustache and rather handsome in a country doctor type of a way, as Lavinia had so eloquently put it to Rose. His appearance was such that they imagined his complexion was usually rubicund, and not the sickly hue of grey it was now. This, coupled with the dark shadows under his eyes, and his skin, which looked taut across his face, gave the overall impression of a man suffering from grief.

'Sit down please, Dr Harrison,' said the inspector, indicating the chair that had been placed on the opposite side of the desk. 'If you don't mind my saying, you don't look at all well. Perhaps you'd like a glass of water?'

Theo's only acknowledgement of the question was to shake his head wearily and pass a hand through his hair. For a moment or two he studied the floor rather than Inspector Bramwell's face. If he was physically present, his mind appeared to be elsewhere, focused on something a long way off in the far distance. The doctor seemed only vaguely conscious of where he was, as if he were just waking from a dream to find that none of it had been real.

'Just for the record, sir, will you give us your full name, please?'

'Theodore Harrison.' Theo said, and then added as an afterthought: 'Doctor.'

He spoke in a flat voice, which gave the impression of the speaker being bored. The inspector frowned. He had a particular dislike of monotone voices for the very reason that such voices did not rise or fall in pitch and as a consequence gave no indication of how the speaker was really feeling. He stared at Theo, trying to take in the measure of the man. He reminded himself that the fellow was a doctor, used to dealing with all types of tragedies and sad cases. In Inspector Bramwell's view a voice with no expression would be a considerable disadvantage to someone in Dr Harrison's profession. He concluded therefore that this was not the doctor's usual voice, but rather his way of coping with his own personal tragedy. There was always the possibility therefore that the man could be provoked into showing some emotion.

'Your middle name too, if you please, Dr Harrison. I take it you have one?'

The doctor made a face.

'Does it by any chance begin with an 'E'?'

'Begin with an 'E'? How the devil did you know that?' The doctor stared at the policeman with his mouth open. 'Oh … never mind. Yes … If you must know, I was christened Theodore Ebenezer Harrison. I've never been particularly fond of the name Ebenezer. Try not to use it if I can. Sounds damned old-fashioned if you ask me. It reminds me of that character in *A Christmas Carol*.'

'But it is your middle name?'

'It is.'

It was not lost on the doctor, even in his befuddled state, that the inspector exchanged a look with his sergeant. He swallowed hard and looked at the floor.

'Tell me about your relationship with Miss Montacute, Dr Harrison.'

'My … my relationship with Miss Montacute?'

'Yes. Was there a love affair between you and Miss Montacute?'

'Certainly not!'

Theo visibly stiffened, and the inspector was relieved to hear the two words uttered loudly and with feeling. It appeared that gone was the man who showed no emotion.

'Come, Dr Harrison, this really will not do. We are aware that an attachment had formed between yourself and Miss Montacute.'

'I wouldn't listen to servants' idle tittle-tattle if I were you, Inspector.'

'No? And yet we find it can be very informative. But as it happens, one or two of Lord Belvedere's guests also advised us of your relationship with Miss Montacute.'

'Did they indeed? People should learn to hold their tongues. If you are so well informed, I am surprised that you bother to ask me about it.'

'It is always as well to have it confirmed from the person most involved in the matter.'

'Very well,' Theo said testily. 'I adored Miss Montacute. Everyone who knew her found her very beguiling.'

'Is that so? Even Miss Brewster?'

'No ... Not Miss Brewster.'

A splash of colour had appeared on the doctor's cheeks, making his face appear less ashen.

'It would be as well to tell us the truth, Dr Harrison,' said Inspector Bramwell, impatiently. 'We've no time to play games. Were you, or were you not, in love with the deceased?'

'Yes ... yes, I was.'

The words were uttered quietly, but with enough emotion for the inspector to pause a moment in his questioning.

'And she with you?'

'I think so ... yes.'

'It has been suggested to us,' said Inspector Bramwell, not altogether truthfully, 'that you formed a relationship with Miss Montacute in an attempt to further your career.'

'No! Who said that?'

This time Theo rose from his seat, his eyes blazing.

'Sit down, please, Dr Harrison. Is it not correct that you aspire to be a fashionable London doctor? A wealthy patient or two would help you on your way, wouldn't it?'

'It is true that I don't want to stay in Sedgwick all my life and be just another country doctor. But that had nothing to do with my relationship with Miss Montacute, I assure you. I loved her, Inspector.'

'Did you indeed? And pray what of Miss Brewster, your fiancée? I take it she did not take too kindly to this attachment?'

'No ... you are right ... I must have hurt her dreadfully. But I'm afraid I wasn't thinking of her feelings. It is awful to say it, but I just didn't care. I daresay you'll think me a rotten sort of a fellow and I suppose I am. I know I behaved very badly, not like a man of honour. I can't explain it. I couldn't think of anything or anyone but Emmeline. She consumed my every thought, Inspector.' Theo put his head in his hands and finally broke down. 'Heaven help me, she still does.'

There was an uncomfortable silence as the policemen waited for the doctor to recover his composure. It took rather longer than either man had anticipated. Sergeant Lane put down his pencil and fumbled inside his double-breasted jacket pocket for a clean handkerchief, which he passed to the man. It appeared that, having finally succumbed to his emotions, Theo Harrison had little inclination to return to the silent, brooding figure of a man he had been before.

'There are those here who think you made a bit of a fool of yourself over Miss Montacute, Dr Harrison,' said the inspector, not altogether kindly. 'They are of the opinion that you behaved disgracefully towards Miss Brewster and made her quite miserable. It made for an unhappy atmosphere, I've been given to understand. Apparently everyone felt it, even the servants.'

'Yes … I suppose they did. I'm not proud of the way I behaved, if that's what you're thinking. I just couldn't help myself. I have never felt before about a woman as I did about Emmeline.'

The inspector snorted.

'I am sure Miss Brewster would be delighted to hear you say that. To know that she never meant anything to you.'

'That's not what I said, Inspector,' Theo said, somewhat defensively. 'As it happens, I was very fond of Miss Brewster. I thought she would make an excellent doctor's wife.'

'Do you think she will take you back, when this business is all over and done with?'

'The awful thing is, Inspector, I think she would.' He gave a rather pathetic laugh. 'She wants me back now, you know. Emmeline is not even dead in the ground and she wants me to go back to her.' He sighed. 'I won't of course.'

'Now tell us about last night, Dr Harrison. Let's start with after dinner, shall we?'

'After dinner? Oh … so Cedric …Lord Belvedere's told you?'

'Told us what, Dr Harrison?'

'About our little talk,' Theo said, a little bitterly. 'As a rule, we didn't tend to linger over the port and cigars. We found it a little awkward because of the count. It was damned difficult to make conversation with the fellow. He was a dab hand at keeping the ladies enthralled. Laughed a good deal with them and flattered them rotten. But he had difficulty joining in our conversations. I don't think our company interested him much.'

'Your talk with Lord Belvedere?' prompted the inspector.

'I am sure I have nothing more to add to that which Lord Belvedere has already told you.'

'Actually, sir, Lord ...' began Sergeant Lane before faltering on receiving a glare from the inspector.

'Even so, sir,' said Inspector Bramwell, ignoring the sergeant's interjection. 'We'd like to have your recollection of the conversation.'

'Very well, Inspector. It was all rather humiliating if you must know. Lord Belvedere told me I was making a damned fool of myself over Miss Montacute. Said everyone was unsettled by it. He informed me that I was making Vera miserable, and that he would not have his guests made upset.'

'I see. Did Lord Belvedere say anything else?'

'He said that I was to resolve the situation, otherwise he would have no alternative but to ask me to leave.'

'I see.'

'I was jolly angry about it at the time, I can tell you. I didn't think it was any of his damned business what I did.' Theo looked down at his hands, clasped in his lap, before looking up. 'If you must know, Inspector, I felt ashamed. To be reprimanded for my conduct by a man eight or ten years my junior I found rather demeaning. Not least because I knew he was right.'

'Tell me about the maze now would you, sir.'

'The maze? What do you want to know about it? You've been to see it yourself, haven't you? It was where Emmeline's body was found ... Oh ... I can't bear it!'

'Please, sir. If you'd just humour me. Had you ever been in the maze before?'

'Of course, a good few times I should think. I grew up in the village of Sedgwick. I've lived here all my life. I'm considerably older than Lord Belvedere and Lady Lavinia, of course, but Miss Brewster is only a few years older than them. They used to play together as children. I've walked with Miss Brewster a few times through the maze when we've been visiting Sedgwick Court.'

'So you would know your way through the maze without using a plan or map?'

'Yes, I suppose so.' Theo looked at the inspector a little warily. 'I can't say I have ever had occasion to walk through the maze by myself. It is not the sort of thing one does. But I daresay I could make a fair stab at making my way to the middle ... and back out again, if that's what you are asking. But if you're suggesting that I had – '

'I'm not suggesting anything at the moment, Dr Harrison,' replied the inspector firmly. 'I am given to understand that after dinner in the drawing room the maze was discussed and a game was proposed for today?'

'Yes ... yes, it was. A silly sort of a game. But I daresay it would have been quite fun. Emmeline was very keen to take part, I remember that. And then she was ... Oh!'

'Now, now, Dr Harrison, calm yourself. You'd do better not to dwell on Miss Montacute's death just now. The best thing you can do for all concerned is to answer my questions as truthfully and accurately as you can.'

'Yes, inspector.' The doctor's voice had returned to its weary state.

'Last night, Dr Harrison. I'd like you to go through your movements if you would. What did you do last night?'

'What did I do?'

'After the others had retired for the night.'

'Oh ... so you know about that too, do you? I say, you do seem very well informed. You appear to know about everything.'

Sergeant Lane dropped his pencil on to the floor and Inspector Bramwell took a deep breath, wondering how best to proceed.

'We know a great deal, sir. But I'd like you to tell me about it in your own words.'

'Very well. I asked Vera to meet me in the library before she followed the others upstairs. I told her I had something important to tell her that wouldn't wait 'til morning.'

'And Miss Brewster obliged?'

'She did, Inspector.' Theo looked down at his hands. 'To tell you the truth, it was awful. You should have seen the look on her face. She thought I was going to say I was sorry about everything and that it was all over with Miss Montacute. That we'd go back to the way we had been.'

'And you didn't say that?'

'No, of course not. Far from it. I told her that I knew I had behaved very badly towards her. That she deserved a far better man than me, and that I was breaking off our engagement as much for her sake as for mine.'

'I see. Now, bear with me if you will, Dr Harrison. Are you saying that you broke off your engagement to Miss Brewster last night?'

Inspector Bramwell had sat up in his chair, and Sergeant Lane had looked up from his notebook. Aware of the interest his words had caused, Theo's cheeks turned crimson.

'Yes. I am. I broke off my engagement with Miss Brewster last night.'

'And how did Miss Brewster take such news? I daresay it came as a bit of a shock, didn't it?'

'I'm afraid, I don't know, Inspector.'

'What do you mean you don't know?' The inspector looked at him incredulously.

'Exactly that, Inspector. I told Miss Brewster I wished to break off our engagement and I left the room.'

Theo glared at the inspector, his cheeks going redder still.

It occurred to Inspector Bramwell that the young man's complexion had changed a great deal during the course of their interview, when compared with the sickly pallor of his skin on entering the room.

'You needn't look at me like that, Inspector. I freely admit I was a coward. A better man than me would have stayed and endured Miss Brewster's tears and recriminations, but I'm afraid I didn't. I'd made up my mind, you see, and I wanted out of it.' He glanced at the carpet. 'And anyway, I thought it would be best for Vera. I thought she'd prefer it. To be left there alone to take it all in.'

The inspector's only comment was to snort.

'You didn't think it might have been better to speak to her in the morning instead of last thing at night?'

'No. I wanted to do it there and then. I've told you. I wanted to get it over and done with. I thought it would be better that way, for Miss Brewster as well as for me. I thought she'd have the whole night to come to terms with it, and that when she came down to breakfast in the morning she would be composed and not too upset.'

The inspector thought of Vera left alone in the library waiting for everyone else to go up to bed so that she might creep upstairs without her tear-stained face being observed. He imagined her lying in her bed, pulling the bedclothes up to her neck, feeling absolutely miserable and dejected. That she had endured a sleepless night he did not doubt for one moment. He stared at the man before him who had caused her such anguish.

'What did you do then, Dr Harrison?'

'I went up to bed.'

'You didn't try and communicate with Miss Montacute to tell her that you had broken off your engagement to Miss Brewster?'

'Of course not, Inspector, it was terribly late.'

'But not too late to break off your engagement to Miss Brewster?'

'I've already told you my reasons for speaking with Miss Brewster when I did,' Theo said coldly.

'When did you speak with Miss Montacute?'

'I didn't, Inspector. I had decided to speak with her straight after breakfast this morning. I was going to tell her I had broken off my engagement to Miss Brewster.' Theo took a deep breath as if he were trying to stifle a sob. 'If you must know, I was going to ask Miss Montacute to marry me.'

'Were you indeed?'

'Yes, I was.' Theo began to sob. 'She'll never know now, will she? She will never know that I had broken off my engagement to Vera and was going to ask her to marry me. She'll never know ...'

'Forgive me, Dr Harrison. But are you quite sure that you didn't arrange to meet with Miss Montacute before breakfast? In the maze for instance?'

'Certainly not! Why should I have arranged to meet Emmeline in there of all places? There are far better places to meet for a romantic assignation if that's what you're getting at. The grounds are full of follies for goodness sake.'

'And yet Miss Montacute was found dead in the maze,' the inspector said, quietly. 'Shall I tell you what I think? I think someone did arrange to meet Miss Montacute in the maze. I think that's why she was there. And do you know what else I think, doctor?'

'No.'

Theo spoke the word hardly above a whisper and seemed to hold his breath.

'I think that person was you.'

'What utter nonsense!'

Theo had risen so violently from his seat that his chair threatened to topple over. 'How dare you suggest such a thing? I loved Miss Montacute, Inspector. I loved her. If you're suggesting I had any hand in her murder, why I'll – '

'Sit down, Dr Harrison. Before you get on to your high horse, there's something I'd like to show you.'

'Oh?'

Theo sat down again, taken aback by the inspector's manner, but equally interested in what he was about to say.

Inspector Bramwell proceeded to pick up an envelope from the desk, the same one Charlie, the footman, had brought into him earlier. He withdrew from it a torn off scrap of paper, and passed it to the doctor.

'Perhaps you'd like to read this out to us, if you will, Dr Harrison.'

Theo held the scrap of paper between his hands. It had obviously been much folded, the consequence of which was to make the words written on it difficult to read. To make matters worse, the ink had been smudged in places, as if the writer had been in a great hurry and had not had the foresight to use a blotter, or alternatively had been too impatient to wait for the ink to quite dry.

Theo held up the paper to his eyes and read each word one at a time, in a disjointed fashion.

'"Meet me in the middle of the maze at a quarter to six tomorrow morning … I enclose a copy of the plan with this note ... Go out by way of the French windows in the study. They are bolted but not locked … Don't be late … I have something of the utmost importance to tell you."'

'Would you be so good as to read out the initials at the bottom of that note?'

'"T … E … H." Oh my God! No!'

'They are your initials are they not, Doctor?'

'Yes … No … Yes. You know full well they are. But I didn't write this note. I tell you I didn't write it!'

'And yet they are your initials, are they not, Doctor? I don't think anyone else in this house has the same initials.'

'Where did you find it?' demanded Theo.

'Folded up inside Miss Montacute's glove. She evidently tucked it inside her glove before she set off for the maze. There was no sign of the plan though.'

'I didn't write that note I tell you.' Theo's face contorted suddenly with a look of pain. 'I didn't write it, but Emmeline would have thought I had, wouldn't she? That's why she went there, isn't it? She thought she was going to meet me!' He held his head in his hands. 'Oh my God, oh my God ...'

'Look at the note again, Dr Harrison. If you didn't write it, do you know who did? Do you recognise the handwriting?'

Theo held the note up to his eyes again. This time the policeman saw him give an involuntary start.

'No ... no, I don't, Inspector.'

'Are you quite certain? You reacted just now as if you had.'

'I don't recognise it.' The doctor fixed the policeman with a cold stare. 'I think I've answered enough of your questions, don't you? I should like to go now, if you please.'

Chapter Twenty-four

'Well, what do you think, sir?' Sergeant Lane asked, as soon as Theo had left the room slamming the door shut behind him. 'Do you think he recognised the handwriting?'

'Oh, he recognised it all right!' snorted the inspector. 'Because it was his own!'

'You don't think it possible that he recognised it as someone else's? '

'No, I don't, Sergeant. I think the man's been lying to us from the moment he sat down in that chair there. Look how he tried to deny that he'd had a relationship with the deceased. Only admitted it when we said the others had told us about it.'

'You could be right, sir.'

'Like as not he's pretending to us that he's recognised the handwriting as being someone else's to try and throw us off the scent,' said Inspector Bramwell, rising from his creaking chair to stretch his legs. 'It must have come as an awful shock to him to discover that we'd found that note. He didn't expect us to. Probably thought the girl had had the good sense to throw it on to the fire before she set off for the maze. I've no doubt it gave him quite a turn having it handed to him like that.'

'You don't like the fellow very much, do you, sir?' enquired Sergeant Lane rather boldly.

'No I don't. Men like that think a lot of themselves. He's rather a handsome fellow, I grant you. But he's a big fish in a small pond and he has ambitions to be a big fish in a large pond. From what we've been told, he treated Miss Brewster very shabbily, very shabbily indeed.'

'He's something of a coward too, isn't he, sir? Fancy just leaving poor Miss Brewster in the library without making sure she was all right.'

'Aye, he's a selfish fellow all right,' agreed the inspector. 'Only thinks of himself I should imagine. And, did you see how he was all up and down like a yo-yo? One moment he could barely bring himself to speak, and the next he was jumping up from his chair threatening to knock it over and shout the place down.'

'He seems to me to have gone all to pieces over Miss Montacute's death though, sir,' Sergeant Lane said. 'Must have thought a lot of her. Do you think he'd be so upset if he had killed her?'

'It strikes me that he is just the sort of a fellow who'd work himself up into a temper and hit a woman, and then regret it afterwards. Do you know what I think happened, Sergeant?'

'What, sir?'

'I think it's just as he says, up to a point. He breaks off his engagement with Miss Brewster in just the manner he says, and then goes upstairs. He wants to go and tell Miss Montacute what he's done, but it's late and he can't do so without the possibility of ruining her reputation. But he doesn't want to have to wait until breakfast. So he scribbles that note to her and pushes it under her door. He probably taps on her door at the same time to make sure she sees it.'

'But I don't understand why he should want to kill her, sir.'

'Don't you, Sergeant? I think he lost his temper. Just as he did in here, jumping up and down. I think they met up in the maze as planned – '

'But why the maze, sir,' interrupted Sergeant Lane. 'Why not meet up in one of the follies as the doctor himself pointed out?'

'Because of that romantic story Lord Belvedere and Lady Lavinia told about that unfortunate maid who got herself lost in the maze waiting for her young man to appear. Dr Harrison had probably heard that story a number of times before, and we've been told that Emmeline Montacute was quite taken with the idea of the maze game. There was little fear that they'd get lost. He had provided Miss Montacute with a plan of the maze and the doctor himself by his own admission knew his way through it.'

'So what do you think happened?'

'I think our doctor told Miss Montacute that he'd broken off his engagement with Miss Brewster and, being the impetuous sort of fellow he appears to be, probably went down on one knee and proposed marriage. He as good as told us that's what he was going to do this morning.'

'Yes, he did. But what happened?'

'I think she took fright, and turned down his proposal. Or possibly she did something much worse from his point of view …'

'What could have been worse than that from his perspective?'

'Remember I said he was a proud fellow who thought a lot of himself? I think she may have laughed at him. I imagine she told him she considered their relationship little more than a dalliance, a mild flirtation if you will, entered into for her own amusement. She probably reminded him who she was. An heiress and a beautiful one at that, with her choice of far more eligible suitors than a country doctor.'

'And you think he flew into a fit of temper because of it and killed her?' asked Sergeant Lane, sounding rather sceptical.

'I certainly think it a possibility. And I think he's regretted it ever since.'

'You may be right of course, sir. But there's something that's worrying me.'

'And what's that, Sergeant?'

'How does the candlestick fit into your story?'

'A very good point, Lane,' sighed the inspector, going back to his chair and sitting down. 'That damned candlestick. How the devil does it fit in? For the life of me I can't imagine why anyone should take such an object with them into the maze.'

'Theo!'

Vera was upon the doctor as soon as he came into the drawing room.

'Vera, not now. Leave me alone, damn you!'

Theo took hold of the woman by the arm and pushed her out of his way with such force that she knocked into an occasional table, which toppled and fell over bringing its contents of a lead crystal vase and a silver-framed photograph down with it. Miraculously the glass in both ornaments did not shatter. But it had been enough of a spectacle to cause all those present to look on with a morbid fascination.

'Harrison!'

Cedric grasped the man roughly by the arm and frogmarched him to the other end of the room. Rose meanwhile went over to Vera who, although shaken, appeared unhurt.

'You must let him be, Vera. Can't you see how upset he is? You're only making matters worse.'

'I just want to help him. To let him know that I'm here for him.'

'Why? Don't you realise, Vera? He doesn't want you to be there for him.'

Vera shrank back from her as if she had been hit. Her bottom lip trembled and she looked pale and drawn.

'When I say he doesn't want you to be there for him, I mean now. I daresay he'll need you later,' Rose said more kindly. 'But please, Vera, see sense. You must give him time.'

It was all Rose could do to keep herself from telling the woman exactly what she thought. In her own opinion Theo had behaved very badly towards Vera and the woman could do much better for herself than settle for a man who had treated her so shabbily. Theo did not deserve Vera's loyalty or devotion. It incensed her that he should know that Vera was eager to take him back and pretend that what had happened between him and Emmeline was no more than a figment of her own vivid imagination. It was on the tip of her tongue to say something to this effect. But looking at Vera now, nodding feebly and looking as if she were about to fall apart, Rose knew it would do no good. Vera would never listen to reason where Theo was concerned.

'I only wanted to speak to him. He was in with the policemen for such a long time, wasn't he? He was in there for much longer than Felix or the count. Why do you think that was, Rose? Do you think they suspect him? Do you think they think he murdered Emmeline?'

'I don't know, Vera. We'll just have to wait and see. But it won't do any good worrying about it.'

'Do you think they'll want to interview me next?'

Vera sounded frightened. She clutched Rose's hand and held it so tightly that it hurt.

'I'm scared, Rose. I'm ever so scared. I don't want to be interviewed. I don't want them to ask me questions about Theo and Emmeline. I won't be able to bear it. I tell you I won't be able to bear it!'

'Ssh, Vera,' Rose said hurriedly, conscious that the woman's voice had risen and that the constable stationed in the corner of the room was eyeing them somewhat suspiciously. 'Don't make a scene. Not now. There's nothing to worry about. It's just routine. The police are interviewing all of us.'

'Will you come in with me, Rose? Please. I don't want to go in there alone. And you know all about being interviewed and murder investigations, don't you?' She pulled at Rose's sleeve so that the girl was obliged to bend her head down so Vera could whisper in her ear. 'I've done something very wicked, Rose. Frightfully wicked. And I'm frightened to tell them about it. Will you come in there with me when they interview me? I want to tell them everything. But I need you to come in with me, otherwise I'll never have the courage to do so. Will you? Say you will?'

'If they allow me to, yes, of course,' Rose said, wondering what Vera had to tell them and whether it would further her own investigations.

'Thank you.' Vera stood up tall, with her shoulders back. She stared fixedly at the door, a grave and determined look upon her face. 'I feel much braver now. Now that I know you'll be coming with me. I want to tell them all about it. It will be such a relief.'

Rose followed Vera's gaze to the door and it seemed to her that together they had willed the door to open. For at that very moment they saw the door handle move, followed by Sergeant Lane entering the room. He scoured those present, his eye settling on Vera, standing there clutching Rose's hand.

'The inspector would like to speak to you next, Miss Brewster. If you'd care to come this way please, miss.'

'I want Miss Simpson to come in with me, Sergeant,' Vera said in a surprisingly firm voice.

'Well, I don't know, miss, whether the inspector will ...'

The policeman's sentence faltered, for Vera had already walked purposefully over to the door and disappeared into the hall beyond, Rose following in her wake, much as Jemima had done in Emmeline's.

'Ah, Miss Brewster, do come in,' said Inspector Bramwell, smiling reassuringly at Vera. He caught sight of Rose and the smile vanished from his lips. 'Ah, Miss Simpson. I didn't see you there. What can I do for you?'

'I asked Miss Simpson to come in with me, Inspector,' answered Vera before Rose was obliged to say anything. 'She has experience of these things, you know.'

'Yes ... I do know.'

'Well, I need her here so that I can answer your questions. If I'm here by myself ... well ... I don't think I will have the necessary courage to answer your questions properly.'

'Courage?' A puzzled look crossed the inspector's face. 'Really, Miss Brewster, you don't need to have courage to answer my questions. I daresay you may find my questions rather intrusive. But I hope you won't find me frightening,' he chuckled. 'Unless of course you have something to hide.'

'That's just it, Inspector. I have. I'd much rather not tell you about it, but I know that I must. Otherwise you'll think Theo had a hand in Emmeline's murder, and he didn't. I promise you he didn't. He'd never hurt anyone. Why, he's a doctor. He saves lives and makes people better. He'd never kill anyone. He couldn't.'

The image of Theo knocking Vera into the table came into Rose's mind unbidden. She remembered too the rough way the doctor had spoken to the woman. He had been trying not to lose his temper, but he had failed to keep it in check. It seemed to her that Theo Harrison was very much the type of man who might hurt someone.

'What makes you believe that we think Dr Harrison murdered Miss Montacute, Miss Brewster?'

The inspector's face now looked rather grave. Rose thought he also looked apprehensive, almost as if he were afraid of what Vera was going to say next.

'He was in here for such a long time,' explained Vera. 'And he looked absolutely awful when he came back into the drawing room, didn't he, Rose?'

'Some people find being interviewed more difficult than others,' said the policeman. 'It's when they try to keep things back or not tell us the whole truth. It does them no good, no good at all.'

'Did Dr Harrison do that?' Vera asked anxiously.

'Now, miss, we're not here to talk about Dr Harrison. We're here to talk about you. Don't worry your head about the doctor.'

'But I love him,' Vera said.

Both her voice and choice of words sounded rather pathetic, and the others stood there awkwardly, not quite knowing how to respond. It was the inspector who recovered first.

'Right, sit down there, if you will please, Miss Brewster.'

'And Miss Simpson, where – '

'It's all right, miss. Miss Simpson can stay as long as she doesn't interrupt. Sergeant, place that chair next to Miss Brewster's, will you.' The inspector turned to fix Rose with a not altogether friendly stare. 'Now, Miss Simpson, I'm allowing you to stay here on account of Miss Brewster seeming to need you here. But I must warn you not – '

'It's all right, Inspector,' Rose said, quickly. 'I've done this before.'

'I'm sure you have. But you needn't think that I'm as tolerant of this sort of thing as Inspector Deacon. Now, Miss Brewster.' The inspector had obviously decided to adopt his kind, fatherly tone again. 'I daresay you'll find this a little distressing, embarrassing even, but I'd like you to tell me about Miss Montacute, if you will.'

'I hated her.'

'Vera! I think you should – '

'Miss Simpson, will you please not interrupt! Go on, please, Miss Brewster.'

'I didn't hate her at first, of course. But I was frightened of her.'

'Perhaps you could explain, Miss Brewster?'

'I was worried when I heard Lavinia had invited an heiress to stay. I shouldn't have been surprised, of course. It was just the sort of thing she would do.' Vera sighed, and pulled at her handkerchief. 'But it changed everything. Theo is very ambitious, Inspector. He thinks he wants to be a doctor in London with a practice in Harley Street. But he wouldn't like that at all, I know he wouldn't. He cares about treating real people, making a difference to ordinary people's lives with his medicine.'

Vera pulled so violently at the material of her handkerchief that Rose wondered whether she would rip it.

'Theo has a weakness for the aristocracy and the landed gentry. He wants to associate with them and have them respect him. He thinks they can help further his career. I knew he'd view Miss Montacute as a potential wealthy patient.'

'Please proceed, Miss Brewster.'

'I thought that was all there was to it at first. Theo trying to secure a rich patient. I didn't think there was any more to it than that. Of course I noticed that they spent a lot of time together, giggling and laughing and that sort of thing. Theo can be quite charming when he wants to be. Then Lavinia said something particularly spiteful ... the day before yesterday, I think it was. Something about Theo enjoying the company of Emmeline rather too much for her liking and that I should make more effort with my dress. You remember, don't you, Rose? You were there, weren't you?'

Rose nodded but said nothing, keen not to catch the inspector's disapproving eye.

'I'd rather been thinking the same thing myself, but hoping that I was wrong. But to find that even Lavinia of all people had noticed. Well, it really was too much. I imagined all sorts of things, you know, about people talking behind my back saying all sorts of horrid things like what a fool I was not to have noticed or put a stop to it. Of course,' Vera averted her gaze to take in the carpet, 'it didn't help that I'd had a bit to drink.'

'I beg your pardon, miss?'

'I'm afraid that when I'm a bit nervous or upset I have a bit to drink. Not so much that I can't walk in a straight line or I slur my words. Nothing like that. I don't think anyone else would really notice. They don't lock the drinks away here at Sedgwick as they do in some houses. They trust their servants here. So you see, it's easy to help oneself to a drink if one wants to.'

'I see.'

'I'm afraid you'll think I was rather beastly to Emmeline. I couldn't get it out of my head that Lavinia was laughing at me. And Emmeline seemed so happy while I was so miserable. It didn't seem fair. So I mentioned the kidnapping. But I had absolutely no idea that Emmeline and Jemima would be so upset. And then Theo ... the way he looked at me ... the way he spoke to me and what he said ... I have never seen him so angry. And then he put his arm around her ... Emmeline, I mean. He cared about her, but he didn't care about me at all. It was awful.'

Vera put her hand to her forehead, as if she were trying to block out the image.

'And then Count Fernand suggested you all play a type of parlour game? Looking at each other's diamonds and the like through his jeweller's lens?'

'Yes. He did. It was awfully kind of him. Of course, it was only Emmeline and Lavinia who had diamonds worth looking at. I don't know what would have happened if he hadn't suggested that entertainment. I'd probably have rushed out of the room and gone up to bed. I might even have packed and left next day before breakfast.' Vera paused and said in a voice hardly above a whisper so that the others only just caught her words: 'I should have done that ... If only I'd done that.'

'Now, I'd like you to go through the events of yesterday for us if you will, Miss Brewster. Shall we start with your walk in the grounds with Miss Simpson yesterday morning? I understand you asked Dr Harrison if he'd care to join you, but that he declined.'

'He said he had work to do,' said Vera. Her voice had taken on a bitter tone. 'I was silly enough to believe him, Inspector. But he lied. He didn't. He just didn't want to walk with me. He wanted to be with *her*.'

'Perhaps you will tell me about this walk, will you, Miss Brewster?'

Vera rubbed her forehead and closed her eyes.

'There isn't much to say, Inspector. At least nothing new to add to what Miss Simpson must already have told you. Let me see. Yes ... we walked in the grounds, didn't we, Rose? I remember us chattering quite happily about one thing or another. I tried to impress upon you how ridiculous Lavinia was being suggesting that Theo was fond of Emmeline. I had quite convinced myself that what I was saying was the truth.'

'And then?'

'We came across Mr Thistlewaite and Miss Wentmore in the gardens. They were sitting on a bench with their backs to us, so they didn't see us. It was all rather embarrassing because they didn't know we were there and they were – '

'Excuse me, Miss Brewster. Miss Simpson, you didn't mention anything about this.'

'Didn't I? I'm sorry, Inspector, I must have forgotten,' Rose said, and then added rather pointedly: 'I rather think you were wanting me to tell you about something else at the time.'

'I'm sorry, Miss Brewster, do go on,' said the inspector, frowning.

'Really. It was all rather sad. They were talking about how they didn't think they could bear to be apart from one another. They were saying that of course they would write, but that it wouldn't be the same thing at all. Then Jemima said something about not having to wait … yes … now what was it? She sounded very serious. Don't you remember, Rose? Now what did she say exactly? Yes … something about what if she could get her hands on some money now.'

'Oh. Did she indeed?'

'Yes, we didn't hear any more. We felt a bit awkward that we had listened in, however unintentionally, to what was obviously a private conversation. I think it was then that we decided to walk down by the lake.'

Vera's voice had suddenly become quieter, and Rose leaned forward in her seat and squeezed the woman's hand.

'It was then that we saw Theo and Emmeline by the lake. It was awful. They were – '

'It's all right, Miss Brewster. Miss Simpson has told us all about it.'

'It was awfully odd in a sad sort of way,' Vera said, her eyes filling with tears. 'Because do you know what kept going through my mind? It was that Theo had lied to me. He had pretended to be busy with his work, when all the time he wasn't. I remember feeling frightfully angry about it. And of course it hurt damnably, Inspector. Seeing Theo and Emmeline like that. So in love. I don't think Theo and I were ever like that.'

'You didn't think to confront Dr Harrison?'

'No. I should have done of course. But it was such a shock. And then before I could do anything they had disappeared. They hadn't seen us, you see. I remember standing there feeling sick and afraid I was going to go to pieces. You were there, Rose, and I suddenly wanted more than anything else in the world to be alone. Part of me wanted to forget what I had seen, and another part of me wanted to think about nothing else.'

'So you went to your room?'

'Yes, I spent all day there. I didn't come down for lunch or tea. Lavinia arranged for my meals to be sent up on a tray, but I didn't eat anything. I just moved the food around on the plate. I felt frightfully lightheaded when I came down for dinner.'

'What happened when you did?'

'Nothing. I don't think Theo had even noticed that I had been absent all day. He didn't come over to me to see if I was feeling better.' Vera looked wearily at Inspector Bramwell. 'That was the excuse I gave, Inspector, for staying in my room.' She sighed. 'It was as if I wasn't there. As if I didn't exist for all the notice they took of me, Theo and Emmeline. I hated them both like poison, parading their feelings for each other for all of us to see. But most of all I hated her. Emmeline Montacute. She could have had any man she wanted and she'd chosen mine.'

Vera laughed, a shrill little laugh that made the others feel uneasy.

'Do you remember, Rose, how concerned you were about me? Do you remember what I said? You were afraid they'd overhear.'

'Vera …'

'Go on Miss Brewster. What did you say to Miss Simpson?'

'I said how much I hated them and I wished they were dead.'

'Did you indeed?'

'I'm afraid I've shocked you, Inspector. But that isn't the worst of it. There's more – '

'Vera!'

'Miss Simpson! Will you please stop interrupting? If you can't keep quiet, I shall ask you to leave.'

'I'm worried about Miss Brewster, Inspector. Vera, have you been drinking?'

'A little bit … yes. But I'm quite all right, Rose. I want to tell the Inspector everything. You heard him, Rose. He wants me to. He doesn't want me to withhold anything.'

'Inspector. I don't think Miss Brewster is feeling quite well.'

'I've only a few more questions to ask her, Miss Simpson, and then she can go.'

'Miss Brewster, Dr Harrison told us that before you retired for the night he asked you to meet him in the library as he had something important to say to you.'

'Yes. He broke off our engagement, if that's what you're referring to?'

'I am.'

'He just announced it. As if … as if it didn't matter. And then he just walked out of the room. He didn't wait to hear what I had to say. He didn't … make certain I was all right. He … he knew how much I loved him. He knew. And he didn't care!' Vera's voice had risen and now she was crying, tears falling freely down her cheeks.

'Inspector, please.'

'All right, Miss Simpson. I only have one more question to ask Miss Brewster. Then she can go.'

The inspector turned his attention to Vera. He withdrew from his pocket a handkerchief, which he passed to her. 'There, miss. Use mine.'

Vera took it and dabbed at her eyes clumsily.

'Now, I want to show you something, Miss Brewster. I want to know whether you recognise the handwriting on this piece of paper here.' He took a scrap of paper from the desk in front of him and handed it to Vera, who looked at it in surprise.

'"Meet me in the middle of the maze at a quarter to six tomorrow morning,"' read Vera. '"I enclose a copy of the plan with this note. Go out by way of the French windows in the study. They are bolted but not locked. Don't be late. I have something of the utmost importance to tell you."'

'You read that very well, Miss Brewster. You obviously didn't have any difficulty reading the handwriting. It's signed at the bottom. Can you see? What does it say?'

'"T. E. H,"' read Vera, again with no hesitation.

'Do you recognise those initials, Miss Brewster?'

'Yes, they're Theo's. Where did you find this note, Inspector?'

'Never you mind about that for the present, miss. Now, do you recognise the handwriting?'

'Yes.'

Rose saw the inspector sit up in his chair and Sergeant Lane put down his pencil and lean forward. There was a silence in the room full of anticipation. Rose wondered whether Vera was aware that the two policemen were hanging on her words.

'Whose handwriting is it, miss?'

'Mine,' said Vera. 'I wrote this note, Inspector.'

Chapter Twenty-five

Rose heard Sergeant Lane drop his pencil.

'You did?' exclaimed the sergeant. 'You wrote that note, Miss Brewster?'

'Yes ... yes, I did.' Vera looked around rather wildly. 'Oh, it's you talking, is it, Sergeant? I'd forgotten you were there.' She returned her attention to the inspector. 'I thought she would have destroyed it. Silly girl. Where did you find it, Inspector?'

'Inside the dead woman's glove,' answered Inspector Bramwell. 'Tell me. If, as you say, you wrote it, why did you put Dr Harrison's initials at the end of this note?'

'I would have thought that was obvious, Inspector. I wanted Emmeline to think the note was from Theo. She wouldn't have gone to the maze otherwise, would she?'

'Miss Brewster. I should warn you that if you're trying to protect Dr – '

'I'm not, Inspector. I wrote that note. You have my word.'

'I think it would be as well to start at the beginning, Miss Brewster,' Inspector Bramwell said gravely. 'Do you wish to have a solicitor present?'

'No, why would I?'

'Vera, I think it would be a good idea.'

'It's all right, Rose. I want to tell them everything. I want to tell them what I did.' She stared at the inspector. 'I suppose the idea came to me after Theo left me alone in the library. I couldn't believe what he'd said or the awful way he had gone about breaking off our engagement. So cruel. Not like him at all.'

Vera pulled at the handkerchief, still clutched in her hand.

'I have been in love with Theo for such a long time, Inspector. I worshiped him. I always knew that I would make him rather a plain, dull little wife. But he needed that, Inspector. Someone like me who was happy to fade into the background and adore him. Someone who could help him stand in the light. Someone – '

'Vera ...'

'Oh … I am going on rather, aren't I, Rose? You are quite right to stop me. What I am trying to say is that I knew I'd make Theo a much better wife than *she* ever could. You never met Emmeline Montacute, Inspector. She was silly and vain. She would never have done for Theo. Don't you see? I was thinking of him all the time. What I did, I did for Theo, not me.'

'It must all have been very upsetting for you,' said the inspector.

'It was. I was devastated. I think I must have sat there for quite a long time, trying to take it all in. A full quarter of an hour, I should imagine. I was trying to think what to do.'

Vera looked up and fixed the policeman with eyes that were bright with emotion.

'Perhaps I should say at this point, Inspector, that I had no intention of giving Theo up. I knew that it was just an infatuation. I knew it would all blow over when Theo came to his senses. But I couldn't wait for that to happen. He might have done something very stupid that he would have lived to regret. He might have run away and married the girl.'

Vera rose from her seat and wandered around the room restlessly, every now and then stopping to examine a picture or an ornament, once even looking in a mirror and patting her hair into place.

'It was no good my trying to reason with Theo, not the sort of mood he was in. But it did occur to me that I could speak to Emmeline. I suppose I should have waited until morning, but I didn't want Theo to see her first. I was afraid about what he might do. Propose to the girl or something awful like that. Of course it was far too late for me to go and tap on her bedroom door and ask to speak to her. And for another thing, I didn't want any of the others to know. For all I knew Jemima or a maid might still be in with her, helping her to undress. And besides, I was afraid it might wake up the others. I didn't want that. Theo would have been furious.'

'It was then that the idea came to you to write that note?'

'Yes, Inspector. I was sitting in the library as you know. Seeing so many old books around me reminded me of the one Lord Belvedere had brought into the drawing room earlier that evening to show us the plan of the maze. Emmeline had been very taken with the idea of the maze. And of course Lavinia had told us that silly tale about the maid who had gone out there to meet her lover. Really, I don't think there's any truth in it, but it did give me an idea.'

'To write this note and sign it with Dr Harrison's initials?'

'Yes. I thought the idea of a romantic assignation would appeal to Emmeline very much. Besides, she would never have gone to meet me in the maze. I had to be sure that she'd go.'

'This note refers to a plan of the maze. Did you enclose one with it?'

'Yes, I made a rough copy of the one from Cedric's book.' Vera blushed. 'I'm afraid I'd had one or two more drinks than I ought, and went a little wrong in one place.'

'What did you do then?'

'I waited in the library. I'd gone to the drawing room to get the book. But I went back to the library to sketch the plan. You see, I knew there'd be notepaper and envelopes there. I waited until I was quite sure that everyone had gone to bed, even the servants. And then I slipped the envelope underneath Emmeline's door. I risked giving it a little tap. You see, I was afraid that she might be asleep and not see the note until the morning.

'And what did you do then?'

'I went back to my own room and waited. I remember being rather pleased to see that it was a full moon. It appeared to be pitch black and yet one could see a little. Does that make any sense, Inspector?'

'Go on please, Miss Brewster.'

'Well, of course, I didn't even try to get some sleep. I have a straight backed chair in my room, and I sat in that and watched the clock. It seemed to take forever for the hours to go by. I think I counted every minute. I can't tell you what a relief it was for me when the time came to set off for the maze.'

'I suppose,' said Inspector Bramwell, 'that you had no idea at this point whether Miss Montacute had seen your note or not?'

'None whatsoever, Inspector. I'd pushed the note right under her door so I didn't know whether Emmeline had picked it up or not. I could only hope that she had. Anyway … where was I? I do wish you'd stop interrupting me, Inspector. You're making me lose my train of thought. I set off for the maze – '

'Vera. I'm sorry to interrupt you,' said Rose, 'but I'd like to ask you just one question.'

'Miss Simpson!'

'I'm sorry, Inspector. But it's important. Vera. Listen to me. Before you set off for the maze, did you go into the dining room and pick up one of the candlesticks from the sideboard?'

'Well, of course I didn't. Why would I have done that? You do say the silliest things, Rose. I say, Inspector, do you think I might have a little drink?'

'I think not, Miss Brewster, unless of course you'd like a glass of water?'

'No, I wouldn't. Very well. Let's see where was I? Ah … yes. I arrived at the maze and went to the middle. Of course I was early for our *rendezvous*, but I still had a jolly long time to wait for Emmeline to arrive. I was beginning to think she hadn't spotted my note after all, and was considering heading back when she came stumbling into the middle of the maze.'

The room was quiet save for the ticking of the clock on the mantelpiece. Rose watched the inspector lean forward in his chair and grip the side of the desk. She imagined he would have liked nothing better than to utter some words of encouragement to prompt Vera to go on with her account.

'I remember her words,' Vera said, very quietly. 'Or at least I think I do. For some reason they've got stuck in my head. She said: "Darling, you silly thing. You made a mistake on your plan. You missed a bit. It took me ever such a long time to work out what you'd done. But I'm here now. Don't you think I was very brave coming out in the dark? I almost didn't. But it was very romantic of you to suggest …" And then her voice trailed off. You see, she'd just realised it was me not Theo.'

'Vera, I really think …'

'She was ever so shocked at first by the deception. And then she was very angry. I tried to explain why I'd done it. I told her how much I loved Theo. How I couldn't live without him. I told her how selfish she was being playing with our lives. I said that I didn't believe she cared anything for him.'

Vera walked back to her seat, and sat down heavily.

'She calmed down then. She told me that she was sorry. She said she knew they had behaved badly, but that she loved Theo and that if he were to ask her to marry him, she would. She looked at me as if she pitied me and I hated her even more. I screamed at her, Inspector. I told her Mr Montacute would never agree to such a match. She said she thought he would because her happiness meant everything to him and that she could never be happy unless she was with Theo.'

'What happened then, Miss Brewster?'

'I struck her.'

'With the candlestick?' enquired the inspector.

'No, I've told you already I didn't take a candlestick with me. There was no candlestick there. Why would there have been?'

'Vera, what do you mean when you say you struck Emmeline?' Rose asked quickly.

'I slapped her hard across the face. She was very shocked, I remember that. And then I did something awful, Rose.'

'What did you do, Miss Brewster?' demanded the inspector.

'She was still holding my plan in her hand and I snatched it from her. I was so angry, you see. I snatched it from her and ran out of the maze. I have never run so fast. I wanted to make sure she couldn't follow me out.' Vera clutched at Rose's hand and gave her a look of desperation. 'Don't you see how wicked I was, Rose? I knew she'd get lost trying to get out of the maze. And I just left her there.'

'Well, what do you make of all that, Sergeant?' asked the inspector as soon as Vera and Rose had left the room. 'I don't know whether the woman's very clever or very stupid.'

'Or very batty or quite drunk,' suggested the sergeant.

'Happen she's all four. I can't make her out at all. One thing's for sure, though, she seems to love that doctor fellow almost to distraction. Having said that, one minute she appears to want to forgive him and the next she hates him. And I'm not altogether sure that story of hers isn't made up in some pathetic attempt to protect him.'

'Well, sir, all I can say is I'm not surprised Dr Harrison gave her the old heave-ho. I found her rather frightening, so I did. And I wouldn't put it past her to have gone back into the maze later with the candlestick to finish the poor girl off. It seems to me it's just the sort of thing she'd do. I could see her coming back to the house, having a couple more drinks, and then going back to the maze, couldn't you? She knew the girl was there, after all. The murderer would have to have known that, wouldn't they? They'd have to have known that Miss Montacute was in the maze.'

As soon as they came out of the study, Vera said: 'I think I'll go and have a little lie down.'

'I think,' said Rose, 'that would be a jolly good idea. But, before you go upstairs, I'd like to ask you one more question.'

'Haven't I answered enough questions in there?' Vera pointed towards the closed study door. 'I seem to have done nothing but talk and talk.'

Vera's mood had become petulant. She was behaving, Rose thought, like a tired child. It occurred to her that the interview had taken a great deal out of the woman and that, coupled with her somewhat inebriated state, meant Vera would soon be asleep.

'It's just one question. What did you do with the plan?'

'The plan? What plan?' Vera asked vaguely. In her mind's eye she was already upstairs, asleep in her bed.

'Oh, Vera. Do try and concentrate. The plan of the maze, of course. What did you think I meant? You said you snatched it out of Emmeline's hand and ran out of the maze with it. What did you do with the plan? Have you still got it?'

'No. I think I threw it away,' said Vera slowly. 'As soon as I got out of the maze I think I screwed it up in my hand and threw it away. It's probably on the ground somewhere.'

'Good lord!' said Cedric, as soon as Rose had recounted to him the salient points of Vera's interview with the policemen. 'What an absolutely rotten thing to do. I half wish I hadn't said anything to Theo now. I take it that Harrison breaking off their engagement was the last straw and was what sent her over the edge?'

'It probably was. And it's my fault, not yours. After all, I told you to have a word with Theo.'

'I should have said something to him much earlier. I only hope that's all Vera did. Leave Emmeline in the maze, I mean.'

By common accord they went into the library, having become thoroughly bored with both the drawing room and the dining room and the company within them. To their relief, the library was empty and they seated themselves comfortably side by side on a great leather Chesterfield sofa. Rose sank back into the seat and leaned her head comfortably on Cedric's shoulder. They sat there curled up beside one another, holding hands in companionable silence. Death seemed far away.

'I don't want this to end, Rose,' said Cedric, at last. 'Sitting here, just the two of us, pretending that a murder hasn't just occurred in the grounds, and that Sedgwick is not crawling with policemen.'

'Yes, it would be nice, wouldn't it, darling? If only we could just click our fingers and have everyone else go away.'

'I expect we'll have Manning or Torridge in here in a minute, asking what to do about dinner.' Cedric sighed. 'I daresay the police will want to interview Jemima and Lavinia before they call it a day. We'll have to put dinner back by an hour at least.'

'What about the servants, when will they have their dinner? They'll be awfully hungry, won't they?'

'They usually have it while we're having our cocktails before dinner. Unlike in some houses where they're made to wait until after all the dinner things are cleared away and the family and guests are having their coffee.'

'Goodness, that would make their meal frightfully late, wouldn't it?'

'It would. But some servants prefer it. They like to have their dinner when they've finished for the night. You should hear Torridge and Manning. They have very different views on the subject.'

'Well, if I were a servant, I don't think I'd want to have to wait for my meal. I'd probably help myself to a few things from the dishes before they were sent up!'

Rose closed her eyes for a moment and thought of Madame Renard's dress shop and the long hours of work she endured there. It occurred to her that there was not so very much difference between her lot and that of Cedric's servants. Her station in life was nearer to theirs than to his.

'I was going to suggest to everyone that we didn't bother dressing for dinner tonight,' Cedric was saying. 'It's likely to be a very short, sombre affair this evening, don't you think?'

'I do. I think everyone will want to go to bed early. It's been such an awful, tiring day. I suppose it's the shock. I don't think anyone will have much of an appetite for conversation.' A thought suddenly occurred to her. 'I say, Cedric, is Lavinia still in her boudoir?'

'Yes, she is. She even took her tea there by herself. Really, one would think she could make more of an effort. She could try and comfort Jemima for a start.'

'Jemima doesn't want comforting. She wants to be left alone by herself. Look at the way she spurned poor Felix's attempts today, and they were as close as anything yesterday.' Rose sighed. 'I think Lavinia's rather annoyed with the inspector for not interviewing her first.'

'Just like Lavinia. Poor old Inspector Bramwell. I wouldn't like to be in his shoes when he finally does interview her. By the way, I've asked Mrs Farrier to prepare rooms for Inspector Bramwell and Sergeant Lane. I thought it would be rather a good idea to keep some police presence here overnight, don't you? God forbid there'll be another murder!'

'Yes. I think that's a very good idea,' said Rose, rather dreamily, her head still on Cedric's shoulder. 'As it happens, I'd rather like to speak to your housekeeper. I have one or two questions to ask her.'

'Would you like me to send for her now?' asked Cedric rather reluctantly.

'No,' said Rose, placing her head more firmly on his shoulder. 'I want to stay like this for as long as possible.'

'So do I. But I say, darling. Do you believe that story of Vera's? It sounds a bit far-fetched all that note business doesn't it? And putting poor old Harrison's initials at the bottom. That really was a bit much.'

'I don't think the police believed Vera at first. They thought it was a rather desperate bid on her part to protect Theo. But, for what it's worth, I believe her.'

'Oh?'

'Yes, it explains one or two things with regard to the way she behaved this morning.'

'Such as?'

'Vera didn't join in the search,' said Rose. 'I caught her smiling when she thought Emmeline hadn't come down to breakfast because she was unwell. But, when she discovered Emmeline was missing, Vera told Lavinia that she had a headache, or some such thing. The truth I think was that she was afraid Emmeline would tell everyone what she had done when they found her, and she didn't want to be there when that happened. Can you imagine how Theo would have reacted?'

'Yes, I can.'

'That's not all. Do you remember that you were afraid that Emmeline might have come to harm because of the cold.'

'Yes, I was.'

'I think the same thought suddenly occurred to Vera, particularly when she saw the blankets and flasks of coffee and brandy we were taking with us on the search. She suddenly realised how irresponsible she'd been to leave Emmeline in the maze. I happened to look up at the house just before we set off. I caught sight of Vera by the window and I remember thinking at the time how worried she looked.'

'But wouldn't she have looked just as worried if, God forbid, she had actually murdered Emmeline in the maze?' asked Cedric.

'Yes, of course. But there's more. You'll remember that, when I came back to the house with Lavinia, Vera came tearing out of the house and asked me what had happened. When I told her Emmeline was dead she fainted, but not before she said something along the lines of: "No, she can't be dead. What have I done? I never meant to ..."'

'Oh, I say! Did she really?'

'Yes. Don't you see what that means?'

'I can't say that I do. It seems to me more like a confession. That she had killed Emmeline after all.'

'Vera thought Emmeline had died from the cold. From exposure or hypothermia or some such thing. Don't you see? She thought she was to blame for the girl's death. Not because she had actually killed her, but because she had left her in the maze.'

'And she was responsible for Emmeline's death in a way, wasn't she? If it hadn't been for her actions, Emmeline would never have gone to the maze in the first place. She'd have stayed safely tucked up in bed instead.'

'But Vera didn't wield the fatal blow,' said Rose. 'At the first opportunity, she asked me if it was true what the servants were saying. Was it true that Emmeline had died from having her head bashed in? That was the eloquent way she put it. I remember being rather shocked. But she wanted reassurance that Emmeline had not died from the cold. And when I told her that she hadn't, she looked relieved.'

'So who did kill Emmeline? Are we any nearer to finding out?'

'I think I may be able to narrow the suspects down a bit further. I would like to have a word with your housekeeper now, if I may?'

'Your wish is my command, my lady. I tell you what, I'll go and get the woman myself rather than ring for her. It'll give me an excuse to find out how the servants are taking all this. Manning and Torridge won't tell me the truth. They'll just assure me that the servants are coping well if I ask them.'

Cedric returned a few minutes later with the housekeeper in tow. Mrs Farrier was a thin, pale woman, dressed all in black, relieved only by white lace cuffs and collar, which accentuated her pallor. Rose thought her dress particularly fitting for a house in mourning, although she assumed it was the woman's usual work attire.

'I hope you don't mind my asking to see you, Mrs Farrier?' said Rose. 'I know you're very busy, particularly in light of what's happened. I daresay some of the young maids are very upset?'

'We all are, miss. Nothing like this has ever happened at Sedgewick before. Not in my lifetime at least.'

'Quite so,' Rose said quickly. 'Now, I wonder if you wouldn't mind answering a question for me. I daresay you'll think my question rather a strange one.'

'I'll do what I can, miss.'

'Would you mind telling me who has which bedroom upstairs … the layout I mean,' said Rose, seeing the look of astonishment on the housekeeper's face. 'For instance, my room is next to Lady Lavinia's. And her room and mine are opposite to Miss Montacute's and Miss Wentmore's. And their two rooms are of course next to one another. Miss Brewster's room is a little further down the corridor. What about the men's corridor? How are the rooms positioned there?'

'Well … let me see. Dr Harrison's and Count Fernand's rooms are next to one another on one side of the corridor, and opposite them are Lord Belvedere's and Mr Thistlewaite's.'

'Which rooms are on the corresponding side of the house to Miss Montacute's and Miss Wentmore's rooms?'

'That would be Dr Harrison's and Count Fernand's.'

'Thank you, Mrs Farrier. That's all I needed to know. You have been most helpful.'

Chapter Twenty-six

'Are you going to tell me what that was all about?' asked Cedric as they made their way back to the drawing room. 'I'm not sure that my housekeeper thought your reasons for wondering which gentleman slept in which room were entirely honourable. If you wanted to know which my room was, you only had to ask me, you know!'

Rose giggled, and then immediately became serious again. She had caught sight of Jemima through the open door, pale and unhappy, and alone. The girl had looked up startled at the sound of laughter.

Rose lowered her voice and said: 'You know very well, darling, that my reasons for asking such things were related to my investigations. I shall tell you about it all in good time once I've been able to think what it all means. I will tell you this, though. Something occurred to me when the policemen were interviewing Vera. I think the number of possible suspects has been narrowed down. I wonder if the same idea has occurred to the police.'

'I didn't have time to ask you before,' said Inspector Bramwell. 'Did you by any chance find anything of interest in Miss Montacute's room or Miss Wentmore's?'

'Nothing I'm afraid, sir,' admitted Sergeant Lane. 'What would you like to do now? We still have to interview Lady Lavinia yet.'

'You're right, Sergeant. Time's marching on. That lot will be wanting to dress for dinner any moment now. I'm surprised that butler fellow hasn't tried to chivvy us along.' He stared at the fire. 'I think it's about time we had a word with Miss Wentmore, don't you? Let's see if we can find out for ourselves if she is who she claims to be. Let's discover whether your Miss Simpson's theory about Jemima Wentmore and the deceased is correct.'

Jemima Wentmore appeared in front of Rose as soon as Cedric had left her side to go and see how Theo Harrison was bearing up.

'Miss Simpson ... Rose, I wondered if I might have a word with you?'

'Yes, of course Jemima, how may I help you?'

'Am I correct in thinking that you accompanied Miss Brewster when she was being interviewed by the policemen?'

'Yes, I went with her.'

'Didn't they mind, the policemen I mean?'

'I think Inspector Bramwell minded very much. But Vera refused to be interviewed unless I was with her. So I suppose he had no choice but to accept it.'

'Did Vera say anything important? Did she say anything about Emmeline's death?'

'I'm afraid I'm not at liberty to discuss Vera's interview,' Rose answered rather primly. 'If you want to know what she said, I suggest you ask her.'

'Please … don't be like that.'

Jemima clung on to her sleeve, and it occurred to Rose that her sleeve had been held on to rather too many times that day already. She wondered how best to disentangle herself from Emmeline's companion.

'Please,' said Jemima. 'I don't mean to sound inquisitive. I was just wondering whether the police were any nearer finding Emmeline's murderer, that's all. It's not that surprising, is it? And … there is something else I wanted to ask you.'

'Oh?'

'Will you come in with me when I'm interviewed?'

'Me? Are you sure you wouldn't prefer Felix to go in with you?'

'No … I … Well, you're used to this sort of thing, aren't you?'

'Yes, all right. I will if you'd like me to.'

'Thank you. Thank you so much. You don't know how grateful I am to you,' Jemima said, her lip trembling.

The door opened and Sergeant Lane walked into the room.

'Miss Wentmore. The inspector would like to interview you now if you'd just come this way.'

'Miss Simpson! What are you doing here?'

This time, Rose noticed, the inspector made little pretence at being polite.

'I should like Miss Simpson to stay with me while I'm being interviewed, Inspector,' answered Jemima nervously. 'I believe you allowed her to be present during your interview with Miss Brewster?'

The inspector snorted and said: 'It would appear, Miss Simpson, that you are fulfilling the role of ladies' chaperone. Stay if you must, but this time please do not try to interrupt the proceedings.'

Sergeant Lane drew up the same chair as before, and Rose sat down beside Jemima, very conscious that her presence was being tolerated by the inspector under sufferance.

'I realise that Miss Montacute's death must have been a great shock to you, Miss Wentmore. You have my sympathies.'

Jemima made no acknowledgement other than to nod slightly and look miserably down at her hands, which were clasped tightly together in her lap.

'For our records I'd like you to give me your full name, miss, if you please.'

'Jemima Mary Wentmore.'

'Mary, eh? Taken a note of that, Sergeant?'

'Yes, sir,' replied Sergeant Lane from his corner.

A puzzled look appeared on Jemima's face as she looked from one policeman to the other. She swallowed hard, and Rose thought that she looked even more apprehensive than before.

'Suppose you tell us how long you've been Miss Montacute's companion?'

'Almost two years, I think … Yes, it would have been two years in March.'

'I understand that you are a distant relative of the Montacutes. Now, just so that I can get it clear in my mind, Mr Montacute employed you as a companion to his daughter, am I right?'

'Yes.'

'So you were paid for your services? You didn't reside in the Montacute establishment on account of your being a member of the family, so to speak?'

'Mr Montacute gave me a very generous allowance,' Jemima said, her cheeks going crimson.

'So you were paid for your services as companion to Miss Montacute?' persisted Inspector Bramwell.

'I suppose I was. I never really thought of it like that.'

'Indeed! You surprise me, Miss Wentmore. This allowance you were given. You say it was generous and yet you dress, if you will forgive me for saying, a little dowdily, a little shabbily even. If I didn't know better, I would have put you down as being a lady's maid. Don't you like fine clothes? Or doesn't your allowance stretch that far?'

'Yes ... no ... yes ... I don't know.'

'You sound rather flustered, if you don't mind my saying, Miss Wentmore. I would have thought my question was a perfectly simple one to answer. Tell me. Did you like Miss Montacute? I don't like to speak ill of the dead but, from what I've heard, she sounded like rather a selfish and vain young lady.'

'She wasn't like that at all, Inspector.'

For the first time Jemima sounded indignant. Her eyes, Rose noticed, were flashing with something akin to anger.

'No? Young Mr Thistlewaite was very vexed at the way Miss Montacute treated you. Said she treated you no better than a servant.'

'He doesn't know what he's talking about.'

'Doesn't he? I have it on good authority that you and he were rather fond of each other. You met in Florence, I understand?'

'Yes.'

'And you are fond of him?'

'I was ... Now I'm not so certain.'

'Oh? And why is that, pray?' The inspector looked interested.

'I'm not interested in anything anymore. Not now that Emmeline's dead. It's all I can think about ... her death. It's all so awful. I can't stand it. I can't stand – '

'That's quite natural, I would imagine,' said the inspector, a touch of sympathy in his voice. 'You were very close, I assume?'

'We were like sisters.'

'Sisters, huh? Well that must have been nice. Company for each other. You almost lived the life of a recluse in Scotland, I understand.'

'What utter nonsense! Of course we didn't. Mr Montacute was always throwing parties and balls.'

'But you didn't leave the house in the Highlands much?'

'We weren't kept prisoners, if that's what you're implying. We were free to come and go as we wished.'

'As long as you were accompanied by Mr Montacute or some of his servants?'

'Mr Montacute was very protective of Emmeline, and with good reason. He was afraid another kidnap attempt would be made. And he was right to be frightened, wasn't he?'

'Was he? Miss Montacute was murdered, not kidnapped. Tell me, Miss Wentmore, whose idea was it that you and Miss Montacute should go to the Continent alone?'

'Emmeline's.'

'Are you certain about that? Mr Montacute's secretary thought it was your idea.'

'Did he?'

'Yes. He seemed very certain, so he did. Now what's the name of the fellow? ... Sugden, is it?'

'Stapleton, Inspector,' said Jemima.

'Ah, that's right, so it is. Now what was I saying? Oh, yes. Stapleton's convinced it was your idea. What do you say to that?'

'Yes ... I remember now. Of course. How stupid of me. He is quite right. It was my idea to go to the Continent. But it was Emmeline's idea to come here to Sedgwick. Silly of me. I was thinking of Sedgwick not the Continent.'

'Confused again, Miss Wentmore? Dear me!'

'I've never been involved in a murder investigation before, Inspector. I'm afraid you're making me feel rather nervous.'

'Am I? Oh, dear. Really, Miss Wentmore, there is no reason for you to be nervous of me unless you committed the deed in question.'

'The deed in question?'

'Killed Miss Montacute.'

'Oh!' Jemima clasped her hand to her mouth and her eyes went very wide.

'Surely you don't think I did it? I loved Emmeline. Why should I wish her dead?'

'Why indeed, Miss Wentmore? Unfortunately for you, I can think of a number of reasons. Shall I go through them one by one? Get them clear in my mind, so to speak.' The inspector did not wait for a response. 'Do you remember poor Mr Thistlewaite for whom you no longer appear to hold any affection? Well, that young man went out of his way to accuse everyone else but you of the murder. Yet you were overheard having a conversation with him in the gardens yesterday, suggesting that you might be able to get hold of a considerable amount of money.'

'Was I? Overheard saying that, I mean?'

'You were. Tell me, Miss Wentmore, do you benefit under the terms of Miss Montacute's will?'

'Yes.'

'Considerably?'

'Very considerably. But I didn't murder my friend, I promise you. And it's not what you think, what I said about the money.'

'What did you mean by it then?'

Jemima stared miserably at the floor and declined to give an answer.

'Very well. If you will not tell us, we can only think the worst. Unfortunately for you, Miss Wentmore, that is not all. We happen to know, for instance, that you stole Miss Montacute's diamond necklace.'

'What did you say, Inspector?' Rose said. It was the first time she had spoken since entering the study.

'Miss Simpson. I almost forgot you were here, you were keeping so quiet. What a pity you have gone and spoilt it. I think I have already told you not to interrupt.'

'But, Inspector –'

'I don't know what you're talking about, Inspector,' Jemima said, a note of panic evident in her voice. 'I didn't steal Emmeline's diamonds.'

'Didn't you? And yet Miss Montacute's jewel box was found hidden on the landing with its lock broken.'

'I don't see why you think that has anything to do with me. I had no need to break the lock. You see, I have the key.'

Jemima produced from her handbag a small brass key which she handed to the inspector. He in turn took out of a drawer in the desk a finely polished mahogany jewellery box with stepped detail to the lid. The wood of the box was smooth except for around the lock. Here the wood was splintered and raw, showing signs of where the lock had been forced. Inspector Bramwell proceeded to open the box to reveal a maroon-coloured, velvet lining.

'Is this Miss Montacute's jewel box?'

'Yes.'

The Inspector took out the top tray and put his hand in the box, from where he retrieved a necklace consisting of yellow diamonds, mounted in platinum and rose gold.

'You found that necklace in the jewellery box even though the lock was broken?' asked Rose in surprise. 'So whoever broke the lock didn't take the diamonds. I wonder why not.'

'We have wondered that ourselves, Miss Simpson. This is the very necklace that I showed you earlier, if you recall. The necklace you identified to us as the one Miss Montacute was wearing the evening before last.'

'I think I said it *looked* like the one Miss Montacute was wearing,' corrected Rose. 'I couldn't swear that it was the same one. Just as I cannot swear now that this necklace is the same one you showed to me earlier.'

'But at the very least, it is remarkably similar to the one Miss Montacute was wearing, is it not? I have also been told that it bears some resemblance to the necklace which forms part of the Montacute Diamonds.'

'It's not that necklace, Inspector, if that's what you're inferring.' Jemima said, shifting awkwardly in her seat. 'The necklace in the Montacute Diamonds collection is made up of much larger yellow diamonds than these, and they are surrounded by many small, white diamonds, which you will see these aren't.'

'I do remember Emmeline mentioning the surrounding of white diamonds,' Rose said helpfully. 'She also said that the Montacute Diamonds were kept at the bank. I don't think this necklace could possibly be from that collection, Inspector.'

'Unless it had been taken from the bank. I assume it is taken out to wear on special occasions?'

'Yes, of course,' said Jemima. 'But this is hardly a special occasion, Inspector. The necklace is not what you think it is.'

'Maybe not. But the diamonds in this necklace are still remarkable, Miss Wentmore. I think they'd be worth stealing, don't you? They'd raise a pretty penny, I'm sure.'

'Actually they wouldn't. I'm afraid you're rather making a fuss about nothing, Inspector,' Jemima said rather wearily. 'I agree the necklace looks very grand. I would go so far as to say that it could even be mistaken for the one from the Montacute Diamonds collection by someone who had not seen the original. But you see this necklace is –'

'A fake. A paste replica, if you will. Is that what you were about to say, Miss Wentmore?' asked Inspector Bramwell, leaning forward to study her closely. 'Because, you're quite right. You see we already know the diamonds in this necklace aren't real. We had an expert look at it as soon as it was found. And he told us just that. A very good fake, but a paste copy nevertheless.'

'If you already knew it was a paste copy,' began Jemima, sounding annoyed, 'then –'

'Just because this necklace is a paste replica, Miss Wentmore, it does not follow that the one Miss Montacute was wearing the night before last was a fake.'

'I'm not sure that I understand what you're saying, Inspector.' Jemima had gone very pale.

'Oh, I think you do, Miss Wentmore. I think you know very well what I'm saying.' The inspector sat back in his chair and studied her. 'Shall I tell you what I believe? Miss Montacute wore the genuine necklace the night before last. If you remember it was examined closely by everyone present by means of looking through a jeweller's loupe. We happen to be of the opinion that at least one person there, the owner of the jeweller's lens, is an expert in diamonds. I am of course referring to Count Fernand, who has confirmed to us that the diamonds in Emmeline's necklace were genuine. He said they were quite fabulous to use his own words.'

'Then he was mistaken,' cried Jemima. 'Only the paste necklace was brought to Sedgwick Court.'

'If that was the case, why was Miss Montacute so keen to take part in a game that would reveal that her diamonds were fake?'

'Perhaps,' suggested Rose, joining in the conversation, 'she viewed it as a bit of a game. Miss Wentmore has just told us that the necklace was a very good paste replica. Perhaps Miss Montacute wanted to see if anyone would notice that the diamonds weren't real.'

'You really will not keep quiet, will you, Miss Simpson?' Inspector Bramwell sighed and frowned at the same time, his small, watery eyes almost disappearing into the deep folds of his face. 'But to answer your point. If Miss Montacute really thought of it as a game, seeing if she could pass off fake diamonds as the genuine article, then would she not have laughed and made a bit of a show of it at the end? Would she not have told everyone how amusing it all was that they had been so easily taken in? But she didn't, did she? She said nothing. She was as keen as anyone to look at the diamonds under the jeweller's lens. And that tells me that Miss Montacute at least believed the necklace to be genuine.'

For a few moments no one said anything at all.

Jemima then explained: 'Emmeline thought that we'd brought the genuine necklace with us. But I was anxious as to its safety. The real necklace is very valuable, Inspector. I didn't think that Mr Montacute would want us to go travelling with it. So at the last moment I substituted the paste necklace for the real one. I didn't tell Emmeline because I knew she would make a fuss about it. If truth be told, I thought it highly unlikely that she'd notice.'

'That's all very well, Miss Wentmore. It even sounds plausible if it were not for the jewellery box.'

'I have told you, Inspector, that it has nothing to do with me. I did not tamper with that box. I had no need to. I have the key.'

'The fingerprints on the jewellery box had been wiped off, as one might expect.'

'There you are, Inspector.' Jemima looked relieved. 'As I said, what has it all to do with me?'

'All the fingerprints except for one or two, Miss Wentmore. And they are yours. Can you explain to me please how that can be if you were not the last person to handle this box?'

Chapter Twenty-seven

Rose glanced at Jemima. The revelation that the inspector had proof that she was the last person to have handled the tampered jewellery box had caused the girl's face to become ashen. She was playing with the material of her skirt, rolling it between her fingers as if the action would afford her more time. All the while she worried with her skirt, she was staring at the desk top in front of her, as if the answer to her dilemma was written on its polished surface.

Finally Jemima took a deep breath and said in a quiet voice devoid of emotion: 'Very well, Inspector. I was the last person to touch that box.' She let out a sigh that was almost pitiful. 'If you must know, I found it in my room this morning when I was dressing. Someone must have put it there. I saw at once that the lock had been forced, but that the necklace was still inside. I wanted to speak to Emmeline about it this morning before breakfast, but there was no answer when I knocked on her door. After breakfast, when we discovered she was missing, I decided to say nothing about the box until she had been found. When we discovered that she had been … murdered …'

'Go on please, miss.'

'Well, naturally all thoughts of the box went completely from my mind. It was only later when I was in my room and saw the box again that I realised what someone was trying to do. They were trying to implicate me in Emmeline's death. I was scared and at my wits end. At the first opportunity, I got rid of the box.'

'That sounds to me a highly improbable story, Miss Wentmore, if you don't mind my saying,' said the inspector at length. 'Shall I tell you what I believe? I think, far from being fond of Miss Montacute, you resented her. She had wealth, beauty and a doting father. She could have everything she wanted. You, on the other hand, had very little in comparison. You were a poor relation who was treated like little more than a servant, expected to wait on a woman to whom you were related.'

'No! You've got it all wrong, Inspector.'

'To make matters worse, the woman in question was vain and selfish, and I suspect a little stupid. Whereas you, Miss Wentmore, I will hazard a guess are of more than average intelligence. It must all have seemed very unfair to you. But for an accident of birth, you would have been the wealthy young lady, and Miss Montacute the servant. As if that were not enough, you were constantly surrounded by the things that you coveted in life, which would never be yours.'

'No!'

'It is true that every now and then you might be permitted to have a taste of, and indulge in, what was beyond your reach, but only at the whim of another. You must have been worried all the time that Miss Montacute would become bored of you as her companion, or would marry and your services no longer be required. And then where would you have been? You were in a very precarious position, Miss Wentmore.'

'It wasn't like that at all, Inspector,' protested Jemima.

'I haven't finished yet, Miss Wentmore. You can have your say at the end. Now, where was I? Ah, yes. Let me put this theory to you. You persuade Miss Montacute to go travelling with you abroad. It provides you with an ideal opportunity to steal her diamond necklace. Before you set off on your travels you substitute the paste necklace for the genuine one. You put the real necklace somewhere safe with a view to pawning it at a later date when you have left the employment of the Montacutes. Your intention meanwhile is to arrange for the paste necklace to be lost or stolen while you are on the Continent. For some unknown reason you do not go through with your plan while abroad, and instead decide to carry it out while you are here at Sedgwick Court.'

'No!' cried Jemima. 'I would never have done such a thing.'

The inspector ignored the interruption and carried on with his tale as if Jemima had not spoken.

'However, there is an added complication, and that is that you fall in love with the penniless Mr Felix Thistlewaite. In a few days' time he is due to go to work in a solicitors firm in London, while you will be returning to the Highlands of Scotland. It is hard to imagine how you could be further apart geographically. The young man is already having doubts as to whether your relationship can survive. You need to act quickly before he becomes immersed in his life in London and forgets you. No doubt you have hidden the genuine necklace somewhere in Scotland and so it is out of your reach here at Sedgwick. You need to get money now which will enable you to move to London if you are to retain Mr Thistlewaite's affections. We have witnesses to your conversation with the young man discussing the supposedly hypothetical question of what would happen if you were to acquire a great deal of money.'

'Have you?' Jemima looked surprised.

'Indeed, Miss Wentmore. In fact, two witnesses. I must say, I am relieved that you do not try to deny that such a conversation took place.'

'Why would I?' Jemima passed a hand through her hair. 'But it is not what you think. None of it is what you think.'

'Then why not tell us what it is?'

'I can't.'

'You are not helping yourself, Miss Wentmore,' the inspector said, looking grim.

'What you are suggesting is horrid. That I somehow managed to entice Emmeline to go into the maze at dead of night to murder her? Why would I? She was my friend. And if I had decided to do something so wicked, wouldn't it have been far easier to have gone to her room and killed her while she was sleeping? My room was next to hers, you know.'

'I do know that, Miss Wentmore. Let us just suppose you did not originally plan to kill Miss Montacute. But you happened instead to hear her leave her room and were quite naturally inquisitive. It would have been very early this morning and not dead of night as you suggest. Undoubtedly you would have been curious to see what she was about. You decide to follow her to see what she is up to. You trail her to the maze and follow her inside, keeping a fair distance between you, so that you are not spotted. You witness her confrontation with Miss Brewster –'

'Miss Brewster?' cried Jemima. 'You mean it was Vera who she was going to meet in the maze? That doesn't make any sense at all. She would never have gone to meet *her*.'

'It is a long story, Miss Wentmore, and one that I do not intend to go into at this time. Let us go back to our story, shall we? We know from Miss Brewster's own lips that she did meet your friend. For our purposes here, suffice to say that you witness Miss Montacute's confrontation with Miss Brewster and the latter's subsequent departure. Miss Montacute is now all alone. And that is when I think the idea occurs to you to kill her. As you have already informed us, you are aware that Miss Montacute has made you a handsome bequest in her will. What better opportunity could you have to do away with her and realise your inheritance? With any luck Miss Brewster or even Dr Harrison will be blamed for the crime. And you will be free to marry Felix Thistlewaite and live a life of relative luxury. What do you say to that, Miss Wentmore?'

Inspector Bramwell sat back in his chair and looked at Jemima, cocking a cynical eye at the young woman in front of him.

'It simply didn't happen,' said Jemima.

'And what about the candlestick?' asked Rose. 'Why should Miss Wentmore take such a thing with her into the maze?'

'You and that damned candlestick, Miss Simpson!' For a moment the inspector looked as if he might lose his temper and burst with exasperation. 'For all we know Miss Wentmore may have thought about killing Miss Montacute before she set off for the maze and so took the candlestick with her.'

'I didn't,' said Jemima. 'I'd never been to the maze until I went there this morning with the others. You must believe me. I didn't do it. I would never have done such a thing. I didn't kill Emmeline.'

Jemima's voice had risen dangerously and become quite shrill. To Rose she seemed to hesitate on the very edge of falling to pieces completely, her aloof and reserved manner about to be utterly destroyed. But on the very brink, she appeared at the very last minute to gather all her energies and pull herself back.

The inspector snorted. 'Well, you would say that, wouldn't you, miss? But as it happens, it is just one of a number of possible theories that we are investigating. You'll be interested to know that we have another theory concerning you.'

'Oh?' Jemima looked apprehensive.

'We were wondering whether you were the real Jemima Wentmore or a clever impostor. Just as we've been wondering whether Count Fernand is a real count.'

If the inspector had slapped her, the effect could not have been more devastating. For one moment Jemima looked as if she might be about to slide off her chair on to the ground. Instead she chose to sink back heavily into her seat, grabbing on to the sides as if to stop herself from falling. She looked to those present as if she wished to disappear into the very fabric of the chair.

Both Inspector Bramwell and Rose looked at Jemima with renewed interest.

'What makes you say that? About me, I mean?' Jemima said at last.

'Tell me, Miss Wentmore,' said the inspector ignoring her question. 'Are you by any chance a jewel thief?'

'What?' cried Jemima. For a moment the woman looked completely bewildered. She took a deep breath and they could see her fighting frantically to regain her composure. 'Why would you think me a thief?'

'Not, why do we doubt you are who you say you are?'

'Well, that is just ridiculous. I wasn't going to dignify that with an answer. But of course I'm Jemima Wentmore. Who do you think I am if I'm not her, Inspector?'

'I've just told you. A jewel thief.'

'I refuse to listen to any more of this nonsense,' said Jemima, rising from her seat. 'You are being absurd.'

'Am I? Sit down if you please, Miss Wentmore. As I said it is only one line of inquiry that we are investigating.'

'You can ask me any question you like about Jemima Wentmore, Inspector,' Jemima said, sitting down and looking indignant. 'I think you'll find I'll be able to answer it to your complete satisfaction.'

'I'm sure you will. You strike me as a very resourceful young woman who would take all necessary steps to ensure that you learned and played your part well. But as it happens, it won't be necessary for me to ask you any questions, Miss Wentmore. You see we will know one way or the other in the next day or so if you are who you claim to be.'

'Oh?'

'Yes, indeed. Mr Montacute is returning from his travels. As soon as his ship docks, his secretary will be bringing him here.'

'To Sedgwick?'

Rose wondered whether it was panic they could hear in Jemima's voice. Certainly all remaining colour had drained from her face, and she was fixing Inspector Bramwell with such a stare that even he was fidgeting in his seat, unused to such unblinking scrutiny.

'Yes, to Sedgwick. I think even you will admit that he of all people will know if you are really Jemima Wentmore.'

'But … I … I don't understand. He was not expected back for another week or two.'

'Then either you have been misinformed, or he has changed his plans.'

'Does … does he know about … Emmeline?'

'Stapleton has gone to meet his ship. The secretary will break the news to him then.'

'Must he? Can't you wait until he arrives at Sedgwick to tell him? I should very much like to break the news to him myself. I don't think you understand how devastated he will be.'

'And you think the news is better coming from you than from his secretary? Why's that, Miss Wentmore?'

'Because he will want to ask me all sorts of questions about Emmeline. How she was feeling, was she happy, that sort of thing. I want to put his mind at rest. I want to tell him that she did not suffer, that –'

'You cannot possibly know that, Miss Wentmore, unless you were there when she was killed,' said the inspector, speaking very quietly.

Jemima flinched but said nothing.

'I should tell you that I find your explanation for wanting to see Mr Montacute highly wanting. It seems to me, Miss Wentmore, that you are playing some sort of a game.'

'I assure you that I am not.' Jemima said.

'Ah, but I think you are. If you are not the real Miss Wentmore you would naturally want to delay Mr Montacute being informed of his daughter's death. Perhaps you are afraid that when his secretary tells him he will say something to the effect that it is quite impossible as he has just left her alive and well in New York.' The inspector held up his hand as Jemima made to protest. 'On the other hand, if you are who you claim to be, perhaps you think Mr Montacute is less likely to blame you for the tragedy if you are able to break the news to him yourself, in your own way. Perhaps it has even occurred to you that in time you may be able to replace his daughter in his affections. You are a relative of Mr Montacute's after all.'

'Or perhaps I just wish to have the opportunity to break the news to him gently. Whatever you may think of me, Inspector, Mr Montacute has been very kind to me and I am very fond of him.'

'Spoken with true feeling, Miss Wentmore. For the life of me, I don't know what to make of you.'

'I don't know what to make of Jemima either,' Rose said.

She was speaking to Cedric over cocktails. While it had been decided not to dress for dinner, few of the guests seemed inclined to indulge in pre-dinner drinks either, preferring instead to keep to their rooms until the very last minute. Rose and Cedric were therefore alone, and were likely to be so for a few minutes more.

'The inspector made quite a good case for why Jemima might have wanted to kill Emmeline, and how she went about it.'

'Did he indeed? But she denied it of course, didn't she?'

'Yes, she did.'

'But, from what you've told me, it sounds as if the inspector's coming around to your way of thinking about her being an impostor,' said Cedric, 'which is good, isn't it?'

'Well, it was obvious to us all that it was a great shock to Jemima when she heard that Mr Montacute was due back from his travels.'

'Well, that will clear everything up, won't it? Poor fellow. What a homecoming. Still, if Jemima isn't Jemima, it stands to reason that Emmeline isn't Emmeline, so perhaps he'll receive some welcome news after all.'

'Oh, Cedric, I'm not so sure that I haven't got it all wrong about Jemima being an impostor,' Rose said, looking rather wistful. 'If only the inspector had asked Jemima the one question that might have thrown some light on it. I would have asked her myself, but unfortunately I had already interrupted the inspector a few times when he was in his stride. I didn't think he would indulge me asking another question.'

'And what question was that?'

'Why Jemima didn't try to put a stop to the relationship developing between Emmeline and Theo Harrison. According to Lavinia, she watched Emmeline like a hawk and reported everything back to Mr Montacute. And he was unlikely to approve of Theo as a prospective son-in-law, was he? No matter how good a doctor Theo is, Mr Montacute would have wanted someone much grander for his daughter, don't you think?'

'Unless his only concern was her happiness. If he doted on the girl as much as everyone says he did, Emmeline needn't have married a rich or influential husband. She had all the wealth she could possibly need. And apart from the way he's behaved towards poor Vera, Harrison's a pretty good sort.'

'If you say so,' said Rose, sounding far from convinced.

'What did you make of Jemima's story about the diamonds?' asked Cedric, deciding to change the subject. 'Sounds jolly odd to me.'

'Well,' said Rose, 'if Jemima was speaking the truth about the necklace always having been a paste replica, it would explain why she looked so apprehensive when the count produced his jeweller's loupe. If you remember, she didn't join in the game.'

'Although, if the inspector's right about the count being a jewel thief, wouldn't he have noticed that the diamonds were fake?'

'Yes, he would. But he might not have said anything. If you remember, he paused before he passed judgement on them. One thing I am certain of though. Emmeline believed them to be genuine. The inspector was quite right that she wouldn't have been able to keep quiet about them not being real. She would have found it awfully funny if the count had mistaken fake diamonds for the real thing.'

'It seems to me that the inspector is accusing everyone of being a jewel thief. I'm rather surprised he hasn't accused me of being one!'

'He is rather, isn't he?'

'I say, that tampered jewellery box is all a bit of a rum go, isn't it? Did you believe Jemima's story about someone putting it in her room?'

'I don't quite know what to make of it,' replied Rose truthfully. 'Although I think I know when Jemima hid the box on the landing. It was when Lavinia and I went to get her on our way back down to the drawing room. I have no doubt Jemima was carrying it in her handbag. She seemed reluctant to leave her room at first, and then all at once she dashed over to one of the windows making some excuse about wanting to see if the maze could be seen from the house.'

'Sounds rather a strange thing to do,' agreed Cedric.

'She almost upset a plant stand in the process. I think she stuffed the jewellery box either in or behind a flower pot. There was a houseplant on the stand, you see. She fiddled with it for a while. At the time I just assumed she was trying to make sure the plant was securely positioned on the plant stand after knocking it. But now I think she was trying to wipe off her fingerprints. Unfortunately for her, your sister was keen to be downstairs. She asked Jemima what she was doing so she had to hurry her task which would explain why she missed wiping off one or two of the fingerprints.'

'That's Lavinia for you,' said Cedric. 'Always impatient. And unfortunately she seems to have taken a bit of a dislike to poor Jemima.'

'It won't be unfortunate if Jemima turns out to be as fake as Emmeline's diamonds. Speaking of Lavinia, I take it she is coming down for dinner. She hasn't decided to eat by herself in her boudoir has she?'

Cedric made a face.

'I told her in no uncertain terms that I expected her to come down for dinner. I said, if nothing else, she owed it to Emmeline. I mentioned that you'd be busy interrogating the guests and that it was her task to keep the conversation flowing so that they wouldn't realise what you were doing. Hello, here's Thistlewaite.'

'I say, I hope I'm not intruding.' Felix said affably, appearing in the doorway. 'Aren't the others down yet? I thought I might be late.'

'What will you have, Felix? I'll do the honours. The servants are having their dinner.'

'A Sidecar, if it's no trouble.' Felix turned to Rose while Cedric moved away to mix the drink. 'I developed rather a taste for the cocktail while I was in Paris. Look here, how's Jemima bearing up? I heard you accompanied her when the police interviewed her. Jolly decent of you. She's taken it all rather badly, I'm afraid. Not surprising of course. I just wish she'd let me speak to her. She's keeping herself to herself, and I'm certain it's not doing her any good. I just want her to know that I'm here for her if she needs me.'

'I'm sure she already knows that,' said Rose. 'She's just shaken up by everything, that's all. Tell me, do you know if it was her idea to go to the Continent or Emmeline's?'

'Oh, Emmeline's to be sure. Jemima was always a little nervous while we were in Florence. I don't think she much liked going against Mr Montacute's wishes. I think she couldn't wait to get back to the safety of their Highland home. Emmeline on the other hand showed no sign of ever wanting to return there. No doubt she had her father wrapped around her little finger. She had no fear of being made homeless when he found out what they'd done.'

'I see.'

'Of course I'm jolly pleased that I met Jemima and all that, but I've been wondering today whether she didn't have the right idea after all, in light of what's happened. It sounds damned ungrateful, I know, but part of me wishes Great Aunt Mabel had never treated me to a European tour. I say,' Felix paused, a look of amusement appearing on his face, 'Lavinia's obviously decided to ignore the suggestion that we didn't dress for dinner tonight!'

Chapter Twenty-eight

'Cedric really needn't look at me like that,' complained Lavinia. 'I am wearing a black dress after all and no diamonds. But I tell you, Rose, I absolutely draw the line at not dressing for dinner. Particularly when one has guests.'

Rose opened her mouth to issue a word of reproach, but thought better of it.

'Now where is Count Fernand?' continued Lavinia. 'I haven't seen much of him at all today, have you? I really do think I need to be flattered and amused tonight. It is all going to be so deadly dull.'

'Lavinia, really! I don't think you are half as awful as you make out.'

'Then you have a better opinion of me, Rose, than I do of myself.' Lavinia turned around to survey the room. 'Oh, have you seen the way Jemima is looking at Vera? If looks could kill! Although perhaps I shouldn't say that in the circumstances.'

'Unfortunately the inspector let slip that it was Vera who enticed Emmeline to go to the maze. I expect Jemima holds her partly to blame for Emmeline's death.'

'Well I never! I wouldn't have thought Vera would have had it in her. If I'd have been in her shoes, I think it would have been Theo I'd have given a good talking to, not Emmeline. Now where is Max? Really, it's too bad. Manning will be calling us to go into dinner any minute.'

'By the way, has the inspector interviewed you yet?' asked Rose. She was rather curious as to what the two of them would have made of each other.

'No, he hasn't. Horrible little man! He isn't a patch on your Inspector Deacon.'

'He isn't *my* Inspector Deacon, Lavinia. But does that mean you've met Inspector Bramwell?'

'Yes. And I didn't like him one little bit. He was frightfully rude to me, you know. I went in to see him just before I went up to dress for dinner. I told him that I thought it was rather too much that he'd kept me waiting so long.'

'I can imagine that went down rather well!' Rose said, smiling in spite of herself.

'He told me in no uncertain terms that he would summon me when he wished to interview me and not before, and that I should run off and get some dinner while I had the chance. And what is more,' Lavinia said indignantly, 'I could have sworn that Sergeant Lane, who up until then I did think was quite a nice man, was trying his hardest not to laugh.'

Lavinia's attention was diverted by the entrance of a man both girls barely recognised, his attire being so very different to what they had become accustomed to him sporting.

'Good gracious!' exclaimed Lavinia. 'That can't be Max, can it? Whatever is he wearing? It looks like an ordinary wool tweed suit to me!'

Count Fernand did indeed look uncomfortable and out of place in the gathering. He was looking around the room rather apprehensively, as if he were afraid that any moment he would be asked to leave or to take his dinner in the servants' quarters.

Rose went over to him and smiled reassuringly. She then proceeded to speak to him in a voice barely above a whisper.

'I want to ask you a question, and I need you to answer me truthfully. Will you?'

'That would depend on your question, Miss Simpson,' replied Count Fernand, cocking an eye at her quizzically. Rose noticed that all traces of a foreign accent had vanished from his voice.

'Did you put Emmeline's jewellery box in Jemima's room?'

'I'm not sure I will answer that question. I don't think it is in my interests to do so.'

'I beg to disagree. I think it is very much in your best interests to do so. But the very fact that you haven't denied placing it there answers my question.'

'I am not a jewel thief, whatever that inspector might think.'

'I never said you were. For what it's worth, I don't think you are. But please do answer my question. Did you put that box in Jemima's room? Was it because someone had placed it in your own room?'

'Yes,' replied Count Fernand, wearily. 'How did you know? I found it in my room first thing this morning when I woke up. The lock had clearly been tampered with. It worried me that the necklace was still there.

I wondered whether it was a fake. I thought someone was trying to implicate me in a theft. The thought even crossed my mind that it might be his lordship. I know he doesn't approve of me and is suspicious of my intentions towards his sister. I thought he might have been trying to discredit me in her eyes.'

'Cedric would never have done such a thing!' cried Rose.

'You are right, of course. I did him a disservice when I thought it was him. But at the time I thought it was only a question of theft.'

'So you decided to put it in Jemima's room?'

'Yes. I thought she was the one person who could not be implicated in the theft. She had a key to the jewellery box. Emmeline had told me so herself. Jemima had no reason to tamper with the box when she could open it with the key.'

'Unless she wanted to divert suspicion from herself,' said Rose.

The count sighed. 'As soon as it was discovered that Emmeline had been murdered, I realised the situation was much more serious than I had first imagined it to be. Someone was trying to implicate me in the girl's death. Hello? I think we're going into dinner.'

'I just have one more question to ask you,' Rose said quickly. 'When you looked at Emmeline's necklace under your jeweller's loupe, did it occur to you that the diamonds might be fake?'

'As it happens that thought did cross my mind. But it didn't seem to make any sense so I dismissed it. I say, the policeman asked me the same question. I was at a loss how best to answer. Tell me. Do you think Emmeline's necklace was genuine?'

'No,' said Rose. 'I think it was a paste replica. I think the real necklace never left Scotland.'

That night Rose found it difficult to get to sleep, which she considered hardly surprising given the circumstances. For one thing, she was sleeping in a different bed than usual. Lavinia had decided that she did not wish to sleep alone with a murderer at large. She had therefore requested that Rose sleep in her dressing room, which joined Lavinia's bedroom by way of a connecting door. The decision had been taken to keep this door open, which was proving far from satisfactory from Rose's perspective. For, somewhat to her surprise, she had discovered that Lavinia had a propensity towards snoring loud enough to shake the house.

Although tired, Rose found that most annoyingly she was fully awake. She lay in her bed thinking how mercilessly she would tease Lavinia in the morning. In the meantime, while sleep eluded her, she gave up her mind to reviewing the events leading up to the murder and its subsequent aftermath. The more she thought and remembered, the more everything seemed to blur into one with sentences and scenes, no matter how separate and disjointed, appearing as if from nowhere, jumbled together and overlapping like a badly put together jigsaw puzzle.

Vera saying how Emmeline behaved like a child in a sweetshop … Emmeline and Jemima walking side by side, a little removed from the others, their heads bent towards each other as if they were sharing a secret … Emmeline giggling and laughing with Theo while Vera looked on ... Cedric carefully and deliberately cleaning the candlestick, and Felix crying out for him to stop what he was doing ... Count Fernand comforting Jemima and leading her out of the maze ... Jemima frightened, always frightened, and anxious and wanting to be back at home ... Vera asking spitefully about the kidnap attempt and Emmeline and Jemima going to pieces over it ... Emmeline's diamonds being hurriedly passed around and around the room. Everyone peering at them except for Jemima and Vera standing apart and alone, as if ostracised … Vera's confession that she had written the note that had summoned Emmeline to meet her fate ... Jemima's evasiveness even when being interviewed.

It all went round and round in Rose's head. Everything swirling together with the odd sentence or scene coming into focus before disappearing into the fog. How long it went on like this, Rose did not know. Later she wondered whether she had been conscious of the shift. For the mist had gradually appeared to get less dense until it cleared. And suddenly Rose knew. She knew the missing link that would unlock the door and let the light in. The light that would reveal once and for all who the murderer was.

If she settled back among her pillows and allowed her exhausted mind to sleep, she was confident that by the morning she would know the identity of the murderer. She sighed, and the sleep that had eluded her for so long at last overtook her in a rush. Lavinia's snores seemed no more than the noise of the wind whistling through the trees.

'Sir! Sir! Wake up!'

'Huh? ... Eh? ...What?'

The inspector somewhat reluctantly gave in to the incessant shaking of his shoulders that thrust him into the land of the conscious. Begrudgingly he half opened bleary, still sleepy eyes and found himself staring at his sergeant. This spectacle in itself was enough to cause him to rouse fully, let alone that he could not at first remember where he was. It was only as his watery eyes began to focus, to take in the strange curtains and unfamiliar dimensions of the room, that he remembered he was at Sedgwick Court.

'What time is it?'

'Nearly six o'clock, sir.'

'What in ...' the inspector sat up and glared at Sergeant Lane, before an awful thought struck him, which had him clinging on to his subordinate's shirt collar, pulling the man down to his level.

'Don't tell me there's been another murder! Not while we've been sleeping under their roof. That really would –'

'No, sir. Nothing like that,' said Sergeant Lane reassuringly.

'Then what's the meaning of waking me up like this? We no doubt have a long day in front of us. I need all the sleep I can get. I'm not getting any younger, you know.'

'If you remember, sir, after we interviewed Miss Wentmore yesterday we thought there was a possibility that Miss Simpson's theory that she was an impostor might prove correct after all.'

'Well, Miss Wentmore was certainly damned evasive,' admitted Inspector Bramwell grudgingly. 'And pretty shaken up at the idea of coming face to face with old Montacute.'

'That's just it, sir. It got me to thinking. I telephoned the station last night and asked them to arrange for a constable to speak with that secretary fellow, Stapleton, and get a physical description of Miss Montacute and Miss Wentmore.'

'Well?'

'To tell you the truth, I'd forgotten all about it until this morning when I myself was rudely awakened from my slumber a half hour ago by a rather annoyed Mr Manning. Apparently the constable obtained a description of the two young ladies last night and intended to telephone us with the information later this morning.'

'Well, what made him change his plans?'

'Stapleton telephoned the station an hour or so ago. Apparently he's received a telephone call from Montacute. The fellow had decided to come home earlier than intended. Would you believe it, his ship docked yesterday. He stayed the night in some hotel or other. Stapleton's a quick fellow. Thought on his feet and hid from his master the panic he was feeling. He told him to come straight here.'

'Good God! Did he tell him why?'

'No. Not the real reason. He just said that Miss Montacute and Miss Wentmore were staying here. He didn't mention anything regarding the murder.'

'Do you know what time he's likely to arrive?'

'Stapleton said it put the wind up Montacute when he discovered Miss Montacute wasn't at home. He wouldn't put it past the old man to have set off for Sedgwick at once.'

'If that's the case —'

'He should be here within the hour, sir.'

Inspector Bramwell showed again how surprisingly agile a man of his physique could be by scrambling out of bed and proceeding to pull on his clothes in a haphazard fashion.

'I'm afraid that's not all, sir.'

'What? There's more? Out with it, Sergeant.'

'The descriptions of the two ladies, sir.'

'What's wrong with them?'

'They don't match our Miss Montacute and Miss Wentmore.'

'What —'

'See here, sir. The real Miss Wentmore is above average height with hair that is dark in colour, so Stapleton says. A striking woman, he called her.'

'That's hardly our dowdy Miss Wentmore,' cried Inspector Bramwell. 'A plain, drab little thing she is. Can't see what that fellow Thistlewaite sees in her.'

'It proves, sir, that the woman purporting to be Jemima Wentmore is not her.'

'It does indeed. It just goes to prove I was right, Lane. She's nothing but a jewel thief. No doubt she was trying to ingratiate herself with Lady Lavinia so she could steal some of her jewels.'

'You think she killed Miss Montacute? Or should I say the woman claiming to be Miss Montacute?'

'I do. The woman was more than likely her accomplice in crime. They no doubt had a falling out over the spoils. Those types always do.'

'Mr Montacute is coming here expecting to see his daughter and her companion,' Sergeant Lane reminded the inspector.

'So he is. We'll have to head him off. And whatever happens don't let anyone tell him about the murder. The last thing we want is for someone to tell him his daughter's dead.'

'Sergeant Lane. What are you doing here? It's awfully early in the morning for you to start your interviews, isn't it?' said Rose, encountering the sergeant outside Jemima's room, which was opposite both her own and Lavinia's.

'Sorry to wake you, miss.' Rose noticed that the policeman was looking a little awkward, as if he did not wish to advertise his presence outside Jemima's room. Either that or he was embarrassed at catching sight of her in her night attire, she decided.

'What is happening, Sergeant?'

Sergeant Lane looked anxiously at Jemima's closed door before moving forward a pace or two. He then proceeded to speak in a whisper.

'You were right, miss. Jemima Wentmore is not Jemima Wentmore. And Mr Montacute is due to arrive any minute now.'

'Mr Montacute,' said Rose rather loudly, 'is due to arrive any minute now?'

'Ssh! Keep your voice down please, miss. You'll wake the young lady pretending to be Miss Wentmore. The inspector is afraid she'll try and make a run for it if she knows Montacute is on his way. He'll be able to unmask her for the impostor that she is, you see.'

They heard the sound of bolts being pulled back and a key being turned in a lock. A moment later, Jemima's bedroom door was flung open and the girl herself appeared. Her face was white and her insipid hair was flowing. This, coupled with her wearing a nightdress in a muted shade, gave her an almost ghostly appearance.

'Mr Montacute is coming here? Now?' She demanded urgently.

'Yes,' said Rose firmly, conscious out of the corner of her eye that the sergeant was glaring at her.

Jemima immediately closed the door and slid back the bolts.

'Now you've gone and done it, miss, and no mistake. She'll be climbing out of her window unless we stop her.'

Rose retreated into her own room as the sergeant ran downstairs to make his way outside. She kept her door ajar. As soon as the policeman was out of sight, Rose ran to Jemima's door and tapped on it rapidly.

'Quickly! Unbolt this door! They think you're trying to escape out of your window. They'll be going to get ladders and all sorts. If you hurry, you can hide in my room. They won't think of looking for you there.'

After a moment's hesitation, the bolts were once again pulled back from the door, the door unlocked and Jemima emerged fully dressed. Without a word she followed Rose into her room.

'You can hide in the wardrobe, if you want to,' said Rose.

'Why are you doing this? Why are you helping me?'

'Because you need a friend, and ... well ... I know who you are.'

'Do you?' Jemima looked scared.

'Don't be frightened. You can trust me. You could trust Sergeant Lane too, you know.'

'No!'

'All right. As you like. They'll be banging on my door in a minute to find out if I've seen you. Quickly. Climb into the wardrobe or under the bed.'

But, before Jemima could do anything of the sort, they heard a commotion in the hall below.

'Is it ...?'

'I'll go and see. You wait here.'

Rose opened her door as silently as she could and crept along the landing so that she was in a positon to look over the bannisters to the hall below. An elderly man in a well-cut suit was in deep discussion with the inspector who, even at this distance, Rose could see was hot and flustered. It was obvious from the elderly man's raised voice and Inspector Bramwell's agitated state that the men were having a disagreement of some kind. Rose took the opportunity to creep back to her room unobserved.

'Come on, quickly,' she said to Jemima.

The girl followed her out until they were at the top of the great staircase peering down.

Everything then seemed to happen very quickly and all at once. Sergeant Lane appeared in the hall. At the same time, Inspector Bramwell happened to look up and caught sight of Jemima cowering behind Rose.

'There she is! Quickly, get her Lane, before she escapes.'

'No!' cried Rose. 'You don't understand. She's –'

'Father!' exclaimed Jemima.

The elderly man looked up, his eyes squinting behind thick lenses.

'Emmeline!' he cried.

Chapter Twenty-nine

'Perhaps, Miss Simpson, you would be good enough to explain things to me,' said Inspector Bramwell, sighing. He looked exasperated and tired, his plump face red and blotchy.

It was some half an hour later and Rose, having abandoned her night attire for a sensible tweed ensemble, was sitting in the study, facing the inspector across the huge polished desk. Besides the policemen, the only other occupant in the room was Cedric, who was sitting beside her, his eyes never leaving her face. Mr Montacute and his daughter had decamped to the library, where Emmeline was acquainting her father with all that had occurred while he had been abroad.

'Well, Inspector. I think we should begin with the fact that the woman that we knew as Jemima Wentmore is in fact Emmeline Montacute,' said Rose.

'And the woman we knew as Emmeline Montacute was actually Jemima Wentmore,' added Cedric. 'Miss Simpson worked it all out, Inspector.'

'Yes,' said Rose, 'but not until last night, or the early hours of this morning, I should say. I had my suspicions that Emmeline and Jemima were not who they professed to be. But it didn't occur to me until a short time ago that they might just have swapped identities.'

'And why pray should they have done that,' asked the inspector, frowning and scratching the side of his head.

'To explain why,' said Rose, 'I think we need to go back to the very beginning. I think it all started long ago with the foiled kidnapping attempt. If you remember, it was very nearly successful. I think Mr Montacute became almost obsessed with the notion that another kidnap attempt would be made on his daughter. As a consequence, he was overly protective towards her. He arranged for them to live in a heavily fortified house in Scotland, with no near neighbours, from which they rarely ventured out. And on the rare occasions that they did, Emmeline was always accompanied by a host of servants or by Mr Montacute himself. Afraid that his daughter would become lonely or bored, Mr Montacute invited a poor relation of a similar age to Emmeline to live with them and be her paid companion. He also organised a number of parties and balls at their residence, but I imagine that the only guests invited were ones that had been closely scrutinised by Mr Montacute himself.'

'A pretty dull existence for a young girl, I'd have thought.' said Cedric. 'It would never have done for someone like my sister.'

'But I'm not sure Emmeline found it dull,' said Rose. 'After all, it was all she had ever known. But I do think Jemima found it dreary.'

'So am I right in thinking that when Montacute decides to go on his travels, the two women decide to do likewise?' said the inspector, sitting back heavily in his chair.

'Yes. They seized the opportunity. Or should I say Jemima did. She managed to persuade Emmeline, who was rather nervous and somewhat reluctant. If you remember, the fear of being kidnapped had been instilled in her from an early age. No doubt at first she refused even to contemplate it no matter how tempted she might have been. That, I think, is when Jemima came up with the suggestion that they swap identities for the duration of their travels. It made Emmeline feel that she was not taking so great a risk.'

'But how did you know that was what they'd done?' asked Sergeant Lane. 'From what I can gather, they both looked and acted their parts very well.'

'A little too well,' said Rose. 'I always thought Emmeline, pretending to be Jemima, looked a little too dowdy and plain. I would imagine the real Jemima would have been given a handsome dress allowance. And Jemima, pretending to be Emmeline, played her part overly enthusiastically. And a chance remark Miss Brewster made remained with me: "... look how much she is enjoying all the attention ... You'd think she'd be used to it by now, wouldn't you? Instead she behaves like a child let loose in a sweetshop." And that was just how the girl we knew as Emmeline behaved for the very good reason that she was not used to all the attention she was receiving as an heiress, and was making the most of it while she had the opportunity to do so.'

'It explains also,' said Cedric, 'why the real Emmeline did not discourage Jemima's relationship with Theo Harrison. The doctor would have made an ideal husband for her companion.'

'And it would also explain the magazine article about Miss Montacute being an accomplished rider, I suppose,' admitted the inspector.

'Yes. There were a number of other things as well,' said Rose. 'The real Jemima was always seeking Emmeline's approval, which seemed rather strange to us all at the time. Once or twice both girls also almost slipped up when referring to Mr Montacute. The real Emmeline of course went to refer to him as father instead of Mr Montacute, and the real Jemima as Mr Montacute instead of father. They both corrected themselves just in time.'

'And the diamond necklace?' asked the inspector. 'What about that?'

'It was only ever a paste replica,' said Rose. 'Jemima wanted to take the real one on their travels but Emmeline, being by nature more cautious, decided to take the fake necklace instead.'

'Do I take it that she omitted to tell Jemima?' asked Cedric.

'Yes, I think she thought Jemima wouldn't notice and so there was no reason to tell her and spoil her enjoyment in wearing the necklace,' said Rose. 'I don't for one moment think she ever imagined that the necklace would be looked at through a jeweller's loupe.'

'But what I don't understand,' said the inspector, 'is why Miss Montacute did not reveal her true identity to us after the murder.'

'I think I can answer that, Inspector,' said Rose, smiling. 'I'm afraid she was suspicious of you.'

'What?' thundered Inspector Bramwell. He sat forward in his chair and grabbed the desk. 'Why should the girl not trust me?'

'You must remember, Inspector, that Miss Montacute has always had a fear of being kidnapped. As soon as she was informed that Jemima was missing, that is what she thought had happened to her. When we discovered that Jemima had been murdered, Emmeline did not know quite what to think. Undoubtedly a part of her hoped that it was as it first appeared to be: Lavinia had killed Jemima. But then we discovered that Jemima had been dead for some hours. So a failed kidnapping attempt was still a real possibility. And rumour had it that some very prominent people, including policemen, Inspector, had been involved in the previous kidnap attempt, although of course nothing was ever proved.'

'You mean to tell me that she thought I was involved in the kidnap and death of Miss Wentmore?' exclaimed the inspector, his eyes watering.

'She thought it a possibility, yes. After Jemima's body was found she was very frightened and did not know whom to trust. She had heard that I had some experience of murder investigations and saw me greeting Sergeant Lane. It was obvious to her that we were already acquainted and that this was a policeman she might be able to trust. She was just beginning to consider confiding her true identity to the police when I informed her of something that was to her very worrying.'

'And what was that?' demanded the inspector.

'I informed her that I did not know you. That I had never met you before. What was more, I told her that Inspector Deacon had been wounded and that you had been brought in to replace him.'

'Are you saying that Miss Montacute thought Inspector Deacon being shot was in some way connected with Miss Wentmore's murder?' asked Sergeant Lane looking incredulous.

'Yes … well, that is to say, I think she thought it was a possibility.'

There was rather an awkward silence that saw the inspector huffing and puffing irritably in his chair.

'Well,' Inspector Bramwell said at last. 'This is all well and good, and no doubt Miss Montacute will corroborate your version of events and offer a few embellishments of her own. But it does not address the fact that we are no nearer knowing the identity of the murderer.'

'Oh, but we are!' cried Rose. 'Don't you see, Inspector? Once we had established the women's true identities, everything else fell into place.'

'No, I definitely don't see,' grumbled Inspector Bramwell. 'Out with it, Miss Simpson. Who do you think is the murderer?'

'Why, Felix Thistlewaite, of course.'

There was a stunned silence as the others took in the news.

'Thistlewaite?' said Cedric at last. 'Are you sure about that, Rose, really? The chap seems such a good egg.'

'I'm afraid I am.'

The inspector glared. 'Well, I for one am far from convinced. Perhaps you will give me your reasons for believing that young Thistlewaite is our murderer.'

'Well, Inspector. I think I shall start at the beginning as I did before.'

'Please do.'

'I suppose it all began on the Continent before they all came to Sedgwick. Inspector, you have been looking for a jewel thief. The most likely person seemed to be Count Fernand, who was rather too obviously not a count. You even wondered if it might be Emmeline, when she was pretending to be Jemima. I think, however, that a successful jewel thief had to be less conspicuous.'

'Just like Thistlewaite, in fact?' said Cedric.

'Yes. An affable young man on a European tour funded by a rich great aunt. He did not pretend to be wealthy or titled. Instead he went out of his way to inform anyone who would listen that he was about to start employment as an articled clerk in a London legal establishment as soon as he returned from his travels.'

'But that wasn't true?' enquired Sergeant Lane.

'No, it was all a lie, including the bit about the rich great aunt. It just provided him with a reason for being on the Continent and staying at an expensive hotel.'

'How do you know all this, Miss Simpson?' asked Inspector Bramwell. 'Is it all conjecture?'

'Well, for one thing he forgot the name of his rich great aunt. He called her both Maud and Mabel. If she had really existed and funded his travels, then surely he'd have remembered her name, wouldn't he?'

'One would have thought so. But I do hope that you have more than that on which to base your accusation, Miss Simpson.' The inspector frowned.

'Indeed, I have, Inspector. But I digress. To return to the Continent. Felix Thistlewaite was no doubt intending to ingratiate himself with either Lady Lavinia or Emmeline Montacute. But, much to his annoyance, he finds that role has been taken by Count Fernand, of whom he is highly suspicious. He settles instead for whom he believes is Jemima Wentmore, but whom we now know is the real Emmeline Montacute. From his perspective, it does not matter so very much which woman he chooses. He only requires an opportunity to discover what jewels the women have brought with them and which are the easiest to steal.'

'But he didn't steal any of their jewels on the Continent.' pointed out Cedric.

'No, he didn't. Quite why, I'm not sure. Perhaps he didn't have an opportunity to do so, or perhaps he thought he'd do better waiting until he came to Sedgwick. I suppose Lavinia has many valuable jewels here?'

'Oh, a lot,' agreed Cedric.

'At Sedgwick, Felix's plans go astray. After dinner one evening, as we all know, Vera makes a scene alluding to the failed kidnap attempt, which results in the count introducing his game of looking at the women's jewels through a jeweller's lens.'

'Felix must have been delighted,' said Cedric. 'It gave him the ideal opportunity to examine both Emmeline's and Lavinia's jewels. We all had a turn with the lens, if you remember?'

'I do. And Felix must have been thrilled as you say, until he discovered that Emmeline's necklace was in fact a paste replica. I think at first he assumed that Jemima, who he believed to be Emmeline, would produce the real necklace at the end of the evening and laugh about them all being taken in by her fake necklace. But as we know she didn't, because she believed it to be genuine.'

'So he decided instead to concentrate his efforts on acquiring Lady Lavinia's jewels?' said Inspector Bramwell. He turned to address Cedric. 'I take it your sister's jewels are genuine, my lord?'

'Yes, of course.'

'But,' said Rose, 'Lavinia had mentioned that evening that you insisted her jewels be kept locked up in your personal safe whenever she was not wearing them.'

'Did she? I'm afraid I don't recall.'

'She did. So you see, Felix Thistlewaite was suddenly faced with the very real possibility that he would not have an opportunity to steal any jewels while at Sedgwick. All his meticulous planning had come to nothing.'

'So what happened next?' asked Sergeant Lane.

'Well, the next evening there was talk of the maze which, as we know prompted Vera to entice Jemima, pretending to be Emmeline, to meet her there in the early hours of the following morning. It was still dark when Jemima set off for the maze. But Vera mentioned there was a full moon. If we believe that Vera did not murder Jemima, someone must have followed Jemima to the maze. Unless it was Emmeline, who might have heard Jemima leave her room, hers being next door, then that person must have been looking out of their window at the time and seen her set off.'

'So that's why you asked my housekeeper who occupied which room,' said Cedric.

'Yes. Other than Lavinia or myself, the only two other people who could have looked out of their windows and seen Jemima setting out was you, Cedric, or Felix Thistlewaite.'

'Well, I assure you I didn't set off after the girl,' said Cedric, with a slight grin.

'I never thought you did,' said Rose. 'But getting back to my theory, I think Felix decided to follow Jemima, who he believed to be Emmeline, because above all else he had been thinking over what to do if he was unable to steal any jewels. And the conclusion he had reached was to kidnap her and hold her for ransom. Her setting off like that gave him the ideal opportunity to carry out his plan. And it would explain something that has been bothering all of us.'

'What?'

'Why someone took a candlestick to the maze. Don't you see? Felix had to act quickly in case he lost sight of Jemima. Remember, he had no idea where she was going. So he picked up the first weapon that came to hand. The knives were all locked away in the butler's pantry, as is custom, but he remembered seeing the candlesticks on the sideboard. He dashed into the dining room, picked up one of the candlesticks, and then ran out of the house, following Jemima to the maze. But I don't think he followed her into the maze itself.'

'Why not?' asked Cedric.

'Well, for one thing he didn't know who Jemima, pretending to be Emmeline, was going to meet. I expect he assumed it was Theo Harrison. Felix needed to wait until Jemima was alone to carry out his plan. So I think he hid at the entrance to the maze and waited for her to come out.'

'It must have occurred to him that he might have been wasting his time,' said Sergeant Lane. 'For all he knew, Miss Wentmore and Dr Harrison might have walked back to the house together.'

'But instead Vera came out alone,' said the inspector.

'Yes. It must have been something of a surprise to him that it was her Jemima was going to meet,' said Rose. 'But fortunately for him, Vera did something when she came out of the maze which enabled Felix to navigate his way to the centre. She threw away the plan of the maze she had drawn for Jemima.'

'So what you are saying is that Thistlewaite picked up the plan and made his way to the centre of the maze where he found Jemima lost and frightened?' said the inspector.

'Yes. He should probably have stayed at the entrance of the maze and waited for Jemima, playing the role of Emmeline, to come out, but I imagine he was impatient. Besides Jemima, you will recall from Miss Brewster's interview, Inspector, did not know her way back out of the maze without the plan. It would have been a long wait.'

'What do you think happened when Felix encountered Jemima in the maze? Whatever made him decide to kill the girl?' asked Cedric.

'I've been thinking about that. I imagine he was not particularly keen on the idea of kidnapping her. But he was desperate. I have no doubt his funds were running out. To begin with I think he would have asked her about the necklace. Jemima of course would have been adamant that it was genuine. Perhaps he was persistent with his questions and she became suspicious. Whatever occurred, I think Felix informed her of his intention to kidnap her.'

'And Jemima panicked and told him she wasn't Emmeline?' said the inspector.

'Yes. If only she had kept quiet she might still have been alive today. But her fatal mistake was not just telling him who she was not, but also who she was. If she had just told him she was an impostor, Felix might have let her go, thinking no real harm had been done. But by telling him who she was, it was obvious that the first thing she would do on reaching the house would be to warn the real Emmeline of the danger she was in. And then of course the police would have been called, and that would have been that.'

'So he killed her to keep her quiet,' said Cedric sadly.

'But it's still all conjecture, Miss Simpson,' complained the inspector. 'I'm not saying you're not right, because I think you may very well be, but there is no real evidence to support your theory.'

'What about the plan that Vera drew for Jemima?' said Rose. 'Of course Felix might have thrown it on to the fire as soon as he got back to his room, but I wouldn't be a bit surprised if it's still in his coat pocket. He hasn't got a valet to see to his clothes. And Vera told us she made a slight mistake when drawing the plan, so if he still has it in his possession we could prove it was the one Vera had drawn.'

Sergeant Lane charged out of the room. They could hear him calling to the constables.

'Wait a minute,' said Cedric. 'Something doesn't make sense. Felix tried to stop me from wiping the fingerprints off the candlestick.'

'No he didn't,' said Rose. 'He waited until you had wiped the candlestick of fingerprints before he made a fuss. Anyway, although Inspector Bramwell and I may disagree on this point, I imagine he wore gloves to wield the candlestick.'

'But what about Emmeline's jewellery box?' asked the inspector. 'I assume it was Thistlewaite who tampered with the lock?'

'Yes. He did it to throw suspicion on the count. He put the box in his room, you see. But fortunately for the count he found it before it was discovered by the police.'

'What a despicable thing to do.' cried Cedric. 'For all Thistlewaite knew he could have been responsible for sending an innocent man to the gallows for *his* crime.'

'Not quite the affable young man he appeared to be,' said Inspector Bramwell grimly.

Chapter Thirty

'Theo! Surely you weren't intending to leave without me?'

Vera, breathless, had just caught up with the doctor on the drive in front of the house. In her haste she had come out without hat, coat and gloves and stood shivering in the weak December sun.

'Go back inside, Vera,' Theo answered, dismissively. 'You'll catch your death dressed like that. Don't worry. I'll send my man back with the car for you just as soon as I've got to my lodgings. He'll take you back to the vicarage.'

'What are you talking about, Theo? We'll leave together of course, the way we came. If you just give me half an hour or so, I'll arrange for my case to be packed and I'll be with you.'

'No, Vera.'

'What do you mean "No, Vera"? Why, you are being quite absurd. It would be a nonsense to leave separately, what would everyone think?'

'What would everyone think?' Theo looked at her in disbelief. 'The truth of course. It's no good, Vera, don't you see? We can't just pretend that nothing's happened. I fell in love with someone else.'

'Don't ... don't say that,' Vera said quickly, almost going so far as to try and cover her ears. 'You were just temporarily besotted, that's all. All the men were. I can't say I'm surprised. She was very pretty and charming, and of course you all thought she was very rich. But you would have got bored of her, I know you would –'

'Vera –'

'No, don't say anything more about it. I don't want us to go over it, it doesn't do any good. It happened, and I don't say that you didn't hurt me very much, but now I just want to forget about it.'

'Vera, it's no use. Oh, if only you wouldn't be so nice about it all. Don't you see that it only makes things worse?' Theo tore at his hair in exasperation. 'I behaved very badly, I know, like a complete rotter and I can't tell you how awfully I feel about it all. You deserved better than that. Why, even Cedric had a go at me about it. He pretty well gave me my marching orders.'

'It doesn't matter, Theo, none of it matters at all now.' Vera clung at the sleeve of his coat and he threw off her hand in an irritated fashion.

'It matters a great deal, Vera. It showed me that I didn't love you, not in the way you love me anyway and certainly not enough for us to get married.'

'I don't care. I don't care if I love you more than you love me. I've always known it. In a couple one party always loves the other more. I love you enough for both of us –'

'No, Vera, it really won't do, not for me, not now I know what it is to really be in love.' He held her hand and spoke more gently. 'If only I could make you understand. When they told me that Emmeline ... I shall always think of her as Emmeline not Jemima ... wasn't an heiress, that she wasn't who she pretended to be, I went to pieces. But not for the reasons everyone assumed. It was because it meant that there would have been no obstacle to us marrying. She wasn't far above me socially as I had thought. The wife of a country doctor might have suited her quite well.'

'What about me?' pleaded Vera, clutching at his hand, 'I'll make you a good wife, you know I will. We belong together, you know we do.'

'No we don't, that's what I've been trying to tell you Vera. I don't doubt for a moment that you think you love me, but it's not real, it's too much. Frankly my dear, it's suffocating. Not only that, I find it rather frightening. Look what it made you do. If you hadn't written that stupid, spiteful note, Emmeline ... no, I must call her Jemima ... would never have been in that maze. And you left her there, Vera, cold and frightened. You left her there to get murdered.'

'But I had no idea that would happen. I wasn't thinking properly. I was so upset ... I ...'

'Yes, and don't you see that only makes it worse,' said Theo more quietly. 'It's my fault. It's all my fault. I know you wouldn't have done what you did if it hadn't been for the way I behaved. The girl is dead because of what we did. Don't you see, Vera? Every time I look at you I'll be reminded of what we did. I can't live my life like that, and neither can you.'

'But I ...'

'And besides, Vera, my dear,' said Theo kindly. 'You deserve a better husband than I will ever be.'

258

'Did you suspect that Felix might be the murderer?' asked Rose, as she and Emmeline walked in the grounds later that day. 'Are you awfully upset?'

'I did rather wonder if it might be him,' admitted Emmeline. 'It was when he joined me in the gardens yesterday. The inspector had permitted us to go outside for some fresh air, if you remember. You were walking in another part of the gardens with Cedric. Felix told me he thought I had killed Jemima. Of course I realise now that he said that to make himself appear innocent in my eyes, but I didn't know that at the time. He said that he would stand by me and protect me the best he could.'

'Did he indeed?'

'Yes, but I remember thinking it rather strange at the time that he should assume I was guilty of Jemima's murder. It made me wonder whether he was really as fond of me as he appeared to be. I suppose it made me a little wary of him. And ... then he made the mistake of referring to Jemima as Jemima not Emmeline.'

'Did he indeed? That was very careless of him.'

'Yes, wasn't it? I thought it might just have been a mistake, but it did make me wonder.'

'Yes, it must have done,' Rose said sympathetically.

'But really I was suspicious of everyone, even you. I didn't know who to trust. I was frightened you see. I didn't know whether Jemima had been killed in mistake for me. Was I really the intended victim? All I could think about was how important it was that no one knew who I really was. I've been frightened ever since I came to Sedgwick that something dreadful would happen. And that it should have happened to Jemima ... I ... I can't bear to think about it.'

'You haven't had a chance to grieve yet,' said Rose, putting her arm around the girl's shoulders. 'You've been too frightened.'

'Yes, you're right. And I can't quite believe that it was only yesterday that it all happened. I'm so glad Father is here. He feels that he is in some way to blame for Jemima's death, you know, which is quite ridiculous. He thinks that, if he hadn't been so protective of me, we wouldn't have felt the need to run away, as he puts it.'

'Oh?'

'Yes. We won't be returning to Scotland, or at least, if we do, only for a little while to arrange matters. We're not going to be hiding ourselves away any more from the rest of the world. Father says he wants me to see more of life. He's even talking about buying a town house in London.'

'I'm so pleased. I think it's just what you need. Perhaps we can meet up when you're in London? You could even come and visit the dress shop where I work.'

'Yes, I should like that very much,' said Emmeline.

'We should invite Vera too,' said Rose. 'I have a feeling that she and Theo won't be getting married. It's the best thing for her, even if she doesn't realise it yet. But she'll need some cheering up.'

'Yes,' agreed Emmeline. 'I might invite her to stay with me for a while in London. Jemima behaved rather badly towards her as far as Dr Harrison was concerned. I'd like to make amends if I can.'

'Darling, do you think it's all over now?' asked Cedric. 'Can I have you all to myself now? Theo and Vera have left, separately as we know. Count Fernand, or whoever he was, has caught a train to London, and Emmeline and her father will be leaving in the next couple of hours. Thistlewaite's been arrested, so there are no loose ends that we need to tie up, are there?'

'No, darling, not that I know of,' said Rose. 'Sergeant Lane told me that they found Vera's plan in Felix's pocket, and that when they showed it to him he went completely to pieces and confessed to everything.'

'Let's hope that Lavinia won't be inviting any more people to stay who she knows absolutely nothing about.'

'Don't be too hard on her, darling.'

'Rose, darling, there's something I've been meaning to ask you. I want to ask you … I mean. I would have done before, but what with Lavinia and her friends turning up like that …'

'Yes?' said Rose, conscious that her heart was beating rather loudly in her chest. Part of her wanted him to go on, and another part of her wanted time to stand still so that she might savour this moment.

'Yes … I … I … You do love me, don't you, Rose? Say that you do. You know how I feel about you. Well, what I have to ask you is this … Will you –'

'Oh, there you two are,' said Lavinia coming across to them. 'Manning told me he'd seen you wandering off to the lake. Are you hiding from everyone?'

'Yes, from you,' said Cedric rather rudely. 'Now, do go away, Lavinia, there's a dear.'

'No, I shan't,' said Lavinia. 'At least, not yet. Is it true that Felix was a jewel thief and murdered Emmeline who was really Jemima? And that Jemima is really Emmeline and that the count isn't a count at all?'

'Yes. Now do go away, Lavinia.'

'So no one was who they appeared to be.' Lavinia said rather sadly. 'I daresay if I had known that Jemima was really Emmeline Montacute then I suppose I might have made a little more effort to get to know her.'

'Go away, Lavinia.'

'Only on the condition that Rose says yes.'

'What?' said Rose. 'But I thought –'

'Well, I think it would be rather nice, don't you? Ceddie and I really don't want to be rumbling around in this house all by ourselves. I think it's a wonderful idea of his inviting you and your mother here for Christmas, don't you?' She smiled at them sweetly. 'That is what you were going to ask Rose, isn't it?'

'Well … yes … among other things,' mumbled Cedric, going rather red and looking at the ground.

'Well,' said Lavinia. 'I'm so glad. Now what shall I do? Shall I join you for a walk by the lake? Or shall I go back to the house?'

'Go back to the house,' said Cedric bluntly.

'Oh, all right. I suppose I should leave the two of you alone so that Cedric can ask you … the other thing, Rose.'

Lavinia smiled sweetly at them again, but this time Rose noticed there was a twinkle in her eye, and that when she ran back to the house she was almost skipping.

Made in the USA
Middletown, DE
07 November 2017